5-24

Restoring the American Dream One Portfolio at a Time

Bob Kolar

AMP&RSAND, INC.

Chicago • New Orleans

ISBN 978-1450795968

Design
David Robson, Robson Design

Published by
Ampersand, Inc.
1050 North State Street
Chicago, Illinois 60610

203 Finland Place
New Orleans, Louisiana 70131

www.ampersandworks.com

5 4 3 2 1

For Sue and the boys

CONTENTS

A NOTE TO THE READER 5

PREFACE 8

PART ONE   **Taking the Mystery Out of Investing**
Chapter One   Get in the Game!...12
Chapter Two   Recognize the Theories.....................................16
Chapter Three   Building Blocks..23
Chapter Four   Gaining Perspective..52
Chapter Five   Think Risk First 61
Chapter Six   The All Important Next Step 84
Chapter Seven   Putting the Pieces Together........................110
Chapter Eight   Looking for More...126
Chapter Nine   What If You Win the Lottery?...................155
Chapter Ten   Dos and Don'ts 168

PART TWO   **Expanding Your Horizons**
Chapter Eleven   Pundits Can Be Detrimental to Your Wealth.....180
Chapter Twelve   When Doing Nothing May Be the Best Move ...184
Chapter Thirteen The Significance of Scarcity....................202
Chapter Fourteen Building on Success.............................222

PART THREE   **Restoring the Promise of a Better Future**
Chapter Fifteen   Financial Security for Everyone 254
Chapter Sixteen   One Portfolio at a Time.............................284

SOURCES AND NOTES..291

INDEX 301

ABOUT THE AUTHOR 311

PREFACE

*An investment in knowledge
always pays the best interest.*

Benjamin Franklin

WE ALL KNOW reading, writing, and arithmetic are the building blocks of a sound education, but given the explosion in technology, computer proficiency has become a valuable addition to the traditional three Rs. The topic of investing, however, does not even come up in conversation, not to mention in our general education curriculum, yet it is critical for our financial security. Investing is something everyone needs to learn and understand, but very few choose to pursue it.

A few years ago, I was looking for a farewell gift for a colleague. Since I had helped this individual develop an investment program, a book about investing seemed a logical choice and a helpful one as well. I soon realized few had been written for the family room and even fewer provided readers with actionable information. The need for such a book was obvious. Many investors seek an understandable approach that helps them with their investment choices today and their retirement decisions tomorrow.

You do not need a college degree in mathematics or economics to understand some basic, time-tested principles. With common sense guidelines, most anyone can improve his or her wealth. If you follow them, you may avoid becoming one of many people who find out they should have started investing a little sooner, should have saved a little more or should have tried a little harder. This book may just become a favorite family reference. Here is a hands-on approach to a subject that, all too often, does not come up until it is much too late to enjoy the benefits.

Understanding historical relationships within the market can remove much of the mystery surrounding the investment world while also iden-tifying some very important dos and don'ts. In the first of three parts, actionable information describing what you might want to do with what you have is provided. The approach is simple, straightforward and effec-tive. Much of the difficulty in achieving investment success results from misunderstanding market relationships, which often leads to emotionally driven actions and poor decision-making.

The second part of the book addresses our national economy and presents some interesting conclusions about the impact of government policies. Some historical realities regarding stock market cycles, government policies, and economic trends are exposed. Sure to stir up a little controversy, the historical facts remain for all to see. Some may suggest that the interpretation of such facts may be misleading, but the documented results provide a very compelling and perhaps even a conclusive argument.

The final part is an answer to a broken promise. While some individuals look to their employers (pensions) for financial security, many others count on the federal government (Social Security). Each of these programs may be helpful, but it is important to understand the limitations and growing concerns about their very survival. Our Social Security system can benefit from the same investment principles presented in the first part of this book. Since the term privatizing conjures up such bitterness, we prefer to "optimize" the Social Security system by revitalizing the program, improving its benefits, and establishing a sound fiscal foundation. This new approach to the optimization of Social Security is fresh and warrants a new mission: *strengthen the economy and improve the financial future for all Americans simultaneously.*

So pull up a nice big comfortable chair, get your favorite beverage, sit back, and enjoy. Some very helpful information is coming your way …

- some technical—trust me, it will be brief
- some historical—sorry, but this is helpful to your understanding, so stick with it
- some actionable—mapping your future, so do read carefully
- some controversial—a road many have not taken, but a path leading to prosperity
- all beneficial—a handy reference tool for the successful investor

The time has come to start putting your money to work—for you!

Bob Kolar
August 2012

PART ONE

Taking the Mystery Out of Investing

CHAPTER ONE

Get in the Game!

I'm thinking it over!
The Jack Benny Show, March 28, 1948

IF YOU HAVE never listened to the Jack Benny radio program, you certainly missed a true classic. The writing was exquisite, the material is timeless, and the characters will live forever. Luckily, many of those great programs are still available for those wanting to know what life was like before the computer, before television, heck, before a whole lot of things. While referred to as the most famous joke in broadcast history, the *Saturday Evening Post* called what follows "one of the three greatest jokes of all time."

Jack Benny's on-air persona was that of a notoriously tightfisted skinflint who even charged houseguests for using the bathrooms in his home! In this scene, Jack is visiting his neighbor Ronald Coleman and borrows Coleman's Oscar to show his butler, Rochester. When Coleman's wife, Benita, asks why he is letting Jack take his Oscar home, Coleman responds, "It might as well be with the rest of my things." As Jack is walking home, a crook jumps out of the bushes brandishing a gun and demands, "Your money or your life!" Jack is silent. Thinking the scene has ended, the audience laughs. However, the frustrated crook again bellows, "I *said*, your money or your life!" After a few more moments of silence Jack blurts out, "I'm thinking it over!" The studio audience erupts.[1]

The lengthy delay before Jack's strange, but very in-character response was timed perfectly. However, delaying the decision to invest is not nearly so funny. In fact, it may be downright costly. While it may sound unbelievable, you can leave your grandson or granddaughter $1 million, with an initial investment of only $3,052. Based on the historical return of 9.32% for the stock market since 1926, that initial

FINANCIAL SECURITY

Excluding illegal activities, how can you achieve financially security? While it might be wonderful if you were born into money, most people are not so privileged. Some may try to marry into money, but most individuals are not so fortunate. Still others may attempt to win the lottery, but most folks are not so lucky. For the rest of us, we must do it the old-fashioned way. We spend less than we earn and invest whatever remains successfully. Money does not buy happiness, but financial security does provide the freedom to choose how to enjoy your retirement, and that, my friends, is priceless.

CHAPTER TWO

Recognize the Theories

*Coincidences, in general, are great stumbling blocks
in the way of that class of thinkers who have been educated
to know nothing of the theory of probabilities.*

The Murders in the Rue Morgue by Edgar Allan Poe, 1841

IF YOU WANT to take the mystery out of investing, start at the beginning. For instance, if you want to learn about mysteries, read the very first detective story written in 1841 by Edgar Allan Poe: *The Murders in the Rue Morgue*. Writing five mysteries, Poe was the first to establish many of the elements still used in mystery writing. In his book *Mysteries and Mystery Writing*, Hillary Waugh lists the 12 tenets. From the inspiring, unconventional detective to the use of secret codes, little has changed since Poe penned his detective novels over a century ago.

Waugh explains that modern mysteries have added only three new elements. The first is the concept of fair play, allowing the reader to have all of the clues. The second is the identification of a motive, explaining why the murder was committed. The final element is presentation style, bringing the reader into the story by showing him what happened rather than withholding the information and telling him about it later.[1]

Just as Poe launched a new genre in writing, all investment strategies evolved from a handful of investment theories. Some of those strategies may put a little smile on your face: the Hemline Indicator, the Super Bowl Indicator, and the Windbag Theory, to name but a few. With as many investment strategies as there are investment advisors, the investment community continually analyzes current thinking. Investment theories endure constant scrutiny and persistent attack. Most investors wonder whether a truly effective investment approach actually exists.

THE FIRM FOUNDATION THEORY

In *The Theory of Investment Value* published in 1934, John Burr Williams advocated the calculation of the underlying, or intrinsic, value of a stock. He believed an investor could improve his investment returns by basing buy and sell decisions on the difference between the calculated intrinsic value of the stock and its existing market price.

The genesis of fundamental analysis, The Firm Foundation Theory compares current characteristics of a stock to its future projections. The fundamental analyst attempts to determine the intrinsic value of a stock based on various factors such as earnings, dividends, growth, or other such measures. When the current price is below the calculated intrinsic value, the stock is a candidate for purchase. This theory suggests the stock market eventually recognizes the intrinsic value of the stock by bidding up its price. Conversely, the stock becomes a candidate for sale when the current price of the stock rises above its calculated intrinsic value.

Critics contend the costs associated with the investigation process may be excessive, or even worse, the analyst may misinterpret the facts and generate misleading growth calculations, incorrect earnings projections, or inaccurate dividend forecasts. Other detractors point out that even if the analyst does assess the key variables correctly, the value estimate of the stock may still be misstated or misinterpreted; the market may have already factored this information into the current price of the stock. Still other opponents argue that rather than "correcting" the price of the stock that is under review, the market may adjust the expectations of the other stocks in that industry relative to the stock under investigation.

This theory became Wall Street gospel with the 1949 publication of *Security Analysis* authored by Benjamin Graham and David Dodd. Most likely, you have heard of its most famous student—Warren Buffett. Despite his success however, many argue that if everyone utilized these concepts and calculated the same value of a stock, no single analyst would be able to gain an advantage over the others.

CASTLE-IN-THE-AIR THEORY

Promoting government intervention to stimulate the economy, John Maynard Keynes gained fame during the depression years with his book *The General Theory of Employment, Interest and Money*. During 1936, he argued that The Firm Foundation Theory required too much effort, cost too much money, and produced too little profit. Keynes suggested rather than trying to calculate intrinsic values, investors should look at investor expectations. He inferred that if you could determine when investors would build their hopes into castles-in-the-air, the successful investor would be able to buy into the market before the stock price goes up.

Since no one knows what influences future earnings or future dividend payments, Keynes theorized most investors were not seeking long-term returns; they were looking to identify short-term changes ahead of the general investing public. If an investor could know that the market was going to move in a certain direction, the investor would be able to generate a profit. In effect, Keynes applied psychological factors, not financial principles, to the stock market.

The Castle-in-the-Air Theory gave rise to technical analysis. Attempting to predict the future by looking at the past, technical analysts construct stock charts to interpret past price and volume changes in an effort to identify distinct patterns. When identified in their early stages, these patterns provide an opportunity to generate an investment profit. In *Irrational Exuberance* published in 2000, Robert Shiller suggested the hysteria surrounding the huge run-up in technology and internet stocks near the end of the twentieth century was a result of psychological factors.

Detractors of technical analysis point to timing issues. Investors take action only after the trends are established. Since the market often moves quickly, the investor may miss the buy or sell signals and thus miss the initial, and often the most significant, movements of the stock. Other rivals of this method argue that even if charting did work, as more investors adopted this approach, the market signals would be weakened since all investors would be taking action at approximately the same time. Trying to anticipate the market signals, traders would become more aggressive in order to beat the others to the market. The earlier the investor acts, however, the less reliable the signal becomes.

EFFICIENT MARKET THEORY

The Efficient Market Theory suggests the stock market is so efficient the price of a stock immediately reflects all public information regarding that company. Therefore, an investor cannot achieve an incremental return from identifying future market trends (technical analysis) or discovering hidden value (fundamental analysis). In effect, price movements in the stock market do not generate useful trends or forecast future price movements. The theory further contends that future returns neither have a relation to, nor are dependent on, past returns.

Through the years, three variations of Efficient Market Theory emerged with each form based on the general premise that future stock prices are difficult, if not impossible, to predict. The strongest form is the purest view and suggests nothing is useful in predicting future prices because the current price already reflects everything known including unpublished developments. The semi-strong form simply states that published information is not a useful predictor of future prices, which implies some unpublished information may be capable of influencing price.

The Random Walk Theory, considered the weakest form of Efficient Market Theory, gained a cult-like following after Burton G. Malkiel's publication of *A Random Walk Down Wall Street* in 1973. He asserted that an efficient market responds almost immediately to new information, making it impossible for investors to use such information in an effort to outperform the market. Since the market incorporates all of the known factors influencing the price of a stock, price changes occur only when new or unexpected data becomes available. This new information may be either good or bad, and thus the subsequent impact on price movement is random. Therefore, investors can only beat the market by chance.

Efficient Market critics point out that biases, trends, and opinions are inherent in the market and these factors distort the prices of stocks in predictable ways, such as the so-called madness of crowds and speculative bubbles. While some opponents concede the market reacts quickly to new public information, they also contend a small window of opportunity to gain an advantage may still exist. Other foes challenge market efficiency because they question the kind of information that affects the price of a stock and how such information influences the value of the company.

MODERN PORTFOLIO THEORY

The beginnings of Modern Portfolio Theory date to 1952. Harry Markowitz pioneered this approach in his book, *Portfolio Selection*. Markowitz argued that a portfolio manager must consider both the expected return and the portfolio risk. He cautioned the concept of risk included both the inherent risk in an individual stock as well as the risk derived from the relationships of those individual stocks within a portfolio. His research revealed that the combination of even the most risky stocks in a portfolio, taken as a whole, could be less risky than any one individual stock within that portfolio.

Markowitz believed rational investors build investment portfolios either to maximize expected returns for a certain degree of risk or to minimize the risk for a specific expected return. For any given holding period, he could graph all of the possible combinations of risk and expected returns ranging from a 100% stock portfolio to a 100% fixed income portfolio. The resulting curve, known as the Efficient Frontier, highlights the optimum holdings at each given risk level.

This theory was further refined through the development of the capital asset pricing model developed by William Sharpe, John Lintner, and Fischer Black in the 1960s. Their model concluded total portfolio risk is actually composed of two distinct risks: (1) Unsystematic risk resulting from factors specific to an individual company, such as product liability issues, management changes, product competition, and so forth. The market does not reward the investor for retaining such risk because diversification can mitigate it. (2) Systematic or market risk is the variability of stocks in general. Beta is the term for the difference between the movement of a particular stock price and the movement of the overall stock market. Diversification cannot eliminate this risk.

Challengers to this theory argue that a single measure of risk is unlikely to address all of the potential factors affecting the movement of a stock price. Other detractors point out that individual stock betas are not stable over time; betas fluctuate in relation to the market against which they are measured. Still other critics cite the potential weaknesses in the underlying calculations, such as expected returns, which may not materialize, or the risk measure may be miscalculated.

THE BENCHMARK

No investment strategy is successful unless it can outperform the market. If the investment approach exceeds the returns of a benchmark portfolio for the same risk and holding period, the positive difference between the two returns represents the value-added for that investment strategy. While many investors may consider the benchmark portfolio to be a proxy for the entire market (S&P 500 Index or the Dow Jones Wilshire 5000 Total Stock Market Index), a more accurate performance assessment is achieved when the benchmark portfolio characteristics match the characteristics of the investment approach being evaluated. For instance, comparing a portfolio of fixed income securities to a benchmark of stocks provides little value in determining the success of such a strategy.

While professional managers argue they can beat the benchmark, the critics point out only a few do and most of those rarely succeed over longer periods. More importantly, though critics may acknowledge that some professional managers do occasionally beat the market, it is almost impossible to identify the winners before they actually become winners.

The inability to outperform the market on a consistent basis spawned an interest in the passive investing approach that gave rise to the popularity of index funds. Sometimes called "buy and hold the market," John Bogle popularized this investment strategy in 1975 when he began the Index Trust for his then fledgling Vanguard Mutual Fund Company. Until that time, the few index funds in existence were available to institutional investors only.

The buy and hold the market strategy does provide a compelling long-term profile. It does not depend on investor sentiment, it does not require stock valuations, it does not matter whether everyone uses it, and it does not rely on any investment strategy. Best of all, it does not require any foresight, only patience.

WHAT DO YOU THINK?

Well that certainly clears it up! Like a good mystery, there are well-meaning experts, clues in plain sight, and even cipher codes (or at least complex formulas). Unfortunately, no definitive solution to this mystery is imminent. The only thing that seems to be reasonably clear is no single investment approach is universally accepted. Accordingly, academia will continue to receive funding for new research to interpret market movements, professors will continue to publish new findings, and Wall Street will continue to seek a competitive advantage. Yes, the mystery continues!

Understanding the shortfalls of various investment theories enables investors to analyze other approaches and provides a foundation upon which to build their investment programs. To paraphrase Poe's detective, C. Auguste Dupin, you must become familiar with the theory of probabilities to improve the underpinnings of your strategy.

CHAPTER THREE

Building Blocks

*There are two kinds of statistics,
the kind you look up and the kind you make up.*
Death of a Doxy by Rex Stout, 1966

CREATED BY REX Stout, the detective genius Nero Wolfe was an obese, orchid-loving gourmet who seldom left the comforts of his New York brownstone. Trained by Wolfe himself, Archie Goodwin performed the investigative legwork. Archie recalled conversations verbatim, memorized crime scenes, and encouraged reluctant suspects to visit the brownstone for further discussions and interrogation. They first appeared in a 1934 novel entitled *Fer-de-Lance*. Thirty-four novels and 39 stories later, Nero Wolfe and Archie Goodwin hold a special place in the mystery genre.

For those preferring the Cliff Notes version, the A&E Network produced a series called *A Nero Wolfe Mystery* that aired for two seasons. The episodes closely followed the plots and dialogue of the original stories and starred Maury Chaykin as Nero Wolfe and Timothy Hutton as Archie Goodwin. Well received by critics, this series is available for your viewing pleasure. For the older crowd, there was a charming, short-lived radio series (1950–1951) starring Sidney Greenstreet as Wolfe that is available for your listening pleasure.

After Wolfe accepted a case, he developed a strategy to gather clues and collect information to unmask the problem at hand. You are no different. After deciding to start an investment program, you must develop an investment plan. Like all plans, you need to understand where you are today, where you want to be tomorrow, and how you are going to get there. It is that last part that causes all the problems.

Understanding five key concepts can improve your investing skill as well as your future success. Return and risk are the marquee players in your investment mystery assuming the roles of Nero Wolfe and Archie Goodwin. All mysteries also have strong supporting players and the investment world is no different. Cost, time and diversification assume the roles of Saul Panzer, Fred Durkin and Orrie Cather—three of New York's finest operatives in the employ of Nero Wolfe. Rounding out the cast of characters are inflation and taxes, obstructionists assuming the roles of the well intentioned but blundering Inspector Cramer, and Sergeant Purley Stebbins.

Based on time-tested principles and grounded in historical evidence, Wolfe might say what follows represents the statistics you look up. The statistics you make up are for the gamblers and speculators. Like a good detective who must chose between fact and fiction, the successful investor must distinguish historical truths from marketing hype.

RETURN: WHAT EVERYONE WANTS

When purchasing stocks, you typically expect to receive a dividend payment and the hope of future growth. For instance, if you purchase a stock for $50 and it pays an annual dividend of $1, your initial rate of return is 2% (the $1 dividend divided by the $50 purchase price). This is where most people begin to hear that little voice asking whether the return is sufficient.

Many investors tend to focus on short-term reality rather than long-term potential. Now suppose U.S. Treasury bonds are paying 3% interest. Well, many investors might say a sure 3% beats 2% anytime, right? Well, that may be true but it is certainly misleading. Common stocks provide upward potential through earnings growth leading to future dividend increases, whereas the interest payment stream associated with bonds remains fixed and does not change.

Suppose three years later, that stock you purchased for $50 raised its dividend 5% each year and the market rewarded its performance by increasing the stock price 5% each year to keep pace with the dividend growth. Assuming the interest and dividends are received in cash and the general interest rates remained unchanged, the interest payments received on the bond over three years would total $4.50 ($1.50 times three years). The combined return of the dividends and stock appreciation would total $11.19 (the 5% annual growth in dividends is $3.31

for three years plus 5% annual price appreciation of $7.88 for the same period). That's quite a difference in the two cumulative returns. The return on the stock investment was $6.69 higher than the bond purchase for an increase of 149%. Assuming the dividend continued to grow at the same rate, the dividend payment would exceed the bond interest payment in nine years.

Corporate earnings provide the opportunity for dividend payments. When purchasing shares of a particular stock, the investor expects (1) the firm will continue to pay annual dividends and those dividends will grow over time, or (2) in lieu of annual dividends, the firm will retain its earnings and invest in the business, ultimately leading to future dividend payments. It is the dividends, or the prospect of future dividends, that make the stock purchase an investment; otherwise, the purchase would be purely speculative. In his book, *Common Sense on Mutual Funds*, John Bogle cites the three key variables that determine the return on equities over the long run.[1]

- the dividend yield at the time of the initial investment
- the subsequent rate of growth in earnings
- the change in the price-to-earnings ratio during the investment period

Linked to fundamental analysis, the first two variables involve forecasting expected annual growth in earnings and dividends over the lifetime of the investment. Interestingly, these first two variables have accounted for almost the entire historical return since 1926—approximately 90% of the total return for the period.

The third variable represents technical analysis. Investors tend to pay more for earnings when their future expectations are optimistic and less when they lose confidence in what the future may bring. With stocks priced at a multiple of 20 times earnings, the mood of the market is generally upbeat and enthusiastic. However, when the multiples are priced at five times earnings, the mood is more somber. Many investors are unsure of the future. Since the price earnings ratio is the price investors are willing to pay for one dollar of earnings, changes in this multiple represent the general mood of the market. For instance, as the multiple falls from 20 to five times earnings, the price of stocks falls 75% (the market goes from paying $20 to paying $5 for $1 of earnings, this is a decrease of $15 or 75% from the original multiple of $20). Moving in the other direction, from five to 20 times earnings, the price of stocks increases 300% (the market goes from paying $5 to paying $20 for the $1 of earnings—an increase of $15 or 300% from the $5 multiple).

Bogle concludes the fundamentals drive the majority of the return. Long-term investors, he contends, place significant weight on dividends because dividends compose almost one-half of the total return in the long run. Speculation, he argues, plays a much smaller role. He stresses that any speculation, whether favorable or not, cannot last forever. Regardless of how compelling the justification may be in the short run, favorable speculative periods inevitably are followed by speculative periods that drive the returns down. The reverse is also true. These speculative swings cancel one another out over the long run. This phenomenon may explain why more experienced investors tend to buy when the market looks its bleakest so they can take that inevitable ride up.

Bogle also applies a similar approach to the long-term government bond market, citing the following variables as the determinants of market returns.

- the interest coupon at the time of the initial investment
- the reinvestment rate
- the end-of-period bond yield

In this approach, fundamental analysis principles appear only in the first variable. The interest coupon on a long-term treasury bond is the yield on the asset over its lifetime. Related to technical analysis, the two remaining variables concern investor sentiment. Driven largely by market expectations, the general level of interest rates directly influences both the reinvestment rate and the value of a bond prior to maturity.

The reinvestment rate is the critical element in determining bond returns. When current interest rates are higher than the initial investment, the value of the bond decreases to adjust the interest rate to current levels. Sometimes confusing to the inexperienced investor, an increase in interest rates lowers the value of a bond, while a decrease in interest rates raises the value of a bond.

Suppose you purchased a bond for $100 paying 3% interest last year, and the current interest rates paid on bonds of similar quality and maturity are 4%. Since the interest payments of a bond do not change, the value of the bond adjusts to reflect the current interest rates. With the current interest rate at 4%, the bond you purchased for $100 paying $3 in interest is now priced at $75 (calculated by dividing the $3 interest payment by 4%, the current interest rate). Thus, the value of the bond decreased from $100 to $75 representing a 25% decline. The importance of the general interest rate environment cannot be overstated. The actions of the Federal Reserve, in turn, have a significant impact on your investments.

RISK: WHAT EVERYONE FEARS

The linkage between risk and return is a basic investment tenet. Increasing the expected return of an investment leads to higher risk, and conversely, reducing the risk leads to lower expected returns for that same investment. The concept of risk intimidates many "would-be" investors and impairs the thought process of more than a few "casual" investors.

Investor sentiment influences the returns of both stocks and bonds. All investors experience the cyclical nature of the stock market; it is unavoidable. Think of some of the events over the past 20 years, and it is no wonder that investors react with so much fear concerning risk. Consider the health care industry when Hillary Clinton attempted to impose a national health care plan that drove stock values down within the entire health care industry; or the rapid devaluation of internet stocks when investors began to realize that these firms could not sustain revenue flows, yet commanded high valuations. The impact of 9/11 affected the airline and travel industries immediately, but soon reverberated throughout the entire market. Ongoing tensions in the Middle East have caused fluctuations in the availability of oil, driving up the price of oil while driving down the price of stocks. Fallout from business scandals such as Enron, WorldCom, Arthur Andersen and Tyco gave rise to a lack of confidence in American business. That moved money out of the stock market, driving prices down. The meltdown of the mortgage market may have begun in the financial and housing sectors, but it soon spread, affecting the entire market.

The investment community defines two broad categories of risk. Market risk, as the name implies, is inherent in the market itself. General market events occurring every day affect all investments to varying degrees, including such events as Federal Reserve actions, changes to the federal tax policy, or national disasters. The other broad category is firm risk. Firm risk relates to specific events or actions unique to individual companies, such as product development, competitive pressures, strikes, or management changes.

In addition to the broad definitions, many very specific risks exist. Specific risks include interest rate risk (movement in the costs of borrowing money), reinvestment risk (inability to reinvest cash flows at the same rates), and call risk (possible bond redemption prior to maturity at unfavorable prices). Other risks include business risk (related to the company's operations or environment), financial risk (inherent in the methods used in financing), and leverage risk (the multiplicative effect from large amounts of debt or derivatives). Still others include economic risk (overall health of the economy of the country or locality), political risk (unfavorable legislation or regulation both home and abroad), and currency risk (unfavorable foreign exchange movements). Additional risks include timing risk (misreading market signals), credit risk (potential default by the issuer), and many more.

Suppose you have an investment opportunity guaranteed to generate a 3% return in one year. Your expected return is 3% because of the guarantee. With the expected return and the actual (guaranteed) return the same, no variability exists and, therefore, no risk is present.

Consider a second investment opportunity with a 50% chance to generate a return of 12% that also carries a 50% chance that a loss of 2% will be incurred a year later. The expected return on this second opportunity is 5%; the calculation is [(50% × 12%) + (50% × -2%)]. The obvious investment dilemma is that the actual return may vary significantly from the expected return. This variation to the expected return is risk and the greater the potential variability, the greater the risk.

A third investment opportunity with a 50% chance to generate a return of 24% also has a 50% chance to lose 6% a year later. The expected return on the third investment is 9%; the calculation is [(50% × 24%) + (50% × -6%)]. The difference between this third opportunity and the expected return on the second investment is that the second carries less risk or variability (the spread between 12% and -2%) than the third investment (the spread between 24% and -6%).

Current financial theory uses standard deviation as the measure of risk. Simply stated, standard deviation measures how far apart the actual return may be from the expected return. Without getting too technical, the concept assumes a normal distribution curve. You may remember the bell-shaped curve from high school or college when teachers used to say they graded on a curve. Well this is that curve! You hated it then and probably don't like it much now either.

With a normal distribution curve, 67.7% of the actual returns fall within one standard deviation, 95% within two standard deviations, and 99.7% within three standard deviations. The three investment examples given above have standard deviations of 0%, 7%, and 15%, respectively. To calculate standard deviation, first compute the difference of each data point (expected return) from the mean (average), and square the result. Next, sum these squared values and divide by the number of data points. Lastly, take the sum and calculate the square root, which equals the standard deviation. Here is how it works with the second investment opportunity:

- subtract the expected return of 12% from expected return of 5% and subtract the expected return of -2% from expected return of 5%.
- square both results:
  $(12\% - 5\% = 7\% \times 7\% = 49\%) + (-2\% - 5\% = -7\% \times -7\% = 49\%)$
- divide the sum of the values by the number of data points
  $(49\% + 49\% = 98\% / 2 = 49\%)$
- calculate the square root of the sum
  $(\sqrt{49\%} = 7\%)$

Putting this into perspective, the first investment is a guaranteed 3% return, there is no risk and the standard deviation is zero. The second investment has an expected return of 5% with a standard deviation of 7%. This means that:

- the second investment has a 68% probability that the actual return will fall within the range of 12% and -2% (the expected return of 5% plus or minus the 7% standard deviation)
- a 95% probability the actual return will fall within the range of 19% and -9% (the expected return of 5% plus or minus two standard deviations—or 2 × 7%), and
- a 99.7% probability that the actual return will fall within the range of 26% and -16% (the expected return of 5% plus or minus three standard deviations—or 3 × 7%)

The third investment has an expected return of 9% with a standard deviation of 15%.

- the third investment has a 68% probability that the actual return will fall within the range of 24% and -6%,
- a 95% probability the actual return will fall between 39% and -21%, and
- a 99.7% probability the actual returns fall between 54% and -36%

When your broker tells you that an investment has an expected return of 15% with a risk (i.e., standard deviation) of 10%, he means that approximately two-thirds of the time, the return will fall between 5% and 25%.

What can we learn from these examples? When comparing investments, the better investment is rarely a clear choice. In our examples, the first investment provides a 3% return with no risk compared to the second investment with an expected return of 5% with some risk and the third investment with an expected return of 9% with even greater risk. The best investment choice depends on your willingness to accept additional risk for a potentially higher return. Understand, however, that this analysis only addresses the probability of higher returns should you be willing to accept additional risk in the hope that those higher returns will be realized. The trade-off between risk and return represent the primary dilemma facing many investors.

Getting a little more personal: which one of the following statements is more troubling to you?

- You did not make a $10,000 investment, and as luck would have it, you missed making a profit of $3,000 in the first year—a 30% gain.
- You did make a $10,000 investment, but unfortunately, things did not quite work out as expected and you lost $3,000 in the first year—now you need a gain of 43% just to break even.

No, this is not a trick question. When discussing investments, many people really believe that they are willing to accept more risk in the hope of achieving a higher return. In reality however, most individuals would rather lose an opportunity to make money than experience the reality of actually losing money. Most people work hard for their money and want to hold onto it. If you are like most rational investors, you would prefer to reduce your risk.

COST: WHAT EVERYONE FORGETS

The concept of risk and return appears frequently in investment literature. Often overlooked is the concept of cost, which is every bit as important. To most investors, however, cost is almost an afterthought because many of the charges come in seemingly small doses, making you believe the expenses are reasonable given the size of the investment.

The one absolute truth about investing that you must remember and never ever forget is this: costs always have a negative impact on your investment returns. Every single dollar paid out in costs is one dollar deducted from your investment returns. This is an indisputable fact, it is plain, it is simple, and it is absolute. Do not be fooled into thinking otherwise.

For the investor in mutual funds, vigilance is critical. Although no-load funds do not charge sales loads (a percentage charge reducing the amount of your deposit), they may incur other expenses and these may be quite costly. In reading the prospectus, make sure you understand the fees that may be charged by the fund in question. Some potential expenses include sales charges (front-end sales commission), deferred sales charges (back-end loads), purchase fees (for new account share-holders), exchange fees (for exchanging funds), account fees (mainte-nance fees on existing accounts), redemption fees (for selling shares), management fees (paid to the investment advisor for portfolio manage-ment), 12b-1 fees (for distribution expenses), and other expenses (annual operating expenses). In addition to these charges, other hidden costs may be harder to identify or are not specifically addressed in the pro-spectus—brokerage commissions and bid-ask spreads, for example.

The mutual fund industry spends millions of dollars advertising their performance but rarely do they discuss their fee structures. Many advertising dollars compare load and no-load funds citing the excellence of one over the other. Within the mutual fund industry, the fees vary widely with some topping 3% excluding sales loads, com-missions and spreads. You need to pay close attention to these costs or you will lose your own hard-earned money and become another victim of this oversight.

If you are purchasing individual equity shares, the brokerage com-mission is an obvious cost. Less conspicuous are the costs associated with the bid-ask spread. The bid price represents the money received for selling the stock, and the ask price is the money you are charged for buying the stock. If you buy a stock currently selling for $30, you pay the asking price, which is somewhat higher than the actual stock price. If you want to sell that same stock, you receive the bid price, which is somewhat lower than the actual stock price. The spread for actively traded stocks ranges from 0.5% to 1.5% of the share price. However, the bid-ask spreads are usually higher if the stocks are thinly traded (low volume).

The costs of trading securities can be deceptive. Consider an investor with a portfolio of 20 stocks valued at $100,000 with each stock position valued at $5,000 and each share valued at $50. The investor trades one-half of his holdings each year. Thus, he sells 10 stocks and then buys 10 different stocks to replace the securities sold—a total of 20 transactions per year. Check the charges:

- assume the discount broker charges $15 per trade and the spread is 1.5% of the share price
- the trading costs are $15 × 20, totaling $300
- the bid-ask spread costs are ½ of 1.5% = 0.75% × the $50 per share price = $0.375 per share × 100 shares = $37.50 × 20 trades = $750
- the annual cost is $300 + $750 total $1,050
- only one-half of the portfolio was traded, so $1,050 ÷ $50,000 = 2.1%

The annual charge for turning over one-half your portfolio is $1,050 or 2.1% of the traded portfolio value. These costs can significantly affect the returns for those day traders on the internet.

In his book *The Four Pillars of Investing,* William Bernstein points out brokerage firms do spend significant amounts of time and money training their staff. However, the training focuses less on investment tools and more on selling techniques. The success of many brokerage houses, he explains, is dependent largely on teaching their trainees and registered reps how to approach a client, pitch ideas and close the sale.[2] So much for placing the client's needs above all else. This information should not be too surprising to you. Stockbrokers want to provide their own children with an education, not yours. This is not to say that stockbrokers are never to be trusted. It simply points out that you need to be cautious when working with them. A favorite phrase of President Reagan's seems appropriate for this situation—trust, but verify.

Unlike homes, or jewelry, or even automobiles, spending higher and higher amounts of money on investment advice is not necessarily indicative of higher quality. Warren Buffett pointed out that Wall Street might be the only place where people arrive in a Rolls Royce to get advice from those who take the subway. Go figure.

TIME: WHAT EVERYONE MISUNDERSTANDS[3]

When someone talks about time, most people tend to look at their watches. Many individuals think solely in the present and not in the long term. Our attention span is becoming shorter and shorter; we are continually seeking faster, if not immediate, gratification. Consider just a few of the changes taking place today—email vs. so-called snail mail, cell phones vs. land-locked lines, fast food vs. fine dining, and texting vs. letter writing. In the investment world, this short-term fixation leads to speculative rather than long-term investment decision-making and that is not a good thing.

In a society obsessed with speed, the concept of long-term may be difficult to grasp. Even our tax code suggests a long-term investment is one that is greater than one year. However, compounding has the mysterious allure of growing even small sums of money into sizeable portfolios. Extending the holding period provides the added appeal of reducing investment risk. On the other hand, the lure of compounding can also become a fatal attraction if long-term cost considerations are ignored. To paraphrase Nero Wolfe's able assistant, Archie Goodwin, compounding is a curious curiosity.

How Time Affects Your Return

Albert Einstein described compound interest as the greatest mathematical discovery of all time. The longer the holding period, the greater the effect compounding has on your investment returns. Suppose you are 25 and expect to retire at 65. Having accumulated $10,000 in savings, you want to know where to invest your money for the next 40 years.

The three types of investments you may be considering are common stocks, long-term treasury bonds, and short-term treasury bills. With all dividends and interest reinvested, the average annual returns since 1926 are 9.3% for equities, 5.0% for U.S. Treasury Bonds, and 3.6% for U.S. Treasury Bills. Figure 3.1 shows how those investment options stack up against one another. After 40 years, the equity portfolio would be worth a little north of $353,000. By contrast, the long-term treasury notes would be worth almost $71,000 while the short-term treasury bills would be worth about $42,000. The all-equity portfolio would generate

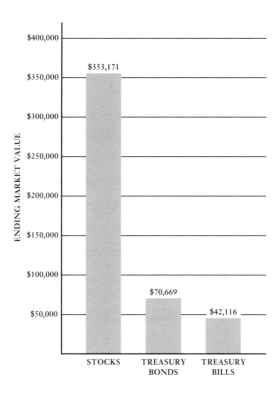

FIGURE 3.1 *Investing $10,000 for Forty Years*

almost five times as much as the long-term treasury notes and over eight times as much as the short-term treasury bills.

While selecting an investment is important, you do not want to procrastinate too long. Figure 3.2 highlights the dramatic effect that delaying the start of your investment program can have on your returns. Example: You and your three brothers each receive $10,000 from your parents. The same parameters exist for each brother—an all-equity portfolio averaging a 9.3% annual return with all dividends reinvested. You decide to invest the money today, but Moe delays investing the money for five years, Larry waits 10 years, and Curly takes 15 years to make up his mind. Forty years later, you have amassed a total of a little over $353,000 while Moe achieved almost $207,000; Larry earned

FIGURE 3.2 *Delaying the $10,000 Investment*

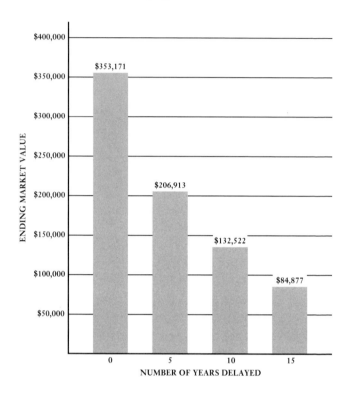

$132,000; and Curly received about $85,000. You do not want to be a stooge; delaying your investment program can be a very, very costly decision. The compounding power of time on an investment is truly a miracle. Not only does time heal all wounds, but time also makes one well heeled.

The size of the investment is not nearly as important as the timing of the investment. The benefit received from compounding even small amounts over long periods is astonishing. Even investing a small amount of money to celebrate the birth of your grandson or granddaughter, when allowed to compound over the life of your grandchild, doubles in value almost 8.5 times. Think of the $3,052 gift to your grandchild growing into the tidy little sum of $1 million when he becomes 65. Can you think of a better way to be remembered?

Here is a fun little fact. Suppose you have an investment with an average annual return of 9%. When you divide 9 into 72, the answer is 8, which also happens to be how many years it will take your investment to double. If you hold on to this investment for 40 years, the investment will double five times (8 divided into the 40-year holding period). Now, say you initially invest $5,000, your money doubles once ($10,000), twice ($20,000), three times ($40,000), four times ($80,000), and now the fifth time ($160,000). Of course, if your average rate of return is 12%, your money doubles every six years, and conversely, when the average rate of return is 7%, your money doubles every 10.3 years. The Rule of 72 is one of those little math exercises that is useful, fun, and a bit impressive. Yes, even math can be fun sometimes.

Now for a more challenging example. Suppose someone tells you he invested $10,000 in a security and five years later the value of the security was $15,000. What was the return? Well with a little math, you figure that if his current trend continues, his investment will double in 10 years. Subtracting the current value of $15,000 from his initial investment of $10,000 equals $5,000. His investment doubles when he achieves a value of $20,000 or an additional $5,000. Given the current trend, getting that $5,000 will require another five years. Therefore, his original investment of $10,000 will double in 10 years and his average annual return will be 7.2%. (divide 10 into 72). Now you will be the hit of the next cocktail party—guaranteed!

The rub, if one exists, is your return really does not accelerate until the third or fourth time your investment doubles because the initial investment amounts are usually small. It is not that larger investments accelerate any faster; it is that the absolute dollar increases may not seem significant. For instance, an initial investment of $3,000 doubles once ($6,000), twice ($12,000), three times ($24,000), and four times ($48,000). Assuming your annual rate of return is 9%, the timeframe to achieve the third and fourth doubling occurs in 24 and 32 years, respectively. Many investors may lose patience and break that compound interest chain. They forget the story of the tortoise and the hare. Do not make that mistake. You need to hold on for the long haul and control your emotions. Do not fall for the "flavor of the month" approach to investing. After all, if it were easy, everyone would be doing it.

How Time Affects Your Risk

In addition to having a significant impact on returns, time also has an important affect on risk. The risk or variability associated with equity returns declines as the investment holding period increases. The good news is, unlike the impact time has on returns, the favorable impact on risk occurs within a relatively short period, making even the most impatient of investors rejoice.

While time significantly reduces risk, time does not eliminate risk. You must remember returns can and do occur outside the normal distribution range. Most assuredly, stock market peaks and troughs are lurking out there and may strike unexpectedly. While all investors prefer that those swings will be neither pronounced nor extended, there are no guarantees. Figure 3.3 presents a series of charts graphically portraying the reduction of risk as the investment holding period increases. If a single picture is worth a thousand words, this series speaks volumes on the impact that time has on stock market risk. For those seeking the bullet points, consider the following facts as you extend the holding period.

The top chart illustrates the unpredictability of annual stock market returns. Since 1926, the highest single year return was a 52.6% gain in 1954 and the worst single year performance was a loss of 43.4% in 1931. The best and the worst years are separated by almost 100 percentage points, suggesting a volatile stock market. Despite such fluctuations, the upward bias in the stock market generates annual gains over 70% of the time. Surprisingly, of the 24 annual losses, over one-half—54%—were only single digit losses. The ensuing charts clearly display that an upward bias in the stock market does exist.

By extending the holding period for the investment to five-year increments, the range or spread of the returns drops to 40%, representing the difference between the high of 28.3% and the low of a 12.7% loss. Additionally, the frequency of losses falls to 12.7% in five-year periods (10 losses in 79 periods), which is a reduction of 56% from reported losses in single year returns. Furthermore, the magnitude of

FIGURE 3.3 *Changes to Volatility as the Investment Period Increases*

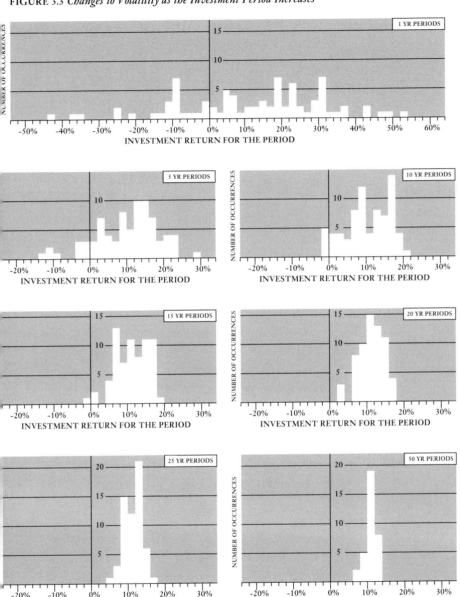

the losses also diminishes as single digit losses now represent 70% of the reported losses—seven of the 10 losses incurred.

When the holding period moves to 10-year increments, the results continue trending favorably. The range of the returns decreases to 22% representing the difference between the high of 20.1% and the low of a 1.7% loss. The frequency of losses falls to 6.8% (five losses in 74 periods) for a decline of 47% from the previous period. Perhaps more important is the losses are not only in the single digits, but every loss is under 2%.

With 15-year periods, the range of the returns drops to 19%, which is the difference between the high of 18.8% and the low of a 0.2% loss. The single, solitary loss represents a frequency of only 1.4% (one loss in 69 periods) and a drop of 78% from the previous period. Again, the loss is under 2%. Extending the holding period to 20 years and beyond eliminates losses entirely.

As the holding periods increase, the dispersion of the returns begins to narrow converging near the historical average return of 9.32%. This movement helps to demonstrate the concept of reversion to the mean, which theorizes that over time the stock market returns tend to remain stable despite short-term fluctuations. Bolstering this concept are the results presented in the final two charts. The 25-year period experienced gains between 4% and 18%, while the 50-year period witnessed the spread narrow still further to between 6% and 14%.

The upward bias of stock market returns and the benefit of reduced risk from longer holding periods are strong incentives for investors. Reinforcing the relative strength of the stock market returns is the fact that the stock market gains ground seven times out of every 10 years. Now that is a batting average even Ty Cobb would envy.[4]

How Time Affects Your Costs

Be cautious. The siren song of wealth creation may lead you to ignore long-term cost considerations. Like the black sheep of the family, the relationship between time and cost is rarely, if ever, spoken about in public. Building on the concept that every single dollar paid out in costs is one dollar deducted from your investment returns, the power of compounding works against you when applied to costs that relentlessly shrink your returns.

As much as you may wish it weren't so, no investor earns the full market return on any investment. Mutual funds incur costs to purchase, manage and sell investments. These expenses reduce the funds' gross earnings and thus reduce the shareholder's profits. When you purchase individual shares though a broker or an advisor, you also incur similar costs, lowering the returns accordingly. Do not be fooled into thinking the charges are relatively small and have little impact; that is exactly what the mutual funds, brokers and advisors want you to believe.

Only a few percentage points can have a devastating effect on the cumulative market returns of an investment over time. For instance, over a 40 year period, those "small, little" annual mutual fund charges can really hurt.

- When mutual fund expenses average 1%, you retain 69% of the market gains.
- When mutual fund expenses average 2%, you retain 47% of the market gains.
- When mutual fund expenses average 3%, you retain 32% of the market gains.

Disclosures such as these will not be forthcoming from the industry any time soon.

Typically, the disclosures provided within the mutual fund industry present their costs as "x" dollars per $1,000 invested. Such reporting disclosures illustrate that a 3% charge for a fund with $1,000 invested would incur an annual expense of $30. This method of disclosure reinforces the belief the expense costs are small and have little impact. You now know differently!

For the skeptics, look at Figure 3.4. Whether reflecting your individual stock buys and sells or your mutual fund all-in costs, a 1% annual cost drastically reduces the market return. After five years, your investment retains only 94% of the market returns. Over the ensuing years however, the retention rate of the market returns decreases dramatically: 90% in 10 years, 82% in 20 years, 75% in 30 years, and only 69% in 40 years. Ouch! Now you understand why you need to be ruthless in holding the line on costs. Why give your money away?

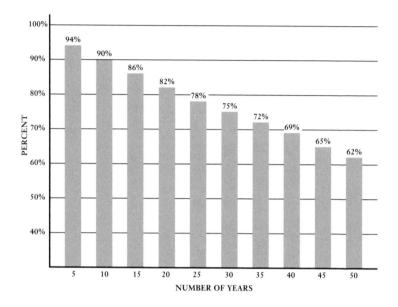

FIGURE 3.4 *Cumulative Percent of Market Return Retained with Costs of 1%*

DIVERSIFICATION: WHAT EVERYONE TRIES TO DO

According to *Webster's Ninth College Dictionary*, risk is the "possibility of loss ... also the degree of probability of such loss." Perhaps a surprise to some, risk does not mean an actual loss. Risk means only the chance of a loss exists.

Some investors view risk as the amount of money they can afford to lose without severely affecting either their financial or emotional well-being. This viewpoint may be easy to understand and may even be accurate, but it remains extremely hard to quantify. At what point does a loss, continued losses, or prolonged losses become an issue? Some may not think about risk at all and others may feel confident about their investments, but when the market begins a steady decline, your portfolio value is going along for the ride. Does your confidence begin to waver? Is your reaction similar to a roller coaster ride just passing the high point on the tracks beginning its downward plunge? Do you remember how you felt on the ride down?

While you are experiencing only paper losses, most investors still feel a bit queasy and tend to lose some objectivity. No actual losses occur until you actually sell investment positions. For those able to avoid selling, there is a chance that the next ride may head northward.

To insulate yourself from dramatic swings in the market, you may want to consider diversification. Reducing investment risk may make those market downturns a bit more bearable for your emotional well-being. Three different portfolio diversification approaches are available. The best choice is the one that makes sense for you. Factors affecting your decision are many, but three of the more important ones are

- your tolerance for risk
- your courage to stay the course and
- your belief in your investment philosophy

Ignore Equity Risk

One approach simply ignores equity risk because equities are historically the best investment alternative. Therefore, if an investor has the financial resources as well as the emotional stability to hold onto an all-stock portfolio through market turbulence, his tenacity can be a very rewarding selection.

However, severe extended market downturns may lead to fears of a potential recession that can change the resolve of even the staunchest, die-hard believers. Fear, with maybe a hint of panic, can have even the most confident of investors making poor, hasty decisions that might affect their portfolio negatively. Emotions are not an investor's friend; they are an enemy equally as destructive as costs, inflation or taxes. Emotional trading typically results in selling at the wrong time and buying at the wrong time—a formula destined for failure.

Diversify Across Equity Sectors

A second approach focuses on reducing risk by broadening the diversification across various sectors in the equity market. Following this approach, you hold a variety of different types of stocks such as large-, medium-, and small-capitalized stocks or perhaps you hold growth and value stocks or maybe you hold domestic and international stocks.

Typically, the purchase of a broad index fund is one method, but other possibilities are available as well.

In his book *Bogle on Investing, The First 50 Years,* John Bogle points out many alternative investments have characteristics considerably more risky than U.S. stocks taken as a group. For instance, business risk is present in new enterprises, financial risk is inherent in real estate, and leverage risk is associated with hedge funds. He goes on to say foreign stocks carry significantly larger risks, such as economic risk in the emerging markets, political risk in many nations, and currency risk in all such markets. Bogle questions the wisdom of reducing short-term volatility risk only to assume substantially greater financial risk of alternative investments.[5]

Sound advice indeed. You need to be cautious in your efforts to diversify. Sometimes, you may actually do more harm than good by unintentionally increasing other risks that may offset your intended purpose. Bogle's concern regarding foreign stocks is an excellent example because in an attempt to reduce U.S. market risk, you will introduce new risks that may be greater than the actual risk you wanted to eliminate. The law of unintended consequences can be very powerful because you do not see it coming; you only recognize it after it arrives.

Diversify Outside of Equity Sectors

Another approach focuses on reducing risk by lowering equity exposure. In other words, you lower the percentage of stocks by adding bonds to your portfolio. Reducing your exposure to stocks reduces your downside risk, but it also reduces your upside potential.

Since no one can accurately predict the future, investment theories analyze past performance in order to package forecasts in doses of probabilities. Probabilities are not guarantees however, and outcomes are never certain. John Bogle suggests investors should determine their asset allocation not on the probabilities of selecting the right allocation, but on the consequences of selecting the wrong allocation.[6] Recall our earlier question regarding the trade-off between risk and reward. Most individuals would much rather lose an opportunity to make money than experience the reality of losing money. Although bond returns may exceed stock returns 40% of the time, the main reason for adding bonds to a portfolio is to protect against the uncertainty of holding stocks.

Much like beauty, risk is in the eye of the beholder. You must decide what approach best fits your needs. Warren Buffett said that risk comes from not knowing what you are doing. Certainly, a key benefit of a balanced investment program is to moderate short-term volatility, but the more important result comes to the investor who has the confidence to stay with his positions in the face of market downturns.

INFLATION: WHAT EVERYONE MUST SURRENDER

Inflation is an increase in the general level of prices. Therefore, inflation risk represents the potential loss in purchasing power. Since inflation treats everyone the same, regardless of circumstances, the most affected segment of society is those people on fixed incomes, such as retirees. Increases in consumer prices also hurt individuals whose incomes remain flat or do not rise at the rate of inflation. Milton Friedman referred to inflation as taxation without legislation.

Inflation was practically non-existent until the end of World War II. Until that time most of the industrialized world was on a gold standard that limited the supply of money and thus inflation. With the adoption of a paper money standard, the world economies eliminated the legal constraints on the issuance of money and linked inflation to political and economic forces. Commissioned to maintain price stability and promote economic growth through effective management of the money supply, the goal of the Federal Reserve was to neutralize deficit spending and other inflationary policies implemented by the federal government.

The relationship between the money supply and consumer prices is undeniable. Well documented in financial literature, high growth in the money supply leads to inflation and restrained growth in the money supply moderates inflation. Like all goods, supply and demand forces determine the price of money. When the money supply increases beyond the number of goods produced, inflationary pressures build, thus linking price levels to the money supply.

For an individual earning 3% in a savings account, no difference exists between paying 100% income tax on his interest income during a period with no inflation and paying zero income taxes during a period with a 3% rate of inflation. In either instance, the individual has no real income because in one the earnings are taxed away while in the other the earnings are eaten away. One is a crime, and the other is an insult. You can figure which is which.

In his book, *Stocks for the Long Run*, Jeremy Siegel provides a definitive study documenting stocks as the best long-term investment for increasing your wealth.[7] In studying the annual real returns on U.S. stocks over the past two centuries, Siegel looks at three periods. The first (1802 to 1870) coincides with the U.S. moving from an agricultural to an industrial economy. The second (1871 to 1925) represents the U.S. becoming a political and economic power. The final period (1926 to the present day) includes the change from post-industrial to a service- and technology-driven economy. Despite the dramatic changes over the past two centuries, the average real rate of return on stocks for each period has been remarkably stable—7.0%, 6.6%, and 6.4%, respectively. The average real return for the past two centuries has been 6.6%.

While stock returns can be very unstable in the short term, the returns are amazingly consistent in the long run (refer to Figure 3.3). Siegel called this stability the "mean reversion" of equity returns. Such stability is even more remarkable considering the many political changes, technological advancements, economic innovations, and social improvements that occurred during the past 200 plus years. Despite the emergence of inflation in the last of the three periods, the average annual real return remained consistent with the first two periods—when inflation was largely non-existent.

Siegel also studied the returns of U.S. Treasury notes and bills during the same period. The average annual real rates of return on long-term treasury bonds for the three periods were 4.8%, 3.7%, and 2.6%, respectively. Similarly, the average annual real rates of return on short-term treasury bills were 5.1%, 3.2%, and 0.8%, respectively. His explanation for the steep decline in the real returns for bonds during the last period was the Great Depression. Following the market collapse, a generation of investors may have shied away from the equity markets preferring the security of U.S. Treasuries, which drove returns down.

An unusual source presented a rather accurate perspective to the inflation debate, Yogi Berra pointed out, "A nickel ain't worth a dime anymore."[8]

TAXES: WHAT EVERYONE LEARNS TO DESPISE

While investors can achieve some protection against inflation, the ravages of taxes pose a more difficult problem. Investors should never base investment decisions solely on tax consequences; however, investors would be wise to understand the tax consequences of their investment decisions. Taxes can help to guide your actions, but taxes must never determine your decisions—perhaps delay a sale due to a pending change in the tax law, or wait to sell an investment until the long-term tax rate applies, or combine several sales that may offset a capital gain, or any number of reasonable actions.

With the tax laws expected to change, favorable tax rates—talk about an oxymoron—still apply to dividend income whereas the marginal income tax rates applies to interest income. You also pay capital gains taxes on the profits earned when selling investments. Short-term capital gains are investments held for less than one year and currently taxed at the marginal income tax rate. Long-term capital gains are investments held for more than one year and taxed at a more favorable rate (there is that phrase again).

If you think capital gains taxes are reasonable, you may want to revisit your assumptions. Capital gains taxes apply to the difference between the purchase price of the stock and the price of that stock when the sale occurs. The tax code penalizes investors during inflationary periods. Suppose your brother, Groucho, invests $1,000 in a non-dividend paying stock for five years. During this period, the inflation rate is relatively moderate at 2% and the stock appreciates 5% annually. Capital gains taxes pertain only to the gain of $276.28 ($1,000 times the 5% annual growth less the purchase price of $1,000). During this period, inflation erodes $117.01 of the purchasing power of the investment. Despite this 42% reduction in purchasing power, the government collects $41.44 ($276.28 profit times the 15% rate) based on the entire capital gain without regard for the loss from inflation. The combination of inflation and capital gain taxes leaves the investor with a real profit of $117.83, an effective tax of 57%! You bet your life this is a devastating hit.

The double taxation of dividends also affects all investors whether large or small. Initially taxed when the corporation reports their annual income, dividends are after-tax payments that are taxed a second time when individual shareholders report their dividend income from that corporation. No wonder President Ronald Reagan was so fond of saying the nine most hated words in the English language: "I'm from the Government, and I'm here to help."

The best advice for managing the taxes on investment earnings is to defer the tax payments for as long as possible. Given the time value of money (the impact of inflation), it is usually cheaper to pay a dollar in the future than to pay that dollar today. Therefore, whenever possible, you need to fund your IRA or Roth accounts, contribute to your 401(k) accounts, and participate in all tax-deferred programs to which you are entitled and can afford. Since these accounts defer taxes until distribution, funding is beneficial even when made with after-tax contributions.

If you are concerned about tax efficiency, you routinely want to review both new and pending changes to the tax laws. In taxable accounts, either long-term capital gains or dividends are the preferred choice since the current tax rates are lower than the marginal income tax rates used on short-term capital gains and interest income. When investing in taxable accounts, you may try to offset "tax losses" by either increasing your savings rate, which is a good thing, or by increasing your investment risk, which definitely is not a good thing. Unfortunately, this may be a circular argument since the greater the investment returns, the larger the tax bill becomes.

Bob Hope said it best: "I love to go to Washington—if only to be near my money."

SOMETHING TO REMEMBER

Individual investors have a very, very powerful weapon in their arsenal that trumps the professional money managers—they have the ability to wait. The professional money manager needs to make investment decisions based on short-term needs, primarily his own. Driven by quarterly performance and annual returns, his compensation focus is on short-term performance indicators. For these reasons, he may assume more risk to achieve performance targets and thus no longer be in alignment with the desires of many individual investors. Successful investors set long-term investment goals and shy away from short-term speculation. As a long-term investor however, you must be able to control your emotions when the market takes an inevitable downward swoon. To quote Nero Wolfe, "I can dodge folly without backing into fear."[9]

Warren Buffett offered an excellent overview of the role the market plays in his investment decisions in the now famous story of Mr. Market as told to him by his friend and mentor, Benjamin Graham.

> Ben Graham, my friend and teacher, long ago described the mental attitude toward market fluctuations that I believe to be most conducive to investment success. He said that you should imagine market quotations as coming from a remarkably accommodating fellow named Mr. Market who is your partner in a private business. Without fail, Mr. Market appears daily and names a price at which he will either buy your interest or sell you his.
>
> Even though the business that the two of you own may have economic characteristics that are stable, Mr. Market's quotations will be anything but. For, sad to say, the poor fellow has incurable emotional problems. At times he feels euphoric and can see only the favorable factors affecting the business. When in that mood, he names a very high buy-sell price because he fears that you will snap up his interest and rob him of imminent gains. At other times, he is depressed and can see nothing but trouble ahead for both the business and the world. On these occasions he will name a very low price, since he is terrified that you will unload your interest on him.
>
> Mr. Market has another endearing characteristic: he doesn't mind being ignored. If his quotation is uninteresting to you today, he will be back with a new one tomorrow. Transactions are strictly at your option. Under these conditions, the more manic-depressive is his behavior, the better for you.
>
> But, like Cinderella at the ball, you must heed one warning or everything will turn into pumpkins and mice: Mr. Market is there to serve you, not to guide you. It is his pocketbook, not his wisdom, you will find useful. If he shows up some day in a particularly foolish mood, you are free to either ignore him or to take advantage of him,

but it will be disastrous if you fall under his influence. Indeed, if you aren't certain that you understand and can value your business far better than Mr. Market, you don't belong in the game. As they say in poker, "if you've been in the game 30 minutes and you don't know who the patsy is, *you're* the patsy."[10]

Read this story again, and file it somewhere in the back of your head—do not forget it. You should never become so obsessed with the daily swings in the market that you lose focus on investment fundamentals. The market is there only to serve you, not to guide you. The short-term is for speculators; the long-term is for serious investors.

Never feel so comfortable that you believe you know the market. No one knows the market. When you begin believing you are infallible, remember these three famous, or rather infamous, dates—September 8, 1929; January 2, 1973; and August 31, 1987. Investors probably felt comfortable when they went to sleep on those particular evenings. In each instance however, the following day started catastrophic declines in the market with some lasting years. After the dust had finally settled, the market decline that started in 1929 finally ended three years later with an 85% loss of value. The 1973 decline finished the following year with a 50% drop. The 1987 decline experienced a 35% loss. Then of course, the most recent decline that began in December 2007 ended more than a year later with a 40% decline in value. Now what were you saying about knowing the market?

Statistical analysis clearly indicates the superiority of stocks in the long run. Stocks have outperformed bonds in all 25-year periods since 1926. Shortening those periods however does reduce the certainty stocks will outperform bonds. For all 10-year time periods stocks have outperformed bonds 85% of the time; for five-year time periods the percentage drops to 76%; and for one-year time periods the percentage is only 61%.

When times are tough, many investors tend to stay away from the market. Unfortunately, this decision can be detrimental to your wealth. With the stock market advancing in seven out of every 10 years, the biggest failures come from either missing the market's upward surges entirely or being under-invested during major upward moves. To take advantage of those upward surges, you always want to be in the market. A balanced portfolio provides you with the confidence to stay the course. You always want to be in the game. In almost half of those years when the market did not advance, the declines were only in single digits often in the 4%–5% range. The risk associated with most bear markets is minimal.

Many studies have analyzed stock market returns over long periods. For instance, being out of the market during the best 30 months of the stock market reduced stock market returns to the level of U.S. Treasury Bills! Now think about that—the return dropped from 9.3% to 4%. Other studies have found deleting the best 50 months of returns eliminated the entire return of the S&P 500. Can anyone really time the market so precisely as to select the best 30 to 50 months over the past 80 years?

Very compelling data indeed, but the stock market is by no means foolproof. Although the market advances seven out of every 10 years, no one can predict which of those years will end with advances or declines. Despite overwhelming evidence that stocks tend to regress to the mean, we still do not know, in advance anyway, the years in which these events will occur. In fact, bonds outperform stocks in four out of every 10 years. No one can foretell the future.

PLAY TO YOUR STRENGTHS

George Santayana said, "Those who cannot remember the past are condemned to repeat it."[11] With history as your guide, you do not want to be a trader or a market timer. You want to stay fully invested, riding out the market swings with a balanced portfolio. You need not be concerned whether you have missed market surges when you are always in the market. As Nero Wolfe opined, "You are to act in the light of experience as guided by intelligence."[12]

CHAPTER FOUR

Gaining Perspective

Long journey always starts with one short step.
Charlie Chan in Shanghai (film), 1935

WHILE MANY MAY know Charlie Chan, far fewer know the author who created this memorable character. Earl Derr Biggers wrote six Chan novels. His first, *The House Without a Key*, was published in 1925. Although not an immediate success, Chan garnered more recognition as more novels appeared. Still, there is little doubt that much of his popularity resulted from the many movies Hollywood produced during the '30s and '40s starring Warner Oland (1931–1938), Sidney Toler (1938–1946), and Roland Winters (1947–1949) in the lead role of that famous Chinese detective.

Being of Chinese ancestry, Hollywood portrayed him in the stereotypical style of the period. In his speech, Chan would replace an "r" with an "l." His use of insightful proverbs demonstrated a depth and understanding of his surroundings, all of which contributed to making Charlie Chan a uniquely unforgettable character for almost two decades. Drawing upon his disarming rhetorical skills, the long journey into the world of investing begins with one short step.

First, you must distinguish savings from investment capital. Savings represents money you have placed in sort of a "holding" pattern. It is your emergency fund and it provides a security cushion, typically representing three to six months of income. Since safety and ease of access are the most important requirements, low risk assets such as savings accounts or money market funds usually house this money. Many also use savings for one-time expenditures such as paying a large tax bill, or buying a car, or replacing a broken appliance. When spending a portion of your savings, you must replenish the funds to maintain your desired safety level. A safety net is extremely important because it protects you in the event of emergencies and other unplanned expenditures.

Investment capital, on the other hand, represents money set aside for longer-term financial needs such as retirement. Although individual circumstances differ, achieving your savings comfort level permits the beginning of an investment program. Everyone, every single investor, must begin an investment program with a retirement portfolio—no excuses, no arguments and no questions. If you have the financial resources, you may want to build a core investment portfolio as well. The tax deferred retirement portfolio is a necessity; the taxable core portfolio is a bonus. The investment choices may be the same for both portfolios, but they need not be.

Always remember investment is not speculation. Speculation is short-term trading and is neither encouraged nor recommended.

THE INVESTMENT LIFE CYCLE

Common sense tells us a 29 year old and a 65 year old have different investment objectives. Decades away from retirement, the younger person can use his wages to offset potential investment losses and, therefore, can maintain a riskier portfolio in the hope of achieving higher returns. The older individual, on the other hand, probably does not have employment income to offset investment losses and needs access to his money sooner since he is either nearing or already in his retirement years. As an individual moves through the various stages of his or her life, investment priorities change based on income needs, financial resources and risk tolerance.

Focus in the early years should be on wealth accumulation. Many graduate from college, start their first job, and enter the workforce. Perhaps some take over a family business or start their own. Soon many buy their first "good" car, perhaps marry, maybe start a family, and purchase their first home. They have a steady income stream; perhaps they are risk takers. The future is in front of them and it looks bright. They want to enjoy life.

Many reach their peak earning years during the transition from early to middle adulthood. Many are paying college tuitions and mortgages and focus on maintaining their lifestyle. All of these factors reduce income options and may reduce their tolerance for risk. In the middle years, their children have grown and may be starting families of their own. Some anxiety begins to appear as many finally begin thinking about their retirement and future needs.

Upon retirement, the distribution stage generally begins. Most are living off their accumulated wealth and presumably Social Security. Many may be enjoying leisure activities, but a good portion also may be worrying about health care costs, housing needs, and other general living expenses. Most are seeking financial security and peace of mind, so their risk tolerance is low.

You want to make sure that you have the flexibility to restructure your portfolio as you move through these stages of your life. The traditional approach suggests a more aggressive portfolio in your earlier years to build your wealth, moving to a more moderate stance during your midlife years to maintain your wealth, and finally leading to a conservative approach in your retirement years. As our Chinese detective friend advises, "Journey of life like a feather in stream—must go with current."[1]

Problems arise when you delay the start of your investment program until later in your life. Perhaps you speculated in the market sustaining frequent or large losses; or maybe you traded too frequently incurring large tax burdens; or maybe it was one of a hundred other reasons. Now you compound your problems by increasing your risk in the hope of achieving higher returns to make up for lost opportunities and lost time. Unfortunately, this approach is fraught with problems and often leads to further frustration and even greater risk taking—a sure fire formula for catastrophe. This is not a good thing.

ESTABLISHING OBJECTIVES

Before deciding on the investments to purchase, you must determine whether you want to own mutual funds, individual securities, or a combination of both. But take a step back. Another issue still needs clarification. Many new investors fail to define their investment objectives. Wanting to make money is much too vague and not quantifiable. Without the ability to measure success, most investors are destined for failure.

First, you need to set realistic goals based on long-term historical markers. Accordingly, you want to target a historically competitive long-term rate of return with minimal risk. You want to avoid the influences of media hype. You never want to become an emotional investor. You do not want to be taking investment advice from friends or relatives.

Second, you have to develop a plan, you need to follow that plan, and you must not stray from that plan. You do not need a lot of money, you do not need to spend hours and hours investigating what to buy, and you do not even need to monitor performance continually. You want to stay invested in a balanced portfolio that will limit your risk in the bad times, but still allow you to enjoy some of the benefits when times are good. Markets are cyclical; they move up as well as down, sometimes rapidly, and sometimes slowly. The stock market goes through four distinct stages: expansion (growth), peak, contraction (recession), and trough. Unfortunately, these stages are identified only after they have occurred and quite often *long* after they have occurred. Never ever try to time the market—it is a loser's game that has taken its toll on many would-be investors.

Finally, you want to concentrate on dividends and interest. Why? Long-term return consists of equal parts dividends and capital appreciation. Yes, almost half of the market's long-term return comes from yield. Let your positions grow through the magic of compounding—remember that $3,052 investment. Keep your costs low, trading to a minimum, and limit portfolio turnover. Concentrate on the long term. Get rich quick ideas rarely work. Your role model is the tortoise not the hare.

OPTION ONE: MUTUAL FUNDS

Conventional wisdom suggests you should stay with mutual funds until you have at least $250,000 to invest. For most new investors, no decision is required because few individuals have that kind of money. So what should you do? Every investor is different. Each situation is unique. Mutual funds provide diversification, professional management, liquidity and convenience. These benefits deserve a closer look.

Diversification helps mitigate risk. Holding investments across equity sectors, or perhaps outside the equity sectors entirely, can achieve diversification. In addition to different industries, equity sectors also refer to large-, medium-, and small-cap stocks or growth and value stocks, or even domestic and international stocks. Most investors are unable to achieve adequate diversification with individual securities and, thus, bear much more risk. Many may be surprised to learn that a volatile mutual fund, such as a sector fund, has less risk exposure than a single position in a conservative blue-chip stock such as Johnson & Johnson.

Professional management ensures fund assets adhere to the basic investment objectives and policies stated for the fund. Fund managers receive compensation based their performance. However, fund managers, as a group, cannot outperform the market—these very fund managers *are* the market—while some overachieve, others will under perform. Professional management provides continuity, consistency, and investment experience.

Liquidity is the hallmark of the mutual fund industry. Valued at the end of each business day, open-end mutual fund shares convert easily into cash or can be exchanged readily for other fund alternatives at a fraction of the cost of individual securities. Depending on the mutual fund, many of these transactions may not incur any charges, allowing you to manage your portfolio efficiently, effectively and inexpensively. Closed-end mutual funds have the same characteristics as individual stocks.

Convenience is another benchmark of the mutual fund industry. While initial purchases require the completion of an application and an acknowledgment you have read the prospectus, future transactions, including exchanges, can occur by phone, online or through the mail. More importantly, you need not spend hours and hours monitoring the management of your investments. Periodic reviews are encouraged, but daily monitoring is not necessary.

Do these benefits go away after achieving the $250,000 threshold? They certainly do not. In fact, most investors, regardless of their wealth, may improve their performance by investing solely in mutual funds. Mutual funds offer many helpful benefits to all investors, but most especially to those investors without large sums of money and those in retirement as well.

OPTION TWO: INDIVIDUAL SECURITIES

If you have more time, more money, more risk tolerance and significantly more emotional fortitude, individual securities may be a consideration. But here are a few issues that should be taken into account before you pick securities.

The main benefit of individual securities is greater control over your portfolio—you decide what to buy or sell and when to buy or sell. On the other hand, mutual funds, by law, must distribute almost all of their dividends and capital gains. The trade-off for this increased control is the significant time commitment necessary to manage your portfolio. You accept responsibility for selecting investments, monitoring performance, and maintaining records for tax reporting.

The capital requirements for building a well-diversified portfolio increase when you go with individual securities. For instance, do you want any single investment to be greater than 5% of your portfolio? Perhaps 3% of your portfolio is better. Maybe 2% is better still. Choosing the first option requires a 20 stock portfolio, choosing the second option requires 33 stocks, and the third option requires 50 stocks. Do you have the time and inclination to manage such a portfolio?

Individual securities possess firm risk as well as market risk. This increased risk may be more unsettling because you are constantly worried about one, two, or even more stocks that may not be performing as expected. You must deal with highly visible performance shortfalls and will need the emotional strength to watch the price swings. It is difficult; do not take it lightly.

Many investors have successfully invested in individual securities. To level the playing field, the investor must make sound choices, keep costs low, trade infrequently, and allow the magic of compounding to work. When choosing this path, you are also choosing to spend more time managing your portfolio. While nothing is wrong with this approach, investing in individual stocks is not necessary. You can accomplish your goals by spending less time, incurring less risk, and enjoying yourself much more.

STAY WITH CONVENIENCE AND SIMPLICITY

Okay, mutual funds are the way to go. To win the investment battle, you must stay focused and well organized, emphasize simplicity and maintain a long-term investment approach. With thousands of mutual funds available in the marketplace, the task of selecting the right funds may seem daunting, but a few simple guidelines can make the job easier.

The use of a single fund group provides maximum flexibility and convenience as you move through the investment life cycle. This does not mean you should sell an old favorite fund, especially if you have a low tax basis (of course, tax concerns do not apply in tax-deferred accounts). If you must own multiple fund families, try to limit your exposure to no more than two or three. Keep exceptions to a minimum.

Stay with larger fund groups that offer investors a wide variety of investment choices. Which fund group do you want to choose? Without question, you want to stay with no-load funds. You certainly do not want to pay someone for the privilege of investing your money! Why give someone $100 only for him to turnaround and invest, say, $95? You start with a loss and you did not even enter the market yet!

Another way to reduce the population is to eliminate entire groups based on undesirable practices or policies. For instance, you want to avoid groups that have hidden sales charges, incur high expenses, generate excessive turnover, or maintain large cash reserves. At a minimum, keep the expenses below 0.75% for equity funds and 0.35% for fixed income funds. Portfolio turnover also needs to be low; look for funds below 50%. Put the power of compounding to work for you. Finally, make sure the fund investment policies are consistent with your objectives.

For simplicity, all mutual fund references and examples used in this book are from the Vanguard Group. Other fund groups are equally suitable to meet your financial needs such as Fidelity, T. Rowe Price and many others. Of course, two of the largest, and perhaps most recognized, fund groups are Fidelity and Vanguard.

Although the overall performances of these no-load funds are similar, with no single group significantly outperforming another, the legal structure of the Vanguard Group is unique. It is truly a mutual fund company because the individual shareholders of each individual fund are the owners of that particular fund. Therefore, the individual fund shareholders, not an outside management company, control the management of the individual funds. Since the overall mutual fund family has neither publicly traded shareholders nor privately controlled ownership, no outside parties are entitled to a portion of the return on the fund's investment results. In other words, there is no additional drain on the profits.

RESEARCHING MUTUAL FUNDS

The Holy Grail of the mutual fund industry is Morningstar. Their reports are available at your local library or online. Morningstar monitors over 1,500 mutual funds providing historical performance information, current holdings, fund analysis, and other background data. Disregard the often-advertised "Morningstar Stars." What makes you think the "Stars" methodology is consistent with your objectives or your financial situation? Instead, you want to use Morningstar for its consistency in presenting data in a way that enables comparison of funds across the mutual fund industry. You can decide which funds fit into your financial plan.

Be cautious about online sources. Many are available; some are good while others are not. However, one point should be uncontestable. Never rely solely on advertising coming from the mutual fund family you are researching. Although there is no suggestion they are misrepresenting facts, data presentation techniques may make comparisons to other investments ineffective and useless. Print ads prepared by mutual fund companies will present their funds in the best light. Often, those advertised returns involve a specific period, such as March 12 through July 5. The reason a fund family uses such specific dates is to promote the performance that, most likely, was better than using a more traditional period such as the second quarter or a calendar year. These specific dates make the ad factually correct, but also a bit misleading and certainly not comparable.

You are investing your hard-earned money. You want comparability, objectivity and history. Retaining copies of the funds you want to monitor enables you to extend the history beyond what is available in the current analysis. In so doing, you can generate an improved historical perspective that tracks performance through various market conditions. Why is this important? Performance in good markets can be misleading, but performance in bad markets is informative. As a long-term investor, you are interested in all types of markets and the fund combinations providing the best long-term performance for your entire portfolio not just the performance of a specific fund.

You often read that past performance is not a guide for future performance. In fact, many financial gurus tell you to disregard history entirely. These assertions are a bit misleading as well. History is certainly not a precursor to future performance when looking at a brief period, such as last month or last year. However, when you look over longer periods, especially those including a recession or a significant downturn, the benefit of past performance increases tremendously, especially when considering passively managed funds. Of special interest is the comparison of past performance to market benchmarks and similar funds. Always understand the need for comparability of the data. Several questions may be helpful. Has the fund merged with another fund? Has the fund manager changed? Have the investment objectives of the fund changed?

Draw on the wisdom of our illustrious detective, Mr. Chan: "Mind like parachute—only function when open."[2]

CHAPTER FIVE

Think Risk First

It is a capital mistake to theorize before one has data.
The Adventures of Sherlock Holmes by Arthur Conan Doyle, 1892

SHERLOCK HOLMES NEEDS no introduction. Arthur Conan Doyle wrote 56 short stories and four novels, resurrecting a London that is gone forever—nineteenth century London complete with dark, foggy cobblestone streets dimly lit by gaslights, Dr. Watson stepping down from a horse-drawn hansom carriage at 221B Baker Street, and Holmes filling his pipe with tobacco taken from the Persian slipper atop the fireplace mantel. Like a fine wine, these classic tales get better with age.

Like many famous literary detectives, Holmes is no stranger to the motion picture industry. Although Jeremy Britt may be more familiar to many as Holmes, there is a particular fondness for the 14 films produced from 1939 to 1946 starring Basil Rathbone as Holmes with Nigel Bruce as his friend and companion, Dr. Watson. They reprised these roles on radio in "The New Adventures of Sherlock Holmes" which aired from 1939 to 1946.

Throughout these engaging stories, Holmes draws upon his keen observation skills, his well-developed attention to detail, and his renowned deductive capabilities to solve the most complex cases. These traits can serve you, an investor, equally as well. Let the most famous fictional character in the world introduce you to the little known concept that follows.

Many investors only purchase equities for their portfolio holdings. They begin investing during bull markets and they tend to forget that markets go up and down. Many individuals enter the bull market believing that investing is rather simple and quite easy. You just buy a stock or an equity fund and watch it go up with the rest of the market. Then surprise, the inevitable market downturn hits and POW! All these new investors go running to the sidelines, trying to avoid losses. Unfortunately, even more seasoned investors may make poor decisions when long running bull markets suddenly end. Perhaps many may not have experienced falling markets, they may not have built a sound portfolio, or they may be trying to time the market. Whatever the reasons for selling their equity holdings, these investors have forgotten the market downturn brings only paper losses. The unintended consequence of their action is to lock in the very losses they are trying to avoid! They let their emotions get the better of them. You will not make that mistake. Why?

Many savvy investors employ a little known secret for their portfolios. You must do the same for yours. As Mr. Holmes might say when he uncovers an interesting clue, "HELLO!" Whatever your age, whatever your risk tolerance, whatever your financial position, your portfolio should be viewed as two separate parts. Stocks or equity mutual funds are one part and fixed income securities, most likely in the form of mutual funds, make up the other part.

SELECTING FIXED INCOME MUTUAL FUNDS

Investors who treat fixed income securities as equities make a huge mistake. You do not want to eek out additional profit by moving into riskier and riskier bonds. Junk bonds are called junk for a reason. You also want to avoid corporate bonds, even the higher quality ones. Think about it. The corporation issuing the bond influences the quality of that bond. When the market goes through difficult times, stocks fluctuate in value primarily based upon projections of the future earnings strength of the company. If that strength is in question, those same market assessments also affect the corporate bonds negatively. At the very time you look to your fixed income holdings to prop up your portfolio, those corporate bonds lose value as the market discounts the future earnings of the underlying company.

Unlike Fannie Mae and Freddie Mac, Ginnie Mae government agencies (GNMA) avoided the mortgage crisis because their conservative investments led to more stable mortgage pools. GNMA guarantees investors the timely payment of principal and interest backed by federally insured loans. While most GNMA funds invest 80% of assets in

Ginnie Mae mortgages, not all funds are alike. For instance, the other 20% of their portfolios may be in derivatives and other exotics or carry long-term debt. This leads to an increase in leverage, subsequently increasing portfolio risk.

Municipal bonds are also a no-no. Too many stories abound concerning current and pending credit problems associated with these securities. Municipalities are finding it increasing difficult to raise local taxes and thus maintain their funding positions. Do not become fooled by the tax benefits offered to municipals; the credit risk exposure more than offsets any tax benefit. Avoiding municipal bonds is a reasonable extension of the sound investment advice that says you should not make investment decisions solely based on taxes. Forewarned is forearmed. Stay away.

U.S. Treasuries provide your portfolio with the insurance policy you seek. When the market gets tough and believe me it will, treasuries provide a welcomed cushion, reducing the magnitude of the decline in your portfolio value and giving you the emotional strength to stay the course. Of course, the opposite is also true. When the market is accelerating to new highs, those same treasuries may dampen your return. However, losing some profit in an up-market is much more preferable to losing your shirt in a down-market. By understanding the role treasuries play in your total portfolio, it is an investment well worth the cost. The safety of treasuries is unquestioned. As a seasoned investor, keep your eye focused on the future. Only buy treasuries for your fixed income portfolio.

Remember, the rationale for holding treasuries is their safety and security. The interest and principal are 100% guaranteed by the full taxing power of the federal government. As an added bonus, you pay no state and local taxes on the interest when these instruments are in taxable accounts (such as your core portfolio). Oh, one more thing you may want to know. The returns on treasuries have actually beaten stocks four in every 10 years. Overall, treasuries make an excellent addition to all portfolios.

THE U.S. TREASURY MARKET

When the U.S. markets experience major declines, the global markets not only suffer the same fate, but they have fewer support mechanisms available to lessen the impact, making foreign markets more risky. The downgrade of U.S. credit in August 2011 was a warning shot. Investors have few options for parking their money while riding out worldwide market volatility. Unpredictability in the U.S. may make investors anxious, but uncertainty in the global markets is even more unnerving.

The treasury market remains the largest and most recognized sector in the investment market. More importantly, U.S. Treasuries remain the safest investment in the world, providing maximum liquidity. With round lot orders of $1 million, there are some rather large players in this arena, most of whom are institutional investors. They understand the near-term is not a major concern, but they also recognize that growing long-term U.S. debt may pose problems in the future.

Changes are necessary to ensure the treasury market remains the safest investment in the world. These adjustments may take many forms, generate a number of new initiatives, and even require structural modifications. However it's done, the economic strength and vitality of the U.S. economy must be restored.

The Structure of the Treasury Market

The Treasury market is actually a combination of two distinct markets. The primary market is the original issuance of securities by the Bureau of Public Debt, an agency within the Treasury Department, through the Federal Reserve. The secondary market comprises the brokerage firms, mutual funds, and investors who trade these securities after their original issuance. The primary and secondary markets operate separately but simultaneously. Since many of the participants are active in both markets, the two effectively appear as a single market.

The Federal Reserve System, or the Fed, is the major force in the market. The Fed is the nation's central bank and acts as the agent for the Treasury Department when issuing new treasury securities. All treasury securities originate from the Fed, and after issuance, all transactions in treasury securities clear through the Fed.

The primary dealers are the next major force in the market. Primary dealer status granted by the Fed, goes to selected large commercial banks and investment houses. Primary dealers perform several essential functions: they bid on all new issues of treasury securities; they bid on and distribute all new issues of debt from federal agencies; and they hold substantial inventories of existing treasuries that require them to maintain liquid markets in those securities. Since they buy securities for and sell securities from their own accounts to their customers, primary dealers act as principals rather than agents.

All other parties below the primary dealers are customers, and they comprise the remainder of the marketplace. Customers of the primary dealers include other banks, financial institutions either domestic or international, mutual funds, brokerages, pension funds, corporations and individuals.

Individual investors are unique in this market because, with certain limitations, they can deal directly with the Fed and the primary dealers. Individual investors can buy new issues of treasury bills, notes and bonds directly from the Fed at its regular auctions. Recent changes allow individuals to sell treasury securities back to the Fed.

Selected U.S. Treasury Securities

Individual investors can buy and sell treasuries in the open market through retail affiliates of primary dealers or through institutions working with primary dealers. Individual investors can also purchase newly issued treasury securities directly from the Federal Reserve without any service charge.

Treasuries come in all sizes and shapes. Their maturities help determine broad market categories. Treasury bills are short-term securities issued with maturities of 13, 26, and 52 weeks. Treasury notes, considered the intermediate range, have maturities ranging from one to 10 years. Treasury bonds have maturities greater than 10 years and are long-term securities.

In addition to these well-known securities, the Treasury offers other instruments as well. Let us look at two of these. Treasury Inflation Protected Securities (TIPS) have a fixed rate of return, but the principal fluctuates according to changes in the inflation rate as

FIGURE 5.1 *Present Value of $1*

YEARS	4.0%	4.5%	5.0%	5.5%	6.0%
5	0.82193	0.80245	0.78353	0.76513	0.74726
10	0.67556	0.64393	0.61391	0.58543	0.55839
15	0.55526	0.51672	0.48102	0.44793	0.41727
20	0.45639	0.41464	0.37689	0.34273	0.31180
25	0.37512	0.33273	0.29530	0.26223	0.23300
30	0.30832	0.26700	0.23138	0.20064	0.17411
40	0.20829	0.17193	0.14205	0.11746	0.09722

indexed by the Consumer Price Index. For this added benefit, the initial yield is slightly lower than conventional treasury securities of the same maturity. The principal amount of the securities increases when consumer prices rise. On the other hand, when prices decline, the Treasury pays back at least the original face value of the securities thereby establishing a floor beneath which the value does not decline.

Separate Trading of Registered Interest and Principal of Securities (STRIPS), or more commonly referred to as zero-coupon treasury bonds, are full-fledged government issues. Created in the secondary market, these securities are not available directly from the government. Sold at a discount and with all their interest paid at maturity, zeros generate "imputed or phantom" interest payments taxed as if distributed annually. The price volatility of zeros, especially longer term zeros, can be quite dramatic. Treasury bills and savings bonds are also zero-coupon securities because they pay interest at maturity.

A FEW BASIC BOND CALCULATIONS

No, this is not about whether a certain British agent prefers his martinis shaken or stirred. Current long-term interest rates and the creditworthiness of the issuer determine the interest rate of a bond at the time of issuance. This interest rate or coupon does not change over the life of the bond. The yield, on the other hand, refers to the actual return on the bond. The yield fluctuates throughout the life of the bond based on interest rate movements within the market.

FIGURE 5.2 *Present Value of an Ordinary Annuity of $1*

YEARS	4.0%	4.5%	5.0%	5.5%	6.0%
5	4.45182	4.38998	4.32948	4.27028	4.21236
10	8.11090	7.91272	7.72173	7.53763	7.36009
15	11.11839	10.73955	10.37966	10.03758	11.11839
20	13.59033	13.00794	12.46221	11.95038	11.46992
25	15.62208	14.82821	14.09394	13.41393	12.78336
30	17.29203	16.28889	15.37245	14.53375	13.76483
40	19.79277	18.40158	17.15909	16.04612	15.04630

The Mechanics of Pricing a Bond

The market price of a bond moves in the opposite direction, or inversely, to the movement of interest rates. Thus, when interest rates are moving higher (inflation) bond prices are moving lower. For instance, suppose you own a $100,000 treasury bond paying 4.5% interest, maturing in 20 years. When government borrowing increases, current long-term interest rates increase. Let's say the rate rises to 5%. Your treasury bond is now worth less than $100,000 because your 4.5% interest payments are below the current market rate of 5%. How much less, you ask.

Bond prices are the sum of two variables. The first variable is the value of the principal payment due at maturity. For the purposes of this example, the bond is not callable. The second variable is the sum of the interest payments received during the life of the bond. While financial calculators speed the process, knowing the underlying concepts is a useful exercise in understanding the overall market.

First, you calculate the present value of $100,000 payable in 20 years at 5% interest. Looking at the present value table in Figure 5.1, the factor is 0.37689. The calculation is $100,000 × 0.37689 = $37,689. The concept of the time value of money is that today's dollars are worth more than tomorrow's dollars because you can invest that money and receive an additional return over the period in question. The present value of $100,000 is much less today than it will be in 20 years. Confusing? Not really. Think of the calculation in reverse. You know the future value; therefore, you are trying to determine the current value that would achieve that future value. Stated differently, you have the option of receiving $37,689 today or $100,000 in 20 years. The two options are equal because investing the $37,689 today at 5% will earn $62,311 over 20 years for a total of $100,000.

Second, you calculate the present value of the $4,500 annual interest payments over the 20-year period, using the current 5% interest rate. Looking at the present value of an ordinary annuity table in Figure 5.2, the factor is 12.46221. You multiply the $4,500 annual interest payment times 12.46221 to determine the present value of $56,080.

Finally, you add the value of the present value of the principal ($37,689) and the present value of the interest payments ($56,080) to give you the current price of the bond. With long-term interest rates rising to 5%, the value of your treasury bond is only $93,769. Selling at a $6,231 discount, your bond has lost value.

Conversely, suppose long-term interest rates fall to 4% because the government has reduced spending and inflation remains under control. Your same treasury bond is now worth $106,795, a premium of $6,795. For the record, the calculation is the sum of the present value of the principal $45,639 (the factor of 0.45639 times $100,000) and the present value of the interest payments $61,156 (the factor of 13.59033 times $4,500). Now, that is a much better scenario.

Calculating the Yield of a Bond

The yield is simply the annual interest payments divided by the current price of the bond. When bond prices rise, the yields fall, and conversely, when bond prices drop, yields increase. The current yield on a bond varies over time due to the fluctuations in interest rates. When you hold the bond until maturity, the yield to maturity at the time of purchase is "locked-in."

Suppose you buy a treasury bond paying 4.5% interest, maturing in 20 years, currently selling for $93,750. The par or face value of the bond is $100,000 paying $4,500 in interest annually. You purchased the bond at a discount of $6,250.

The current yield on this bond is 4.8% (divide the annual interest payment $4,500 by the current price $93,760). If you hold this bond until maturity however, your actual yield-to-maturity would be slightly higher: 5.0%. Since the bond sold at a discount, you receive the par value of $100,000 at maturity rather than the $93,750 you paid for the bond.

The reverse occurs when you purchase a bond at a premium. In this case, the treasury bond matures in 15 years, but also pays interest at 4.5% annually. This bond is currently selling for $105,550, a premium of $5,550.

The current yield on this bond is 4.3% (divide the annual interest payment $4,500 by the current price $105,550). If you hold this bond until maturity however, your yield-to-maturity would be slightly lower: 4.0%. Since the bond sold at a premium, you receive the par value of $100,000 at maturity, but you paid $5,550 more than the par value.

Some bonds have callable features meaning the issuer has the right to redeem the bonds prior to the stated maturity date. Since redemption of the bond may occur prior to maturity, the yield-to-maturity calculation is misleading. When bonds are callable, the calculation is renamed yield-to-call and simply changes the maturity date to the call date.

When a bond is selling at a ...

- discount, the coupon or stated interest rate < current yield < yield-to-maturity
- premium, the coupon rate > current yield > yield-to-maturity
- par value, the coupon rate = current yield = yield-to-maturity

Understanding Risk

Having an understanding of the relationships among interest rates, price and yield sheds some light on several risk concepts discussed earlier—interest rate risk, reinvestment risk and inflation risk.

Interest rate risk (or price risk) is the possibility that the price of a bond will fall due to an increase in the general level of interest rates. The longer the maturity of the bond, the greater the interest rate risk because the longer the period to maturity, the greater the chance of a change in price for a given change in interest rates.

Reinvestment risk is the possibility that future interest and principal payments will be less than the current interest rates when reinvested. With regard to interest payments, this risk increases as maturities lengthen because the longer maturities increase the potential for a fall in the general level of interest rates. In terms of principal payments, the shorter maturities actually increase this risk because frequent rollovers increase the chance of lower interest rates over a long period. In other words, rather than rolling over a shorter-term bond, say every two or three years, you can purchase a longer-term bond of eight or nine years which generally provides a higher interest rate than the shorter-term bonds. When bonds possess call features, this risk increases as well.

Inflation risk (or purchasing power risk) is the potential erosion of the real return due to a sustained increase in the general level of prices. The longer the maturity of the bond, the greater the risk becomes since the longer time horizon provides more opportunity for actual inflation to exceed the fixed interest rate. Investing in inflation-protected securities, such as TIPS, may mitigate this risk somewhat.

Often referred to as risk-free investments, even treasuries are not immune to the aforementioned risks. On the plus side, however, treasuries are not subject to credit risk, liquidity risk or a whole host of other risks typically associated with other fixed income investments.

DOING A LITTLE HOMEWORK[1]

Now that you know what to purchase for your portfolio, you need to do some research. Not to worry, the research is not very taxing (no pun intended) and you do not need to spend hours and hours analyzing what to do.

Obtain a current copy of the *Morningstar Mutual Funds* book from your local library. You also may want to see a copy of the *Morningstar Mutual Funds Resource Guide* to familiarize yourself with the information presented. Due to the constraints of publication, some information is dated but that is not a hindrance. You are seeking directional information such as trends, holdings and long-term performance. Time is on your side.

Figure 5.3 presents a copy of the Morningstar analysis page for the Vanguard Intermediate Term U.S. Treasury Fund.[2] You want to familiarize yourself with the presentation format to facilitate your research. Not in any particular order of importance, the following items are helpful in analyzing fixed income funds.

FIGURE 5.3

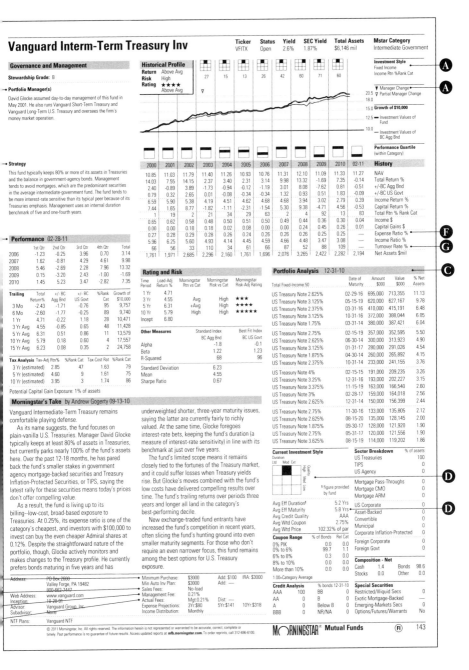

Ⓐ *Area:* Governance and Management

Section: Portfolio Manager(s)

Glance at the chart to the right of this box for any arrows indicating management changes. Also, look at the investment style boxes to the right at the top of the graph. The boxes highlight the investment style through the years. You are looking for consistency. Since these changes may influence the characteristics, holdings and performance of the fund, you want to confirm that the fund remains an appropriate selection for your portfolio objectives.

Ⓑ *Area:* Governance and Management

Section: Strategy

Review the stated objectives, buying characteristics and expected risks of the fund. Sometimes the fund also provides their evaluation benchmarks.

Ⓒ *Area:* Portfolio Analysis

Section: Sector Breakdown

Verify that the securities held within this fund are consistent with the fund strategy. Never assume the name of the fund accurately describes the securities held. Do not take anything for granted; you do not want to assume anything. Remember, "When you assume you make an *ASS* out of *U* and *ME*." Verify what percentage of the securities are, in fact, U.S. Treasuries.

Ⓓ *Area:* Portfolio Analysis

Section: Current Investment Style

Topic: Avg Eff Maturity

Check the average effective maturity of the fund's security holdings. Verify that the maturities of the securities held within this fund are consistent with the fund strategy. You do not want to purchase a fund with a strategy of holding short-term securities only to find out the fund holds instruments with an average maturity of 10 years.

ⓔ *Area:* Performance:

Section: Trailing Periods

Look at the average returns for the five, 10 and 15 year categories. Compare these returns to benchmarks such as the market indexes listed or similarly invested funds. Look for consistent earnings performance. Absolute earnings may be misleading because market conditions can affect the absolute returns significantly. Remember you want to counter-balance your total portfolio.

ⓕ *Area:* History

Section: Expense Ratio %

Check the average operating costs over the past three years. The operating costs for a fixed income fund should be under 0.35%. If higher, look elsewhere. More so than equity funds, the differences in the returns for fixed income funds of similar maturities is directly attributable to either expenses or risk. While *lowering the costs* favorably affects returns, *lowering the quality* of investment holdings increases risk, which is exactly what you do not want to do. Be sure you know which it is! The expense ratio pertains solely to asset-based expenses. Excluded from the expense ratio calculation are those expenses not tied to the asset base. Expenses such as portfolio transaction fees, brokerage costs and sales charges are volume or activity driven.

ⓖ *Area:* History

Section: Turnover Ratio %

Keep turnover low because portfolio transactions generate trading costs. Since these costs are not included in the expense ratio, many investors do not realize the significance of the turnover number. Fixed income fund turnover is not as meaningful, however. For instance, short-term bond funds holding treasury bills have significantly more activity because the bills mature in less than one year. Bond funds may also utilize cash management techniques that increase turnover.

Ⓗ *Area:* Operations

Section: Minimum Purchase

The smallest investment amount the fund accepts to establish a new account. After deciding which funds to purchase for your portfolio, the minimum purchase requirements dictate the total dollars needed to implement your plan. If you do not have sufficient funds to implement your entire program, you may need to stage purchases and temporarily adjust percentages.

Ⓘ *Area:* Operations

Section: Sales Fees

Always refer to the fund's prospectus for up-to-the-minute expense information. Sales fees, also called loads, come in many different sizes and shapes.

- *12b-1 fees* pay distribution and marketing costs typically capped at 1% of average net assets
- *Deferred loads, contingent deferred sales charges, or back-end loads* are deductions from the proceeds of sold fund shares and usually decrease to zero over time
- *Initial sales loads or front-end loads* are deductions from each new investment in the fund and usually discounted or waived for large investments and/or investors
- *Service fees* are part of the 12b-1 charges paid to financial planners or brokers for various types of services
- *Redemption fees* are deductions taken from fund withdrawals occurring before a predetermined period; these fees go back into the fund itself

Ⓙ *Area:* Operations

Section: Management Fees

The maximum percentage deducted from the fund's average net assets to pay for their advisors. Individual funds can base these charges on a flat fee, fixed percentage, or even as a percentage of the gross income generated.

FIGURE 5.4 *Selected Data for Vanguard Fixed Income Funds*

THROUGH YEAR END 2010

	TOTAL BOND INDEX	SHORT TERM U.S. TREAS	INTERMEDIATE U.S. TREAS	LONG TERM U.S. TREAS
Percent of U.S. Treasuries	34%	100%	100%	100%
Average Effective Maturity	6.9 yrs	2.3 yrs	5.8 yrs	22.2 yrs
Total Returns: 5 years	5.7%	4.5%	6.3%	5.5%
10 years	5.6%	4.3%	6.1%	6.4%
15 years	5.8%	4.8%	6.1%	6.5%
Expense Ratio (avg last 3 yrs)	0.21%	0.22%	0.25%	0.25%
Turnover Ratio (avg last 3 yrs)	70%	129%	83%	65%

Source: Morningstar Mutual Funds

🅚 *Area:* Operations

Section: Actual Fees

The prior year's actual charges paid for management and distribution services incurred by the shareholders.

MAKING THE RIGHT CHOICES

Unlike equities, bonds do not trade on exchanges. Dominated by large bond brokers, the bond market is neither efficient nor especially liquid. As a result, bond index funds are more expensive because they incur a larger performance drag relative to equity index funds. Index funds within the bond market generally focus on the entire market rather than specific segments. Accordingly, index funds may not be the best choice for the fixed income side of your portfolio.

Figure 5.4 summarizes selected data for several Vanguard fixed income funds. As you would expect, the Bond Index benchmark holds a much smaller portion of treasuries, is the lowest cost, and maintains an intermediate range maturity. The treasury funds hold a majority of their investments in treasuries with no fund currently holding less than 100%. Surprisingly, the expenses are not only reasonable but each treasury fund is only slightly higher than the benchmark index fund. While the return for the short-term treasury fund is below the broad market index, the average maturities of the two funds are significantly different (4.5 years). The Intermediate treasury fund holding similar maturities to the benchmark outperformed the index fund in each of the three return categories, and the long-term treasury outperformed the benchmark as well. A little closer look is in order.

Figure 5.5 presents the annual returns generated by each of the four mutual funds. The Total Bond Market Index generated annual loses only once in the past 19 years. The Short Term Treasury fund had one loss, the Intermediate Term Treasury fund reported three losses, and the Long Term Treasury fund posted four losses during the same 19 years.

It is rather interesting to highlight the returns for the treasury funds in the year following the losses. Except for one instance, the return in the following year was more than double the loss reported in the previous year and, in some instances, significantly greater. Remember the story about losing 50% on an investment means you must make 100% the next time just to break even. Well, in these particular instances that did indeed occur. Of the eight losses reported within all the funds, the return in the following year was substantially higher, enabling the fund to recover the loss and to report solid two-year performance numbers as well. This is definitely a good batting average.

Now let us look at the long-term performance of these funds. As expected, the returns increase as the maturity lengthens, consistent with the general concept of risk and return. The annualized returns for both the intermediate- and long-term treasury funds outperformed the benchmark index in the 10, 15, and 19 year periods. While the intermediate fund also outperformed the benchmark in the five year period, the long-term fund trailed the benchmark. The annualized returns for the short-term treasury fund trailed the benchmark index by approximately 1% in each category. That is consistent with the significantly shorter holding period of the fund. Even with the added safety and security of the treasuries, their performance was more than competitive on all fronts.

Do you recall the concept of standard deviation? The short-term treasury fund reported a total return of 5.1% over the 19 years with a standard deviation of 3.3%. Approximately two-thirds of the time, the expected annual return for the fund should be between 1.8% and 8.4%.

Unfortunately, no statistical programs are able to predict the actual return, only the probable return. Do not try to time the market. Overconfidence can have some dire consequences. Just ask the "undefeated" New England Patriots about Super Bowl XLII (New York Giants 17, New England 14). Ouch!!

BUILDING THE FIXED INCOME SIDE
OF YOUR PORTFOLIO

Do not be fooled by the pundits. They are always looking at the short- or near-term in their analyses—this investment is expected to outperform the market over the next six months, or this investment is a good place to put your money now, or this investment is in the next big growth area. The problem is that you are not building a short-term portfolio and even if you were, those pundits do not know your financial situation. Perhaps most important of all is those pundits are not exactly batting 1.000 with their recommendations. You want an all-weather portfolio because you want to sleep through those loud thunderstorms, severe hailstorms, and even record snowfalls.

Short-term speculation, excessive trading, and market timing are recipes for disaster because they mean higher trading costs, more taxes (in your core portfolio but not in your retirement portfolio), and little to no compounding. The fixed income side of the portfolio is your insurance policy. It is the roof over your head, the foundation under your feet, and the walls that protect you. The equities, on the other hand, are your belongings. It is what you talk about; it is what people see. But it is your fixed income securities that let you hold onto these possessions. They are your protection against the elements.

You want to own treasuries, and only treasuries, for the fixed income side of your portfolio. The first step is to construct a mix of treasury funds that will generate a competitive return against a broad market of fixed income securities while providing stability for the total portfolio.

In order to be competitive with a broad mix of fixed income securities, you want to own a reasonable portion of the *Long Term U.S. Treasury Fund* to boost your return. Longer term fixed income funds are more sensitive to interest rate movements, leading to returns that are more volatile. The fund reported annual losses four times in the last

19 years or once every 4.75 years, which is 21% of the time. Despite this volatility, if you had purchased this fund the year before each reported loss (the worst time to purchase), the two-year compound annual return would have been 10.0%, 6.0%, 4.6%, and -2.1%. The fund recovered three of the four losses in less than one year, and almost two-thirds of the remaining shortfall pending the current year results. Not bad at all. When coupled with a 7.5% annual rate of return over the last 19 years, this fund is a solid candidate for your portfolio. Suggested holdings for the fixed income side of your portfolio are 20% to 40%.

The *Intermediate Term U.S. Treasury Fund* needs to be the largest portion of your fixed income portfolio. Why? Under normal yield curve conditions, the intermediate term maturities typically provide the best risk-reward return. Despite conventional wisdom, which says the returns of treasuries lag the overall fixed income securities of similar maturities due to their lower risk, the total return of the intermediate maturity treasury fund actually performed significantly better than the benchmark index in each five-year period. The fund reported losses three times in the past 19 years or once every 6.3 years. In the year following the reported loss, the fund generated a return well over three times the loss of the preceding year. As before, if you had purchased this fund the year before each reported loss (again, the worst time to purchase), the two-year compound annual return would have been 7.3%, 4.9%, and 2.7%. Okay, this fund must be included in your fixed income portfolio. The annual rate of return of 6.6% over the entire 19 years makes this a very good fund to own. This fund needs to be the largest percentage within the fixed income side of your portfolio—40% to 75%.

With such a modest return, what about the *Short Term U.S. Treasury Fund?* The return is not the driving factor; it is the stability offered. Just like those old Brylcreem commercials, a little dab will do ya'. The primary purpose of the fixed income side of your portfolio is to provide some insurance against significant market downturns. A good return is simply icing on the cake. Since they fluctuate within a narrow range, short-term treasuries act as a buffer for your longer term treasury holdings. Since its inception 19 years ago, this fund has posted an annual loss only once. Following that loss, the fund regained that loss and then some, posting a two-year compound annual return of 5.6%. In fact, during the entire 19-year run, this fund has posted a very respectable annual rate of return of 5.1%. This fund also needs to be in your portfolio, but in moderation. Suggested percentages for the fixed income side of your portfolio are 10% to 25%.

There is much to like about an *Inflation Protected Securities Fund*—upside protection against inflation and a floor against deflation. However, mutual funds are not individual securities. Many of these funds had not been in existence during inflationary periods, which makes it difficult to document whether they will perform as advertised or even as expected. The daily price swings in a mutual fund reflects moves in the Consumer Price Index (CPI) as well as the general level of interest rates. For instance, when inflation occurs, interest rates rise, pushing bond prices down. It is reasonable to believe the demand for TIPS (Treasury Inflation-Protected Securities) will increase thereby providing some support to prices. Without history to test this hypothesis, TIPS are not a viable candidate at this time. Inflation protection comes at the expense of lower interest payments to fixed income securities of similar maturities. Downside protection is available by holding short-term treasuries in your portfolio. Although not recommended currently, any holdings of TIPS should reduce the percentage of your holdings that are in short-term treasuries.

You always want to err on the side of caution, use long-term history as a guide, and position your portfolio to ride out market turbulence. Certainly, the percentage allocated to various treasury funds will adjust to your specific situation. The suggested fixed income side of your portfolio includes the following treasury funds.

- 20% Short-term treasuries
- 50% Intermediate-term treasuries
- 30% Long-term treasuries

Remember these percentages are not against your total portfolio but the fixed income side of your portfolio. As you will see later, percentages change as you move through your investment life cycle, but more on that later.

FIGURE 5.5 *Selected Vanguard Fixed Income Funds*

ANNUAL PERFORMANCE

	1992	1993	1994	1995	1996	1997	1998	1999	2000	2001	2002	2003	2004	2005	2006	2007	2008	2009	2010
Total Bond Market Index	7.1%	9.7%	-2.7%	18.2%	3.6%	9.4%	8.6%	-0.8%	11.4%	8.4%	8.3%	4.0%	4.2%	2.4%	4.3%	6.9%	5.1%	5.9%	6.4%
Short Term U.S. Treasury	6.8%	6.3%	-0.5%	12.1%	4.4%	6.5%	7.4%	1.9%	8.8%	7.8%	8.0%	2.4%	1.0%	1.8%	3.8%	7.9%	6.7%	1.4%	2.6%
Intermediate U.S. Treasury	7.8%	11.4%	-4.3%	20.4%	1.9%	9.0%	10.6%	-3.5%	14.0%	7.6%	14.2%	2.4%	3.4%	2.3%	3.1%	10.0%	13.3%	-1.7%	7.4%
Long Term U.S. Treasury	7.4%	16.8%	-7.0%	30.1%	-1.3%	13.9%	13.1%	-8.7%	19.7%	4.3%	16.7%	2.7%	7.1%	6.6%	1.7%	9.2%	22.5%	-12.1%	8.9%
**Fixed Income Portfolio	7.5%	12.0%	-4.4%	21.7%	1.5%	10.0%	10.7%	-4.0%	14.7%	6.6%	13.7%	2.5%	4.0%	3.5%	2.8%	9.3%	14.8%	-4.2%	6.9%

**FIXED INCOME PORTFOLIO

	Allocation
Short Term U.S. Treasury	20%
Intermed U.S. Treasury	50%
Long Tm U.S. Treasury	30%
	100%

COMPOUNDED ANNUAL PERFORMANCE

	ANNUALIZED RETURNS				STANDARD DEVIATION
	5 YRS	10 YRS	15 YRS	19 YRS	
Total Bond Market Index	5.7%	5.6%	5.8%	6.2%	4.5%
Short Term U.S. Treasury	4.5%	4.3%	4.8%	5.1%	3.3%
Intermediate U.S. Treasury	6.3%	6.1%	6.1%	6.6%	6.6%
Long Term U.S. Treasury	5.5%	6.4%	6.5%	7.5%	10.9%
**Fixed Income Portfolio	5.7%	5.9%	6.0%	6.6%	7.1%
Performance Differential	0.02%	0.29%	0.19%	0.35%	-2.5%
(between the Fixed Income Portfolio and the Total Bond Portfolio)					

Figure 5.5 also compares the performance of a fixed income portfolio against the benchmark index. Surprise, surprise! The fixed income portfolio, comprised entirely of treasuries, outperformed the benchmark in each of the periods analyzed with only a modest increase in volatility. While outperforming the benchmark 58% of the time on an annual basis, our treasury model portfolio improves this ratio to 63% for every two-year period, 68% for each three-year period, and 95% for all five-year periods. Analyzing the annual losses provides some comfort to the resiliency of the treasury model portfolio. If you had purchased this fund the year before each of the three reported losses (yes, again, the worst time to purchase), the two-year return would have been 7.9%, 4.9%, and 1.2%.

The annual rate of return of 6.6% over the entire 19 years makes our treasury model portfolio a winning combination. With a standard deviation of 7.1%, the annual expected return of this portfolio is between -0.5% and 13.7%. When you get an insurance policy providing such a return with rock solid safety, you do not let the train leave the station without being safely aboard. Like the Polar Express, enjoy the ride!

If you do not have sufficient funds to implement this program in its entirety, do not worry. Purchase the short-term treasuries first because this fund maximizes your insurance. The first concern is always safety and never returns. Short-term treasuries are not as volatile and they do not lose money. This is important because many investors might get scared off from holding fixed income securities should they begin to falter. You know better. You know the plan and you know why fixed income securities are such an important part of your portfolio. Next, purchase one-half the intermediate treasuries for stability and consistency. Then purchase the long-term treasuries to bolster your long-term returns. Finally, purchase the remaining half of the intermediate treasuries.

You need a solid foundation to protect your returns during those inevitable market swings. All successful investors have a common set of characteristics. They maintain a plan, they understand the laws of compound interest, they are patient, and they avoid taking big hits. The treasury model portfolio successfully accomplishes each of these objectives.

STAYING THE COURSE—U.S. TREASURIES

An old baseball adage says you cannot win the pennant in April, but you sure can lose it. While this may sound crazy, it actually shows good sense. When a team falls too far behind, it will not be able to overtake the leader by making up that lost ground. In most divisions, teams usually need to win approximately 95 games for a reasonable chance at the playoffs. Assume your team starts the season with a record of five wins and 20 losses. Over the remaining 137 games, it needs to win 90 games for a .657 winning percentage; it is not impossible, but it is a very tall order. The same is true for your portfolio. You have seen the impact a delay can have on the long-term return of your portfolio. Equally important is to avoid potentially large losses by assuming more risk than is required. Why fall behind when you can avoid it?

There is a constant struggle between risk and reward. Many investors think more of the reward side of the equation because it aligns with the promise of riches. Unfortunately, many investors tend to disregard or rationalize risk until the inevitable day-of-reckoning comes knocking on the door. The difference between most investors and you is that you now understand the risk and you are going to be ready for that day. A veteran ballplayer understands that there are 162 games in a season, and it is filled with many ups and downs. More importantly, he also understands that the odds are in his favor if he focuses on what he can control: he plays his game, sticks with it, and executes accordingly. You need to do the same.

Staying the course refers not only to adhering to your plan, but also to controlling your emotions and not being influenced by media pundits, advertising hype, water-cooler talk, or hundreds of other "gurus" peddling their advice. This is wise counsel and it applies whether markets are growing or heading down. You need to control your emotions in all markets. When markets are declining, many novice investors who joined the crowd when markets were at their highest are devastated. They forget that the markets are cyclical and forget to maintain their positions in treasuries. Then that darn market goes into a tailspin and those investors soon realize their insurance policy has not kept pace with their portfolio. You, however, will not make that mistake.

A balanced portfolio is your best protection. No one can tell you when the market is going to change. Do not wait for the stock market to tank before you take action. It will be too late. Do it now and stay with your positions.

As the famous detective Sherlock Holmes noted, "Unwelcome truths are not popular."[3]

CHAPTER SIX

The All Important Next Step

The problem with putting two and two together is that sometimes you get four, and sometimes you get twenty-two.
The Thin Man by Dashiell Hammett, 1934

THE THIN MAN, published in 1934, was the last of five novels written by Dashiell Hammett—arguably his finest detective story based on the technical merits of detective fiction. It was not, however, his most famous work or even his most famous detective. Set in Prohibition-era New York, Nick Charles, a retired detective, returns from San Francisco with his wealthy socialite wife, Nora, for a vacation around Christmas time.

The story became the basis for a reasonably successful radio series (1941–1950) as well as a short-lived television series (1957–1959). It gained much notoriety from a successful series of six feature films (1934–1945) starring William Powell as Nick Charles and Myrna Loy as Nora Charles. Produced as light comedy, these films revived the careers of both leading actors.

In *Mysteries and Mystery Writing,* Hillary Waugh shares interesting background about this successful film series. With their careers fading and their contracts ending after their next film, MGM planned to drop both William Powell and Myrna Loy. The husband and wife screen-writing team of Albert Hackett and Frances Goodrich also needed to write one more film to complete their contractual obligations before leaving Hollywood for Europe. MGM decided to put the four of them together to speed their departures. Waugh explains that with little need to accommodate MGM executives, the writers developed the script based on their desires. He went on to say that since it was a minor film, management paid little attention to the daily clips. After the film was finished, MGM executives finally reviewed it. While they were outraged at the comedic undertone, Waugh points out that the movie audiences loved both the movie and its stars. Both Powell and Loy received long-term contracts, starred in five more *Thin Man* movies, and many other films on their own. You just never know what is around the corner.[1]

The same holds true with the stock market. Your investment plan must consider the uncertainties. Separating capital between savings and investment provides one layer of safety. Beginning a retirement portfolio, and for some maybe even a core investment portfolio, is another level of safety. Recognizing a very, very important aspect for every portfolio is yet another level of safety—a fixed income side and an equities side. The fixed income side contains only treasury securities functioning much like an insurance policy, enabling you to stay the course through the difficult times.

THE EQUITY MARKET IN MUTUAL FUNDS

Now to the equity side of your portfolio. You always want to own equities. Yes, that is correct; you always want to hold equities. Even in the worst of times, equities are essential. The question is what percentage of your portfolio should be in equities?

Over many cycles, equities provide significantly better long-term returns than fixed income investments. Unfortunately, many investors regularly equate action (i.e., trading in and out of positions) with profits. The truth is just the opposite; you do not want a lot of action in your portfolio. You only need to follow a handful of investments. Frequent trading is counter-productive because it breaks the chain of compounding—one of the key principles of successful investors.

Small-, Medium-, and Large-Cap Funds

When looking at the total market, splitting it into segments dictated by the size of the company is common. Market capitalization, or market cap, is the value of all outstanding shares of a corporation times its current price per share. Therefore, a company that has five million shares outstanding and trading at $100 per share has a market cap of $500 million.

How is the market split? The most common method is to divide the market by absolute values. Companies with a market cap in excess of $10 billion are called large-cap stocks. Mid-cap stocks are valued between $2 and $10 billion, and small-cap stocks are below $2 billion. Rather than using fixed market cap cutoffs, Morningstar uses percentiles. The largest 1% of U.S. companies are giant-caps, the next 4% are large-caps, the next 15% are mid-caps, the next 30% are small-caps, and the bottom 50% are micro-caps. Using the Morningstar market format:

- the large-cap category equals 5%
  (the combined totals of the giant- and large-caps)
- the mid-cap category is 15%
- the small-cap firms equal 80%
  (the combined totals of the small and micro-caps)

Why are these categories important? They are a key way to diversify a portfolio because these broad groups react differently to changing market conditions. When looking at the total market capitalization, large-cap stocks account for approximately 70% of the total dollar value with mid-cap stocks making up approximately 20% and small-cap stocks the remaining 10%. Hence, the market tends to mirror the large-cap segment.

Small-cap stocks are more volatile or risky because small companies do not have the financial strength of the larger corporations. Without a financial cushion, small-caps find it more difficult to withstand sustained market downturns, periodic operating troubles, and long-term internal problems. Despite these risks, small-caps offer superior growth potential because their higher debt ratios generate greater leverage on their earnings growth. While companies such as P&G, Microsoft and Exxon Mobil were small-caps at some point, the ability to uncover such success stories is difficult, time consuming, and fraught with many unsuccessful selections.

Mid-cap stocks have many of the same characteristics as small-caps. Greater financial stability, however, enables many mid-caps to withstand the inevitable market downturns, annoying operating troubles, and irritating internal problems. Arguably, mid-caps have become the sweet spot for investors because they offer better risk-reward opportunities. These companies have withstood the test of time, and have "graduated" from small-cap status.

Large-cap stocks tend to move in lockstep with the larger indexes because the corporations held in large-cap funds also compose a major portion of broad market indexes. Much like a huge ship on the ocean, strength and size provide security and stability, but those same characteristics also limit maneuverability and reaction time when market conditions change. Accordingly, for the strength and security of large-caps, an investor may sacrifice rapid growth opportunities.

During economic recoveries, small- and mid-cap stocks are expected to outperform the market because their size and narrower focus enable them to position their businesses better as the market picks up steam. Large-cap stocks tend to react more slowly as their internal operations require more time and effort to adjust to the market. Seasoned investors consider large mega-cap funds as little more than quasi-index funds. Due to the size of their asset base, these funds are limited primarily to purchasing giant- and large-cap stocks since those stocks can support the large purchases. Thus, giant- and large-cap stocks compose a significantly larger portion of those portfolios.

During market contractions, the financial strength of small-cap stocks raises concerns and limits their available options, whereas mid-cap stocks may be more insulated from such concerns and can weather some of these gyrations. These funds typically feel the market crunch first as their funding opportunities are squeezed. On the other hand, the financial strength of large-cap stocks enables many of them to withstand all but the most severe market conditions and to meet the challenges of operational and internal issues successfully.

Of course, market expectations, company performance, and reality rarely turn out as planned. With anomalies always present, the stock market is never a sure thing. Never assume you know how the market will react. Nothing is guaranteed and no one knows what will occur before it actually does.

Growth and Value Funds

Another common approach to the market is to split stocks into growth and value segments. *Growth funds* seek long-term capital appreciation, with dividend income a non-factor. The expectation of future growth drives their price higher thereby making these stocks expensive relative to their current earnings. Since expectations and growth are sometimes hard to achieve and even more difficult to sustain, these funds tend to have shorter time horizons and may trade more frequently, increasing fund turnover and fund expenses. As you might expect, growth funds tend to hold higher concentrations in industries such as technology, health care and consumer services.

Value funds, on the other hand, represent a combination of growth and income. These funds concentrate on stocks with above-average yields (dividend payouts) and below-average price-earnings ratios. Traditionally, these funds seek companies viewed as undervalued or out-of-favor. The justification for the undervaluation varies by fund and even by manager. Perhaps the entire industry is struggling, the company's financial statements are weak, the firm's balance sheet indicates perceived opportunities, or a host of other factors as determined by the fund advisor. Since company turnarounds can take time, value funds tend to have a long time horizon that corresponds to lower portfolio turnover and lower expenses. Value funds tend to concentrate in industries such as financial services, energy and utilities.

During bear markets, value funds are expected to do better because there is less price risk at the time of purchase. With much of their downside loss already built into the lower price, these stocks are expected to fall less than the market during a general decline. Partially offsetting this benefit, however, is the heavier concentration in interest-rate sensitive sectors (financial services, utilities), which may generate more volatility than anticipated during extended or severe market downturns.

During economic recoveries, growth funds tend to outperform value funds for the very reasons they are named growth stocks. When a recovery affects specific industries rather than a broad market upswing, some growth funds may outperform others. Again, no one can consistently predict what the market will do over the long term. Sometimes the ride is fun, and sometimes you fall off.

Specialty Funds

Specialty funds typically include investments in companies within a single industry such as health care, financial services, energy or utilities, to name a few. Some funds may limit investments to specific segments within a single industry such as biotechnology, drugs, managed care, hospitals or equipment in the healthcare field. This concentration within a specific segment or single industry constrains broad market diversification and thus increases the risk exposure of the fund.

Specialty funds represent a more aggressive investment approach and typically generate higher price volatility than mainstream funds. Similar to the characteristics of growth funds, specialty funds tend to have higher prices than their underlying earnings growth, generate higher turnover as they concentrate on short-term performance, and incur greater expenses due to greater transaction volume. These funds often are invested in speculative companies, raising the overall risk exposures for the fund.

The impact of market swings on specialty funds is based on the underlying industry held in their portfolios. With limited exposure to the general market, specialty funds can generate dramatic ups and downs, especially when market moves are focused on the industries held by the funds. Since the market is cyclical, these funds can outperform the market at times. Even a broken clock is correct twice a day!

Hybrid Funds

Hybrid funds are a combination of stocks and bonds. *Balanced funds* are a reasonably fixed portfolio allocation between stocks and bonds. *Asset Allocation funds* have stock and bond allocations that reflect existing market conditions. *Life Cycle or Target Date funds* have a time horizon and as that date approaches, the fund's stock and bond allocations are adjusted toward more conservative positions.

Balanced funds tend to hold up well during market downturns because the bond holdings provide a cushion against falling prices. Over longer periods, however, balanced funds lag behind pure stock funds because those bond positions also act as a drag on performance when stock prices are rising.

Asset allocation fund managers assume they can forecast the market correctly and shift their holdings to take advantage of their forecasts. As we know, however, no one can accurately predict the market over the long run. Furthermore, the cost of moving assets to coincide with forecasts leads to higher expenses than either the balanced or the life cycle funds incur.

With life cycle (or target date) funds, you must accept the fund's asset allocation mix. To improve performance, these funds tend to hold significantly riskier investments. Even as the theoretical target date approaches, the holdings in many of the funds continue to include positions in riskier assets to compensate fund holders who remain invested in the fund beyond the original target date.

While hybrid funds make sense conceptually, you have to accept their portfolio mix, their market concentrations, and their attempts at market timing. A wise man once said if you want to hold a stock fund, hold it; if you want to own a bond fund, hold it—just don't mix the two into a single fund. A better approach, and one that you control, is to build a portfolio that you want to own rather than a portfolio that someone else wants you to own.

Domestic and International Funds

The parameters that determine whether a fund is domestic or international vary. Morningstar defines a domestic fund as one with a minimum of 70% of domestic stocks among their total equity holdings. International funds, according to Morningstar, have a minimum of 40% of their total equity holdings in foreign stocks. These percentages are an average of a fund's holdings over the past three years. International funds are sorted into still narrower segments such as region, country specific and world funds.

Today the conventional wisdom is that investors should diversify their portfolios by holding international funds because domestic markets are entering a sustained period of slow growth. The belief is that foreign markets are generating significant future growth opportunities. The problem with conventional wisdom is that it is generally misleading and sometimes just wrong.

Even if you are convinced that foreign markets may outperform domestic markets, you are taking on considerably more risk when you add international funds. An example: when the returns from foreign markets are converted from local currency to U.S. dollars, the returns reflect fluctuations in the value of the U.S. dollar versus other currencies. In other words, when the U.S. dollar is weak, returns earned by U.S. investors in international markets are enhanced, but when the dollar is strong, those returns are reduced. In addition to currency risk, foreign funds also carry sovereign risk whereby a nation may default on its financial obligations, the risk of political instability and even the possibility of war. Considering the issues, it is difficult to justify the incremental risk associated with international funds. Investors always need to think about the risk before considering the return an investment may generate.

Passive and Active Funds

Passive or index funds are designed to replicate the performance of a particular market benchmark by holding a representative sampling of investments that compose that benchmark. All other funds are categorized as active funds because the fund portfolio advisors actively make investment decisions regarding their portfolio holdings.

Index funds are unique for several reasons. Since the funds replicate a benchmark target by investing either in all the stocks in that market index or a representative sampling of those stocks, index funds provide *predictable performance.* Since the funds remain virtually 100% invested regardless of the economic conditions, the *fully invested* index funds eliminate the drag on performance associated with holding cash. With no need to trade the stocks, index funds incur *low expense ratios.* With only two reasons to sell stock—a company has been dropped from the benchmark or cash is needed to meet redemption requests—index funds have *low portfolio turnover rates.* With the fund turnover being low, significant capital gains are not realized or distributed, making index funds *tax efficient.*

Critics claim that index funds provide only average returns. This argument falsely implies that index returns are average and, of course, investors can do better than average. In fact, study after study confirms the majority of actively managed stock funds fail to outperform the market index funds on a consistent basis. How can this be? To outperform an index fund, an active manager's portfolio must differ from the benchmark. It must hold a different number of stocks, hold stocks at different weights from the benchmark, or some combination of both. In addition to the risks of poor stock selection and bad timing, actively managed funds hold cash to execute these transactions, incurring additional expenses.

Because they hold cash, actively managed funds tend to lag their benchmarks during bull markets. Assume a fund holds 10% in cash and the market grows 25%. Further, assume the fund earns 3% on its cash holdings and 25% on its stock holdings. The fund's rate of return would be 22.8% (10% cash × 3% return + 90% stocks × 25% market growth). At a 22.8% return, this actively managed fund would have lagged the market by more than two full percentage points.

When the market is declining, many equity funds must meet redemption requests thereby drawing down their cash positions. In more severe bear markets, equity funds may need to sell some stock positions in order to meet the demand, which incurs additional expense. Both actively managed and index funds seem to suffer the same fate, but actively managed funds have the added risk of stock selection—choosing which stock positions to liquidate.

All investors, taken collectively, match the broad market average before considering costs. If one investor makes a 10% profit, another investor or group of investors must lose 10%. The market is a zero-sum game, which means the losers offset the winners. Zero-sum makes it considerably more difficult to outperform the benchmark index fund for any extended period.

Every fund must be able to pay expenses that include advisory fees, operating costs, distribution costs, and transaction fees. The average expense ratio for actively managed stock funds is approximately 1.45% with brokerage costs adding another 0.30% totaling 1.75%. For index funds, the average expense ratio is approximately 0.55% with brokerage costs adding 0.13% totaling 0.68%, less than half the cost of actively managed funds. These costs do not include the trading cost components (e.g., bid-ask spreads). Based on the previous example, the average active fund holding 10% cash would need a 28.7% return—or a 14.8% improvement over the market—to match the return of an average index fund. While such an improvement is achievable in any given year, performing at this level over a number of years is unrealistic. Large amounts of cash and higher operating costs put actively managed funds at a distinct disadvantage over index funds.

While active management does offer the opportunity to outperform a given benchmark, it does so at the cost of higher expenses and the risk of underperformance due to stock selection errors. Indexing, on the other hand, may not offer the ability to outperform a benchmark, but the low expenses and avoidance of stock selection errors allows index funds to outperform a majority of similarly positioned actively managed funds over the long term.

Mix and Match

Now that we looked at a few ways to segment the equity market, the choices significantly increase when combining various types of segments. For instance, perhaps you are looking for a large-cap value fund that holds domestic companies in an index fund. This search is not as intimidating as it sounds.

The antithesis of market segmentation is the broad index fund. Holding the entire market is, in effect, a mix-and-match approach. Many actively managed funds try to outperform index funds through the creation of blended funds that hold both growth and value funds. The premise of these funds is to limit the volatility of a particular market segment when it is out of favor, but they still remain susceptible to problems associated with actively managed funds. You accept their asset allocation mix; you accept larger costs due to cash holdings and increased trading; and you accept the risk of stock selection error. Conceptually appealing, but performance hindered.

You always want to hold some equity funds regardless of market conditions. It may be very difficult emotionally to hold onto equity positions when the market is in a tailspin, but every bull market starts in the throes of a recession. Remember that the stock market advances seven out of every 10 years, with almost half of those down years being in the single digits. The biggest failures do not come from being in the market during a market downturn, but from either missing the upward surges of the market entirely or being under-invested during those major upward moves. Knowing when market surges are coming on is the difficulty. Mostly we only see those market surges in the rear view mirror!

DOING A LITTLE HOMEWORK[2]

Once again, off to the library to get the *Morningstar Mutual Funds* book. Figure 6.1 presents a copy of the Morningstar analysis page for the Vanguard 500 Index Fund.[3] Again, not in any particular order, the following items are helpful in analyzing equity funds.

A *Area:* Governance and Management
Section: Portfolio Manager(s)
Glance at the chart to the right of this box for any arrows indicating management changes. Also, look at the investment style boxes to the right at the top of the graph. The boxes highlight the investment style through the years. You are looking for consistency. Since these changes may influence the characteristics, holdings and performance of the fund, you want to confirm that the fund meets your portfolio objectives.

B *Area:* Governance and Management
Section: Strategy
Review the stated objectives, buying characteristics and expected risk of the fund. Sometimes the evaluation benchmarks are provided.

C *Area:* Performance
Section: Trailing Periods
Look at the average returns for five-, 10-, and 15-year categories. Compare these returns to benchmarks such as the listed market indexes or similarly invested funds. Look for consistent earnings performance. Absolute earnings may be misleading because market conditions can affect the absolute returns significantly. Remember you want counterbalancing for your total portfolio.

FIGURE 6.1

D *Area:* History
Section: Expense Ratio %
Check the average operating costs over the past three years. The operating costs for an equity fund will vary considerably based on its strategy. With index funds, expenses need to be below 0.35%, while all other equity funds need to be below 0.75% including specialty and international funds. Each dollar paid out in expenses is one dollar less in returns, and the compounding effect can be devastating. Higher expenses also lead to riskier investments because the fund needs to offset the higher costs and compete with other funds. The expense ratio pertains solely to asset-based expenses. Excluded from the expense ratio calculation are those expenses not tied to the asset base. Expenses such as portfolio transaction fees, brokerage costs and sales charges are volume or activity driven.

E *Area:* History
Section: Turnover Ratio %
Keep turnover low because portfolio transactions generate trading costs. Since these costs are not included in the expense ratio, many investors do not realize the significance of the turnover number. Turnover also results in taxable events. Fund strategy influences this number. For most equity funds, the turnover needs to be below 50%; however, small-cap stock funds and high-growth funds tend to be higher. Caution is advised. Try to keep the turnover below 75% and monitor the fund's performance. Review the past few years; some funds may exceed your target number in a single year, but stay within the range on average. In your tax-deferred accounts turnover is not a taxable event, just an expensive one.

F *Area:* Operations
Section: Minimum Purchase
The smallest investment amount the fund accepts to establish a new account. After deciding which funds to purchase for your portfolio, the minimum purchase requirements dictate the total dollars needed to implement your plan. If you do not have sufficient funds to implement

your entire program, you may need to stage purchases and temporarily adjust percentages.

❼ *Area:* Operations
Section: Sales Fees
Always refer to the fund's prospectus for up-to-the-minute expense information. Sales fees, also called loads, come in many different sizes and shapes.

- *12b-1 fees* pay distribution and marketing costs typically capped at 1% of average net assets
- *deferred loads, contingent deferred sales charges, or back-end loads* are deductions from the proceeds of sold fund shares and usually decrease to zero over time
- *initial sales loads or front-end loads* are deductions from each new investment in the fund and are usually discounted or waived for large investments and/or investors
- *service fees* are part of the 12b-1 charges paid to financial planners or brokers for various types of services
- *redemption fees* are deductions taken from fund withdrawals occurring before a predetermined period; they go back into the fund itself

❽ *Area:* Operations
Section: Management Fees
The maximum percentage deducted from the fund's average net assets to pay for their advisors. Individual funds can base these charges on a flat fee, fixed percentage, or even as a percentage of gross income generated.

❾ *Area:* Operations
Section: Actual Fees
The prior year's actual charges paid for management and distribution services incurred by the shareholders.

J *Area:* Portfolio Analysis
Section: Individual Stocks
Identifies the total number of stocks held in the portfolio and lists the top 20 equity holdings. For the top 20, it provides the fund weightings for the individual stocks, if any of the stocks have had recent share changes, and the stock performance. It can provide a peek at the fund's stock picking and selection prowess as well as the activity of these top holdings.

K *Area:* Portfolio Analysis
Section: Current Investment Style
The style box highlights the focus of the fund's investment program. Does the fund invest in large-cap, mid-cap, or small-cap stocks? Does the fund concentrate on growth, blended, or value stocks? Review the style boxes across the top of the page to determine the fund's consistency in its investment approach. Consider funds maintaining a consistent style. Surprises are not a good thing.

L *Area:* Portfolio Analysis
Section: Market Cap %
Indicates the percentage of holdings allocated to giant-cap, large-cap, mid-cap, small-cap, and micro-cap stocks. When building your portfolio, understand the mix of your entire portfolio in order to evaluate expectations with actual results.

M *Area:* Portfolio Analysis
Section: Sector Weightings
Verify the securities within this fund are consistent with the fund strategy. Do not assume the name of the fund accurately describes the equities held. In addition to listing the proportions of industry sectors held within the fund, Morningstar further splits the sectors into three broader economic groupings—cyclical, defensive and sensitive. The industry analysis provides a quick view of where the fund is investing and how it differs from the benchmark. The economic spheres provide a glimpse of what management expects and how the portfolio may perform in various market conditions.

N *Area:* Portfolio Analysis

Section: Composition Information

Check the percentage of cash held in the portfolio. Compare this cash percentage with the annual percentage of equity stocks held, found underneath the style boxes at the top of the page. Subtracting the style box percentage from 100 provides an approximation of the cash percentage held. Large percentages of cash may imply the fund is in a defensive mode, or perhaps trying to time the market, or possibly paying redemptions. Whatever the rational, large cash percentages are a drag on performance and returns suffer. This is especially true of funds that hold large percentages of cash year after year.

The foreign stock percentage appears here as well. When building your portfolio, it is useful to determine your exposure to foreign equities. This information is especially important if international funds are in your portfolio because your actual allocations may just be a little larger than you may have thought.

NARROWING THE FIELD

One of the often-cited dilemmas associated with investing in mutual funds is the sheer volume of choices available. What are you to do? First, selectively prune away those funds that do not fit into your long-term investment objectives. Since you are building a balanced portfolio, eliminate any mutual funds containing both stocks and bonds. Why hold a fund trying to perform the same task as your portfolio? Thus, you eliminate balanced funds, asset allocation funds, life cycle funds and target-dated funds.

As a reminder, do not invest in any funds with loads—either front- or back-loaded. Never ever invest in loaded funds; this must be crystal clear. While on the subject, stay away from closed-end or Exchange Traded Funds (ETF) funds as well. Like loaded funds, these funds are usually over-priced, under-achievers in the long run. You can do better elsewhere.

Avoid specialty funds as well. With their holdings concentrated in a single industry and, sometimes even in a segment of that industry, these funds are just too risky. Often these specialty funds prey on the unsuspecting investor. The cyclical nature of the market does make various sectors of the market a winner from time to time. After just such a period, these funds tout their superior performance, but as General George S. Patton commented, "All glory is fleeting." Still skeptical? Consider the banking industry, the commodity industry or even gold. The growth may be real, but not long lasting. You are not a market timer and you do not want to become one. With that said, the only industry that may provide sustained long-term growth and potentially be a sector play is healthcare. Stay as diversified as possible within the industry by choosing a fund that invests across all of the major healthcare segments. Avoid placing bets on narrower segments such as delivery segments or even biotech stocks. The point here is to avoid narrowly focused bets on any market segment of any sort, in any industry, for any period. Healthcare, as a whole, has been the only sector with solid performance over the long run (note the term "as a whole"). Be warned, however. This industry is under heavy assault politically. The full market impact of ObamaCare has yet to be determined.

International funds are another over-hyped area. The sales pitch is you must own foreign equities to diversify your risk properly. Do not be fooled. Foreign markets follow U.S. markets and the increased risk far outweighs any perceived benefits. Remember conventional wisdom. Many experts cite market-driven opportunities in foreign markets such as access to new markets, growth in disposable income, pent-up demand and so forth. If true, why are large, multi-national U.S. firms that boast significant sales and profits coming from overseas operations not providing sufficient portfolio exposure to this growth opportunity? Other experts claim the foreign market opportunities come from the small market niches available only to local firms. If true, other than significantly more risk, is this any different from U.S. small-cap funds? Enter at your own peril!

These suggestions eliminate a large chunk of mutual funds, but a little more paring is still necessary. First, stay away from funds that are less than five years old. Funds that have not been in a down market are a concern because there is no history of resiliency—the recovery time needed to recoup losses. Next, eliminate funds with operating expenses over 0.75%. To be fair, look at the last several years and calculate an average. High expenses not only lower the returns but also increase risk. Next, eliminate funds with turnover ratios exceeding 75%. As before, look at the last several years and calculate an average. High turnover increases cost and increases risk, neither of which is a good thing. Finally, eliminate funds that hold significant amounts of cash, say 7% to 10% of assets. Again, look at the last several years and calculate an average. Cash is a drag on performance.

With the remaining funds, you need to look at long-term performance against appropriate market benchmarks. Typically, large-cap funds, whether growth- or value-oriented, mimic the overall market. The question is: does the return compensate for the increased costs? Mid- and small-cap funds tend to be more volatile than the market. Here, the same question applies but with an additional caveat: does the return also compensate for the increased risk?

MOVING TOWARD INDEX FUNDS

Did you know a large-cap index fund, over the long term, usually ranks third out of any 10 randomly selected diversified, large-cap funds? Despite what you may read in the financial news columns or hear on the financial news networks, index funds are not average performers. Once again, conventional wisdom is misleading. In reality, an index fund is a much better-than-average performer. How can that be? Well, based on pure performance, an index fund would likely be in the middle of the pack because the market is a zero-sum game—winners offset losers and what remains is the market. What the pundits fail to explain is the impact of fees, loads and taxes. Deducting all such expenses from the performance of all funds moves the ranking achieved by index funds significantly higher. Why? Index funds have minimal fees, low turnover, no sales charges, and remain fully invested. These advantages, without question, make index funds better-than-average performers.

Figure 6.2 highlights these very points. Each of the selected Vanguard index funds maintains rock bottom expense ratios, extremely low turnover, and hold little or no cash. As you might expect, the Small-Cap Index Fund sports the highest expenses at 0.13% while the Mid-Cap Index Fund posted the highest turnover at 20%. Still, each fund is well below actively managed funds. Index funds, by far, are the most cost-

FIGURE 6.2 *Selected Data for Certain Vanguard Index Funds*

THROUGH YEAR END 2010

	TOTAL STOCK MARKET INDEX	SMALL-CAP INDEX FUND	MID-CAP INDEX FUND	INDEX 500 FUND
Percent of Large-Cap	71%	0%	10%	88%
Percent of Mid-Cap	20%	32%	89%	12%
Percent of Small-Cap	9%	68%	1%	0%
Total Returns: 5 years	2.9%	5.4%	4.3%	2.2%
10 years	2.5%	7.2%	6.8%	1.3%
15 years	7.0%	8.6%	n/a	6.7%
Expense Ratio (avg last 3 yrs)	0.07%	0.13%	0.12%	0.07%
Turnover Ratio (avg last 3 yrs)	5%	13%	20%	8%
Percent of Cash (avg past 3 years)	0.4%	0.3%	0.2%	0.2%

Source: Morningstar Mutual Funds

effective way to invest in mutual funds. Since each of the funds remains fully invested, the potential drag on performance is non-existent.

Despite what the fund name suggests, the actual portfolio holdings may include stocks that are outside the expected population. For instance, the Small-Cap Index Fund holds mid-cap stocks, the Mid-Cap Index Fund maintains positions in both large- and small-cap stocks, and the Index 500 Fund owns mid-cap stocks. Always check the market capitalization to avoid surprises.

Given the similarity of their holdings, the returns of the both the Index 500 and Total Stock Market Fund for each period are similar. Since the Total Stock Market Fund allocates 71% of its holdings to large-cap stocks, it is reasonable to expect the Index 500 Fund to post similar performance numbers. The Mid- and Small-Cap Index Funds, on the other hand, generate more divergent returns. In fact, both the Mid- and Small-Cap Index Funds outperformed their large-cap sibling, and both funds accomplished these returns with less volatility over the period under review.

BUILDING THE EQUITY SIDE OF YOUR PORTFOLIO

If experience is the best teacher, the year 2008 provided an excellent example for all investors to learn about the volatility of the stock market. Many investors took their money out of the market and some might never return. Do not be one of these individuals. The Great Depression was, by far, the worst economic collapse in U.S. history. Yet, if investors had remained in the market and owned a broad index fund, their losses would have been recovered by 1936. Since a second recession followed in 1937, investors remaining in an all-equity portfolio did not recover their losses until 1944. Until you actually sell an investment, your portfolio incurs only paper losses. The best way to stay invested in the market is to maintain a balanced portfolio.

When investing, focus on the long term to maximize the value of compounding. Unfortunately, most investors jump around, destroy the compound interest chain, and lose substantial savings opportunities in the process. These investors are chasing performance in an effort to beat the market. The problem is, more often than not, the active investor rarely finds the next big winner and continues to fall further and further behind in the long-term investment game. You know better. You want to stay in the market and you want to stick with equity index funds.

The total stock market includes approximately 70% large-cap stocks, 20% mid-cap stocks and 10% small-cap stocks. Weighting the mix slightly more toward small- and mid-cap stocks can enhance overall performance. Why? Intuitively, the life cycle of a company is similar to the life cycle of a product: introduction, growth, maturity and decline. The introduction phase is comparable to small-cap stocks: opportunities abound, financing is lean and risks are high. Unfortunately, a number of these companies do not succeed. The growth stage corresponds to mid-cap stocks: niches identified, sales and profits rising and competitive risks mitigated. While a few of these companies may close their doors, many will continue to grow and prosper after weathering the difficult early years. The maturity stage is analogous to large-cap stocks: market share maintained, steady sales and profit performance, and risk factors effectively managed.

Just as managers try to select winning products for their companies, investors attempt to identify successful companies for their portfolios early in the cycle as well. The earlier you select a winner, the less expense you incur and the longer you can ride the winner upward. Overweighting both the small- and mid-caps provides just such an opportunity. Since the risk-reward ratio for small-caps is not as compelling, the small-cap over-weighting should be less than the mid-caps. Thus, the 33% targeted weighting for mid-caps is approximately 65% greater than the overall market, while the 12% targeted weighting for small-caps is approximately 50% higher than the overall market. Reducing the large-cap allocation lowers the percentage of old, safe names that may be getting a bit long in the tooth. The 55% targeted weighting for large-caps is about 25% lower than their overall market weighting.

Analyzing the market cap and sector weightings for each fund confirms that the actual percentages in your portfolio are reasonably consistent with your targeted objectives. Never assume the fund name describes the actual holdings within the fund. Figure 6.3 presents the findings.

To achieve the suggested target allocations, the equity side of your portfolio might be as follows:

- 60% of the Vanguard 500 Index Fund
- 25% of the Vanguard Mid-Cap Index Fund
- 15% of the Vanguard Small-Cap Index Fund

Based on the individual weightings within each fund, the equity side of your portfolio holds the approximate weighting of the targeted allocations—55% in large-cap, 34% in mid-cap, and 11% in small-cap stocks. The over-weighting in both the small- and mid-caps provides more upward potential in expanding markets. While contracting markets may pose a risk, the treasury side of the portfolio minimizes downside risk. With over 75% of the large-cap market allocation intact (55% versus 71% of the total market), the portfolio performance remains closely tied to the overall market.

As the weightings shift over time, the integrity of your investment program should remain intact because the same market dynamics influencing the composition of the individual index funds also affect the total

FIGURE 6.3

MARKET CAPITALIZATION

MARKET CAPITALIZATION	SMALL-CAP INDEX 15%	MID-CAP INDEX 25%	500 INDEX 60%	STOCK MODEL PORTFOLIO	TOTAL STOCK INDEX	PORTFOLIO DIFFERENCE TO INDEX
Giant	—	—	51.7%	31.0%	41.0%	-10.0%
Large	0.1%	10.2%	36.0%	24.2%	30.2%	-6.0%
Mid	31.8%	88.5%	12.1%	34.2%	19.7%	14.5%
Small	53.5%	1.3%	0.2%	8.5%	6.6%	1.9%
Micro	14.6%	—	—	2.2%	2.5%	-0.3%
TOTALS	100.0%	100.0%	100.0%	100.0%	100.0%	0.0%

SECTOR WEIGHTING

SECTOR WEIGHTINGS	SMALL-CAP INDEX 10%	MID-CAP INDEX 30%	500 INDEX 60%	STOCK MODEL PORTFOLIO	TOTAL STOCK INDEX	PORTFOLIO DIFFERENCE TO INDEX
Basic Materials	6.8%	7.2%	3.4%	4.9%	4.1%	0.8%
Consumer Cyclical	13.8%	14.5%	9.4%	11.4%	10.4%	1.0%
Financial Services	12.2%	10.7%	15.0%	13.5%	14.0%	-0.5%
Real Estate	7.5%	6.1%	1.5%	3.5%	2.7%	0.8%
Cyclical	**40.4%**	**38.5%**	**29.4%**	**33.2%**	**31.2%**	**2.0%**
Communication Services	1.4%	2.9%	4.2%	3.5%	3.9%	-0.4%
Energy	6.4%	9.5%	11.8%	10.6%	10.9%	-0.4%
Industrials	16.9%	14.6%	12.2%	13.4%	12.9%	0.5%
Technology	17.9%	13.9%	17.3%	16.3%	17.1%	-0.8%
Sensitive	**42.5%**	**40.8%**	**45.5%**	**43.8%**	**44.9%**	**-1.1%**
Consumer Defensive	3.9%	5.7%	11.2%	8.8%	9.8%	-1.0%
Healthcare	10.0%	9.7%	10.7%	10.3%	10.8%	-0.5%
Utilities	3.3%	5.2%	3.3%	3.8%	3.3%	0.6%
Defensive	**17.1%**	**20.7%**	**25.2%**	**23.0%**	**23.9%**	**-0.9%**
TOTALS	100.0%	100.0%	100.0%	100.0%	100.0%	0.0%

Source: Morningstar Mutual Funds

market benchmark. However, you still want to review these allocations periodically to verify your targeted model allocations remain reasonably accurate. As a general guideline, holdings for the equity side of your portfolio include small-cap stocks between 5% and 15%, mid-caps between 20% and 35%, and large-caps between 50% and 75%. Minor variations are okay.

Since each individual index fund selection maintains a blend of both growth- and value-oriented stocks, the risk is primarily with the market capitalization. For instance, selecting a small-cap growth fund magnifies risk because of risk associated with small-cap funds (financial strength) plus the risk inherent in growth-funds (greater volatility, increased costs, and higher turnover). The blended fund limits the cyclical impact of holding growth- or value-stocks when either is out of favor. The cyclical impact associated with market capitalization remains. Since our model portfolio over-weights small- and mid-cap stocks, the portfolio performance may suffer when large-caps are in vogue.

The higher percentages of small- and mid-cap holdings within the model portfolio account for the slight overweighting in cyclical stocks which is offset equally between both the sensitive and defensive stocks. Drilling down into the specific sectors indicates the largest difference is a 1% variance posted in two different sectors offsetting each other. The overweighting in consumer cyclical sector includes retail stores, auto manufacturers, residential construction firms, restaurants, and entertainment companies. The underweighting of the consumer defensive sector includes household, personal products, packaging, food and beverage manufacturers, and tobacco companies. The relative consistency with the overall market weightings allows the model portfolio to mimic overall market performance even during narrower rallies that are limited to specific market sectors.

The final piece of the puzzle appears in Figure 6.4. Our stock model portfolio outperforms the benchmark in each of the five-, 10-, 15-, and 19-year periods with less volatility. Looking at the individual funds, the Small-Cap Index Fund provided strong growth across all periods while the Mid-Cap Index Fund contributed significantly in the five-year period, enabling our portfolio to surpass the benchmark. Despite the traumatic market collapse of 2008, the 19-year returns for our stock

FIGURE 6.4 *Stock Model Portfolio Performance*

ANNUAL PERFORMANCE

	1992	1993	1994	1995	1996	1997	1998	1999	2000	2001	2002	2003	2004	2005	2006	2007	2008	2009	2010
Total Stock Market Index	10.4%	10.6%	-0.2%	35.8%	21.0%	31.0%	23.3%	23.8%	-10.6%	-11.0%	-21.0%	31.4%	12.5%	6.0%	15.5%	5.5%	-37.0%	28.7%	17.1%
500 Index Fund	7.4%	9.9%	1.2%	37.5%	22.9%	33.2%	28.6%	21.1%	-9.1%	-12.0%	-22.2%	28.5%	10.7%	4.8%	15.6%	5.4%	-37.0%	26.5%	14.9%
Mid-Cap Index Fund	n/a	n/a	n/a	n/a	n/a	n/a	8.8%	15.4%	18.2%	-0.5%	-14.6%	34.1%	20.4%	13.9%	13.6%	6.0%	-41.8%	40.2%	25.5%
Small-Cap Index Fund	18.2%	18.7%	-0.5%	28.7%	18.1%	24.6%	-2.6%	23.1%	-2.7%	3.1%	-20.0%	45.6%	19.9%	7.4%	15.7%	1.2%	-36.1%	36.1%	27.7%
****Stock Market Portfolio**	9.6%	11.7%	0.8%	35.7%	21.9%	31.5%	19.0%	20.0%	-1.3%	-6.9%	-19.9%	32.5%	14.5%	7.4%	15.1%	4.9%	-38.1%	31.4%	19.5%

COMPOUNDED ANNUAL PERFORMANCE

	5 YRS	ANNUALIZED RETURNS 10 YRS	15 YRS	19 YRS	STANDARD DEVIATION
Total Stock Market Index	2.9%	2.5%	7.0%	8.3%	19.2%
500 Index Fund	2.2%	1.3%	6.7%	8.0%	19.5%
Mid-Cap Index Fund	4.3%	6.8%	n/a	n/a	21.2%
Small-Cap Index Fund	5.4%	7.2%	8.6%	10.1%	19.5%
****Stock Market Portfolio**	3.3%	3.6%	8.1%	9.3%	18.7%
Performance Differential (between the Stock Market Portfolio and the Total Bond Portfolio)	0.3%	1.2%	1.1%	1.0%	0.6%

**STOCK MARKET PORTFOLIO

	Allocation	*ADJ**
500 Index Fund	60%	80%
Mid-Cap Index Fund	25%	n/a
Small-Cap Index Fund	15%	20%
	100%	100%

*ADJ adjusts the allocation percentages for the years in which the Mid-Cap Index did not exist (opened in 1998). The adjustment distributes the Mid-Cap allocation into the two existing funds holding constant the relationship of those two funds. The 60%–15% split between the Large and Small-Cap funds are applied to the entire population changing the split to 80%–20%.

model portfolio is 9.3%, which is remarkably similar to the historical performance of the stock market.

The returns of the five- and 10-year periods were significantly lower than the historical averages but remained positive. During the 19-year period, the market experienced two major declines of almost 40%—the first was the three-year period 2000 to 2002 and the second was in 2008. Our stock model portfolio reported losses 21% of the time on an annual basis (4 of 19 times), the frequency of losses declined to 7% for each five year period (1 of 15 times), and experienced no losses for the 10- and 15-year periods (0 of 10 and 0 of 5 times). Furthermore, the volatility of the returns declined from 18.7% annually to 8.7%, 4.7%, and 2.0% for the five-, 10- and 15- year periods. As the volatility decreases by approximately 50% in each five-year increment, the average annual returns are reasonably consistent, ending at 9.3% for the 15-year periods. Thus, as the holding period expanded, the returns normalized to the historical trends. Time really is on your side.

Stick with equity index funds. Over the long run, you will be happy with your selections as well as your returns. Bumps in the road always occur and craters may even appear at times, but you still need to stay with your positions. Let history be your guide.

STAYING THE COURSE—EQUITIES

Interestingly, when the stock market is flying high, no one wants to hold fixed income securities. Perhaps not so surprisingly, when the stock market is tanking, no one wants to hold stocks. Do you think there might be a pattern here? Is it your emotions, the need for instant gratification or a lack of historical perspective? Whatever the reason, resist it. You know markets are cyclical, the economy moves through stages and history repeats itself.

With the recent market collapse on your mind, you may want to consider the following question: of the following scenarios, which is the most preferable?

> ***Door One:*** You had a portfolio of $250,000 fully invested in the stock market—one year later the stock market tanks and your

portfolio is valued at $175,000 but two years later the stock market roars back and your portfolio is now valued at $290,000.

Door Two: You had a portfolio of $250,000 fully invested in U.S. Treasuries—one year later the stock market tanks but your portfolio improves slightly and is valued at $275,000 and two years later the stock market roars back and your portfolio is now valued at $290,000.

This is not a trick question. While both portfolios end with exactly the same value, the rides were quite different. Which of the two rides is more desirable? There is no right or wrong answer; there is only your answer. It is probably correct to assume most individuals would prefer the second option. It is also probably correct that most investors would be emotionally distraught with option one when their portfolio value dropped 30% in a single year. Some of those investors may have withdrawn their funds from the stock market, locking in their losses rather than holding onto their positions for an opportunity to recover their paper losses.

No matter how prophetic the phrase "staying the course" may be, this advice is difficult to put into practice and even harder to maintain during those big market declines or extended downturns. For these reasons, a balanced portfolio is crucial to your investment success and to your peace of mind. While a balanced portfolio may dampen some gains when the good times roll, a balanced portfolio also softens the losses when the bad times hit home. Your choice now is to make the deal. Will you go for door number one, door number two, or door number three? Door number three?

CHAPTER SEVEN

Putting the Pieces Together

The stuff that dreams are made of.
The Maltese Falcon (film), 1941

PUBLISHED IN 1930 and perhaps America's best detective novel, *The Maltese Falcon* was the third of five novels written by Dashiell Hammett. The novel introduces San Francisco detective Sam Spade, a no-nonsense, hard-driving loner who is the very definition of the private eye. True to his code of ethics, Spade is the quintessential tough guy dominating every scene and every situation regardless of whether he is actually in control or not.

Many may remember the classic film of the same name considered by many film historians as the first of the film noir genre to come out of Hollywood. Released in 1941, *The Maltese Falcon* stars Humphrey Bogart as Sam Spade, Mary Astor as his client, and Sidney Greenstreet in the role of Kaspur Gutman. Filled with intrigue, deception and greed, the film portrays unforgettable characters, contains vivid dialogue, and provides many memorable scenes.

A key difference between the book and the film is the last line. Suggested by Humphrey Bogart, the now famous line paraphrases a speech from Shakespeare's *The Tempest*. One of the most famous lines in motion picture history is a perfect lead-in for this chapter. Like the black bird, your investment program is the stuff that dreams are made of.

When solving a mystery, the protagonist gathers facts, recognizes misdirection, explains inconsistencies and avoids emotional entanglements. This approach equally applies to developing an investment program. The plain truth is, over the long run, approximately 80% of large, well-diversified mutual funds generate returns plus or minus 2% of the S&P 500. In reality, most funds closely mimic the returns of the overall market. Yes, most mutual funds are average performers.

A WINNING STRATEGY

History tells us the stock market posts a profit seven out of every 10 years and treasuries outperform the stock market four in every 10 years. It is not possible to forecast the actual years, but history does show that treasuries tend to move in the opposite direction of stocks thereby making treasuries an excellent counter-balancing investment. History establishes realistic expectations to gauge potential performance targets. History also suggests staying in the market allows the investor to take advantage of the market's upward bias.

The problem encountered by most investors is the ability to withstand the emotional strain of watching their portfolio lose money during market slides, often referred to as market corrections. Successful investors focus on the long term, exercise discipline, and emphasize patience. They understand a balanced portfolio is the tool of choice. Tracking their investment life cycle is a winning strategy.

When you eliminate confusion, you improve the probability of success. Experienced investors place a premium on what *not* to do, perhaps even more than on what *to* do. Far too many investors put their capital at risk to improve their yield by a single percentage point or even less. Rather than moving toward the safety of treasury securities, these so-called investors choose riskier, more speculative investments. Do not reach for that higher yield. A loss of 50% requires your next investment to earn 100% to breakeven.

Many of these same investors attempt to recoup their investment losses too rapidly. They turn to riskier and riskier investment choices in the hope of scoring a big win. In fact, they fall further and further behind. Remember Warren Buffett's investing guidelines—rule number one is not to lose money and rule number two is not to forget rule number one. Put the odds in your favor, protect your capital, and sleep well tonight.

When reviewing fund performance, too many novice investors move toward yesterday's winners. Regardless of the fund chosen—growth or income, large- or small-cap, domestic or international—it is important to remember that performance moves in cycles. When a particular style is in favor, a manager may occasionally stand out. Understanding the cyclical nature of the market leads investors to two important questions: can they identify the fund that is expected to outperform the market? And can they select the manager within that fund population who is expected to outperform the rest? You know the answer. No one has tomorrow's newspaper and no one has an accurate crystal ball. Unfortunately, yesterday's hero can quickly become tomorrow's bum.

Many investors forget history. Many more fail to remember the concept of "regression to the mean"—a powerful force in the stock market. Markets move in cycles. Although the lengths of those cycles are unknown, there is comfort in knowing that cycles occur. Neither long-running bull nor long-running bear markets last forever; change happens eventually. Avoid being caught up in either the euphoria of the bull or the despondency of the bear. Stay focused and you will maintain a balanced investment approach.

BUILDING YOUR INVESTMENT PROGRAM

The last chapter ended with a reference to Door Number Three. The first door contained an all-equity portfolio, and the second door proposed an all-treasury portfolio. The third door combines the long-term growth prospects of equities with the counter-balancing safety of treasuries. This investment program (Figure 7.1) recognizes the importance of adjusting allocations between stocks and treasuries as you move through the various stages of your investment life cycle.

No rules exist defining the correct ages for investing for retirement. As a general guideline, young investors are 40 years of age and under, middle-aged investors are roughly between 40 and 60 years of age, early retirement coincides with ages between 60 and 70, and late retirement begins after age 70. While moving through the various columns at a faster pace is fine, slowing the pace of the program may not be such a good idea due to the increased risk relative to your age. Always think risk before reward.

You may find it helpful to think about the columns as an investment style rather than an aged-based program. The investment model can

FIGURE 7.1 *Investment Program Utilizing Selected Vanguard Funds*

		YOUNG INVESTOR	MIDDLE-AGED INVESTOR	EARLY RETIREMENT INVESTOR	LATE RETIREMENT INVESTOR
EQUITIES		**80%**	**60%**	**40%**	**25%**
	MODEL				
500 Index	60%	48%	36%	24%	15.0%
Mid-Cap Index	25%	20%	15%	10%	6.3%
Small-Cap Index	15%	12%	9%	6%	3.8%
U.S. TREASURIES		**20%**	**40%**	**60%**	**75%**
	MODEL				
Short Term	20%	4%	8%	12%	15.0%
Intermediate Term	50%	10%	20%	30%	37.5%
Long Term	30%	6%	12%	18%	22.5%
		100%	100%	100%	100%

act as a framework for selecting a portfolio allocation that matches your comfort level. Rather than associating the descriptions with a chronological age, the columns can be linked to an investment style—young investors are more aggressive, middle-aged investors are more moderate, early retirement investors lean toward being more conservative, and late retirement investors are risk averse. Growing older lessens risk tolerance because you will be moving from wealth generation to capital preservation. Test your risk tolerance by combining your financial situation with your view of uncertainty in the market.

An important takeaway from this model is the minimum percentage you need to hold in either treasury or equity securities. Regardless of how young or aggressive you may be, never fall below the 20% mark in treasuries. Learned behavior is a powerful tool; start early and develop an appreciation for holding treasuries. You will be grateful—guaranteed. On the other side of the portfolio, never fall below 25% in equities even after you pass the wonderful milestone of 70 years young. After all, we are on the 100-year plan. Markets are cyclical and as devastating as a recession can be, the ravages of inflation are equally disastrous. Only equities can provide the growth potential to offset inflation. Fixed securities are just that—fixed. Hold onto equities.

The primary or bolded percentages located in the shaded area represent the overall splits between the two sides of your portfolio. Apply this primary percentage (the bold number in the shaded area) to the secondary percentages of the two individual fund models developed in the preceding chapters (the percentages to the right of the individual funds, underneath the word model) to determine the actionable percentage holdings for each individual fund within the portfolio.

For example, the young investor holds 80% of his portfolio in equities. Multiply this number by the percentages of the equity model components. The portfolio holds 48% in the 500 Index Fund (multiply 80% × 60% = 48%); it holds 20% in the Mid-Cap Index Fund (multiply 80% × 25% = 20%); and it holds 12% in the Small-Cap Index Fund (multiply 80% × 15% = 12%). The remaining 20% of the portfolio goes to treasuries. Therefore, the portfolio holds 4% in the Short-Term Treasury Fund (multiply 20% × 20% = 4%); it holds 10% in the Intermediate-Term Treasury Fund (multiply 20% × 50% = 10%); and it holds 6% in the Long-Term Treasury Fund (multiply 20% × 30% = 6%). Follow the same process to obtain the individual fund allocations for the other portfolios presented in Figure 7.1.

The equities side of the portfolio does not employ a single, fully integrated total market index fund. Using market-cap defined index funds allows more flexibility in selection and enables you to overweight the small- and mid-cap stocks in your portfolio. Constructed with maturity-defined funds, the treasury side of the portfolio creates a quasi-index fund. The allocation combines the greater return opportunities of long-term maturities with the stability of short-term treasuries and the income characteristics of the intermediate maturities. Net, net—you want to index stocks, not bonds.

The investment program provides a simple, straightforward approach for your model portfolio that will mature right along with you. The model assumes greater risk during the earlier years because you are a long way from retirement, thus allowing time to recover should the market sustain a major cyclical downturn. The late retirement investor has begun taking distributions from his retirement portfolio and, therefore, has little time to recover from major market downturns. This program works in either retirement (tax deferred) or core (taxable) portfolios.

PERFORMANCE OF YOUR INVESTMENT PROGRAM

Turning to the all-important issue of performance, benchmarks must provide an equitable comparison. For instance, comparing small-cap stocks to a large-cap stock benchmark may lead to incorrect conclusions and poor investment decisions. Does a patient diagnosed with cancer have the physicians prescribe a medication regimen for heart disease? Why would he? To avoid misleading readings, measure the equity side of the portfolio against the Total Stock Market Index and the treasury side against the Total Bond Market Index. Both benchmarks replicate the entire market within each broad category. As we learned earlier, no investment strategy is successful unless it can outperform the overall market.

Figure 7.2 compares the four model portfolios to their comparably weighted benchmark portfolios. For the young investor portfolio holding 80% equities and 20% treasuries, the corresponding benchmark is 80% Total Stock Market Index and 20% Total Bond Market Index. For the middle-aged investor portfolio holding 60% equities and 40% treasuries, the corresponding benchmark is 60% Total Stock Market Index and 40% Total Bond Market Index. The remaining portfolios follow the same approach.

Each of the investment model portfolios outperformed their respective benchmarks for the five-, 10-, 15-, and 19-year periods—with less risk. Now let that sink in for a moment. Every one of the investment model portfolios outperformed its respective benchmark for the five-, 10-, 15- and 19-year periods. Each portfolio accomplished this feat with lower risk than its benchmark. Not bad, not bad at all.

Analyzing the performance of the base portfolios explains what actually occurred. Presented above the double line in Figure 7.2, the base portfolios show two sides of the model portfolios before applying the primary percentages to the individual fund holdings. In other words, the base portfolios are 100% invested in either treasuries (i.e., the treasury model portfolio) or equities (i.e., the stock model portfolio). A year-to-year comparison indicates the treasury model portfolio outperformed

FIGURE 7.2 *Model Portfolio Performance*

ANNUAL PERFORMANCE

	1992	1993	1994	1995	1996	1997	1998	1999	2000	2001	2002	2003	2004	2005	2006	2007	2008	2009	2010
Total Bond Market Index	7.1%	9.7%	-2.7%	18.2%	3.6%	9.4%	8.6%	-0.8%	11.4%	8.4%	8.3%	4.0%	4.2%	2.4%	4.3%	6.9%	5.1%	5.9%	6.4%
U.S. Treasury Model Portfolio	7.5%	12.0%	-4.4%	21.7%	1.5%	10.0%	10.7%	-4.0%	14.7%	6.6%	13.7%	2.5%	4.0%	3.5%	2.8%	9.3%	14.8%	-4.2%	6.9%
Total Stock Market Index	10.4%	10.6%	-0.2%	35.8%	21.0%	31.0%	23.3%	23.8%	-10.6%	-11.0%	-21.0%	31.4%	12.5%	6.0%	15.5%	5.5%	-37.0%	28.7%	17.1%
Stock Model Portfolio	9.6%	11.7%	0.8%	35.7%	21.9%	31.5%	19.0%	20.0%	-1.3%	-6.9%	-19.9%	32.5%	14.5%	7.4%	15.1%	4.9%	-38.1%	31.4%	19.5%
Young Investor Benchmark	9.8%	10.4%	-0.7%	32.3%	17.5%	26.7%	20.3%	18.9%	-6.2%	-7.1%	-15.1%	25.9%	10.9%	5.3%	13.3%	5.8%	-28.6%	24.1%	15.0%
Young Investor Portfolio	9.2%	11.7%	-0.2%	32.9%	17.8%	27.2%	17.3%	15.2%	1.9%	-4.2%	-13.2%	26.5%	12.4%	6.7%	12.7%	5.8%	-27.5%	24.3%	17.0%
Middle-Aged Benchmark	9.1%	10.3%	-1.2%	28.7%	14.0%	22.4%	17.4%	14.0%	-1.8%	-3.2%	-9.3%	20.4%	9.2%	4.5%	11.0%	6.1%	-20.2%	19.6%	12.8%
Middle-Aged Portfolio	8.7%	11.8%	-1.2%	30.1%	13.7%	22.9%	15.7%	10.4%	5.1%	-1.5%	-6.5%	20.5%	10.3%	5.9%	10.2%	6.7%	-16.9%	17.2%	14.4%
Early Retirement Benchmark	8.4%	10.1%	-1.7%	25.2%	10.5%	18.1%	14.5%	9.1%	2.6%	0.7%	-3.4%	14.9%	7.6%	3.8%	8.8%	6.3%	-11.8%	15.0%	10.7%
Early Retirement Portfolio	8.3%	11.9%	-2.3%	27.3%	9.6%	18.6%	14.0%	5.6%	8.3%	1.2%	0.2%	14.5%	8.2%	5.1%	7.8%	7.6%	-6.4%	10.0%	11.9%
Late Retirement Benchmark	8.0%	9.9%	-2.0%	22.6%	7.9%	14.8%	12.3%	5.4%	5.9%	3.6%	1.0%	10.8%	6.3%	3.3%	7.1%	6.6%	-5.5%	11.6%	9.1%
Late Retirement Portfolio	8.0%	11.9%	-3.1%	25.2%	6.6%	15.3%	12.8%	2.0%	10.7%	3.3%	5.3%	10.0%	6.7%	4.5%	5.9%	8.2%	1.5%	4.7%	10.0%

COMPOUNDED ANNUAL PERFORMANCE

	ANNUALIZED RETURNS				STANDARD DEVIATION
	5 YRS	10 YRS	15 YRS	19 YRS	
Total Bond Market Index	5.7%	5.6%	5.8%	6.2%	4.5%
U.S. Treasury Model Portfolio	5.7%	5.9%	6.0%	6.6%	7.1%
Total Stock Market Index	2.9%	2.5%	7.0%	8.3%	19.2%
Stock Model Portfolio	3.3%	3.6%	8.1%	9.3%	18.7%
Young Investor Benchmark	4.1%	3.5%	7.2%	8.2%	15.5%
Young Investor Portfolio	4.7%	4.7%	8.2%	9.2%	14.6%
Middle-Aged Benchmark	4.9%	4.3%	7.1%	8.0%	11.9%
Middle-Aged Portfolio	5.5%	5.4%	8.0%	8.8%	10.8%
Early Retirement Benchmark	5.4%	4.9%	6.9%	7.5%	8.4%
Early Retirement Portfolio	6.0%	5.8%	7.6%	8.2%	7.6%
Late Retirement Benchmark	5.6%	5.3%	6.6%	7.1%	6.2%
Late Retirement Portfolio	6.0%	6.0%	7.1%	7.7%	6.1%

**MODEL PORTFOLIOS

	U.S. Treas	Stocks
Young Portfolio	20%	80%
Middle-Aged Portfolio	40%	60%
Early Retirement Portfolio	60%	40%
Late Retirement Portfolio	75%	25%

the Total Bond Index in only 11 of the 19 years, just a little over half of the time. The stock model portfolio, on the other hand, exceeded the Total Stock Market Index in 13 of the 19 years—a 68% success rate. These results seem a bit more ordinary than extraordinary. So how was it that the integrated model portfolios performed far better than their respective benchmarks?

The key drivers of the performance were the five calendar years in which the total stock market posted losses. Approximately one out of every four years the market lost ground, and it was during those periods the model portfolios out-paced the performance of their respective benchmarks to create separation and generate a more favorable overall return. A closer examination of the two sides of the portfolio provide an interesting, if not surprising, insight into the driving force of this performance.

The cumulative difference during these market declines was a positive 3.0% for the treasury model portfolio, equivalent to a 0.8% annual return during the 19-year period (the calculation is five years divided by 19 years equaling 26.3%, then multiply 26.3% by 3.0% to arrive at 0.8%). Since the average annual return for the treasury model portfolio was 6.6% versus 6.2% for the benchmark, the performance difference relates entirely to those years during which the market declined. Coincidently, the stock model portfolio posted almost exactly the same performance differential versus the total stock market during those market declines—a positive 0.8%. The average annual return for the stock model portfolio was 9.3% versus 8.3% for the benchmark. Again, the entire difference relates to the performance generated during those years when the market declined.

For the treasury portfolio, this spurt is consistent with historical performance patterns. Whenever the stock market takes a big hit or experiences an extended decline, a flight to security occurs. Linus, of *Peanuts*[1] fame, may have had his blanket, but experienced investors hold onto treasury securities. Corporate bonds will not hold up well during extended or deep market declines. Investors move to the safety and security of treasuries, thereby driving the prices higher and the yields lower. Due to their safety, treasuries tend to lag the overall bond market, which explains their lackluster performance during stock market upswings. The treasury model portfolio performed exactly as expected vis-à-vis the benchmark as well as the stock market.

The stock model portfolio outperformed the total stock market due primarily to the over-weighting in mid- and small-cap stocks. You know the stock market moves in cycles, and during this particular period, the large-cap stocks faltered, leading to a positive differential for our stock model portfolio over its benchmark. Had the downturn hit mid-cap stocks harder, our stock model portfolio most likely would have underperformed the benchmark.

While the four individual model portfolios have different primary splits between total equities and total treasuries, the model portfolios retain the same secondary percentage allocations within the two base portfolios. Therefore, each model portfolio performance is consistent with the relationship between the base portfolios and the respective benchmarks. Protecting downside risk, the treasury holdings coun-ter-balanced the equity side of the portfolio during severe market downturns.

Especially noteworthy was the performance of the late retirement portfolio in 2008 when the stock market declined a tumultuous 37%. The late retirement portfolio posted a positive 1.5% return. This may not seem like a whole lot, but then again, it was a whole lot more than most. More importantly, this portfolio followed Buffett's rule number one and did not lose money. Before you flock to this portfolio, however, it is good to recognize that the late retirement portfolio is not for every investor. The purpose of this portfolio is preservation of capital and the performance was right on target. Yes, it did not lose money, but the heavy concentration of treasuries are a drag on performance during up markets, as evidenced in 2009 when the portfolio generated a modest 4.7% return. While respectable, the return was well below its sibling portfolios. Designed for risk averse, ultra-conservative investors and individuals in their later years of retirement, the late retirement port-folio is not for everyone. Younger, more aggressive investors seeking wealth generation should select portfolios holding higher percentages of equities. Those portfolios may have more risk, but they also hold the potential for greater rewards.

As expected, portfolios holding larger treasury percentages are less volatile (standard deviation). For example, the young investor and middle-aged portfolios have posted losses in four of the 19 years or about once every five years (21% of the time). Whereas the early retirement portfolio experienced two losses in the last 19 years (11% of the time), and the late retirement portfolio reported only one loss during this period (5% of the time). Also as expected, the reduced risk generated lower returns over the long run, but each model portfolio still outperformed its respective benchmark.

The longer the investment horizon, the more likely historical norms will begin to appear and the portfolio risk will begin to diminish. Looking at the last 19 years, the stock market declined five times while posting 14 gains, which is consistent with the historical norm of seven out of every 10 years. While this information is useful, investors cannot consistently forecast the specific years in which downturns may occur, but more importantly, the upward bias of the market tends to reward those portfolios holding a greater percentage of stocks. Although stocks carry high short-term risk, time moderates that risk. The variability of one-year returns within each model portfolio decreases significantly as the time horizon lengthens. In fact, none of the individual model portfolios experienced a single loss in the five-, 10-, or 15-year increments. Perhaps this explains why Warren Buffett's favorite holding period is forever. Still, never forget that probability is not to be mistaken for certainty.

Some may be nervous about the 37% fall in the stock market during 2008. Well it is perfectly normal to be concerned; after all, it is your money and you should always put risk before reward. On two separate occasions during the past 19 years, the stock market gave back almost 40% of its value. Despite these two significant downturns, the annual compound growth rate for both of the equity-dominated model portfolios was 9.2% and 8.8%. The two treasury-dominated model portfolios posted returns of 8.3% and 7.7%. All the model portfolios generated very solid performances by any evaluation measure.

MANAGING YOUR INVESTMENT PROGRAM

The strength of any plan lies in its execution. Execution improves when you have easy-to-implement and easy-to-understand programs.

Eliminating confusion and promoting consistency greatly enhances the probability of success. This investment program does just that.

When beginning any program, you may have difficulty in establishing the optimum percentages of the investment model that you have chosen because of insufficient investment capital. Not to worry. A few basic guidelines will help. First, the primary split between equities and treasuries is the most crucial; the secondary splits between the individual funds within either the equities or treasury categories can occur over time. Accordingly, start with the funding of your equity position if you are either a young or middle-aged investor, but if you are in either early or late retirement, be sure to begin with your treasury position. The rationale is simple—the majority of your holdings are equities in the first two portfolios, but treasuries dominate the second two. Funding your largest position first is the most logical course of action as you purchase the specific funds within each category. For example, you have $3,000 to invest and you are a young investor. Your first priority is to purchase an equity fund and the largest allocated position is the 500 Index Fund. Whenever possible use new, incremental capital to purchase the remaining funds within the portfolio. However, there may be times when you do not have sufficient capital to complete the purchase of all the individual funds within the portfolio at the designated percentage allocations. In these situations, your primary objective is to maintain the primary equity/treasury percentage; this is the most important split. The secondary allocations to the specific funds are less important, and you may purchase those funds over time.

You should review the allocation percentages annually to determine if any adjustments are necessary. Pick a date and review the portfolio at the same time each year. However, when the market is going through an especially volatile period, it is a good idea to check your allocations more frequently. Minor variations of less than 3% to 5% are reasonable. Whenever possible, try to adjust the percentages with new money rather than shifting dollars between funds. Accordingly, the most appropriate review period is the time you normally fund your accounts.

When shifting into another portfolio, you may consider managing the change over a period of time. Since it is unlikely you will be adding new capital to effect every portfolio change, you may stagger the shift over a three- to five-year span. If you are moving from the young investor to the middle-aged portfolio, the equity allocation falls from 80% to 60%. You may want to avoid redistributing the entire 20% in a single, large transaction. Why? Perhaps the market may be experiencing a major decline, thereby requiring you to sell a larger portion of your shares, or maybe this is your core (taxable) portfolio and you want to avoid a huge tax bill. A more extended three- to five-year approach also may allow you to offset a portion of the changes with new, incremental capital, thus lowering the amount you need to transfer between funds.

What are you to do if the market tanks? Preferably nothing, but many may find their emotions making such an option difficult. In those hopefully few instances, consider shifting your current portfolio one column to the right. Choosing this path indicates your investment approach is more style driven than age or proximity to retirement. Say you are a middle-aged investor, but you are uncomfortable having the majority of your assets in equities. Your investment style is probably more conservative than moderate. If that is the case, you will want to move toward the asset allocation percentages outlined in the early retirement portfolio. You do not want to move out of equities only to move back later when you perceive it is safe. Those reactions suggest you are trying to time the market and you know that is a losing proposition. It is a sure fire way to buy high and sell low—the exact opposite of what you want. You never want to be a market timer. If you decide to move to a more conservative portfolio, do not switch back. You feel uncomfortable with the risk level of the previous portfolio, so stay with the new portfolio even when the market recovers.

Hopping from portfolio to portfolio will only break the compound interest chain and, if you are in taxable accounts, generate larger tax bills. Always remember that time in the market is more important than timing the market.

Before moving on, Figure 7.3 presents the expected earnings for each individual model portfolio. The calculation assumes you initially invest $3,000 when you turn 21, and subsequently invest an additional $1,000 each year until you are 70 years of age. The young investor portfolio (aggressive) achieves $1.12 million; the middle-aged portfolio (moderate) realizes $0.98 million; the early retirement portfolio

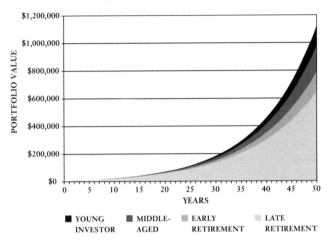

FIGURE 7.3 *Investing $3,000 at Age 21 and Adding $1,000 Annually*

(conservative) finishes at $0.78 million and the late retirement portfolio (ultra-conservative) ends with $0.65 million. Following the recommended approach of moving to successive portfolios throughout your lifetime, the value of the portfolio achieves $0.95 million. A nice number, don't you think?

PERHAPS YOU OWN A MUTUAL FUND

For the new investor, starting an investment program requires only the desire to begin and, of course, money to invest. For someone having a few investment holdings, the process becomes a bit more complicated. Perhaps you may have an old favorite or two. What are you to do?

First and foremost, you do not want to hold onto a favorite fund for emotional reasons. However, if you want to keep an old friend because it has performed well over the years, that is perfectly fine. The investment model provides the flexibility to accommodate an old favorite when appropriate. In so doing, you always want to maintain the proper balance between the equity and fixed income sides of the model portfolio throughout your lifetime.

Suppose you are a middle-aged investor holding an equity fund that you do not want to sell. The middle-aged investor model portfolio holds

60% in equities and 40% in treasuries. By adjusting the allocations within the equity side of the model portfolio, you can integrate that old favorite into the model portfolio.

Assume your favorite fund represents 10% of your equity portfolio and the fund holds only large-cap stocks. Since the equity allocation to the large-cap 500 Index Fund is 60%, a quick check suggests the allocation becomes 50% with your favorite equity fund adding the remaining 10%. Carrying this calculation to the total portfolio, the allocation of the 500 Index Fund becomes 30% (multiply 60% × 50% = 30%) and your favorite fund adds 6% (multiply 60% × 10% = 6%). Therefore, your portfolio maintains the desired 36% allocation to large-cap equities for the middle-aged portfolio model.

The preceding example simplifies the process slightly. In actuality, you must identify the percentages of large-, mid-, and small-cap stocks held within your favorite equity fund. After identifying the market capitalization percentages, you calculate the new market cap percentages for the revised model portfolio that now also holds your favorite fund. Referring to Figure 6.3, compare the new model portfolio percentages to the targeted percentages of 55% large-cap, 33% mid-cap, and 12% small-cap. In this example, assuming the fund holds 100% large-caps, the new capitalization percentages are now 56%, 33%, and 11% for the large-, mid- and small-cap stock positions, respectively. Since each of the new percentages are within 1% of the targets, no change to the current weightings for the three Vanguard Index funds is necessary.

The model can accommodate exceptions, but the greater the percentage of exceptions to the model, the greater the probability that deviations from expected performance may occur. Preferably, exceptions should be less than 5%, but certainly not more than 10% of the model portfolio.

STAYING THE COURSE—A BALANCED PORTFOLIO

So there you have it—Door Number Three. A balanced portfolio provides downside protection when the market is in turmoil, but it also offers upside potential when the market is booming. Experienced investors always think risk first when making investment decisions because they understand losing 50% of an investment requires a 100% return just to get even. Their investment goal is not to earn the highest return possible, but rather, to earn a competitive return with minimal risk. You want to be an investor, not a speculator.

Remaining fully invested regardless of market gyrations ensures investors are not going to miss the next upward surge in the market by being either under funded or entirely out of the market. The balanced portfolio also takes full advantage of the miracle of compounding. The hidden secret behind the success of long-term compounding is the concept of dollar-cost averaging. Rather than trying to time the market, you use the market movements to your advantage. Routinely reinvesting the interest, dividends, and capital gain distributions from your mutual funds enables you to purchase more shares when the market is undervalued and fewer shares when the market is overvalued. Over time however, the average cost per share is lower than the mutual fund's average price per share during the same period.

In exchange for these inherent benefits, the investor must become emotionally detached from reacting to either the negative doom and gloom or the unwarranted euphoria emanating from the media pundits. The investor also must ignore the promotional hype generated by investment companies, stockbrokers, and especially friends and neighbors.

Holding your positions in the face of falling prices is emotionally difficult, and yet it is one of the key reasons to maintain a balanced portfolio. In football, you think of a balanced attack that can score in the air or on the ground. In baseball, you think of a balance between power and speed. Why should investing be any different? You need a balanced portfolio to stay the course. The long-term return for the stock market is 9.3%, and it was sufficient to grow a $3,052 investment into $1 million. Had you followed the recommended approach of moving to successive portfolios throughout your lifetime, the same $3,052 investment would have grown to over $838,000. To reach the magic $1 million target, your initial investment would need to be $3,641. Therefore, for the small addition of $589, you still can achieve $1 million by the time you enter retirement. How do you define success?

You have the tools and the knowledge to become successful without becoming obsessed with over analysis and time-consuming research.

Separating savings from your investment capital provides you with a safety net for emergencies. Your investment program is not stagnant; the program evolves as you move through your investment life cycle. When properly planned, the portfolio shifts occur over a period of time rather than a point in time and, hopefully, with new money. These shifts are fine-tuning in nature, not massive overhauls. You need not move beyond mutual funds to be a successful investor. The diversity and convenience offered by mutual funds is appropriate and recommended for both your retirement (tax deferred) and core (taxable) portfolios.

Stay focused, stay invested, and stay the course because dreams can be made of this stuff.

CHAPTER EIGHT

Looking for More

Think about it. Think about it hard.
Gunsmoke (television series), 1950s

As RADIO GAVE way to television in the '50s, many radio programs tried to take on the challenges of the new medium. One of the best and most successful was *Gunsmoke*. Regarded as one of the finest radio dramas of all time, the series starred William Conrad in the role of Marshall Matt Dillon and it aired 480 performances during its nine-year run (1952–1961). The television series starred James Arness in the role of the Marshall and 633 episodes were produced during its 20-year run (1955–1975). *Gunsmoke* was one of the longest running prime time dramas in the history of television. Recognized for its crisp writing and solid acting, the radio and television stories dealt with the problems of frontier life, often requiring the sound judgment and bold action of Marshall Dillon.

To accommodate the new television audience, program executives decided to recast all of the leading roles and soften the image of two prominent supporting characters. Rather than presenting her as the owner of a bordello, Kitty Russell became the proprietor of a saloon. While Doc Adams remained a bit cantankerous, he became a warmer, more laid-back character. Despite the changes, *Gunsmoke* was not an immediate success. However, beginning in its third season and for the next four years, *Gunsmoke* was the top rated program on television. Following its success, other Westerns joined the prime-time network schedule, but *Gunsmoke* outlasted all of them.

Many of those radio programs from the '40s tried to make the jump to the new medium, but only a few retained their audiences and far fewer could claim to be a success. As the saying goes, be careful what you wish for. Making a transition to investing in individual stocks rather than mutual funds is a major undertaking.

LOOK BEFORE YOU LEAP

The main benefit of purchasing individual securities is greater control of your investment choices. You decide what and when to sell as well as what and when to buy. The trade-off for greater control of your investment decisions is increased risk, expanded time commitments, and greater capital requirements. How will these trade-offs affect your investment plan?

Purchasing U.S. Treasuries as individual securities is not appropriate for most investors. Unlike stocks, trading in and out of treasuries is a costly and unnecessary process. Individual treasuries are beneficial when the investor can hold the security until maturity thereby riding out periodic market fluctuations. The mutual fund alternative is actually the superior choice because you may participate in capital appreciation while maintaining the flexibility in the duration of your holdings. Unless you have significant wealth, stay with mutual funds offering short-, intermediate-, and long-term options. Okay, enough said. This chapter refers solely to owning individual stocks and does not suggest owning individual treasury securities.

Portfolio Size

When holding individual securities, each position is susceptible not only to market risk but to firm risk as well. Your individual selections are front and center, reminding you each day that they are either winning or losing. Clearly, individual stocks are more volatile than mutual funds. Having the emotional strength to ignore this volatility can be a difficult task; do not take it lightly. If you are unsettled and uneasy with market gyrations, you may not be a good candidate to hold individual positions in stocks

How many stocks do you need to own in a well-diversified portfolio? Well, if you own just one stock, it provides no diversification. You can double your diversification by adding another stock. To double your diversification again, you must also double your holdings to four stocks. In other words, each time you double the number of stocks you hold, you double the diversification. By holding 16 stocks, your portfolio achieves almost 90% of the market diversification. Doubling your holdings to 32 stocks provides a little over 90% of the market diversification, and doubling once more to 64 stocks achieves about 93% of the market diversification. For clarification, owning 64 stocks does not achieve adequate diversification; owning 64 stocks spread over different industries does. You can further improve the properties of diversification by blending growth-oriented companies with more mature, value-oriented firms.

You may want to consider the concentration of a single investment. For instance, what impact do you want a single stock investment to have on your portfolio: 5%, 3%, 2%, or what? Choosing the 5% option requires a 20 stock portfolio, choosing the 3% option requires holding 33 stocks, the 2% option requires holding 50 stocks. With a 64 stock portfolio, the exposure of any single stock holding is limited to only 1.6%.

At this point, a few obvious questions arise.

How many stocks should you hold in a portfolio?
How many stocks will you have to follow to find that number of reasonably good investments?
How much capital will be required to build such a stock portfolio?

The best way to address the first question is to consider two options. First, if you are building a stand-alone stock portfolio, the minimum number of stocks you need to consider is 50, but the preference would be to hold 64 to provide adequate diversification and reduce the risk of owning any single stock to less than 2%. The second option, which is the recommended approach, is to incorporate the stock portfolio into the model. In so doing, you can reduce the number of stocks in your portfolio to a more manageable 16 to 20 companies.

As for the second question, the most accurate answer is as many as it takes. A more definitive answer is not possible. While you may hope that the first 16 or 20 stocks you review are viable investment candidates, do you really think that will happen? Of course not, but knowing how many companies you may need to research is impossible. When analyzing individual stocks, you may find a good investment in one out of every three companies under review, maybe one out of every four, or maybe more. Do not forget this analysis is an ongoing task. You must monitor your holdings continually and be ready to make changes when necessary, which requires monitoring a population of possible candidates. Managing an individual stock portfolio takes time, takes effort, but offers no guarantees.

As for the last question, a few simple assumptions help to estimate the capital requirements. You need to hold a minimum of 100 shares for each stock in your portfolio. If you assume the average price of a stock is $50.00 it becomes a simple calculation. For instance, for a 20 stock portfolio the capital required would be $100,000 (multiply the 20 stocks times 100 shares times $50 per share) and for a 64 stock portfolio your capital needs would grow to $320,000 (multiply the 64 stocks times 100 shares times $50 per share). If you cannot or do not want to commit such an amount of money, you would do better to stay with mutual funds.

Focus on the Future
Now is the time to recall the story of Mr. Market—he is there to serve you, not to guide you. You do not want to fall into the trap of making decisions by watching the market. Do not be fooled into thinking a stock is a bargain simply because it is selling sharply off its high price. There may be very good reasons the stock is moving downward. The reverse is also true. Do not be fooled into making a quick decision to buy a stock when it is rising rapidly. Not only may the growth be unsustainable, but you also may be buying into a speculative bubble.

The problem many investors make when investing in individual stocks is they try to find the next Apple or Microsoft before everyone else. Your goal needs to be more realistic. You want to find solid companies at attractive prices providing good, but not necessarily spectacular, results. It is far easier to find solid, well-established companies promising years of good results than to find companies achieving spectacular results. Spectacular growth is difficult to achieve in the marketplace, but it is even more difficult to identify in the investment game. Stay focused and set realistic goals.

A Strategy to Sell

The question of selling an investment is almost irrelevant with equity index funds because you stay fully invested in the market. While you do reduce your equity holdings as you move through the investment life cycle, selling shares in an index mutual fund is not nearly the same as selling an individual stock position.

Selling an individual stock can be a very difficult task for some individuals. Why? Some investors may feel an attachment toward a company or maybe they do not want to admit to a bad purchase. The reason does not matter. If individual stocks are not performing, you must take action because you now control your investments. Monitoring your investments does not mean you are a trader; it simply makes you a prudent investor because you recognize no one is infallible. Occasionally you will select a loser or, at least, a less than stellar performer. However, if you do your homework upfront, selling an investment position is the exception, not the rule.

INCORPORATING STOCKS INTO YOUR MODEL

For those still undeterred, individual stocks may be an option for your core (taxable) portfolio but stick with mutual funds in your retirement program. Rather than considering such a move as a new direction, you want to position individual stocks as an extension of your investment model. Each side of the portfolio maintains a primary percentage allocated to equities and treasuries. The primary percentages do not change. The secondary allocations, however, require modification to accommodate the addition of individual stocks within the revised program model.

When the value of the core portfolio approaches $100,000, you may consider developing a common stock portfolio. Until achieving that threshold, you want to invest exclusively in mutual funds. With the majority of the portfolio diversified in mutual funds, you may accumulate your stock positions over time, reducing risk and building confidence. Unlike learning to swim, you do not want to jump in. This is not the time to sink or swim.

Figure 8.1 presents an investment plan with individual stocks as the primary focus of an equity investment program. This model enables

FIGURE 8.1 *Core (Taxable) Investment Program Including Individual Stocks*

OPTIONAL APPROACH

		YOUNG INVESTOR	MIDDLE-AGED INVESTOR	EARLY RETIREMENT INVESTOR	LATE RETIREMENT INVESTOR
EQUITIES		**80%**	**60%**	**40%**	**25%**
	MODEL				
Individual Securities	30%	24%	24%	24%	25%
500 Index	30%	24%	18%	8%	n/a
Mid-Cap Index	25%	20%	18%	8%	n/a
Small-Cap Index	15%	12%	n/a	n/a	n/a
U.S. TREASURIES		**20%**	**40%**	**60%**	**75%**
	MODEL				
Short Term	20%	4%	8%	12%	15%
Intermediate Term	50%	10%	20%	30%	38%
Long Term	30%	6%	12%	18%	23%
		100%	100%	100%	100%

you to begin selecting individual stocks while still maintaining equity mutual funds as your core equity investments. This allows time to determine whether buying individual stocks is an appropriate approach. First-hand experience remains the best teacher enabling you to assess your skills, judge your time commitments, and evaluate your results without committing your entire equity investment portfolio at the outset. Over time, you may elect to continue with individual stocks, hold only a few stocks, or return entirely to equity mutual funds. Always think risk before return.

Before looking at the changes, first review what has not changed. Treasury allocations are exactly the same; you do not want to adjust anything on this side of your portfolio. You always want to maintain your insurance policy regardless of your investment approach. You always want to remember the first two rules of investing: the first is not to lose money and the second is not to forget the first rule. Never, never compromise your safety. You always want to maintain your treasury positions.

With respect to the equity side of your portfolio, you always want to consider risk before potential reward. When you think risk first, you may avoid a very slippery slope. You know how it goes. For the chance to make another half percentage point, you rationalize your principles—you increase your risk, put your capital in jeopardy, and all too often, you regret your decision. Stick to your plan, do not deviate, and maintain your percentages.

Individual stocks, for the young investor, represent approximately 30% of the equity side of your portfolio. Some may believe this percentage is light, but it provides time to build your portfolio. In most instances, you do not have sufficient capital to purchase the entire stock portfolio (the entire 24% of the total portfolio). You most likely will need to purchase one stock, then another, and so forth until you complete the portfolio. Retaining 70% of the equity side (or 56% of your total portfolio) in equity index mutual funds allows you to stay diversified while building your individual stock positions. This diversity enables you to hold as few as 16 to 20 individual stock positions, limiting your exposure from 1.2% to 1.5% of the total portfolio per stock position.

Individual stocks, for the middle-aged investor, remains at 24% of the total portfolio, but increases to 40% within the equity side. By this time, you have established your individual stock portfolio, and you can begin reducing your mutual fund holdings over time. Since it is the most volatile, the small stock index fund is the first fund affected. As you begin to position the portfolio for retirement, you move toward more stable investments.

Starting in early retirement, the individual stock portfolio again remains at 24% of the total portfolio, but increases to 60% on the equity side. After eliminating the small-cap fund, reduce both the mid-cap and 500 Index Fund to 8% to accommodate the increase in the individual stock percentage. As you enter retirement, you seek more control over your investments by reducing your equity mutual funds. The overall portfolio risk continues downward since the primary percentages allocated to the treasury side now represent 60% of the total portfolio.

As you move into late retirement, the individual stock portfolio actually increases by a single point to 25% of the total portfolio, but now represents 100% of the equity side. With 75% of the total portfolio invested in treasury funds, you want to hold individual stocks as a buffer against inflation. With all equity mutual funds eliminated, your risk in holding only individual stocks is minimal. No position exceeds 1.5% of the entire portfolio since 75% of the portfolio is invested in treasuries.

After purchasing individual stocks, suppose you decide individual stocks are not the way to proceed? That is okay. Should you decide to hold no individual stocks, the correction is relatively simple—resume the original model percentages described in Figure 7.1. It is also okay to retain a few individual stocks in your portfolio. If this is the case, a few adjustments are in order.

Let's say you are a young investor and want to hold four individual stocks as part of your portfolio. You start with the model equity allocations presented in Figure 8.1. To reduce your risk of holding individual stocks, you decide to limit your exposure to no more than 2% of your entire portfolio to any individual company and you limit your purchases to only the large-cap category. The model allocates 30% of your equity portfolio to individual stocks or 24% of your total portfolio. The 2% exposure limitation on your total portfolio changes the allocation to 8% (4 stocks × 2%). The remaining 16% moves to the large-cap Index 500 Fund adjusting the allocation to 40%. To calculate this change, multiply 80% (primary equities allocation) times 30% (model allocation for individual securities) which equals 24% and add 16% for your adjusted individual stock percentage.

One additional modification is necessary for middle-aged, early retirement, or late retirement investors. You must move to the original model presented in Figure 7.1 because this model maintains exposure to the entire market rather than focusing on individual stocks. Assuming the same facts as before, you are a middle-aged investor. Individual stocks at 8% reduce the 500 Index allocation to 28%, leaving the allocations for the Mid-Cap Index (15%) and the Small-Cap Index (9%) unchanged. For the early retirement investor, individual stocks at 8% reduce the 500 Index to 16%. For the late retirement investor, individual stocks at 8% reduce the 500 Index to 7%. Thus, your portfolio is consistent with the model presented in Figure 7.1: 60% large-cap (8% individual stocks plus 52% Index 500 Fund), 25% mid-cap, and 15% small-cap equities adjusted for your stage in the life cycle.

BUILDING YOUR STOCK PORTFOLIO

One of the key premises advocated within these pages is the overpowering evidence that consistently beating the market is an extremely difficult task, even for the professionals. Nevertheless, you want to buy individual stocks. To be a successful, you will need to exploit the most important advantage you have over the professional money manager—a long-term perspective. To retain a long-term view, concentrate on lower risk companies that can weather the cyclical swings of the market. Focus on established firms such as big, blue-chip companies that have a history of paying dividends and increasing those dividend payments over time. Your goal is not to earn the highest return possible; your goal is to generate a good return with minimal risk.

In a *Forbes Magazine* article, John Bogle suggested buying the 50 largest companies in the S&P 500 and then never buying another stock. He went on to say that if a stock is lost in a merger, do not replace it. Thomas Easton, the author of the article, asked Professor Jeremy Siegel to calculate whether the portfolio performance would suffer from solely buying large companies. Siegel determined the return would have been a fraction of a point better than the entire market. Bogle cautioned that many of the 50 stocks may be overpriced when purchased, but he explained the prices are not material when holding the stocks for 50 years.[1]

Holding a stock position in 50 companies requires a significant capital investment—something like $250,000. That is, most likely, beyond the scope of many investors. If you are a young investor, your required portfolio value would be over $1.0 million (divide the $250,000 in stocks by the 24% allocation in Figure 8.1). Okay, this program is out of reach to many, if not most, investors.

Bogle's approach does provide several insights that all investors can apply when building a stock portfolio. His strategy focuses on low turnover and large, well-established companies emphasizing dividends and low risk. Seems a bit familiar, doesn't it?

Trade Infrequently to Emphasize the Power of Compounding

Few individual investors understand how devastating active trading can be to long-term total returns. Although the stock market has provided a

FIGURE 8.2 *Staying in the Market*

NUMBER OF YEARS	0	1	2	3	4 RECESSION	5 RECESSION	6 RECOVERY	7 RECOVERY	8	9	10
ANNUAL MARKET RETURN		10%	10%	10%	-15%	-15%	20%	20%	10%	10%	10%
BUY AND HOLD											
Investment	$100	$110	$121	$133	$113	$96	$115	$138	$152	$168	$184
Avg Annual Return		10.0%	10.0%	10.0%	3.1%	-0.8%	2.4%	4.8%	5.4%	5.9%	6.3%
TIME THE MARKET											
Investment	$100	$110	$121	$133	$113	OUT OF	MARKET	$111	$122	$134	$148
Avg Annual Return		10.0%	10.0%	10.0%	3.1%	OUT OF	MARKET	1.5%	2.5%	3.3%	4.0%
Investment Loss %								-20%	-20%	-20%	-20%

9.3% long-term total return, that number does not include trading costs, bid-ask spreads, or taxes. As an individual investor, you must absorb these costs, and they can only reduce your total return.

You want to sell infrequently keeping your portfolio turnover to less than 10% per year. You want to stick with a buy-and-hold approach with only occasional pruning. This allows your money to grow through the miracle of compounding. When you decide to sell a stock position, you also have to replace it with another stock. In other words, you have to double your costs! Even with discount brokers, these charges add up quickly. Sell only when necessary and never try to time the market.

In addition to correctly choosing the stock to buy and to sell, you must make two more decisions correctly when you try to time the market. Those decisions are *when* to sell your stock and *when* to buy a replacement stock. No, it is not the same decision.

Many people think it wise to "lock in" their profits during market downturns. Figure 8.2 shows the result of staying in the market through a market downturn compared to getting out and reentering later. The example assumes you are out of the market for two years—missing half of the recession as well as half of the recovery, which are generous assumptions. It also assumes you will pay only 2% in trading costs to sell and buy which, again, is a generous assumption.

What are the results? By trying to time the market, your investment return is 20% lower than it would have been had you simply stayed in the stock market. The average annual return is 2.3 percentage points lower than staying in the market. Even if you park the money in a money market account earning 2% while you wait for the market to turnaround, your annual return is still 1.9% lower than staying in the market. Now, consider multiplying this number by your own portfolio value. This is not a pretty sight, and, in fact, it is downright scary! The percentages stay the same, but the dollars lost are based on your portfolio value. The conclusions are obvious—do not be a trader or a timer. Stay fully invested.

Size Does Matter

The concept of size matters most when comparing a company to its competitors within its industry rather than with the overall market. The benefits provided by large companies relate to the concept of scale, which is the ability to offset increasing costs against a larger inventory of goods or services. Of course, this concept is most obvious in companies having significant fixed cost requirements. Consider industries requiring investment in heavy machinery (steel, automobiles, oil) or large, expansive distribution networks (FedEx, Coke, P&G). The greater the percentage of fixed costs to variable costs, the more consolidated the industry tends to be or will become. By definition, industry consolidation provides the opportunity to allocate fixed costs to larger and larger inventories, reducing the unit costs of those products and thereby generating higher margins.

As an outgrowth of size, large companies tend to be well established, well financed, and well managed. They have been around for a long time, they have weathered a storm or two, and they tend to be less volatile. In the stock market, volatility is determined by calculating the standard deviation that measures the variation between the returns of a particular stock over time. Market professionals use the capital asset pricing model (CAPM) to determine the risk, or beta, of an individual stock. Based on a regression analysis, beta is a measure of the price movement of a particular stock compared to the price movement of the entire stock market.

Companies with a beta of 1.0 expect their stock prices to move in the same proportion as the overall stock market. Therefore, when the market gains 10%, the stock price also gains 10%. Conversely, when the market loses 10%, the stock price goes down 10% as well. Firms with a beta of 1.2 are more volatile. Their stocks are expected to move 20% more than the market does. Thus, when the market gains 10%, the stock price goes up 12%, but should the market lose 10%, the stock price drops by 12%. Businesses with a beta of 0.7 are less volatile. These stocks move only 70% relative to the market move. Accordingly, when the market gains 10%, the stock price gains only 7%; but when the market loses 10%, the stock price suffers only a 7% loss.

The less volatile the stocks in your portfolio, the more likely you can stay fully invested during those inevitable market downturns and sleep a little easier, too. Over time, the stock market advances seven out of every 10 years. You want to stay invested to take advantage of major upward moves. You may increase your comfort level by buying stocks with betas of 1.0 or less.

Dividends Key to Successful Investing

The historical 9.3% average annual return for stocks is equally divided between dividend growth and capital appreciation. By mid-2008 however, the dividend payout ratio on the S&P 500 Index had dropped to 30% from the historical norms of 40% to 60%. Furthermore, the dividend yield sank to 1.8%, well below the historical norm of 3.5%. Conventional wisdom is that dividends are out of favor, passé, and irrelevant.

Several recent studies challenge this interpretation. Robert Arnott and Clifford Asness published an article in the January/February 2003 issue of the *Financial Analysts Journal* in which they concluded that historical evidence strongly suggests that expected earnings growth is fastest when current dividend payout ratios are high, and slowest when the payout ratios are low.[2] The study went on to say companies paying higher dividends usually are confident in their ability to provide strong earnings growth in the future. Firms with low payout ratios, on the other hand, may indicate that those companies are holding earnings in so-called contingency funds to protect against future developments, or the current managers of those companies may be empire building in the hope of higher executive compensation down the road.

Ping Zhou and William Roland published a follow-up study in the May/June 2006 issue of the *Financial Analysts Journal* confirming those findings. The authors conducted their own testing and verified that high dividend payout companies tend to experience strong, not weak, future earnings growth.[3] Both studies were not intended to dispute the evidence on companies in the early stages of growth that typically pay little to no dividends (remember the life cycle of companies). The studies focused on stocks in their mid-growth phase and listed in the S&P 500 Index.

Another study performed by Stanley Block for the May 2009 issue of the *AAII Journal* documented that firms in the Dow Jones Industrial Average with dividend yields of over 2% generated better capital appreciation performance than those companies with yields under 2%. The study also suggested stocks paying abnormally high dividends of 6% or more may not be sustainable and indicate potential future concerns. The study exempted normally high dividend yielding sectors, such as utilities and REITs, from such warnings.[4]

The cornerstone of any stock portfolio must be dividend-paying stocks. You want to select either (1) higher yielding stocks with modest annual dividend increases or (2) stocks with modest yields but strong dividend growth potential. The first criterion leans toward value-oriented stocks while the second pushes you toward growth-oriented stocks. Your position in the investment life cycle guides the portfolio weighting. Generally, if you are a young investor, you need to hold more dividend growth stocks; middle-aged investors need a more even split between the two or a slight over-weighting toward dividend growth; both retirement portfolios need to concentrate more on current yield stocks. Do not ignore that one-half of long-term stock returns come from those regular, old, boring dividend checks. Jurassic Park lives on.

A strategy rich in dividends promotes investment in big, blue-chip stocks—those with a history of uninterrupted dividends and prospects for continued dividend increases. It is best to avoid companies that do not regularly increase dividends. Exceptions to this general rule are companies that have improved their operations and restarted regular dividend increases or firms that have just begun paying dividends for the first time. If you do your homework and construct a portfolio of dividend winners, your quarterly dividends will grow larger and larger through the years.

Interestingly, professional money managers and big mutual fund managers generally cannot use this strategy. Why? Evaluated on their quarter-to-quarter performance and yearly results, many of these professionals receive their compensation based on short-term results. A dividend approach requires a long-term perspective that rewards patience, not action. Too many investors fail to realize a simple mathematical fact. Suppose you purchase a stock with a current dividend yield of 2% and the company increases its dividend payment 10% annually. After 10 years, the dividend yield on that original investment would grow to 5.2%. Adding the expected capital appreciation during those same 10 years, the original purchase would generate an annual return of 11.9%. Chalk up another one for the tortoise over the hare.

DRIPs Reduce Cost While Promoting Growth

Dividend Reinvestment Plans (DRIPs) are a convenient, cost-effective approach to managing individual stocks. Most DRIP plans allow you to make cash payments for additional shares, many offer initial stock purchases through the plan, and a few even provide discounts on additional share purchases. In addition to holding shares in book entry form, most DRIP plans allow you to sell your shares well below normal brokerage fee charges. The shareholder typically receives these services at little or no cost.

Rather than trying to time the market, invest on a regular basis to promote a forced savings approach that adds discipline to your investment strategy. It also takes advantage of dollar-cost averaging, a proven strategy to improve the results of your investment dollars by using the market ups and downs to your advantage.

Dollar-cost averaging is a key benefit of a DRIP program, allowing you to reinvest your dividends and promoting the power of compounding. When you invest the same amount of money at regular intervals over a long period, you need not be concerned about timing the market. Dollar-cost averaging allows you to ride out market volatility because the results show little difference whether the program began during a bull or bear market. A systematic investment of a fixed dollar amount forces you to purchase more shares when the market is undervalued and fewer shares when the market is overvalued. The average cost per share is lower than the investment's average price per share during the same period.

Before making your initial share purchase, you want to verify whether you can purchase shares directly through the DRIP program. If not, you want to check the minimum number of shares required to join the DRIP program (typically, call Shareholder Services for the answer). If you must first own the shares before joining the DRIP plan, contact your broker to purchase the minimum number of shares. Although purchases in 100 share lots are cheaper on a per share basis, it will not be cheaper in total dollars spent. Therefore, pay the higher per share fees and instruct your broker to register the shares in your name and send you the certificate. Once you are a shareholder of record, you may contact the company to request enrollment forms for their DRIP plan. When you receive the enrollment kit, simply follow the application instructions to join. Once enrolled, you can mail your stock certificates to the plan for safekeeping.

TARGETING PORTFOLIO CANDIDATES

You are doing something right when Benjamin Graham applies an approach similar to the plan you implement. In his classic work *The Intelligent Investor*, Graham proposed several rules for the defensive investor who he defined as either an inexperienced investor or an individual who lacks the time to understand the entire investment process. He believed investors need adequate, but not excessive, diversification. He wanted to limit stock purchases to conservatively financed blue chips with a history of uninterrupted dividend payments. Lastly, he suggested an upper limit on the price to pay for a stock based on its average earnings.[5]

Based on his experiences, Graham believed paying too high a price for a good quality stock was not the major risk confronting the average investor. The major risk to an investor, he believed, was purchasing a low quality stock during favorable market conditions. He feared the investor would assume incorrectly that current good earnings were equivalent to earning power, which would continue into the future.[6] How many people do you know who entered the market during boom times thinking it was easy to make money, only to be hurt when the market corrected itself?

Understand Your Goals

When selecting individual stocks for your portfolio, the most important guideline is to purchase quality companies. The portfolio needs to hold high quality, well-established companies with a history of solid performance regardless of the economic environment. Speculative, high-risk companies have no place in your portfolio.

Capital gains are much less dependable than current income/dividends. Furthermore, current income helps to cushion the portfolio from market volatility. When markets are falling, new cash from dividends is constantly flowing into the portfolio to purchase additional shares at deflated prices. Stocks with rising dividend income streams can contribute significantly to the total return of the portfolio. Over the long term, dividends provide almost half of the return for a typical common stock.

A portfolio with a higher yield than the overall stock market is most likely to be less volatile than the overall market. In a well-balanced portfolio of 16 to 20 stocks, not every investment need have a high dividend yield. Some may not even pay a dividend at all. However, the total yield of the entire portfolio should average above the current overall stock market yield.

The majority of the portfolio holdings needs to be stocks that not only pay a dividend but also have not reduced that dividend during the past 10 years. The stocks must provide an above average dividend yield with a solid record of earnings and the potential for continued growth. Remember your goal is not to earn the highest return possible, but to generate a good return with minimal risk. Accordingly, robust growth is not necessary, but avoiding companies that lose money is very desirable.

To Buy or Not to Buy

With apologies to William Shakespeare, the purchase of individual stocks for your portfolio is a major responsibility. Figure 8.3 presents a few selected companies.

Some of these companies may not pay dividends and some may have cut their dividends. Although those dividend cutters are not candidates for your portfolio today, it may be helpful to monitor them to provide longer term trending data from which to evaluate future performance.

FIGURE 8.3 *Selected Individual Stocks*

LISTED BY INDUSTRY AND COMPANY

HEALTH CARE
Abbott Laboratories
Amgen
Bard
Baxter International
Becton Dickinson
Bristol-Myers Squibb
Eli Lilly
Johnson & Johnson
Medtronic
Merck (Schering-Plough)
Owens & Minor
Pfizer (Wyeth)
Stryker

CONSUMER GOODS
Archer Daniels Midland
Brown-Forman
Campbell Soup
Clorox
Coca Cola
Colgate-Palmolive
ConAgra Foods
General Mills
Heinz
Hershey Foods
Kellogg
Kimberly-Clark
Kraft Foods
McCormick & Co.
Molson Coors
PepsiCo
Procter & Gamble
Sara Lee
Smuckers
Sysco
Tootsie Roll

CONSUMER SERVICES
Harley-Davidson
McDonalds
Walgreen
Wal-Mart Stores

FINANCIALS
Berkshire Hathaway
Northern Trust Company
Wells Fargo
Wilmington Trust

BUSINESS SERVICES
Burlington Northern
CSX Corporation
Federal Express
Kansas City Southern
Norfolk Southern
Union Pacific
United Parcel Service

INDUSTRIAL MATERIALS
Boeing Company
Caterpillar
Deere
Dow Chemical
DuPont
Emerson Electric
General Dynamics
General Electric
Illinois Tool Works
International Paper
Lockheed Martin
Northrup Grumman
Raytheon
3M Company
United Technologies
Weyerhaeuser

SOFTWARE
Automatic Data Processing
Microsoft
Oracle

HARDWARE
Apple
Applied Materials
Dell
EMC Corporation
Hewlett Packard
IBM
Intel
Texas Instruments

MEDIA
Walt Disney

TELECOMMUNICATIONS
AT&T
Cisco Systems
Verizon Communications

ENERGY
Chevron Texaco
Conoco Philips
Exxon-Mobil

UTILITIES
American States Water
Aqua America
Black Hills Corporation
California Water
DPL, Inc.
FPL Group, Inc.
National Fuel Gas
Peidmont Gas

You must do your homework. The list is neither all-inclusive nor exclusive; it is only a starting point.

Stocks are quite different from mutual funds. Individual companies require monitoring because individual stock performance can change overnight, even the blue chips. Perhaps some of the companies on this list have merged, or been acquired, or have downsized, or even ceased operations. For instance, both General Electric (GE) and Pfizer (PFE) have cut their dividends. Until they restore their dividend growth record for a minimum of 10 years, neither company is a candidate for purchase. Seeking competitive advantages, some companies may choose to consolidate such as the mergers of Pfizer/Wyeth and Merck/Schering-Plough. Regardless of the hype associated with the merger, the company is not a candidate for purchase until sufficient performance trending is available. What looks good today may not tomorrow; new names may be added while old friends may be dropped. Stay vigilant and stay focused.

Some Guidelines

You need to concentrate on dividend paying stocks offering DRIP plans. Although you may select some companies that do not provide DRIP plans, you want to concentrate your purchases on companies paying dividends. While you can own a company paying no dividends, be cautious. Large companies occasionally spin-off or divest operations to form new companies. Many of these spin-offs may offer DRIP plans, but you do not want to add them to your portfolio until their performance can be vetted for a minimum of five years and preferably longer. You always want to put safety first.

You want to focus exclusively on companies with powerful franchises, dominant market share positions, or unique intellectual properties. These companies tend to hold up well during tough economic times because they gain even more customers as others falter. Companies with a dominant market position also have the ability to raise their prices higher than the rate of inflation. As the market leader, they can set the price base. Due to their industry status, these companies may seem expensive and you may even overpay in the short run. Over time, this slight premium becomes negligible when they deliver the expected growth. Your individual stocks are long-term investments and should be going strong well into the future.

You want to target a 15% to 20% premium over the long-term return of the market as compensation for the incremental workload associated with individual stocks. Achieving only market returns is not a prudent trade-off for the added efforts associated with individual stocks. Accordingly, the long-term stock market return of 9.3% translates to a target return of 11.2% for your portfolio. This is a long-term goal, not an annual target. You want to put the power of compounding on your side. Look for companies providing either a current dividend yield of 15% higher than the current Dow yield or a projected 10% growth in dividends. You can earn a better return with less risk by investing in lower yielding stocks that regularly boost their dividend payouts. The secret is the compounding power of those increasing dividend payments.

Rather than merely chasing higher yields, investors must identify stocks of companies that increase their dividends year in and year out. This dividend-rich strategy works for individual investors because it separates the steady achievers from the rest of the field. A predictable and steady increase of the dividend indicates management rewards its shareholders. Furthermore, their dividend policy tends to provide a safety net under the stock price. This approach focuses primarily on big, blue-chip companies paying at least some current dividend with the potential for future dividend increases.

While steady dividend growth may indicate a potentially good company, you need to analyze other attributes to complete the profile. This review needs to concentrate on data trends. You are seeking quality, sustainability, and long-term achievement. These attributes include, but are not limited to, a record of increasing dividends for 10 years or more, dividend payouts below 60% of earnings, increasing book values, returns on equity above 15%, increasing sales growth, steady or increasing margins, low debt ratios with long term debt below 40%, and reasonable P/E ratios.

Quality investments have one overriding characteristic that separates them from the rest of the pack—consistency over the long run. No investment can continually grow month-to-month, quarter-to-quarter, or even year-to-year. All investments flounder at times, but what separates the good companies is the ability to post consistent results over time. When you look at three-, five-, and 10-year periods of compound growth, you want reasonably consistent results and, hopefully, a small uptick. Again, you are not looking for a shooting star; you are looking for the North Star. You want a consistent, stable, and steady performer that will be around for years to come. You really do want to hold that investment forever.

Speculative stocks are for more seasoned investors who have the ability to withstand extreme price volatility. If you go this route, you may get some big winners, but you may also incur some large losses. Since these speculative portfolios can lose some or all of your investment capital, there is no place for such a program here.

Initially, you want to concentrate on those industries that hold up well through all business cycles, maintain an easily understood business model, and retain a well-defined, secure demand for their products and services. Examples of these industries include oil, medical products and supplies, drugs, beverages, food, and household products. These industries tend to deliver the goods year after year while routinely increasing their dividends. You may purchase more than one stock from each industry, but it would be best to limit your purchases to no more than 12 companies from these seven industries.

While few may be blue-chip holdings, the often-overlooked stodgy utilities continue to pay steady, but unspectacular, dividends. The water, gas, and electric utilities are viable candidates with the water industry being the best risk-reward candidate. Utilities are regulated companies, and therefore, some of the evaluation criteria require adjustment. For instance, debt ratios and dividend payouts are much higher. Avoid utilities with substantial nuclear power resources. While these companies tend to have lower operating costs, nuclear waste disposal is a very significant issue posing not only costly compliance requirements but also potentially catastrophic risk in the event of radioactive contamination. Look for utilities with an evenly distributed client base among residential, commercial, industrial, and government customers. Limit your portfolio selections to no more than three utilities and no more than two companies from the same industry.

To complete your portfolio you may need to move beyond these industries. You want diversification and you need to expand your search into more cyclical industries with greater volatility. That is okay. You must remain selective, do your homework, and stick to the guidelines. A shotgun approach to identifying good investment opportunities is neither desirable nor practical. You want to select quality companies with solid performance while avoiding those that have been erratic in raising dividends, have a record of cutting dividends, or have increased debt without a legitimate business reason.

USEFUL VALUATION FACTORS

Dividends

The total return of a stock includes both its current dividend yield and future price appreciation. Over time, stock prices tend to match dividend increases for large, blue-chip companies. In other words, if you pick a company providing 10% increases in its annual dividends, you can expect increases in its stock price to average 10% per year also. Of course, dividend increases and stock price appreciation do not move in lockstep. The growth of a given stock price may outpace the growth rate of the company's dividend increases periodically, and for a time, the opposite may also occur.

Stock price appreciation tends to follow dividend growth rates in the large, stable companies; many experienced investors build portfolios with companies providing current dividends (yield) with the potential for future dividend increases. In so doing, they position themselves to achieve consistent long-term investment results.

Many companies use excess cash to buy back their shares, improving the earnings for their remaining shares rather than paying dividends. Dividends are paid with after-tax earnings and shareholders pay tax on the dividends received, so double taxation occurs on all dividends paid. This double taxation leads to shareholder acceptance of share repurchases in lieu of higher dividends. In severely down markets, however, share repurchases are a poor management decision. Many shareholders prefer the reinstatement of those old, boring dividend payments.

Value companies typically include those that pay higher dividends. Growth companies tend to include those that pay lower or no dividends because they reinvest their earnings in the business.

Book Value

When looking at a balance sheet, assets equal liabilities plus equity. When subtracting total liabilities from total assets, what remains is stockholders' equity. Since stockholders' equity represents what the company is worth after liquidation, assuming all the values stated on the balance sheet are accurate, some analysts use the terms net worth, intrinsic value, or book value.

Over time, a correlation exists between book value growth and share price growth because increasing book value typically increases the intrinsic value of the company as well. Growing book value through expanding profits, improving returns on assets, or acquiring companies below book value adds economic value to the company. However, you need to watch for companies that grow their book value through other, less desirable methods. Increasing the outstanding number of shares, acquiring companies at a premium to their book value, hoarding cash for future contingencies, or implementing significant accounting changes do not add economic value to the company.

Return on Equity (ROE)

ROE is the current year's earnings per share as a percent of the most recently released shareholder equity or book value per share. Warren Buffett has long believed ROE is the primary test of managerial economic performance and a better precursor to long-term performance than earnings per share. He points out companies can employ a number of devices or mechanisms to distort the actual accounting earnings and thus artificially improve performance by showing consistent gains. Those mechanisms are not readily available for the manipulation of ROE.

Since debt reduces shareholder equity, high ROE achieved with little or no debt is more valued than similar ROE with high debt. Compare ROE performance for companies in the same industries only. The infrastructure within certain industries may alter the balance sheets of competing firms making ROE comparisons across industries misleading or even incorrect. Watch for companies with stock buybacks because reductions in the number of outstanding shares generate higher ROE values. Since ROE performance tends to follow the business cycle, avoid making projections based on artificially high rates due to the cyclical nature of the company. You also want to be aware of inflated ROE numbers due to one-time charges such as restructuring, asset sales, or one-time gains.

Sales Revenue

It all starts with sales revenue. Without sales, there are no profits, there are no dividends, and there are no returns for your investment dollars. Rapid sales growth can occur when the product or service is so popular and in such demand, the product sells itself. Rapid sales growth can also occur when the demand for a particular product is greater than the supply of such a product, which leads to higher prices and higher sales. Neither of these two scenarios is sustainable over the long term. The former leads to greater competition because more players enter the market; the latter reallocates industry resources to correct the supply/demand imbalance.

Dominant players in those industries can exploit such market inequities longer because they may be able to create barriers to entering the market. When the competition finally does enter the market, the dominant players are able to find new products or services, thereby restarting this process. You want companies that can continually expand sales, providing consistent, sustainable growth over time.

Profit Margin

The profit margin percentage (calculated by dividing net income by total sales) indicates how much money the company is making on every revenue dollar collected. Expanding sales with lower margins may indicate the company has lowered prices to stimulate sales; or the company may have added incremental resources to support the sales growth, driving their costs higher and their profits lower.

You want to own companies that routinely reduce costs and improve productivity. You want to own companies that create innovative ways to repackage existing products and services. You want to own companies that enter new markets with their existing products and services. These factors lead to higher sales while reducing or limiting costs, thereby improving margins. Look for profit margins that consistently grow.

You also want to watch for temporary margin improvements occurring when a company initiates a restructuring program to bring costs in line with sales. Good management, however, does not implement cost-cutting initiatives. Good management routinely tackles unnecessary and excessive spending in good times as well as bad. Some firms can expand margins through increased sales volume that does not proportionately increase their costs. When fixed costs dominate the cost structure more than variable costs, the company can allocate a greater portion of costs to a larger sales volume generating a higher profit margin per product.

Debt to Total Capital

Obviously, the more long-term debt a company has relative to its net worth, the more risk the company accepts. Conventional wisdom calls companies with debt ratios greater than 60% highly leveraged (excluding the utility industries). Although no absolute benchmark exists, you want companies with debt to total capital ratios below 25%, but ratios up to 40% may be acceptable. You can blend higher leveraged firms with more conservatively managed companies within your portfolio. A few higher leveraged companies are okay, but limit your exposure to these firms.

When long-term debt is a relatively cheap source of capital and the company can use these funds to produce significant returns, the judicious use of debt can have a positive impact on the returns. Coincidently, companies with little or no debt can become takeover targets because their unused debt capacity can finance the takeover, thereby limiting the exposure of the buying company.

Debt does influence ROE. Although a company may be generating significant earnings, you must ask whether these gains are coming at the expense of an ever more highly leveraged balance sheet. You want to look at the trends of both debt and ROE when comparing similar companies. You can gain valuable insights into the competitive and investment value of each.

The Price/Earnings Ratio

The most common measure used to evaluate whether a stock is over-priced or relatively cheap is the price to earnings ratio (P/E). Comparing it to the market as a whole, to other companies in the same industry, and to the company itself (trending data) is a wise decision. The price investors pay for those earnings provides a glimpse of investor sentiment because investors tend to pay more for earnings when their expectations are high and less when they lose confidence.

Sometimes overlooked is the price to cash flow ratio (P/CF). Looking at both the company's P/E and P/CF ratios allows you to make better comparisons. In fact, you may uncover some reasonable values by comparing cash flow growth rates to price/earnings growth rates. Cash flow, which is the sum of the reported earnings and depreciation, is a good indicator of the company's internal cash generating ability. For instance, when the P/E ratio of a company seems overpriced, the cash flow ratios may indicate high growth, thereby providing some evidence that the "overvalued" P/E ratio may be justified.

SELLING AN INVESTMENT

First, you must distinguish need from want. Emergencies occur, tragedies happen, and life throws you an occasional curve. Should your financial situation change, you must revise your needs and, if necessary, you may need to liquidate some or even all of your holdings. These scenarios are outside the normal course of an investment program and therefore are not part of this discussion.

The concept of want is operational in nature. In other words, what guidelines or monitoring techniques are appropriate to determine whether you need to sell a currently held stock? Much of the financial literature and many investment advisors instruct investors to have a sell strategy typically based on some trigger—your investment achieves "x" profit or the stock P/E exceeds "y" or the price falls below "z" or some other criteria that acts as the trigger. Unfortunately, the notion of selling when a so-called trigger happens is wrong on the merits. You are not speculating in high-risk investments, you are investing in large, stable blue-chip companies with a history of performance. Your goal is not to sell your investments; your goal is hold onto them for as long as you can.

There are exceptions. One sure-fire sell signal is a cut in dividends. You do not want to own any dividend cutters. Before you buy any stock, the company must have a 10-year record of increasing its dividend payments. Should a company cut dividends on a stock you currently own, you want to sell your position. Once sold, you may monitor the stock, but you do not want to buy it back until that 10 year performance has been restored. For companies that stop increasing their dividend payments and hold dividends flat, you need only monitor the company to see if the decision is a temporary setback or the precursor to more draconian measures.

Aside from such situations, selling becomes a much more subjective exercise. Regrettably, no rules exist providing you, or any investor, with a reliable, objective system for selling stock. The key word in this statement is "reliable." Triggers may be objective, but they may not be the most accurate approach. Nothing is foolproof and exceptions always arise.

Since your portfolio focuses on long-term, quality companies, you have a bit more latitude in holding on to less-than-stellar performers. That does not mean you hold on to losers, it means you give them time to generate the returns you had expected while you reevaluate your assumptions. Has anything changed to adjust your expectations? The typical evaluation period is one to two years, but more time may be appropriate when the market is down or when the company is performing consistently with historical trends or industry standards.

Every investor will make occasional mistakes, not to worry. Investment losses do occur, but you want to minimize both the number and magnitude of those losses. You want to recognize your mistakes as early as possible and jettison them from your portfolio. Investors may find it difficult to sell stocks at a loss because they may not want to admit mistakes. You need to understand investing is a long-term game. You want to move on so you can restart the compounding chain.

Your goal is to allow your winners to "run for the roses" for as long as possible, perhaps forever. However, your dividend-rich portfolio has certain characteristics that may contradict or, at least, conflict with potential sell decisions. The first few years are the most crucial to your portfolio holdings. Consider three types of investment performance: losers, winners, and marginal performers. The losers are easy to identify; the stock underperforms expectations, underachieves the market, and trails its industry competition. The winners are also easy to identify; you just sit back and enjoy the ride. The marginal performers are more difficult to assess.

An often-overlooked benefit of those marginal stocks is their dividend payment. If you have held a stock for 10 or more years, the dividend yield on your original investment has most likely risen to well over 6% and, in some cases, may even approach 8% or 9%. Now assuming there is no deterioration in the company's fundamentals and the trending data does not indicate potential problems, do you sell or not? Again, there is no right or wrong answer.

Even when the company growth has slowed, you may not want to sell. Why? First, you most likely are receiving a hefty dividend yield despite the slower growth and the stock may retain some appreciation potential. Second, despite the slowing growth projections, these dominant companies may rekindle their historical growth patterns. They may develop new products, enter new markets, or acquire other companies. Some questions also arise. What alternative investments are under consideration? Do they hold the same long-term prospects? How do these alternatives fit with your other portfolio holdings? What is wrong with just holding that very juicy dividend paying stock? Perhaps a "bird in the hand" is a timely thought to consider.

You want to maintain the discipline to purchase a new stock only after first selling an existing position. If you want to increase the number of stocks in your portfolio that is okay, but you need to do so with your eyes open, understanding the consequences rather than the fear of selling a position. It is perfectly fine to take your time in making sell decisions. Ignore the daily gyrations of the market; a good idea today is still going to be good idea tomorrow and even next week. Do not forget to hold portfolio turnover to a minimum.

You also want to invest equally in each stock. Over time, some positions may grow faster than others distorting the percentages allocated to the stocks in your portfolio. Add new money to those stocks that are lagging to equalize positions. Not only does this maintain the percentage relationship within the portfolio and thus the risk; it also encourages purchasing the stock when the price is lower, which follows the famous buy low, sell high adage. Of course, you only invest new money after verifying that the fundamentals remain sound.

STAYING THE COURSE—INDIVIDUAL STOCKS

No individual stock investment program is foolproof. No one has all the answers. More importantly, the best individual stock investment program is the one that works for you, not your neighbor, not your broker, but you. Like most things in life, success is heavily contingent upon your efforts. When buying individual stocks, you must understand the tradeoffs. You will spend significantly more time researching potential stock candidates. You will spend significantly more time monitoring current portfolio holdings. You will need more capital to provide adequate diversification when holding individual stocks. You will increase your portfolio risk since individual stocks introduce firm risk while also raising market risk concerns.

While the mutual fund portfolio targets market returns, an individual stock portfolio must generate returns 20% higher to compensate for the increased efforts associated with stock selection and portfolio management. Neither approach comes with a guarantee, but one has the benefit of history while the other concentrates on hard work and knowledge. Only you can determine if this trade-off fits your needs. Remembering the advice of Marshal Dillon, you want to think about it hard because individual stock investing is not for everyone.

If you remain determined to proceed, you want to work to your strengths. Without a doubt, the best weapon in your arsenal is time. Time is the great equalizer when comparing your portfolio to those of professional money managers. When you buy a stock, your goal is to garner a good return with minimal risk. To accomplish this goal, you must consider price and quality. You want to focus on quality, blue-chip companies purchased at reasonable prices.

Unfortunately, these big companies with the best potential are rarely available at an attractive price. Again, that is okay. You may purchase stocks at higher prices than you want to pay because you are holding them for the long term, which you assume is forever. Of course, you may also wait for something to happen that negatively affects the stock price. The best time to purchase stocks is during a recession because the stock market always generates its biggest gains coming out of the throes of a recession. You have all heard that you buy on the bad news, sell on the good. Well, it is probably not such a good idea to be a seller on bad news nor is it a good idea to move out of the market in a weakening business environment.

You want to sell infrequently, keeping your portfolio turnover low. Not only does this keep your costs low, but low turnover also allows your money to grow through the miracle of compound growth. Time is your ally, patience is your friend, and Mr. Market is your teacher.

You want to stay focused, set realistic goals, and always look at risk before rewards. In *The Intelligent Investor*, Benjamin Graham provided some encouraging words for all investors. The average investor, he said, should limit his or her ambitions and confine activities to safe, defensive investments. He went on to say that achieving satisfactory investment results is easier than most people realize but achieving superior results is harder than it looks.[7]

CHAPTER NINE

What If You Win the Lottery?

I think this is the beginning of a beautiful friendship.
Casablanca (film), 1942

Is THERE ANYONE who has not seen the movie *Casablanca*? Set in French-occupied Morocco during World War II, Rick's Café Américain is the setting for intrigue, espionage, and of course, romance. Shot in just seven weeks with multiple script rewrites, expectations for the movie were mediocre at best. Released in 1942, Michael Curtiz directed *Casablanca* and it starred Humphrey Bogart as Rick Blaine, Ingrid Bergman as Ilsa Lund, and Claude Rains as Captain Louis Renault. The movie boasted many, many character actors from the Warner Bros. back lot. Despite the rushed production, the film always ranks in the top five of the greatest movies ever made by Hollywood.

In the final scene of the movie, Rick and Captain Renault are walking across the wet runway into the foggy night with a heavy mist surrounding them. Rick tells Renault, "I think this is the beginning of a beautiful friendship." A fitting end to the many script rewrites, Producer Hal B. Wallis wrote this final line after completion of the shooting. He needed to bring Bogart back to the studio to dub the line into the film over a month after production ended.

To everyone's surprise, *Casablanca* received eight Academy Award nominations, winning three including Best Picture, Best Director, and Best Adapted Screenplay. Oh yes, the song "As Time Goes By" ranks as the second best song in the American Film Institute's 100 Best Songs.

As a testament to the film's durability, *Casablanca* enjoys the most remembered quotes in the American Film Institute's Top 100 Film

Quotes, with a total of six. Perhaps you may recall the scenes for some of these memorable lines.

Ranked # 5: "Here's looking at you, kid."
Ranked # 20: "I think this is the beginning of a beautiful friendship."
Ranked # 28: "Play it, Sam. Play 'As Time Goes By.'" (Often misquoted as "Play it again, Sam.")
Ranked # 32: "Round up the usual suspects."
Ranked # 43: "We'll always have Paris."
Ranked # 67: "Of all the gin joints in all the towns in all the world, she walks into mine."

Unlike *Casablanca*, this chapter most likely will be skipped. After all, how many of us actually win the lottery? Still, you never know what the future holds.

PROCEED WITH CAUTION

All too often, people who come into large sums of money lose perspective. Once again, those silly emotions get in the way and you make rash judgments, spend foolishly, and most likely obtain expensive, and sometimes, questionable advice. None of these scenarios bodes well for you, many of them are unnecessary, and some may be very, very costly. Even if you have never been wealthy (you define what wealthy means to you), there is a simple, safe, and effective way to invest any windfall regardless of size. Would you be surprised if this entire process required only a few hours at most? Better still, it does not even involve the stock market! What? Say it ain't so, Joe.[1]

It is true. In reality, the wealthier you are, the less you need to invest in the stock market. Why? Most likely, your personal needs no longer require wealth generation. As we grow older, most of us become more concerned about capital preservation. When you acquire a significant amount of money, the main investment objective changes to ensuring you do not lose what you now have.

INVEST IN TREASURIES, NOT EQUITIES

Hey, wait a minute! Doesn't the investment program call for a balance between stocks and bonds? Why the change? Really, there is no change in the program. Just as you have skipped the part about working a lifetime, your wealth enables you to skip a few steps in the model.

Early in life, you need to build capital or wealth. As your wealth increases, your risk tolerance grows smaller, so you move more of your wealth into treasuries. When you reach retirement, the preservation of your wealth is more important than growing your wealth, thereby making your risk tolerance even lower. The model directs you to maintain 25% of your wealth in stocks to protect you from the ravages of inflation.

When you receive a sizeable lump sum of money, it changes your life. You become more conservative and more risk averse, so your portfolio takes on retirement stage characteristics. Your concern is more towards maintenance and preservation rather than growth and risk. With a sizeable windfall, you should invest in treasuries then put the interest stream from treasuries into the equities side of your portfolio. This approach may seem a bit backwards, but then your wealth creation is also a bit backwards. You already achieved your wealth. Now you need to keep it, not create it.

MAXIMIZING INCOME AND PRESERVING CAPITAL

The goal is to provide as much income as possible without affecting your principal. You are in this for the long haul and you want to ensure your capital stays with you for the entire ride. For this reason, U.S. Treasuries are the instrument of choice. Now you want to maximize your income with treasury securities.

A bond ladder strategy minimizes the reinvestment risk associated with bonds while managing the cash flows received from those bonds. Purchasing individual treasuries scheduled to mature at staggered dates in the future provides liquidity. For instance, you might buy equal amounts of treasuries due in one year, two years, three years, and so on.

Reinvestment risk is the possibility that future interest and principal payments, when received, will earn less than the current rates. Although a bond ladder does not provide as much income as buying only the highest yielding, long-term treasuries, it does provide diversification and therefore reduces overall risk. For example, a surge in interest rates would drive down the prices on long-term treasuries, producing capital losses for those investors who need to sell before maturity. When rates surge, the bond ladder allows you access to new money from the staggered maturities, which are available to spend or to reinvest at the new higher rates. A bond ladder also provides some protection if rates fall because some higher yields are locked in on the longer maturities. Accordingly, a bond ladder strategy balances reinvestment opportunity with market risk.

A bond ladder allows you to manage your cash flows. For instance, if you want to guarantee a monthly income stream from the interest payments on your treasuries, select treasuries with payment dates corresponding to each month of the year. Since the majority of treasuries pay interest semi-annually, you need a minimum of six bonds to complete the 12-month cycle—January/July payments, February/August payments, March/September payments, April/October payments, May/November payments, and June/December payments.

In addition to monthly interest payments, you have created a relatively liquid asset that will provide access to cash because of steadily maturing treasuries. In other words, by staggering the maturity dates over a period of time, one of your treasury placements will mature every year or so, providing access to those funds. You may choose to reinvest the entire amount, or only a portion, or even none at all depending on your financial needs at the time.

Why Not Mutual Funds?

The dynamics of the investment model changed. You are no longer investing periodically to build wealth; you are investing a lump sum to preserve wealth. You no longer need to shift investments between the two sides of your portfolio. More specifically, you no longer require the fixed income side of the mutual fund portfolio. For the equity side of your portfolio, be sure to stick with mutual funds.

In exchange for the benefits of mutual funds, you relinquish control. Control was not the priority in developing your retirement (tax deferred) portfolio nor was it important in your core (taxable) portfolio since both focused on wealth generation. With your newly acquired wealth however, control means everything. You cannot build an investment bond ladder with mutual funds. Funds are a diversified, managed portfolio of investment instruments. The fund manager is continually buying and selling positions to accommodate capital flows into the fund as well as the distributions out of the fund, all based on his interpretation of market indicators. Therefore, a mutual fund cannot provide specific maturity dates such as one year, two years, and so on. Funds can only provide a broad time horizon identified as short, intermediate, or long term.

Building a ladder with individual treasury positions, you can manage your portfolio and avoid the capital gains or losses associated with mutual funds. When you hold the treasuries to maturity, there are no capital losses except in the rare case of a default by the issuer, but that does not occur with treasuries.

BUILDING A BOND LADDER

Now suppose you are a teacher earning $50,000 and you have just won the lottery with a payout of $25,000,000!! You decide on the lump sum payout, and the after tax amount is approximately $10,000,000. Of course, the actual payout amount varies based on your state income taxes and future federal income tax law changes. After you catch your breath, what do you do?

You want to open an account with the Treasury so that you can purchase the treasury securities directly from the Federal Reserve. The $5 million purchase limit per auction may require more time and a little inconvenience as you stage your purchases over time, but it is certainly worth the return and therefore worth the wait. After all, you probably have a little more free time on your hands now anyway.

Maintaining Liquidity

Your portfolio transactions may be similar to those presented in Figure 9.1. You want to spread the total amount of your investment over a 10-year period. You want to avoid maturities beyond 10 years because 20- or 30-year maturities limit your access to the funds and usually do not provide an adequate return for the length of the maturity. Granted

FIGURE 9.1 Building A Treasury Ladder

TERM	AUCTION	ISSUE	MATURITY	RATE	YIELD	PRICE	INVESTMENT	INTEREST
2 year	5/29/07	5/31/07	5/31/09	4.8750%	4.8860%	99.97928	1,000,000	48,750.00
5 year	5/30/07	5/31/07	3/15/12	4.7500%	4.8180%	99.70103	2,500,000	118,750.00
10 year	6/12/07	6/15/07	5/15/17	4.5000%	5.2300%	94.39913	2,500,000	112,500.00
26 weeks	6/11/07	6/14/07	12/13/07		4.9640%	94.39913	4,000,000	198,560.00
						ORIGINAL ALLOCATIONS	10,000,000	478,560.00
								4.786%
26 weeks	12/17/07	12/20/07	6/19/08		3.3910%	94.39913	4,000,000	135,640.00
	5/29/07	5/31/07	5/31/09	4.8750%	4.8860%	99.97928	1,000,000	48,750.00
	5/30/07	5/31/07	3/15/12	4.7500%	4.8180%	99.70103	2,500,000	118,750.00
	6/12/07	6/15/07	5/15/17	4.5000%	5.2300%	94.39913	2,500,000	112,500.00
						ROLLOVER T-BILLS	10,000,000	415,640.00
								4.156%
UPDATED TERM								
< 1 year	5/29/07	5/31/07	5/31/09	4.8750%	4.8860%	99.97928	1,000,000	48,750.00
1 year	7/1/08	7/3/08	7/2/09		2.3680%	97.67950	2,000,000	47,360.00
2 year	6/24/08	6/30/08	6/30/10	2.8750%	2.9220%	99.90934	1,000,000	28,750.00
4 year	5/30/07	5/31/07	3/15/12	4.7500%	4.8180%	99.70103	2,500,000	118,750.00
5 year	6/26/08	6/30/08	6/30/13	3.3750%	3.4400%	99.70374	1,000,000	33,750.00
9 year	6/12/07	6/15/07	5/15/17	4.5000%	5.2300%	94.39913	2,500,000	112,500.00
						ALLOCATE T-BILLS	10,000,000	389,860.00
								3.899%

Source: www.treasurydirect.gov

you may give up some income when long rates are high, but your goal is to maximize your income for a given level of risk.

Ideally, you want to allocate equal amounts of money to each year within the 10 year period. Our teacher, therefore, would purchase 10 individual securities for $1 million each, maturating in one year, two years, three years, through 10 years. As you will soon find out, that task is usually not possible in a single auction or even multiple auctions over a short period.

In the example, the majority of treasury offerings is in maturities of less than one year, with periodic auctions of two-, five-, and 10-year notes. Given these parameters, meeting the original investment goals requires two separate auctions. At the first auction, 25% is invested in both the five- and 10-year notes. At the second auction, 10% is invested in two-year notes and the remaining 40% in short-term bills. Although a bit more concentrated, the allocations approximate your intended goal with 50% invested for five years or beyond, 10% invested for two years, and the remainder held for 26 weeks since no 52-week bills are available. The heavier weighting in treasury bills gives you the flexibility to reinvest the funds in other maturities when these bills mature.

In the next section, the treasury bills roll over for another 26 weeks. With only six months passing since the original auctions, the treasury did not offer any maturities that provided sufficient spacing between our existing maturities. With another 26 weeks before these treasury bills mature, there will be a bit more spacing between the maturities, which should allow you to reinvest at least a portion of these funds.

When the treasury bills mature in the final section, enough time will have passed to allow the purchase of one-year bills and two- and five-year notes. The first column lists the updated or effective maturities and they show the funds maturing in less than one year, one, two, four, five, and nine years. As the various investments mature, look to fill those missing rungs in the ladder in $1 million increments. It does not have to be exactly $1 million, but do try to spread your investment reasonably across the 10-year timeframe. In other words, you want to try to place half the funds beyond five years to take advantage of the higher rates of a normal yield curve. When you are concentrating purchases in a few years, be sure you have placed sufficient funds in the one- to two-year maturity range because you want to ensure liquidity in the event you need access to your funds.

Reinvestment Risk

Figure 9.1 shows the potential for reinvestment risk. The allocation for the two original auctions provided an annual return of almost 4.8%, but within one year, the annual return fell to 3.9% as you reinvested a portion of the short-term funds. The benefit of the ladder strategy is also on display in Figure 9.1. Since you locked in the higher rates of the five- and 10-year notes, you have cushioned yourself, for a while at least, from the falling rates. The period presented in Figure 9.1 represents the time of the stock market meltdown from sub-prime loans that caused a flight to the security of treasury instruments. This capital flight caused the prices on treasuries to rise considerably while the yields dramatically fell.

The benefit of spreading your maturities enables you to hold onto those higher yields typically provided with longer-term maturities. Of course, the longer the recession or the higher the U.S. debt, the lower the interest rates. Again, this is secondary to preservation of capital. The markets are cyclical; it may take some time, but the market will eventually turn that corner.

Now, about that Windfall

Getting back to that teacher earning $50,000, he or she has just given him or herself a raise to the tune of almost $400,000 pre-tax. Here is some other goods news—treasury interest is exempt from state income taxes. Only you can decide whether you are wealthy or not, but you still want to adhere to the investment model guidelines. To provide a little discipline, you want to invest one-half of the interest in money market funds and the other half in equities, preferably mutual funds according to our investment model. If you decide to quit working, increase the percentage in money market funds to two-thirds of the interest and put the remaining one-third in equities.

The percentages are only guidelines and you most likely will need to readjust them after you become accustomed to your new lifestyle. Always put preservation of capital at the top of your list. The "unused"

FIGURE 9.2 *Potential Earnings from Lottery Winnings*

LOTTERY WINNINGS	APPROXIMATE TAKE HOME	INTEREST PERCENTAGE				
		1%	2%	3%	4%	5%
$ 2,500,000	$ 1,000,000	$ 10,000	$ 20,000	$ 30,000	$ 40,000	$ 50,000
$ 6,250,000	$ 2,500,000	$ 25,000	$ 50,000	$ 75,000	$ 100,000	$ 125,000
$ 12,500,000	$ 5,000,000	$ 50,000	$ 100,000	$ 150,000	$ 200,000	$ 250,000
$ 25,000,000	$10,000,000	$100,000	$ 200,000	$ 300,000	$ 400,000	$ 500,000
$ 50,000,000	$20,000,000	$200,000	$ 400,000	$ 600,000	$ 800,000	$1,000,000
$ 75,000,000	$30,000,000	$300,000	$ 600,000	$ 900,000	$1,200,000	$1,500,000
$100,000,000	$40,000,000	$400,000	$ 800,000	$1,200,000	$1,600,000	$2,000,000
$125,000,000	$50,000,000	$500,000	$1,000,000	$1,500,000	$2,000,000	$2,500,000

portion from the interest you receive should be earmarked for the purchase of equities to get to the 25% level of the investment model, but do not reduce the principal of your treasury holdings. Let the equity position build from your unused interest earnings only.

Figure 9.2 presents the potential earnings available for various levels of lottery winnings at different interest rates. Historically, treasury interest yields fluctuate between 2% and 5%. Of course, exceptions beyond these ranges do occur especially when inflation becomes excessive.

If your wealth is approaching the bottom portion of Figure 9.2, you may be inclined to overweight the portion of funds allocated to longer maturities. When the interest rates on longer maturities are favorable, say in the 4.5%+ range, you may want to move a higher portion of your funds into these maturities to lock in those rates. Be cautious, however. You still want to retain shorter maturities for stability of capital and access to funds should an emergency arise.

How often have you heard of a lottery winner who has gone broke or star athletes who have squandered their earnings through bad investments or dishonest investment advisors? Scanning the potential earnings in Figure 9.2, you can quickly ascertain the magnitude of the interest payments. One may assume most individuals would be able to live quite comfortably on $400,000 to $500,000 per year. Of even greater value is the principal that passes to your children or other designated heirs. This is a powerful motivation for a sensible, low-risk investment program.

Unfortunately, many individuals lose perspective when they acquire such large amounts of money. They incorrectly believe it will last forever regardless of how much they spend or how they invest. Most take needless risks, accept dubious investment advice, and throw logic out the window. Do not lose your good judgment; you want to stay focused, you want to preserve your capital, and you want to build a ladder to your future.

U.S. TREASURIES

When constructing your bond ladder, you only want to use U.S. Treasury Bills or Notes. When using bond ladders, the concept is to hold each individual security until maturity because the staggered maturity dates provide sufficient liquidity. Since you know you may be holding some of these bonds for 10 years, you want to make sure your principal is not at risk. Make no mistake; the only diversification you are interested in is the diversification of maturity dates. Do not deviate from treasuries; you want to sleep at night. You do not want to put your principal at risk. Case closed.

You also want to purchase your treasuries directly from the Federal Reserve. Not only is the Treasury Direct program as convenient as mutual funds, but there are no fees or charges for buying or holding your treasury securities. You cannot beat that! You do not want to use a dealer or broker and pay needless, expensive commissions.

Establishing a Treasury Direct Account [2]

To open an account, you need a Social Security number, a U.S. address of record, either a checking or savings account, an email address, and a web browser. Simply log onto the Treasury website (www.treasury direct.gov), follow the instructions, enter your information as directed, and within minutes you have an account.

This account allows you purchase and hold treasury bills, notes, bonds, inflation-protected securities, and savings bonds. You are able to purchase, re-invest, and sell securities as well as perform account maintenance online. Treasury Direct charges neither a transaction fee nor a maintenance fee. When selling treasury securities prior to their maturity through SellDirect, a small fee does apply. The account also allows you to participate directly in the auction process.

The Auction Process[3]

The Treasury sells bills, notes, bonds, and TIPS through regular public auctions that determine the rate for these securities. Several days prior to the auction, the Treasury announces the auction amount, the maturity dates, and other details. As an individual, you have two types of bidding options. With the non-competitive bid, you agree to purchase treasury securities at the rate set at the auction. Non-competitive bids are limited to total purchases of $5 million in a single auction. With a competitive bid, you specify the rate you will accept for the treasury securities requested. Competitive bids are limited to a maximum of 35% of the total amount of treasuries offered in the auction. Institutional investors generally submit competitive bids, but experienced individuals may also participate.

When the auction closes, the Treasury accepts all of the non-competitive bids. Then, the Treasury accepts the competitive bids in ascending order of their yields until the total of accepted bids equals the total amount of the treasury securities offered. In other words, they accept the lowest yields first because the Treasury receives the most funds for a given yield.

STAYING THE COURSE—A TREASURY LADDER

For those fortunate few who have won the lottery, you have passed "Go" and you certainly have collected much more than $200. While the investment program remains useful, you have skipped quite a number of steps. Your investment focus turns to capital preservation, risk mitigation, and income generation.

Bond laddering is one of the smartest investment concepts available. Laddering is a time-tested, low-risk approach that many, many successful individuals use. It is a very simple strategy to execute, it is understandable, it is easy to explain, and it mitigates reinvestment risk. Oh yes, it also works. Simplicity is always a key factor of any successful investment plan. When you understand the investment program, you will gain confidence in yourself and in the plan as well.

When you try to maximize income from treasury securities, you typically expose your portfolio to capital fluctuation. Higher income generally, but not always, comes from securities with longer maturities which are more vulnerable to price fluctuations. When balancing capital stability and income, you need to manage maturities while also monitoring the income generated. Here are a few helpful hints.

- If two reasonably identical treasury securities provide the same income, you always want to select the one with the shorter maturity. The longer maturity does not compensate you for holding the security longer. In fact, the longer maturity increases your risk of capital fluctuation.
- When building your portfolio ladder, you want to stagger the securities maturities. In other words, your portfolio holds securities with escalating maturities of one year, two years, three years, and so on. This approach balances the stability of the shorter maturities with the income generation of the longer maturities.
- If the Treasury auctions do not offer a complete series of maturities, you may need to concentrate your purchases into fewer years. You want to hold about half of your total investment in maturities beyond five years even if this means only two holdings (the five- and 10-year periods). When this approach is required, be sure to hold a good portion in short-term treasury bills and one-year notes to provide stability and access to your funds.
- The key to using an investment ladder is to buy and hold longer-term treasury securities while reinvesting the shorter-term treasury bills and one- or two-year treasury notes. This allows you to hold the higher paying, longer-term treasuries without losing either the capital stability or the access to your funds since you are constantly reinvesting your short-term treasuries. As the longer-term treasuries near maturity, you simply extend your purchases to fill in the maturities.

There you have it. When you have attained sufficient wealth, your goal is to minimize risk while maximizing income. Treasuries provide you with safety, security, and a steady income. What more can anyone ask? Okay, okay, that is why you are still maintaining that 25% in equities. You want to maintain that inflation hedge equities provide, but you are only investing the unused portion of your interest payments in stocks, even if it takes awhile to get to the appropriate percentages. Do not dip into that capital; time is definitely on your side. Yes, this is definitely the start of a beautiful friendship.

CHAPTER TEN

Dos and Don'ts

...he exhibited complete, overwhelming and colossal indifference.
Seabiscuit by Laura Hillenbrand, 2001

IT HAS BEEN said that luck is merely the intersection of preparation and opportunity. That was never more true than some 75 years ago when, in 1936, an unlikely cast of characters came together to inspire America during some of the darkest hours in our history. As the Great Depression continued to devastate the economy, keeping millions of Americans unemployed, this group of misfits formed an unlikely alliance and gave the nation new hope that the little guy can rise up off the mat and successfully compete with the privileged power brokers.

From her marvelous book entitled *Seabiscuit*, Laura Hillenbrand brought several historical characters to life for a new generation to admire. Despite the ongoing ravages of a Depression, she showed how they utilized their individual abilities to resurrect themselves. There was Red Pollard, abandoned as a child and a below-average jockey. She described Tom Smith as a quiet, introverted trainer who learned his skills on the American frontier. She told us how Charles Howard started his career as a bicycle mechanic, but went on to create an automobile empire in the American West. Then she introduced Seabiscuit, an undersized, disappointing horse unable to straighten his knees whose favorite pastimes were eating and sleeping. Misunderstood, mishandled, and mistreated, Seabiscuit competed only in the lowest levels of racing until these three men discovered, or perhaps unleashed, his hidden talent.[1]

The date was November 1, 1938; the place was the Pimlico Racetrack; and the result was historic. On that date, America witnessed what is still considered the greatest horserace in history. In a match race, the sentimental favorite, Seabiscuit, a supposedly untested little horse from the inferior West Coast racing circuit, challenged War Admiral, the highly celebrated Triple Crown winner from the East Coast racing establishment.

Since Seabiscuit was a much smaller horse and a notoriously slow starter out of the gate, Hillenbrand explained that Smith feared he might not be able to catch up with the huge strides of War Admiral, who usually broke out to an early lead. Smith decided to retrain Seabiscuit for this race—in just two short weeks! His strategy was to take the early lead, allow War Admiral to catch him near the final turn, and then turn Seabiscuit loose. Although risky, Smith knew Seabiscuit was a strong, tenacious champion who would not quit.[2] He knew once War Admiral caught up and became a challenge in the race, the 'Biscuit would give the Admiral the old evil eye and run him into the ground.

During the post parade, the heavily favored War Admiral took the walk majestically, looking almost regal. Seabiscuit, on the other hand, looked like a milk-truck horse. Hillenbrand cited that Shirley Povich of *The Washington Post* thought he exhibited complete, overwhelming and colossal indifference.[3] When the race ended, however, Seabiscuit had won by four lengths and solidified his place in history.[4]

After sustaining a career ending and almost life threatening injury, an aging Seabiscuit returned for one more ride into the record books. The second largest crowd in horseracing history at the time attended the return of the beloved Seabiscuit at the Santa Anita "One Hundred Grander" on March 2, 1940. Riding in the one race he had not won, Seabiscuit breezed into history and retirement with his final win.

Just as Seabiscuit was misunderstood and considered mediocre, index funds and treasury securities also are thought to be inferior. These investments are only average performers, so the argument goes. Well, by understanding the ravages of cost, applying the benefits of diversification, and allowing time to work its magic, you too might just breeze into retirement.

REVIEWING WHAT TO DO

We started this journey hoping you would not become one of the many people who find out that they should have started a little sooner, should have saved a little more, and should have tried a little harder. You now have a better understanding of the rules of the road, and you are ready to go out on your own.

Use a Little Common Sense

There may be as many investment strategies as investment advisors, but one common denominator exists in every single strategy. The one consistent and common element is the evaluation of all strategies against the market benchmark. No investment philosophy consistently overachieves the benchmark strategy. Oh, it can be done for a year, maybe two, and perhaps even five, but you are investing for a lifetime.

The market is a zero-sum game. For every winner there is a loser. Even the most experienced investors are unable to outfox and outmaneuver other investors with such frequency as to outperform the market over the long term. The buy and hold market strategy provides a compelling long-term investment profile depending neither on investor sentiment nor on stock valuations. The buy-and-hold market strategy requires only patience, not foresight.

What could be better than that? You need not take time to evaluate companies, to monitor performance, or to make timely buy and sell decisions. This simple, low maintenance strategy may be just what the doctor ordered. Sherlock Holmes noted, "When you have eliminated the impossible, whatever remains, however improbable, must be the truth."[5]

Set Realistic Goals Based on History

The biggest fallacy promoted by investment advisors is that index funds provide only average returns, and they of course can do better. However, study after study confirms the majority of actively managed stock funds fail to outperform the market index funds on a consistent, long-term basis. In fact, a large-cap index fund, over the long term, most likely ranks third out of any 10 randomly selected, actively managed, diversified, large-cap fund. How can this be? To outperform an index fund, you must hold a different number of stocks, at different weights from the benchmark, or some combination of both. Now to this add the risks of poor stock selection, incorrect timing, the need to hold cash to execute these transactions, and you realize why actively managed funds fall short.

In reality, an index fund is a much better-than-average performer. Based on performance, an index fund will most likely be in the middle of the pack because the market is a zero-sum game—winners offset losers and what remains is the market. What investment advisors fail to explain is that after deducting the fees, loads, and taxes from the performance of all managed funds, the ranking achieved by index funds moves up significantly. Index funds have minimal fees, low turnover, no sales charges, and remain fully invested. Because of these advantages, index funds are without question better-than-average performers.

Therefore, any attempt to beat the market incurs additional risk. While experienced investors think about risk, new investors think about reward. Youth and inexperience often lead to consequences associated with losing positions. The investment field is littered with those who have disregarded the risks of investing. Experienced investors set realistic goals based on historical market returns. They understand no one earns 100% of the market. Savvy investors understand investment losses of 20%, 40%, and 50% require gains of 25%, 67%, and 100% just to break even. Always put the concept of risk first when making investment decisions. Your investment goal is not to earn the highest return possible; your goal is to earn the market return with minimal risk when investing in mutual funds. When investing in individual stocks however, your goal is to earn 20% more than the market return to compensate for the additional workload.

Stay Fully Invested in a Balanced Portfolio

Historically, the biggest investment failures occur from either missing the market's upward moves entirely or being under-invested during those major upward surges. Successful investors realize a balanced portfolio consisting of equities on one side and treasuries on the other allows you to remain fully invested in all types of markets. Equities provide the wealth increases in growing markets while treasuries provide the stability in contracting markets. When the markets are reeling, the market always experiences capital flight into treasury securities. Successful investors also realize continually changing plans destroys the continuity of any program and promotes emotional considerations rather than reasoned buying techniques. They stick with their balanced plan.

The purpose behind splitting your portfolio into two parts is to provide stability by counter-balancing your returns between stock and fixed income positions. In 14 of the 15 years that the S&P 500 has posted losses since 1941, intermediate-term treasury notes have posted gains. Treasuries have provided an astounding 93% success rate in counter balancing portfolios and the only exception was a loss of less than a single percentage point. Those are definitely good odds.

The investment model provides a simple, straightforward approach to improving wealth generation while maintaining capital preservation. The primary allocations assigned to the two sides of the portfolio are a function of your risk tolerance, proximity to retirement, and financial stability. Veteran investors realize one size does not fit all. The percentage allocations change as you move through your investment life cycle. The model assumes greater risk during the earlier years when you are a long way from retirement, thus allowing time to recover should the market sustain a major cyclical downfall. The late retirement investor who has begun taking distributions from his retirement portfolio has little time to recover from a major market downturn.

You need go no further than investing in mutual funds. The program model recommends equity index funds on the one side and a blend of short-, intermediate-, and long-term treasury funds on the other. Although other options may be used, these options should be within the parameters of the overall model. For instance, wanting to own individual securities can incorporate such an option into the model. However, you need to recognize that such a move leads to greater risk exposure, expanded time commitments, and increased capital requirements. The model also provides a framework for individuals receiving significant lump sum payments who may begin seeking capital preservation techniques.

Focus on Long Term Results

Individual investors have a very, very powerful weapon that trumps the professional money managers. They have the ability to wait. Successful investors set long-term investment goals and shy away from short-term speculation. Professionals, on the other hand, receive compensation based on quarterly performance and annual returns. They may take on more risk to achieve personal objectives that may be inconsistent with the objectives of individual investors.

Albert Einstein described compound interest as the greatest mathematical discovery of all time. The longer the holding period, the greater the power of compounding your investment returns. Always emphasize dividends and interest when constructing your portfolio.

Current income is much more dependable than capital gains, and current income helps to cushion a portfolio against market volatility. When markets are falling, new cash from interest and dividends is constantly flowing into the portfolio to purchase additional shares at deflated prices. A growing income stream significantly contributes to the total return of the portfolio. With almost half of the long-term return coming from dividends and interest (yield), let your positions grow with the magic of compounding—remember that million-dollar nest egg funded with a measly $3,052 deposit. When you double the value of your investment every eight years, the impact of the fourth, fifth, and even sixth doubling has a truly magical impact on the dollar value of your portfolio. Allow your positions to grow; you do not want to break this compounding chain.

You always want to emphasize low cost and low turnover because every single dollar paid out in costs is one dollar deducted from your pocketbook. Costs always have a negative impact on investment returns and these costs can be debilitating over time. Stay with no load mutual funds that maintain low expense ratios and low turnover. Turnover is the hidden cost in mutual funds because it leads to trading costs that are not included in the operating costs reported by the fund. Individual stocks are no exception. You want to keep your commissions and turnover low. Warren Buffett reminded us that Wall Street makes money on activity; you make your money on inactivity. Resist the temptation to continuously buy and sell stocks; trading activity is counter productive.

Reinvesting dividends and interest provides significant cost advantages and mimics dollar-cost averaging techniques. You want to concentrate on the long-term. You know get rich quick ideas rarely work. Time and patience have an uncanny way of making ordinary people look like investment geniuses. Your role model is the tortoise not the hare. Slow and steady wins the race.

Emphasize Discipline and Patience

Although things are never as bad as they seem or as good as they appear, most people realize this fact only in hindsight. As events unfold, you may find controlling your emotions is a rather difficult task and yet controlling your emotions is exactly what you need to do when investing. It is neither wise nor useful to watch the daily performance of your investments. You must always remember Mr. Market—*he is there to serve you, not guide you.*

When purchasing your initial positions, you need to stay patient. Every investment choice does not immediately go up, nor does it immediately go down. It does not matter, because you are selecting investments for the long run not the short term. Stick with your positions to allow time for the compounding magic to work for you. Do not overreact to an immediate drop in the value of your purchase.

When the market heads south, you need to remain fully invested. Selling your stock positions during a market downturn will only lock in your paper losses and ensure that you sell low while probably buying high. A balanced portfolio is your best insurance against emotional selling and general panic. The dollar-cost averaging approach allows you to purchase increasingly more shares at deflated prices thereby creating increasingly higher value when the market recovers, raising the value of your holdings.

When the market moves upward, you also need to stay disciplined. You do not want to wander off the reservation in the good times and lose sight of your portfolio parameters. Just because the market is booming, it does not mean you want to add to your equity positions. You want to remain balanced with treasuries. Nothing lasts forever and history tells us that a drop in the stock market soon follows a stock market boom. Avoid the trap; stick with a balanced, all-weather portfolio.

Stay the Course

All bull markets begin in the throes of a recession. You want to be in the market to take advantage of those upward surges. Why? Many studies highlight the benefit of staying fully invested. Being out of the market and missing the best 30, 60, or 90 days substantially decreases your total return. Those best days typically represent less than 1% of the entire period. Do you really believe you can select those exact days to be in the market? The message is clear—stay invested.

Over time, the stock market advances seven out of every 10 years. You always want to be in the game. While statistically significant, stocks are not a sure thing so you need to counter-balance your portfolio with treasuries. Stocks have outperformed bonds in all 25-year periods. However, shortening those periods reduces the certainty that stocks outperform bonds. For all 10-year time periods, stocks outperform bonds 83% of the time; for five-year periods, the percentage drops to 74%; and for one-year periods, the percentage is only 61%. The message is clearer—stay invested in a balanced portfolio.

Time is on your side. Time gives you the wonder of compounding which allows even modest sums of money to grow into extraordinary amounts of wealth. Time also gives you the mitigation of risk, which decreases the variability of stock market returns in a relatively short period. Unfortunately, time also gives you the devastation of compounding should you ignore the warnings of low cost and low turnover. Warren Buffett once said that he makes most of his money while sleeping. The only thing left to say is good night and sweet dreams.

REVIEWING WHAT NOT TO DO
Successful investors implement a low maintenance investment program that places a premium on what not to do. In fact, what you do not do is just as important, and perhaps even more so, than what you do.

Don't Take Unnecessary Risks
You do not want to own corporate bonds or municipal bonds. You do not want to purchase new issues, futures, short sales, or options. You do not want to use margin accounts. You certainly do not want to buy exotics or hybrids. Why? You always think risk first, and these investments have elevated risk factors. In a misguided effort to increase returns, you increase your potential for loss. There are no guarantees; never put your capital at risk.

Compounding these problems, inexperienced investors often try to recover their losses by turning to riskier and riskier investment choices. These speculative investments lead to still further setbacks. Never put reward in front of risk. All too often it leads to unwanted and costly results.

Don't Be a Market Timer

You do not want to be a market timer. You want to stay invested in a balanced portfolio, limiting your risk in the bad times while enjoying some of the benefits when times are good. Markets are cyclical. They move up as well as down, sometimes rapidly and other times slowly. While there is certainty in knowing that market cycles change, uncertainty exists because no one knows exactly when those cycles will change. In fact, definitively defining either the start or the end of a market cycle occurs only after the cycle has long passed. Never ever try to time the market—it is a loser's game that has taken its toll on many would-be investors.

Don't Listen to the Hype

You do not want to follow the media hype whether the hype is favorable or not. You do not want to follow the crowd. You never want to become an emotional investor. You do not want to listen to media pundits, financial writers, and especially stockbrokers. They always look to the short- or near-term in their analyses. You do not want to own speculative investments. Tune out the noise.

Be wary of the promotional hype generated by mutual fund groups touting their funds. Some of their print ads present fund returns using date specific data that is misleading. Always check the fine print. With the ever-increasing number of new funds and the cyclical nature of the market, mutual fund groups always can identify one or two funds to promote as the darlings of the market. Do not be fooled, do not think short term, and do not believe what you hear. Do your homework.

You do not want to take investment advice from friends, relatives, or business associates. Most, if not all, people avoid talking about their failures, especially when discussing their investments. Keep this in mind the next time someone is touting his or her winners. Strangely, their losers are never mentioned and, more likely than not, they far outweigh their successes.

Don't Forget the Obvious
What are the most important "don'ts" to remember as you go out on your own? The answer, of course, is rule number one that says don't lose money, and rule number two that says don't forget rule number one.

SOME FINAL THOUGHTS
For words of encouragement, we turn to Warren Buffett. In writing the preface to Benjamin Graham's *The Intelligent Investor,* he informs us that successful long-term investors do not require exceptional intelligence, extraordinary business acumen, or even inside information. He reveals that investors need only a sound, rational plan for making investment decisions and the ability to keep emotions from clouding that judgment.[6]

As for the sound, rational plan part of the equation, the investment model achieves that objective. As for your emotions, you have a homework assignment but with a helpful hint: you may want to follow Seabiscuit's lead. When the market is in turmoil, you simply need to show complete, overwhelming, and colossal indifference.

A fully invested, balanced portfolio approach allows history to instruct, patience to guide, and time to reward. Get in the game to enjoy many happy returns.

PART TWO

Expanding Your Horizons

CHAPTER ELEVEN

Pundits Can Be Detrimental to Your Wealth

We are drowning in information but starved for knowledge.[1]

John Naisbett

HAVE YOU EVER asked someone how the market is doing? Most likely, the reply was something like the market was up or it was down. While today's market closing may address the question, it provides little information and practically no insight into the market.

Compare that response with a question about the weather. The response probably included the expected temperature, the possibility of precipitation, and the likelihood of sun or clouds. Would it surprise anyone to learn most weather forecasts are not wrong? But most are not entirely correct either? Pay close attention the next time you listen to a forecast. It includes such specific details as partly cloudy, partly sunny, a 20% chance of showers, a 30% possibility of snow, and so on. Especially helpful are the forecasters who point out if the coming weather front passes a little more to the south or a little more to the north, the storm may miss us entirely. Weather forecasts contain so many qualifiers that regardless of the actual weather conditions that follow, their forecasts are at least partially correct.

Think about these two scenarios for a moment. Most people listen to the evening weather forecast to determine what to wear the next day. Many make decisions based on information filtered through some sort of evaluation criteria. Now consider that most individuals and many investors have limited working knowledge of the market. Most have difficulty deciphering the financial news or understanding economic trends. Yet which is more important, the weather or the economy?

TOO MUCH OF A GOOD THING

Today, information is everywhere. Whether print media, internet websites, broadcast news outlets, or any number of other venues, the amount of information available today is staggering. One of the problems with this growing access to information is the illusion that all information is equally reliable. The term information, itself, implies something of value thus making it more useful to the recipient. Many people accept information because they assume it was properly researched, analyzed, and documented. Mark Twain once quipped, "If you don't read the newspaper, you are uninformed; if you do read the newspaper, you are misinformed."

As our attention span becomes shorter and shorter, the competition for that time intensifies. Competing for audiences, news outlets use 10 second sound bites, internet pop-ups, and newswire catch phrases, keeping you interested rather than keeping you informed. Just look at newsprint headlines or listen to the newscast promos. Their intention is to titillate, not to enlighten. The in-depth, hard-hitting articles of the past, such as the analytical pieces that instruct or the documented exposés that inform, are now the exception rather than the rule.

With the number of news sources available, the consumer must be more vigilant regarding the accuracy of the information disseminated. Too often opinion is confused with fact. Whether intentional or not, in their haste to be the first with the story, perhaps they fail to vet the information fully or conduct a thorough background investigation or perform important fact checks. Information does not mean knowledge. A more informed consumer must perform his or her own due diligence regarding the reliability of the information received. No place is this more evident than with the economy.

INFORMATION YES, KNOWLEDGE NO

For those investors believing they can consistently outperform the market, the following chapters may be very enlightening. Beyond its sheer size, the complexities of the economy make it both formidable and intimidating. Consider what influences the marketplace—almost anything and probably everything! In addition to those normally expected factors such as interest rates, money supply, availability of credit, unemployment levels, a whole host of other unrelated factors can play a significant role, including weather conditions, natural disasters, terrorism, strikes, and so forth. More exasperating is the realization that no one knows when these events may occur, the severity of the disruptions, or the duration of the problems. Some factors may even offset other factors to some degree, adding a new dimension to consider. Include inevitable meddling by our politicians and you get a recipe for a witches' brew like no other.

Trying to time the market in such a minefield is not only a losing proposition, but can be an expensive one as well. Never time the market. As an investor, you want to limit your risks whenever possible so you always think risk before return. Surprises lurk out there waiting to turn good markets into bad nightmares. Do you remember the technology bubble of 2000 that triggered a long running bear market? Or the housing bubble of 2006–2007 that led to a worldwide credit crisis and the "Great Recession?"

TAKING THE NEXT STEP

Parts Two and Three of this book turn to a macro perspective. Providing a basic understanding of business cycles and interest rates is beneficial to everyone, not just investors. Often heard on the financial news broadcasts and frequently seen in print, many commonly cited market indicators need further clarification. Introducing a few economic concepts may provide insight into the various influences affecting consumer behavior. A historical roadmap may aid in understanding current economic activities while opening a dialogue on a strange obsession: avoiding historically successful market solutions.

Typically, investment books target individuals with investing knowledge or the financial resources to begin investing. Understanding the need to build a future is also true for those working families living paycheck-to-paycheck who may be unable to save enough money to start a retirement portfolio. What are they to do?

Historical trends and time-tested guidelines helped validate the investment model. The same model can help solve the looming crisis in the Social Security system. Often meaning the difference between poverty and self-sufficiency, millions of Americans depend on Social Security. Objective analysis, clear thinking, and a long-term focus are critical to confronting the problems of Social Security. Success is rooted in defining the appropriate goals of the program, avoiding the mistakes of the past, garnering the support of the public, and constructing an unbiased solution void of politics. Effectively implemented, a sound Social Security system can provide a solid foundation for economic growth and prosperity.

What follows are some interesting conclusions for you to consider, to ponder, and yes even to argue. After all, isn't that the fun of reading and learning new concepts—to promote discussion and meaningful conversations? Stay with it. You just might learn a few historical curiosities and some important facts as well.

CHAPTER TWELVE

When Doing Nothing May Be the Best Move

Wall Street people learn nothing and forget everything.
Benjamin Graham

YOU NOW HAVE an investment model that can grow old with you. The model combines inflation protection with financial security while providing historical market returns at minimal risk. Staying fully invested with the balanced portfolio model reduces costs and retains the compound interest chain. Even better, the model requires little time to implement and only a minimum effort to monitor. Why does such a program work so well? Markets are inherently cyclical. While they do go down, markets gain ground in seven out of every 10 years. Patience is rewarded, but the ride may occasionally hit a speed bump and at times even a pothole.

When you listen to the news, do you notice how often the newscasters describe the economic news with words such as surprising, startling, sudden, unanticipated, unexpected, unforeseen, and unpredicted? Whether the topic is the stock market, unemployment, inflation, GDP, consumer spending or whatever, these so-called experts always seem to be surprised. Whatever the reason for their astonishment, you definitely do not want to base any investment decision on the insights of these so-called experts.

The economy is far too huge and far too complex for anyone to forecast short-term changes consistently. The market does not operate in a controlled environment. At any given time, many factors affect the market simultaneously—some help, some hurt, some offset, and some may have no impact at all. Having a basic understanding of several key concepts allows you to do some due diligence for yourself.

THE BUSINESS CYCLE

The business cycle acts as a report card aggregating the actions of all businesses to assess the current economic climate. Although every business cycle is different, each business cycle contains the same four phases—expansion, peak, contraction and trough. The expansion and contraction phases occur over a period typically defined in months. The peak and trough phases are specific points in time defined as month and year. Most references to the business cycle focus either on the duration of the expansion or the length of the contraction.

The expansion phase, known also as recovery or growth phase, starts when the economic indicators begin to rise. The early stages of an expansion are difficult to differentiate from the existing contraction because the unemployed are still unable to find jobs, retailers are trying to reduce inventories and manufacturers have not seen any significant increase in orders. After a few months, the economy gains strength and the growth becomes more robust.

The expansion ends when the peak, or the highest point in the business cycle, occurs. Unfortunately, the confirmation of the business cycle peak rarely occurs until it has passed, often when the economy already shows the effects of downward movement.

The contraction phase, known also as a recession, begins when the economic indicators start to decline. Businesses begin to experience a softening of their sales and profits begin to weaken. In an effort to offset this downturn and achieve their profit targets, many businesses reduce production, delay expansion plans and stop capital investment projects. The result of such moves affects other businesses across many industries, creating a market slowdown.

Called the trough, the lowest point in the business cycle marks the end of the business cycle. Like the peak, the identification of the business cycle trough rarely occurs until long after it has passed with the economy already showing signs of a recovery.

A common misconception often heard in the media is a recession occurs when the real Gross Domestic Product (GDP) declines for two consecutive quarters. The task of actually dating business cycles is the responsibility of the National Bureau of Economic Research (NBER), a private research organization founded in 1920. The bureau focuses on a range of indicators to determine the actual turning points of a business cycle. Significant emphasis is placed on the monthly indicators, but consideration also is given to the depth of the decline in economic activity. An analysis of the activities surrounding domestic production is another factor to be included. Since the actual dating of the business cycles has political and economic implications, the Business Cycle Dating Committee of the NBER is very deliberate in confirming the actual dates of the various phases of the business cycle. The official announcements typically do not take place until long after the business cycle phases occur, allowing for a thorough analysis of all pertinent data.[1]

Figure 12.1 presents a history of U.S. Business Cycles. Understandably, every major advance in the stock market always begins when the business climate is bad and the public sentiment is negative. Since 1919, the average contraction lasts 14 months, but can range from six to 18 months (excluding the Great Depression). After six months of economic contraction, the stock market usually tends to be near the bottom. Getting into the market is relatively inexpensive at this point because, based on long-term prospects, many businesses are undervalued. Since 1919, the average expansion lasts 50 months, but can range from 10 to 120 months. Moving out of the stock market is much more difficult during expansion. The time span for bull markets varies considerably more than for bear markets, and often many false signals occur before the bull market truly departs. These false signals are reported as market corrections.

In *Stocks for the Long Run*, Jeremy Siegel points out that since 1802, even if an investor were able to switch into treasury bills at the exact business cycle peak and then switch back into stocks at the exact business cycle trough, his portfolio return over the buy and hold strategy would be negligible. Siegel goes on to say if the investor missed the peak and trough by a single month, he would have lost 0.6% per year compared to the buy and hold strategy. Siegel also points out the data indicate that an investor buying stocks before the trough of the cycle outperforms an investor selling stock an equal number of months before the peak of the cycle, which he credits to the historically longer duration of expansions.[2]

FIGURE 12.1 *U.S. Business Cycle Expansions and Contractions*[1]

CONTRACTIONS (RECESSIONS) START AT THE PEAK OF A BUSINESS CYCLE AND END AT THE TROUGH.

BUSINESS CYCLE REFERENCE DATES		DURATION IN MONTHS			
Peak	Trough	Contraction	Expansion	Cycle	
Quarterly dates are in parentheses		*Peak to Trough*	*Previous trough to this peak*	*Trough from previous trough*	*Peak from previous peak*
	December 1854 (IV)	—	—	—	—
June 1857 (II)	December 1858 (IV)	18	30	48	—
October 1860 (III)	June 1861 (III)	8	22	30	40
April 1865 (I)	December 1867 (I)	32	46	78	54
June 1869 (II)	December 1870 (IV)	18	18	36	50
October 1873 (III)	March 1879 (I)	65	34	99	52
March 1882 (I)	May 1885 (II)	38	36	74	101
March 1887 (II)	April 1888 (I)	13	22	35	60
July 1890 (III)	May 1891 (II)	10	27	37	40
January 1893 (I)	June 1894 (II)	17	20	37	30
December 1895 (IV)	June 1897 (II)	18	18	36	35
June 1899 (III)	December 1900 (IV)	18	24	42	42
September 1902 (IV)	August 1904 (III)	23	21	44	39
May 1907 (II)	June 1908 (II)	13	33	46	56
January 1910 (I)	January 1912 (IV)	24	19	43	32
January 1913 (I)	December 1914 (IV)	23	12	35	36
August 1918 (III)	March 1919 (I)	7	44	51	67
January 1920 (I)	July 1921 (III)	18	10	28	17
May 1923 (II)	July 1924 (III)	14	22	36	40
October 1926 (III)	November 1927 (IV)	13	27	40	41
August 1929 (III)	March 1933 (I)	43	21	64	34
May 1937 (II)	June 1938 (II)	13	50	63	93
February 1945 (I)	October 1945 (IV)	8	80	88	93
November 1948 (IV)	October 1949 (IV)	11	37	48	45
July 1953 (II)	May 1954 (II)	10	45	55	56
August 1957 (III)	April 1958 (II)	8	39	47	49
April 1960 (II)	February 1961 (I)	10	24	34	32
December 1969 (IV)	November 1970 (IV)	11	106	117	116
November 1973 (IV)	March 1975 (I)	16	36	52	47
January 1980 (I)	July 1980 (III)	6	58	64	74
July 1981 (III)	November 1982 (IV)	16	12	28	18
July 1990 (III)	March 1991(I)	8	92	100	108
March 2001 (I)	November 2001 (IV)	8	120	128	128
December 2007 (IV)	June 2009 (II)	18	73	91	81
	Average, all cycles:				
	1854–2009 (33 cycles)	17	39	56	55*
	1854–1919 (16 cycles)	22	27	48	49**
	1919–2009 (17 cycles)	14	50	64	63

*31 cycles   **15 cycles

[1] The NBER does not define a recession in terms of two consecutive quarters of decline in real GDP. Rather, a recession is a significant decline in economic activity spread across the economy, lasting more than a few months, normally visible in real GDP, real income, employment, industrial production, and wholesale-retail sales. For more information, see the latest announcement from the NBER's Business Cycle Dating Committee.

Source: National Bureau of Economic Research, Inc. www.nber.org/cycles/#announcements

THE STOCK MARKET CYCLE

Since they tend to move in the same direction, many people confuse the stock market with the business cycle. The stock market performs well when the economy is growing, and it performs poorly when the economy is contracting. When discussing the stock market, the terms expansion and contraction are referred to as bull and bear markets. In reality, the stock market is actually a leading indicator of the business cycle and tends to precede economic changes by as many as six months. Why? Since the stock market reacts more to profit expectations than reported earnings, many of the moves in the stock market precede the assessment of the business cycle that focuses on actual reported data.

While the stock market moves downward prior to a recession and rises before a recovery, it is not a perfect indicator. The stock market reacts to real and perceived changes in profits, the general level and direction of interest rates, and anticipated government regulations and policy initiatives. The primary drivers of stock market moves are predictions, forecasts and estimates. The thing about expectations is that they may be correct, but they may also be misleading because they are only educated guesses about the future.

THE INFLATION CYCLE

One of the best guides to longer-term movements in the stock market is the rate of inflation. When inflation is low, it is a plus for both the stock and bond markets. Low inflation tends to lead to lower stock yields not due to reductions in the dividends, but rather the result of rising stock prices, which lowers the yield. With bonds, the lower yields also are indicative of higher prices. The major factors affecting bond pricing are inflation, inflation momentum and the perception about future inflation. Perhaps redundant, but it is an accurate assessment nonetheless.

Each new inflationary cycle has three stages. Identifying the first two stages helps to provide an early warning sign for the higher prices that are soon to follow. Since long-term trends are more important than monthly blips, watch the most recent three- and six-month changes as well as year-over-year moves.

The inflationary cycle begins when *crude materials prices* begin to rise. These raw materials are entering the economy for the first time, and the increased prices eventually work themselves down the road. An upward tick in inflation shows up here long before it turns up on your supermarket shelves. Crude or raw materials are unprocessed food and non-food items such as cattle, hogs, milk, coal, gas, oil, and so forth. Crude prices are volatile and since weather conditions affect many of the items, you want to concentrate on the overall trend rather than the individual monthly moves, either up or down.

Increases in *wholesale or producer prices* indicate the arrival of the second stage of the inflation cycle. With raw materials costing more, the wholesalers most likely will raise their prices on the products sold to retailers. Based on their existing profit margins however, some whole-salers may be able to absorb short-term or periodic increases. Since they are much less volatile than the crude material prices, trends in wholesale prices confirm the direction of inflation. When wholesale prices are going up, consumer prices are sure to follow.

The Consumer Price Index (CPI) monitors the final stage of the inflationary cycle. Just as wholesalers raised their prices to retailers, retailers increase their prices to the consumer. As a result, the CPI begins to move higher. Any increase in the cost of doing business ulti-mately affects the consumer's pocketbook in the form of higher prices because all businesses need to maintain their profit margins to stay competitive in the marketplace.

The CPI moves in the opposite direction to stock prices. When the consumer price index is falling, stock prices tend to rise because con-sumers have more disposable income that may move into the markets, driving stock prices up. Conversely, when the CPI goes up, stock prices tend to fall.

INTEREST RATES PLAY A MAJOR ROLE

Perhaps the single most important factor affecting the overall economy is interest rates. Why are they so important to the stock market? Interest rates are the key to discounting future cash flows of stocks and critical to establishing the yield on bonds. Stocks and bonds continually compete for your investment dollar. When interest rates rise, bonds become more attractive thus encouraging you to sell stocks. As interest rates fall, the returns on stocks improve relative to bonds, pushing you toward stocks.

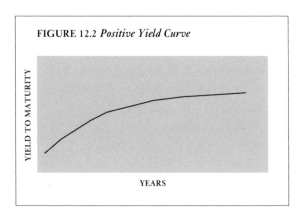

FIGURE 12.2 *Positive Yield Curve*

YIELD TO MATURITY

YEARS

Moreover, interest rates also play a significant role in the business cycle. Many businesses need access to outside funding. The cost and availability of those funds is linked directly to interest rates. While most of their financing comes from revenues generated from product sales, many businesses may still seek outside funding to expand operations, open new markets or make other capital investments.

The *momentum* of rate changes helps to identify the potential for a reversal of the current trend. For instance, when interest rates have been dropping and then begin to stabilize, this loss of momentum may indicate the trend is about to reverse and interest rates may begin to rise. A loss of momentum in interest rate hikes, on the other hand, suggests interest rates may soon stabilize and are about to decline.

The *divergence* or the difference between short- and longer-term rates is another key component. The stock market performs poorly whenever short-term rates are higher than long-term rates. The weak performance typically occurs regardless of the level of interest rates or the direction of the trend. Conversely, the stock market tends to do well when longer-term money is more expensive than short-term money.

For a quick check on the economy, the inflation-adjusted real rate of return is a good monitoring tool. Simply subtract the Consumer Price Index (a proxy for the inflation rate) from the 90-day Treasury bill rate (considered the risk free rate of return). When the inflation rate is higher, the negative real interest rate signals inflationary pressure in the economy. Without a real return on money instruments, many investors

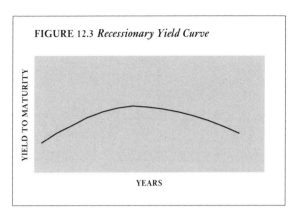

FIGURE 12.3 *Recessionary Yield Curve*

move into non-interest bearing investments such as precious metals that tend to increase in value during inflationary times.

Understanding Treasury Yield Curves

The Fed may be able to influence short-term rates, but long-term rates are another story. The bond market sets long-term rates based on economic, inflationary and political factors, both domestically and internationally, all of which are well beyond the control of the Fed.

For any given period, bonds offer a certain yield to maturity that can be calculated and plotted on a graph. The span of those yields for all maturities represents the yield curve. The yield curve presents not only the range of yields available, but it also provides a picture of the interest rate structure reflecting the state of the economy.

A positive yield curve represents a normal economy showing no significant inflationary or recessionary pressures. Presented in Figure 12.2, a positive yield curve shows gradually increasing bond yields as the maturities extend farther into the future. Consistent with the concept of risk and return, this interest rate environment encourages investors to extend their maturities to obtain the higher yields offered on the longer term bonds.

Figure 12.3 presents the yield curve of a business cycle recession. As competing investments become less profitable with the softening business cycle, investors tend to move out of the stock market, preferring the safety of treasuries. This demand increases bond prices, which

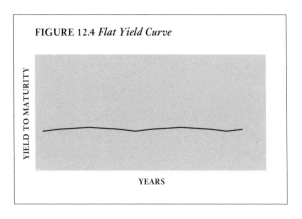

FIGURE 12.4 *Flat Yield Curve*

lowers yields. Typically, the Fed adds money to the economy to avoid a deepening recession that tends to lower interest rates, adding further to the price gains in bonds. Since the impact affects long-term bonds more dramatically, the point of highest return shifts to the earlier years.

Figure 12.4 depicts a flat yield curve. As you might expect, the yields are essentially the same for all maturities. This curve typically indicates an economy that is in transition. However, it may also signal an inflationary recession more commonly referred to as stagflation, which characterized the economy during the Carter Administration. Since the economy does not function well with the same yields for both short- and long-term money, investors move to shorter maturities to reduce risk.

The negative or inverse yield curve is the hallmark of inflation and a precursor to a market downturn. As Figure 12.5 indicates, short-term bonds provide higher yields than long-term bonds, the exact opposite of a normal curve. When the economy starts to overheat, the Fed attempts to combat the inflationary pressures by reducing the money supply that leads to higher interest rates. While all rates rise, the Fed actions initially raise short-term rates, but as the inflationary pressures continue to intensify, the long-term bonds suffer the largest price declines.

INDEX OF LEADING INDICATORS

Frequently cited in the media, the Index of Leading Indicators corroborates the direction in which the economy is moving. A common rule-of-thumb suggests three consecutive declines in this index are an

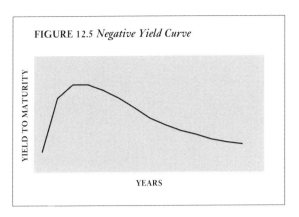

FIGURE 12.5 *Negative Yield Curve*

YIELD TO MATURITY

YEARS

early warning sign of a recession, while three straight increases suggest a recovery may be underway. Released one month after compilation, the timeliness of the data is a concern. Since revisions to previous data releases frequently occur, trending information also remains uncertain.

When evaluating the data, the magnitude of the changes provides some indication of the reliability of the indicator. For instance, the size of the percentage change shows the depth or strength of the change. The diffusion or breadth of the changes indicates how many other indicators support the foreseen change. The number of months the trend has continued reveals the duration of the move. The greater the depth, the larger the diffusion, and the longer the duration helps to indicate the probability of the pending change.

The Money Supply

The money supply is the total amount of money circulating within the banking system. In the short run, growth in the money supply generally leads to lower interest rates because money is more readily available. It also tends to stimulate consumer demand for durable goods and benefits the housing market as well since lower interest rates make those larger purchases more affordable. The increased demand for durable goods leads to production increases and income growth as employers hire more staff to meet the growing demand. The opposite occurs when the money supply decreases.

Problems arise when the growth in the money supply is excessive. For instance, if the growth rate exceeds the existing rate of inflation for an extended period, the relatively easy access to money fuels a higher demand. When demand outstrips production capacity, inflationary pressures result.

The Average Weekly Hours Worked by Manufacturing Workers

When the economy is expanding, manufacturers increase overtime for workers and expand the hours in the workweek in order to produce more products to meet increased demand. When an economic slowdown occurs, manufacturers begin to cut overtime and shorten the workweek.

Businesses tend to adjust the work hours of existing employees in response to initial economic changes because these moves are immediate and less costly in the short run. However, as the economic conditions become more defined, those businesses may prefer to change the size of their staffing needs by hiring new workers in an expanding market or laying off existing employees in a contracting economy.

The Interest Rate Spread

Subtracting the federal funds rate from the 10-year Treasury bond rate provides a snapshot of the yield curve. Through its monetary policy, the Federal Reserve attempts to influence economic activity. For instance, suppose the Fed wants to tighten credit. To do that, it would drive up short-term interest rates to the point where the yield curve becomes inverted. When short-term rates are higher than longer-term rates, it often indicates a recession may be on the way. If the Fed wants to loosen credit, it would push short-term interest rates lower, restoring a more normal yield curve, which tends to generate stronger economic activity.

Manufacturers' New Orders, Consumer Goods and Materials

New orders are not necessarily a timely indicator of manufacturing activity because existing inventory fills those initial new orders. Unfilled orders may be a better indicator of future production. Since the production process begins with order placement, monitor the monthly trends, looking for strength and consistency. When orders are growing, production activity increases, replenishing depleted inventories and meeting the demand of continued growth in new orders. The production activity in turn promotes greater employment and higher income levels.

Index of Supplier Deliveries

Also referred to as vendor performance, this component tracks supplier deliveries. When deliveries slow down, manufacturers are busy and unable to fill orders quickly. Slower deliveries indicate increased demand and economic growth. In contrast, faster deliveries suggest a slowing economy because producers are not as busy and can fill orders more rapidly.

The S&P 500 Stock Index

Since the stock market moves primarily on the expectations of profits and interest rates, the S&P 500 index is a good snapshot of investor sentiment about the future. For instance, when investors forecast improving profits, stock prices move higher. Conversely, if investors predict lower profits, the market softens and many investors may sell their stock positions to take profits, resulting in a decline in the stock market.

The Average Weekly Initial Claims for Unemployment Insurance

The number of new claims filed for unemployment insurance is a better indicator of the economic climate than either total employment or unemployment. Always look at the trend rather than weekly figures even when looking at the four-week moving average. While claims are a good indicator of economic activity, the lead-time can be several months.

Do not confuse this figure with the total unemployment rate. During a recession, many people actually drop out of the labor force because they become frustrated finding no employment and simply stop looking for a job. No longer part of the workforce, these individuals do not count as unemployed which leads to an understated unemployment rate during a recession. In the early stages of a recovery, the growth in the labor force accelerates since many of these missing individuals re-enter the labor force as the economy picks up and job opportunities improve. Since it may take some time for these individuals to find employment, the early stages of a recovery may actually show an increase in unemployment. To keep pace with the population growth, the economy needs to create approximately 100,000 jobs per month just to maintain a steady unemployment rate.

The Index of Consumer Expectations

Consumer spending makes up more than two-thirds of the real Gross Domestic Product (GDP). GDP represents products produced within the borders of a country (location driven) whereas Gross National Product (GNP) represents products produced by firms owned by the country's citizens (ownership driven).

The actual retail spending figures may not immediately reflect the monthly changes in the consumer confidence numbers. Therefore, look at the trend in the direction of the consumer confidence series rather than a single monthly change. The index tends to increase rapidly near business cycle peaks when employment prospects are improving. A drop in consumer confidence suggests the economy is weakening and corporate profits could move lower, which may lead to a decline in the stock market.

Building Permits, New Private Housing Units

New building permits are a good indicator of both economic momentum and interest rates. While high interest rates typically slow the housing market, lower rates tend to accelerate demand. Low rates usually occur near the end of an economic slowdown and into the early stages of recovery because the demand for credit is still in the early stages, not yet putting undue pressure on rates. The lower mortgage rates coupled with rising consumer confidence of the business cycle provide favorable conditions for the housing market. Builders recognize these trends and take out more building permits to create more housing inventory. Accordingly, housing construction tends to preclude a recovery, and housing permits precede construction. When the housing market begins to climb, it is one of the earliest signs of an economic recovery.

Conversely, housing permits generally decline toward the end of an economic expansion. The combination of rising interest rates and growing concern about the strength of the economy typically dampens housing purchases, which increases the inventory of available homes thereby causing a decline in issued permits. When the housing market starts to fall over several months, it has an enormous ripple effect throughout the U.S. economy.

Manufacturers' New Orders, Non-Defense Capital Goods

Similar to new orders for consumer goods, manufacturers' new orders are not necessarily a timely indicator of manufacturing activity because existing inventory fills those initial new orders. Unfilled orders may be a better indicator of future production.

Non-defense capital goods orders suggest how businesses view the current conditions. Purchasing new equipment to expand and modernize their production facilities indicates a positive outlook about the economy. These orders lead to higher employment and increased income resulting from the increased production process activity. Construction spending usually lags behind new housing starts by several months. When construction spending rises for more than three months, this may indicate a rising trend in other economic indicators.

INDEX OF COINCIDENT INDICATORS

The Index of Coincident Indicators is another commonly cited measure in the media, but it provides information about the current state of the economy. Changes in the yearly momentum of this index moves with the economy. When the economy is expanding, the indicator is moving higher, but when the economy is contracting, the indicator is declining. As with the leading indicators, the greater the depth, the larger the diffusion, and the longer the duration helps to corroborate the strength of the current economic climate.

Employees on Non-Agricultural Payrolls

Sometimes referred to as payroll employment, it includes both full- and part-time employees, but it does not distinguish between the two. The component reflects the net change between the actual hiring and firing of employees, so look at the trends of year-to-year job growth as well as the monthly momentum. The changes in manufacturing employment precede changes in production momentum.

Personal Income Less Transfer Payments

This component represents the value of income received from all sources, inflation adjusted, excluding transfer payments such as Social Security. A derivative of this measure is disposable personal income calculated by subtracting personal income taxes from personal income. The growth in personal income accelerates during expansions leading to increased consumer demand and slows during downturns negatively affecting consumer demand.

The Index of Industrial Production

The index tracks product inventories, values of shipments, and employment levels in the manufacturing industries. Industrial production is primarily demand-driven. Unexpected changes in demand that either exceeds or falls short of current output levels is reflected in changes to existing inventory levels. Strong demand reduces inventory, leading to increased production to replenish inventory levels and meet the unexpected demand. Weak demand, on the other hand, results in slower inventory turnover, raising the inventory levels, which slows production to reduce unnecessary inventory carrying costs. Changes in new factory orders reflect changes in demand, but the initial impact of either increased or decreased demand (orders) is first seen on inventory levels and secondly in the production cycle.

When the index is higher than last year and continues to move higher, the economy is growing. When the index is higher than last year but the monthly gains are smaller, the economy is weakening. Once momentum in the industrial production index begins to slow, interest rates begin to rise because many businesses experience diminishing revenues, which pushes firms to begin borrowing, increasing credit demand, and therefore cost.

Manufacturing and Trade Sales

Sales at the manufacturing, wholesale and retail level move in the same direction as the economy. The level of aggregate sales always exceeds GDP because some products and services are double-counted (e.g., temporary additions to wholesale inventories and retail sales). Strong consumer spending figures indicate a healthy economy and most likely lead to greater corporate profits.

INDEX OF LAGGING INDICATORS

Since certain sectors of the economy lag the business cycle, this index declines as the economy starts to expand. Conversely, the index increases when the economy falls into a contraction. Mainly used to determine turning points in the business cycle, these indicators appear only occasionally in the media.

The Average Prime Rate Charged by Banks

Traditionally viewed as the rate banks loan to their best customers, some bank customers are able to borrow below this rate. Still important however, the prime rate acts as a benchmark for many loan products. Due to this significance, rate changes occur after a trend has taken place. Cuts in the prime rate provide the best environment for strong stock market performances. During these times, capital becomes more available and consumers are optimistic.

The Change in the Consumer Price Index for Services

The services component of the Consumer Price Index (CPI) is much slower in reacting to price changes than the other components, thereby making it a lagging indicator. The largest service grouping is housing and other household services. Since many of these services are contractually driven, the impact of price changes, either up or down, do not immediately appear. These delays often cause the index to register increases in the initial months of a recession and decreases in the initial months of an expansion.

Consumer Installment Credit Outstanding to Personal Income Ratio

When an economic downturn hits, unemployment increases, which leads to a reduction in personal income. Although consumers cut back on purchases, the outstanding debt remains. Since incomes have fallen, consumers may have to reduce their debt payments temporarily. Thus, the ratio remains high—lagging the economy. When an expansion begins, employment picks up after the economy continues to grow, which raises incomes and provides more security for consumers to spend money.

Ratio of Manufacturing and Trade Inventories to Sales

Inventories can climb when demand for products increases or is projected to increase. Both of these factors reflect a positive economic scenario. However, inventories can also increase because an unexpected economic slowdown hits. Unable to sell products and incapable of immediately shutting down production, inventories begin to rise. Comparing inventories to sales provides clues as to whether the inventory buildup is positive or negative. For instance, when inventories and sales are both increasing, it is a good sign of economic activity. When inventories are increasing but sales declining, it implies the economy may be slowing and it may lead to production cuts, reduced worker hours, job losses and delays in capital spending.

Commercial and Industrial Loans Outstanding

When economic growth slows, corporations increase their borrowing to offset decreased revenues. The increased loan demand causes interest rates to rise, exacerbating the negative effects on the economy. On the other hand, when the year-to-year numbers are decreasing, the trend in interest rates is also likely to be down, indicating favorable expectations for the economy. If loan demand picks up dramatically, the potential for a new round of interest rate hikes can cause problems for the economy.

The Change in Labor Cost per Unit of Output in Manufacturing

The ratio of output to hours worked is a measure of productivity. Many factors influence hourly output including, but not limited to, capital investment, changes in technology, capacity utilization, the work force and even management. Unit labor costs increase when hourly wages rise without an offsetting gain in hourly output. As long as productivity increases, wages can rise without putting upward pressure on unit labor costs and inflation. During economic downturns, productivity tends to decline, as producers are slow to layoff workers despite curtailed production.

The Average Duration of Unemployment

This measure reflects the average length of time that unemployed or laid-off individuals have been looking for work. When the economy rebounds, employers typically delay hiring new workers preferring instead to expand hours and overtime for their existing workforce. The hiring of new workers usually occurs when businesses can no longer keep up with demand.

LOOKING FOR DIRECTION

Whether a business cycle, stock market cycle, or inflation cycle, a common theme appears. In a free market economy, the market does seem to be self-correcting or, for those more skeptical, self-adjusting. Consumer behaviors are key economic drivers. During economic expansions, for instance, investors are optimistic, individuals become risk-takers and consumers are enthusiastic shoppers. During economic contractions however, investors are more cautious, individuals are more risk averse and consumers become apathetic. Often, consumer behavior accelerates the directional moves that occur in the market.

In addition to consumer behavior, the intangibles are the so-called wild cards. While natural disasters such as droughts or massive storms typically have little long-lasting impact, the self-inflicted remedies initiated by the government may have a much longer influence on the duration and severity of the various cycles. Given the market's ability to revitalize itself, government officials should be careful when tinkering. While most politicians want to be viewed as doing something, the majority of the time it may actually be more beneficial to do very little and allow the market to correct itself. Misreading business cycles can lead to misguided programs that adversely influence the market, causing unintended consequences.

As an investor, you want to use the market cycles to your benefit. Always being in the market with a balanced portfolio allows you to take advantage of the upward bias in the market. You do not want to be a market timer, moving in and out of the market, trying to identify the specific funds or individual securities that may be tomorrow's stars. You want to be concerned with the long-term rather than the individual winners or losers within a particular business cycle.

CHAPTER THIRTEEN

The Significance of Scarcity

Government's view of the economy could be summed up in a few short phrases: If it moves, tax it. If it keeps moving, regulate it. And if it stops moving, subsidize it.

Ronald Reagan

ALMOST THIRTY YEARS ago, Willis Peterson, then a professor at the University of Minnesota, frequently asked his students why we study economics. The answer he sought summarizes the importance of economics then, and remains so to this day. Professor Peterson reduced economics to a single word—scarcity. He explained that individual human wants are greater than the resources available to satisfy those wants, and since resources are scarce, people must economize. Peterson went on to say that if all resources, including time, were unlimited, there would be no need for economics. People could be as wasteful as they pleased, and still they would be able to satisfy their wants.[1]

The scarcity of resources places a finite limit on production as well as consumption. Decisions, therefore, are inevitable when choosing among the various alternatives. Effectively utilizing these scarce resources enables a nation, a business, or an individual to prosper. With millions and millions of transactions occurring every moment of every day throughout the nation, you soon realize the economic system is not only immense, but extremely complex as well.

In his book, *Basic Economics: A Citizen's Guide to the Economy,* Thomas Sowell provides a detailed look at economic theory and describes in plain language the workings of economic teachings.[2] Following his template, here is a common sense look at how some of the key pieces fit together, providing a much-needed perspective on such an important subject.

ECONOMICS IMPACT EVERYONE

Every transaction involves a buyer and a seller interacting with one another in an attempt to improve their respective positions in that transaction. With millions and millions of transactions occurring daily, the flow of information is crucial. In a free market system, the allocation of resources is determined primarily through profit and loss statements (P&L). In other words, firms continue to produce those goods and services that generate profits, but discontinue goods and services that trigger losses. As profits grow, competition soon follows. Competition brings more choices. Consumers then select from those alternatives, driving the demand higher for the items chosen and allocating more resources to the items purchased. The pricing mechanism plays a vital role in the efficient use of resources.

Consider this simple example: you sell chocolate chip cookies at a local farmers' market charging $4.00 per cookie. When the summer season begins, you are the only seller of cookies and you sell your entire inventory before mid-afternoon. At the next market, you again sell your entire inventory. When a new vendor appears at the same market selling his chocolate chip cookies for $3.00, he sells his entire inventory while you sell only half of your stock. Although you have a better tasting cookie made with real ingredients, most market visitors decide to buy the cheaper cookies. The following week, the new vendor again sells his entire stock, but you only sell about a third of your inventory. You need to do something.

Supply and demand principles allow you to use the framework of the pricing system to gather information. Prices tend to increase when goods are in short supply and fall when goods are plentiful. The pricing mechanism helps consumers prioritize their spending budgets, which sends a message about the value perceptions of the goods and services available. For manufacturers and retailers, prices drive profits. Profits result when revenues are greater than costs.

Returning to the cookie example, you decide to lower your price to $3.25, and both you and the other vendor sell about half of your inventories. The following week you reduce your price further to $2.75, but the other vendor reduces his price to $2.50. At the end of the day, you sell your entire inventory, but the other vendor sells about half of his inventory. What happened? Through their purchases, the consumers indicated that your cookie is a better value at $2.75 than the cheaper cookie at $2.50. If the total cost of your cookie is below the $2.75 price, you most likely will continue selling your product at this price since you are earning a profit. However, if your cost per cookie is greater than $2.75, you undoubtedly will stop selling cookies because you are losing money. Should the other vendor further reduce his price, consumers may go for the lower price cookie. Consumers send a very persuasive message regarding price and quality through their spending habits. Of course, price reductions cannot continue indefinitely. Each baker must pay for ingredients and other related expenses such as entry fees, baking equipment, and staff while still earning some profit as well. Now consider this simple example being reenacted millions and millions of times each day throughout the nation. Given that consumer spending makes up about two-thirds of Gross Domestic Product (GDP), the importance of consumer spending cannot be overstated.

How many small businesses are in your neighborhood today? How many of those same small businesses were around five years ago, or 10? When you were growing up, your local community probably supported hardware stores, bookstores, stationery stores, candy stores, small grocery stores, repair shops, and a host of other small "mom-and-pop" businesses. Over time, many small business owners were unable to compete effectively against the big box stores. Why? Many of these small business owners sold products manufactured by others, which enabled the larger regional or national chains to gain a cost advantage through volume purchases. The chains lowered prices to their customers. In addition to falling margins, small entrepreneurs saw other costs begin to rise including wages, rents, utilities, and the other costs as well. Having to raise their prices, the small business owners became more expensive in the eyes of their customers, outweighing the value of the convenience they offered. Ultimately, many small businesses continued to lose money, forcing them ultimately to shut down.

These economic circumstances are not limited to small businesses. Remember A&P? Not too long ago, it was the largest grocery chain in America. Have you even heard the name? Montgomery Ward and Sears were two of the largest retailers in America in the very recent past, and yet, the former closed its doors years ago and the latter is just a fraction of the size it once was. Look at a list of companies in the S&P 500 today, and compare that list to the companies in the S&P 500 just five years ago. Even the benchmark Dow Jones Industrial Average has undergone changes over the years. You can think of large regional businesses that at one point were thriving, but now have ceased operations, drastically reduced their size, or perhaps merged with another business. Large and small businesses alike succumb ultimately to the same P&L conundrum largely driven by consumer apathy.

LABOR IS JUST ANOTHER RESOURCE

Contrary to the writings of Karl Marx, labor is not the ultimate source of prosperity for a society. One need only turn to the many Third World countries that have an abundance of labor. Unfortunately, they can boast neither a robust nor a profitable economic climate. Given the quantity of available labor, Mexico should enjoy a vibrant economy and yet many of its citizens cross the border to work illegally in the U.S. If labor were the sole source of prosperity, why are these people fleeing their homeland? Successful economies use resources effectively, combining not only labor, but capital and management as well.

In a free market, labor is just another resource subject to the principles of supply and demand. The labor force tries to earn as much as possible, while employers try to pay as little as possible. Some may look at this conflict as unfair, but others see it as normal economic behavior. For instance, higher salaried management positions require training and experience which limits the supply of such individuals thereby raising their prices (salaries). Conversely, assembly line workers require fewer skills and less experience, which allows access to a larger supply of capable individuals, thus lowering their prices (salaries).

Although the scarcity in executive candidates leads to higher salaries, employers seek to place upper limits on their salaries by looking at the value-added for the position. An employer is not going to pay $100,000 to someone contributing only $25,000 to profits. This value relationship between wages and productivity occurs at every level in the organization and the concept is critical to a company wanting to sustain their profitability. In our cookie example, would you pay the same wages to the baker who develops your cookie recipes and to the clerk selling the cookies at the farmers' market? No business can survive for very long when it pays more for any component than that component contributes to the profits of the business. This value concept is a major reason why many businesses move their operations and jobs overseas.

Consider the impact minimum wage laws have on employers. This artificial price for labor typically is set at a level that exceeds the contribution to profit. The employer has the option to continue paying for services that generate a net loss per employee, or the employer can eliminate those positions and push the work onto the remaining employees. If this were your business, what would you do? Of course, you would eliminate the positions, assuming you want to remain in business. While larger firms that hire people for lower level positions may be able to retain some of the jobs, they most likely will hold the number to minimum levels. Minimum wage laws affect small local businesses the most because they have so little excess profits. Your sons or daughters may not find as many job opportunities during the summer or after school. Remember your summer job at McDonalds or the movie theater? Gone and soon to be forgotten.

Another example is labor unions. The most visible union today may be the United Auto Workers, but many unions exist in many industries. Most of the media coverage involving labor unions focuses on higher wages and improved benefit packages for rank-and-file members. The very same media virtually ignores the economic reality of these negotiations. Unions increase the cost of products, reduce the competitiveness of the manufacturer, and hasten the move to lower cost locations (business-speak for overseas) by those manufacturers. Just consider the number of manufacturing plants still in existence in the U.S. While labor is just one element of product costs, it is usually the largest. Although seeking ways to hold costs in check, manufacturers may have no alternative but to raise the price of their products, thus affecting the desirability of their product to the consumer. As the consumer begins to purchase cheaper alternatives, the manufacturer moves much of the production overseas to remain competitive and hold on to its customers. Do you purchase the higher priced item or the less expensive product? Most consumers spend money based, at least somewhat, on price. Today, it is difficult to find any product manufactured entirely in the U.S. including higher-end luxury items. One of the key factors is the cost differential of labor around the world. In the end, the consumer ultimately casts the deciding vote.

YOU ALWAYS NEED CAPITAL

Providing an efficient flow of capital and an effective method to fund new ventures, financial institutions are critical to economic prosperity. Acting as intermediaries, they enable the transfer of capital between unrelated parties facilitating economic development. When individuals purchase stocks and bonds, the infusion of capital is obvious. Equally important, and perhaps even more so, are the many checking and savings account deposits in your local banks, savings and loans, and other financial institutions. In order to compensate you for the use of your funds, these institutions need to put the funds to work earning a profit from which they repay you. Think about the mortgage on your home, the small business loan to a local business, the construction loan for a new housing development, or the many other loans to individuals and businesses that provide the necessary funding to start new ventures, expand existing businesses, or finance ongoing operations.

The pricing mechanism driving these transactions is the return on investment. You, the investor (consumer), want compensation for temporarily depositing your money with the institution, which takes the form of interest or dividends. In effect, you supply the capital and the borrowers represent the demand. The profit enjoyed by the financial institution is the difference between the rate they pay you for supplying the funds and the rate they charge borrowers for lending the funds.

Speculators also can act as intermediaries when they enter into contracts to buy or sell goods at prices determined today for delivery in the future. Maligned for periodic run-ups in the price of oil, speculators are a favorite target in the media. Such an assessment, however, dismisses the point of this economic transaction. Referring to the cookie example, suppose you need capital to purchase a new oven, but the bank is unwilling to lend the money based on the revenue you hope to earn at the next farmers' market. Too many variables exist to accurately forecast your revenue, including weather conditions (will rain cancel or shorten the event?), competition (will more cookie sellers appear, undercutting your price?), and demand (will fewer people attend the event?). What are you to do? You enter into a contract with a speculator who buys all of your cookies at a set price for delivery at the next farmers' market. Thus, the speculator provides you the contracted funds enabling you to buy your equipment regardless of what happens at the next farmers' market. Your decision to transfer the risk is based primarily on your estimate of the future expected price less the contract price you receive from the speculator.

Many may believe speculators raise or inflate overall market prices. For speculators to influence the market, they would need to control a significant portion of that entire market. In our cookie example, had the same speculator purchased all the chocolate chip cookies from all the vendors at the farmers' market, the speculator can set whatever price he desires because he controls the entire market (all the cookies at the market). The consumers, however, still may decide the price is too high, reducing their purchases or eliminating their purchases altogether. While such pricing monopolies are theoretically possible, the global markets are far too complex and dynamic, thus making such a proposition rather difficult.

When receiving a pre-approval for a mortgage, many buyers chose to pay an additional fee to lock-in a mortgage rate today. In so doing, they avoid the market risk of a potentially higher mortgage rate when their application is approved sometime in the future. Regardless of the underlying product of a futures contract such as a mortgage rate, the economic benefit facilitates the flow of goods and services in the market. In effect, these transactions match the strengths and expertise of the respective parties. In the cookie example, you are the expert at baking cookies while the speculator is the so-called expert at understanding the financial aspects of the market. Each focuses on strengths and this efficiently allocates market resources.

THE KEY DRIVER IS PROFITS

Recently, business and, more specifically, corporate executives have come under increasing attacks in the media and from government officials. In a free market system, companies stay in business only when they achieve profits. Consumers largely determine those profits through their purchasing decisions. The role of business is to establish a model that fosters creativity, encourages innovation, and rewards risk taking. Think about Robert Goizueta who made sugar water a household word—Coca Cola; or Ray Kroc who made hamburgers into an empire—McDonalds; or Jack Welch who showed how to consolidate unrelated businesses into a cohesive corporate juggernaut—General Electric. Many such stories exist. There are technology innovators like Microsoft, Apple, and Google, leaders in bringing global information to their users. There are manufacturers like Pfizer, Merck, and Johnson & Johnson, major worldwide leaders in the healthcare industry. There are facilitators like IBM, Intel and Cisco, major players in improving efficiency and productivity. There are logistics experts like FedEx and UPS, pioneers in worldwide distribution networks, bringing the world a little closer.

The biggest difference between a business executive and a government official is one receives directions from the market, fulfilling its needs and the other gives directions to the market, forcing its compliance. The private sector encourages risk taking. By visualizing how certain resources can be commercially viable, it combines various resources to manufacture goods efficiently, and creates distribution networks to facilitate the transfer of those goods. Seeing how unrelated resources can create viable products, business executives produce profits for their companies by fulfilling consumer needs and advancing economic output. Referring again to the cookie example, the individual creating the recipes must determine the ingredients to use, the proper proportions to mix, the time to bake, the quantity to bake, and the distribution channels to facilitate deliveries. If you are successful, perhaps you may become the next Mrs. Fields.

As Sowell points out, profits are crucial to the success of individual businesses but the prospect of profits is critical to a robust economy. One sustains the other. New businesses continually enter the market in the hope of achieving success and building wealth. They may have a new idea, an improved product, a less costly manufacturing process, or a more efficient distribution network, but each competes for limited resources and only the best survive as judged by the consumer. This process efficiently allocates economic resources, creating opportunities and growth for the entire economy.[3]

The private ownership of those profits is the driving force pushing the economy forward. Entrepreneurs seek the next breakthrough and businesses strive to deliver products to consumers. These actions create jobs, kick-starting the economic cycle. Jobs provide the income to purchase goods and services. Those purchases provide a roadmap for suppliers to distribute the desired goods, requiring manufacturers to purchase the appropriate resources to create those goods. Successful products promote competition, more consumer choices, greater innovation, and an expanding economic cycle.

EXPANDING GEOGRAPHICALLY

When overseas firms can produce better and cheaper goods, international trade benefits the consumer. Do you drive a Toyota or Honda automobile? Do you own a Samsung TV or a kitchen appliance from Miele? Do you occasionally drink a Heineken, a Guinness, or maybe Smithwick's? Do you prefer French wines and fine champagne? Not many people think about the company or their employees when purchasing a product. You more likely think about the quality, dependability and cost of what you purchase. As with any economic transaction, when you and many others stop buying the products of a company it reduces their profits, which may eliminate more than a few jobs; look no further than GM or Chrysler. Do you remember Zenith televisions, IBM computers, or instant Polaroid cameras? Closer to home, do you remember Eversharp ballpoint pens, Hydrox chocolate sandwich cookies, or Lotus 123?

While consumers rarely, if ever, consider the employees when they purchase products, international trade conjures up some of the most heated debates. Consider the controversy surrounding the North American Free Trade Agreement (NAFTA). Who can forget Ross Perot's now infamous phrase about a "giant sucking sound" when referring to his belief that many U.S. jobs would be lost. Years ago, when someone referred to something made in Japan it was assumed to be poor quality, but today Japanese products are considered some of the finest in the world. Now, China has become the manufacturing capital of the world making many of the products sold in America and throughout the world, including many high-end products. It is relatively easy to inflame public sentiment regarding national pride, American made goods, and American jobs … well, at least until you go into any store to buy something for yourself.

When you were working your way through college, you had little money, few possessions and probably owed a fair amount of debt. You may have lived at home or found roommates to share an apartment. You may not have had much money, but neither did your friends so you all made the best of it. Fast forward to graduation and your first job. What happens? Naturally, you begin to spend some of the money you are now earning. This scenario is similar to many impoverished countries whose citizens welcome the opportunity to supply the labor in the manufacture and production of goods. Many corporations pursuing these workers are also thrilled because the labor costs are significantly below the U.S. market, thus lowering costs and improving profits. The part many people forget is what happens with the newly created income within these countries? Similar to what you did after graduation, these workers become consumers and their numbers are sufficiently large to generate new demand for products, which may lead to more jobs to produce new incremental economic growth.

The other side of the free trade debate is protectionism. Countries trying to protect a particular industry within their borders impose tariffs on foreign imports. Suppose you want to buy a shovel and competition has driven out all but two manufacturers, leaving only two different shovels available for purchase. A U.S. manufacturer makes one of the shovels and it produces other garden tools as well. A foreign company produces the other shovel, which is its only product. There is no appreciable difference between the two shovels. Since the foreign firm produces only shovels, it is able to achieve certain economies of scale, allowing a lower price. The U.S. firm, seeing sales falling, lobbies the government to impose a tariff on the import of shovels. That increases the foreign shovel price, making it more expensive than the domestic model. Which shovel are you going to buy now? Most people are going to buy the less expensive one, which is the American shovel. What is the economic result? The U.S. firm continues making shovels rather than shifting its resources to other garden tools. The consumer pays the higher price. If sales drop significantly, the foreign company may leave the market entirely. The consumer also may have lost an opportunity to purchase those other garden tools at lower prices had the American company reallocated resources away from the shovel, possibly gaining economies of scale on those garden tools. The net loser is the consumer.

How often have you heard about the huge deficits in the U.S. "balance of trade?" Politicians and businesses alike continually use this information as fodder for campaign pieces and for arousing public opinion against foreign imports. While this may be factual, it is also misleading and does not represent all of the facts. The total output of the U.S. consists of both goods and services and it is no surprise to anyone that the U.S. economy produces more services than goods. The *"balance of trade"* number only includes the goods portion of the U.S. economy, thereby eliminating over half of the economy. The *"balance of payments"* number includes both goods and services. This number shows significant improvement over the balance of trade.

Coupled with balance of trade is the concept of a debtor nation. When foreign countries invest here, the U.S. obviously owes that money to those countries which, by definition, makes the U.S. a debtor. Similar to your deposits in a financial institution, foreign sourced deposits in U.S. banks and corporations create more jobs for American workers and more goods for American consumers. In fact, the more prosperous the U.S. economy, the more foreign capital flows into U.S. markets. Of course, the U.S. balance of payments deficits, in turn, grows higher and the international debt increases further. Not to worry, this is a good thing leading to a more robust economy.

Not all capital inflows are equal, however. Foreign investment capital redirected into the private sector promotes economic growth, which benefits the economy. When the inflow of foreign investment finances government debt, complications may arise. While funding debt enables the government to continue operations, it may delay the government from addressing fundamental issues, or it may create a growing dependence on those foreign investors. It is not difficult to understand the difference between investors wanting to place funds in the U.S. to participate in a robust economy, and investors buying larger portions of an ever-increasing debt to finance government largesse. The former creates real economic wealth, but the latter promotes the inefficient use of resources, reducing economic output.

HOW GOVERNMENT FITS INTO THE MIX

The government plays a major, if not vital, role in a free market economy. Whether you agree or disagree with the magnitude of its involvement, the government does enable the private sector to function by establishing a framework of laws. The key role played by the government is not only the enforcement of those laws, but also the consistent application of those laws. Neither the parties nor the subject matter should influence decisions made in court proceedings. To do so would be harmful to the economy and destructive to the nation. The rule of law must govern all judicial outcomes. The Constitution asserts the role of government is to provide equality of opportunity, not equality of outcome—a very, very important distinction.

The recent government involvement in the bankruptcies of General Motors and Chrysler have threatened long standing laws that provide secured bondholders with first priority on all claims during bankruptcy proceedings. The government maintained the restructuring occurred outside the bankruptcy courts and therefore violated no laws. Whether technically correct or not, the message is quite clear. Ownership rights are under attack, and more importantly, the rights of creditors seem to have little standing in the Obama administration. Potential investors may think twice about investing in American companies. Why invest or extend credit if your rights are in jeopardy, as evidenced with GM and Chrysler? The longer-term consequences of these actions may lead to lower investment capital from foreign entities, as they may consider the U.S. market neither safe nor secure.

The American business concept of property rights and private ownership is the core foundation of capitalism and the free market system.

You have the individual freedom to own a home, own the wages you receive, spend your wealth however you wish, and live your life in the fashion you desire. Private ownership provides incentives to work and to save. When you lived at home, how did you treat your parents' car when you borrowed it? Were you concerned when you scratched the furniture or spilled something on the carpet? How many glasses or dishes did you break? You probably were not exactly careful about the way you treated those possessions. When you grew a little older and purchased many of those same items with your hard-earned money, you most likely handled them with a little more care.

Well the same is true in business. Corporations (property owners) do not want to jeopardize their profits by not policing the quality of their products or the safety of their production processes. They understand selling defective or dangerous products does not make good business sense because product problems influence consumers to seek better alternatives. Consider the potential consequences if you sold bad cookies at the farmers' market. The immediate reaction would be consumers discarding them or, perhaps worse, getting sick from eating the cookies. The longer-term considerations may include the loss of existing customers (concern over product quality), the loss of potential customers (negative word-of-mouth campaign about the quality), or the loss of ongoing sales (impact on other products and other distribution outlets). You, as the owner, would not risk the potential impact on long-term profitability just to sell a few more cookies today.

Looking at some past headlines for real life examples, when Perrier had issues with product quality, its market share dropped as many consumers purchased competing products. Unfortunately for Perrier, some of those consumers never returned even after Perrier eliminated the problem. Do you recall the impact on Tylenol sales during the reported incidents of poison-laced capsules, or the recent troubles with salmonella associated with several different types of vegetables, or the gas pedal problems occurring in Toyota models? Many such examples exist. Consider the product recalls announced in your local media outlets encouraging you to throw out or return affected product for a full refund. These companies are trying to avoid major catastrophes by providing rapid responses to potential problems. The fear of losing everything, the potential legal consequences, or simply promoting customer goodwill are powerful incentives for owners to do the right thing as quickly as possible.

With the ever-increasing number of special interest groups and lobbyists, some government actions may lead to conflicting policies or unintended consequences. Consider several policies endorsed by the U.S. government: reduce the dependency on foreign oil, curb global warming, and seek alternative fuels. Biofuels are at the intersection of these three policies. Through tax subsidies and fuel mandates, the federal government strongly supports the use of grains (such as wheat, corn, soybeans) in the production of biofuels. The growing prosperity in China, India, and other countries also increases demand for these same grains as food products. This increased demand has driven the price of these grains higher and higher. The impact on the world food supply has been alarming, as many poorer countries can no longer afford the higher prices. The tragedy of the policy is both the fuel savings and the environmental benefit derived from biofuels are negligible at best and the production process is quite costly. Despite the problems, the government continues to subsidize the siphoning off of these grains for the production of biofuels.

Enacted separately, three seemingly reasonable regulations created a firestorm within the banking industry. Encouraging home ownership, the government guaranteed mortgages for low-income buyers. Stressing the need for stronger banks, the government also enacted aggressive bank capitalization standards (ratios) to avoid future bank failures. Intended to promote confidence in corporate financial statements, the government required large, publicly traded corporations to mark-to-market, requiring the valuation of corporate assets at their current market values. Taken individually, the regulations are well intentioned, but the application of the regulations creates inconsistent messages. The large commercial banks that want to remove low-income loans from their balance sheets package these loans to sell in the secondary markets. Guaranteed by the federal government, these loans received AAA ratings and became investment instruments for the global financial community. When the low-income homeowners began to delay payments, miss deadlines, and even default entirely, the housing market began to collapse, causing a domino effect throughout the economy. The mark-to-market regulations require the write-down of mortgage loan portfolios to current market valuations without considering those homeowners who have continued making their mortgage payments. Why is this a potential problem? If the loan is current (the homeowner is paying his mortgage), the asset value should be the amount of the loan. Based upon the known facts, the loan will be repaid, thus making a devaluation of the underlying asset (the home) unnecessary and potentially misleading. Arbitrarily forcing such accounting changes may severely affect the lending practices within the banking industry. The newly revised capitalization ratios of regional, community, and local banks lowered the ratings of many banks, creating fear of more failures, further compromising the economy. Responding to the new regulations, banks implemented restrictive lending practices in an effort to shore up their capitalization ratios. Despite the intent to strengthen the banks, the government initiated new stimulus programs and offered new plans to help impacted homeowners. Once again, the good intentions of the federal government created unintended consequences, severely affecting the market.

Some people question whether politicians actually focus on the public interest as opposed to their personal agendas. Consider the peace dividend after the fall of the Soviet Union. The government sought to close many of the armed forces training bases scattered throughout the U.S. Although it seemed that everyone favored these closings, politicians did not want to close any bases within their voting districts—surprise, surprise. Drawing upon a more recent example, the staunchest political supporters of wind and turbine power seem to be reluctant to build such facilities near their homes even when independent testing supported these locations as the most beneficial. Consider the number of unrelated amendments attached to pieces of legislation voted on in Congress often referred to as "pork barrel spending." Politicians often add these spending bills to benefit their constituents or political supporters as rewards for their continued support. Everybody does it, right? Disconnected from economic realties, politicians give new meaning to the phrase—do as I say, not as I do. Milton Friedman articulated the effects of government intervention rather succinctly when he observed, "The government solution to a problem is usually as bad as the problem."

WHAT ABOUT GOVERNMENT FINANCING

The federal government's impact on the economy is not limited to the enforcement of the rule of law, the protection of private property rights, or the enactment of new laws and regulations. The financial activities of the government play a very significant role. While the government may generate some revenue from the sale of public assets, the primary revenue source is and always will be the collection of taxes.

A common mistake concerning income taxes is the assumption that raising the income tax rate by a certain percentage generates a commensurate increase in tax collections by an equal percentage. Raising taxes 10% does not generate a 10% increase in tax revenues. With human behavior being what it is, many individuals find ways to avoid paying a new tax increase. In addition to reducing the expected tax revenues, tax increases redirect or even misallocate resources. The larger the proposed increase, the more likely wealthy individuals will hire financial experts to find ways to avoid those tax increases legally. Such a reaction is a rational response. Consider your reaction when the price of an item you regularly purchase increases. Most likely, you try to reduce your purchase quantities, perhaps you seek other alternatives, or maybe you forego the purchases entirely.

Raising taxes reduces disposable income, which decreases consumer spending. With less money to spend, consumer purchases may move toward necessity items and staple goods, shifting consumer demand. Depending upon the scope and magnitude of the tax changes, these market shifts may be more long lasting and may extend into other industry sectors as well. The softening economy may lead to other less desirable consequences such as rising unemployment, more severe downturns, or even potential recessions.

Taxes are a very strange phenomenon. The government may decide to start or increase the rates for such items as personal income taxes, corporate income taxes, utility use taxes, municipal fees, Social Security taxes, sales taxes, real estate taxes, fuel taxes, and on and on and on. When the government supposedly levies a new tax targeted at someone or something, the consumer ultimately pays the new taxes, including corporate income taxes! Yes, that is correct. The taxes paid by corporations are part of their cost of doing business and become part of the product costs passed onto the consumer. When the government continually tries to affect corporate behavior through tax increases, the business passes such costs onto the consumer. If the product cannot support this price increase, the corporation may pursue cutting expenses by shifting production overseas. When you want to affect the behavior of your son or daughter, do you penalize or do you reward him or her?

A budget surplus occurs when current tax revenues exceed current spending, and a deficit arises when current tax revenues are not sufficient to offset the current level of government spending. When tax revenues fall short of spending, the sale of government bonds offsets the shortfall. The accumulation of such annual budget deficits at the federal level is the national debt. The outstanding bonds sold to cover the annual deficits are claims against future tax revenues. Granted the government can roll over portions of the maturing debt into new bond issues, but this simply delays the actual payment of those borrowings.

Government debt can be good and it can be bad as well. When individuals carry debt for instance, the ability of the borrower to repay the funds helps to determine the appropriate level of debt an individual may carry. When buying a home or an automobile, most individuals take on debt to enjoy the use of those purchases. In such cases, the debt is a good thing, provided the individual has the resources to repay the loan. If an individual is spending money that he cannot afford to repay, it is a bad thing since it can lead to significant financial troubles and possibly imprisonment.

The government must adhere to similar principles, but politics often enters into the equation. Interest group politics guides many government officials to avoid consideration of funding cuts for any program and, in many cases, even holding spending to prior year levels. Comparing the national debt to the Gross Domestic Product (GDP) indicates the relative burden on the economy. While conventional wisdom focuses on taxes to pay for government programs, the visibility of the impact on paychecks poses significant political hurdles to increasing taxes. Debt financing, on the other hand, relieves much of this political pressure. Deferring the payments into the future masks the real impact, making debt financing a tempting aphrodisiac to over-spending for political interests. When left unchecked, this spending can escalate to dangerous, unsustainable levels.

During good economic times, tax revenues are growing and the outlook is upbeat. Our politicians take this opportunity to reward their constituents with pork barrel spending, new or expanded entitlement programs, or other "feel-good" initiatives. During economic downturns however, these built-in programs are difficult, if not impossible, to scale back without severe political ramifications. When the debt levels become excessive, the government may need to raise the interest rates on new bond offerings as well as existing debt rollovers. The rising interest rates on government bonds influence the entire market by forcing higher rates on the entire fixed income market, leading to tighter money, reduced credit, and less consumer spending. These are precursors to a slowing economy or worse.

The debt burden is further complicated when we are borrowing from foreign entities rather than just ourselves. When foreign countries are financing a significant portion of government debt, it magnifies the potential issues. Should these countries lose confidence in our ability or our intent to repay the debt, they may stop buying our bonds, or worse, they may start dumping their existing bond holdings, which would have disastrous consequences in the financial markets. Some of these countries may attempt to exert political pressure on the government, creating still other international concerns, further disrupting our economy and the global marketplace.

Interestingly, many politicians and even more media pundits suggest the only ways to reduce the rising deficits are to raise taxes, reduce spending, or some combination of both. What is sad about such rhetoric is whether they truly do not know another alternative or they simply choose to ignore the better solution. The better answer is a growing economy that allows the government to collect larger amounts of tax revenues, reduce the debt percentage relative to GDP, and foster investor confidence in the future. A strong economy leads to increased investment, job growth, and a lower interest rate environment.

LOOKING BACK IN HISTORY

Surprisingly, a strong economy does not always generate goodwill throughout the entire country. While everyone may seek prosperity, those individuals, groups, or regions not participating in the economic upswing pose a concern. Promoting these inequities as unfair, politicians propose government solutions to remedy the situation, often leading to unintended consequences.

As stated in the beginning of this chapter, the definition of economics is learning to deal with scarcity. Thus, the efficient allocation of resources, by definition, requires certain areas to lose access to some resources. Regardless of the economic or political system, allocations of limited resources are a necessity. This is an indisputable fact. The unknown is whether the chosen allocation system raises the overall standard of living for the country. Who is best equipped to decide such allocations—a centralized government seeking to solidify power through legislation that rewards their supporters, or the private sector amassing wealth through the buying decisions of the consuming public?

The CBS series "*You Are There*" first appeared on radio in 1947 with John Daly as host. The program moved to television in 1953 lasting four years with Walter Cronkite as the commentator. This educational series showed dramatic recreations of historic events that were occasionally presented in grade school classrooms. Each episode closed with its signature line, "… and you were there." Well, perhaps a history lesson is necessary again. Presenting an objective assessment, history can teach an appreciation of the accomplishments of the past while providing anticipation of future achievements.

During the early part of the twentieth century, the world experienced the rise of many forms of political structures such as fascism, socialism, and communism. Despite the lofty rhetoric of a centralized power structure, their economies were unable to match the success of capitalism where the consumer directs the allocation of resources. People or entities do not willingly give up their resources. Unfortunately, many centralized governments often use force to acquire additional resources or limit the loss of their existing resources, which may lead to destruction and war. Capitalism, on the other hand, influences consumers to purchase products, shifting resources to profitable businesses, which often leads to innovation and progress, raising the standard of living for all.

While the United States has the most formidable military power the world has ever known, its economic strength strikes the most fear in our enemies. Capitalism has begun to spread throughout the world, creating individual wealth, improving living conditions, and fostering economic cooperation wherever it is tried. Whether nation-states or fanatical factions, the tyrannical powers see their influence eroding in the face of this grass-roots movement toward capitalism.

Some view the U.S. as using a disproportionately larger share of the world's resources, but a more accurate accounting is necessary. While representing about 6% of the world's land and population, the U.S. represents almost 30% of the world's Gross Domestic Product, more than three times its closest competitor. An even more startling revelation is that the United States accomplished these feats in less than 300 years—a relative upstart in the historical context of other nations and civilizations that have existed far, far longer. While this accomplishment epitomizes the very concept of economics, the contributions made by the U.S. far outweigh the economic considerations.

As pointed out by John Steele Gordon in *An Empire of Wealth: The Epic History of American Economic Power,* this economic power enabled the United States to save the Union in the 1860s, save the world in the 1940s, and stand down the Soviet Union in the 1980s.[4] This economic strength also permitted the U.S. to be the first responder to the world's natural disasters wherever they occur, the food supplier to the impoverished of the world, the healthcare provider to those in need, and the defender of free people everywhere. The U.S. has given more money, provided more humanitarian aid, and sacrificed more of their sons and daughters in countries around the world than any nation in history.

Capitalism may not be perfect, but its successes are irrefutable and impressive. The concept of private ownership, which is at the heart of the free market system, is a very powerful incentive. To paraphrase Winston Churchill, capitalism may be the worst economic system, except for all the others.

CHAPTER FOURTEEN

Building on Success

Government is not reason; it is not eloquent; it is a force.
Like fire, it is a dangerous servant and a fearful master.
George Washington

OVER TWO HUNDRED years ago, Adam Smith wrote *The Wealth of Nations* (1776) in which he described the economic benefit of individuals pursuing their own personal wealth in local businesses rather than a centralized government directing the flow of industry. Defending the virtues of low taxes, he also warned that higher tax rates negatively affect behavior. For most of our history, income taxes were non-existent, and when instituted, taxes rarely approached 10%.

As the nation entered the twentieth century, America would soon be engaged in the first of two world wars and sandwiched between those conflicts was the Great Depression. This economic catastrophe changed America not only in the way we look at the economy but, more subtly, in the way politicians look at their constituents. America in the twentieth century and in the early years of the 21st century is vastly different from the America of the first 100 plus years.

THE TURNING POINT

Many historians, economists and scholars attribute the beginnings of the worldwide depression to the aftermath of the First World War that devastated the European continent and fostered resentment among its participants. The U.S. became creditor to the free world, amassing debt in excess of $24 billion, almost one-half of which was loans to European countries financing the war. Sowing the seeds of economic disaster, the federal government pursued a number of misguided programs, enabling those seeds to grow and flourish.

Several recently published books have critically analyzed the historic years of the Roosevelt Presidency and its impact on the economic issues of the day. *FDR's Folly,* written by Jim Powell, explains many of the federal programs of his presidency and their impact on the nation. *The Forgotten Man*, written by Amity Shlaes, suggests FDR did not understand the prosperity of the '20s, which contributed to errors in his federal intervention that prolonged the Depression. *New Deal or Raw Deal?*, written by Burton Folsom Jr., contends the legacy of his presidency continues to harm our economy and our politics. Let's look at some of the historical points from these scholarly works.[1]

The Great Depression

When Western Europe began rebuilding infrastructure and industrial capacity, stabilizing their currencies from the ravages of inflation became a struggle. Much of their capital flowed out of their countries seeking the stability of the U.S. economy. With the Fed following a relaxed gold standard and maintaining a low discount rate, the money supply expanded throughout most of the decade following the war, thus driving down interest rates. Seeking higher returns, much of the domestic and foreign money moved into the U.S. stock market, increasing speculative pressures. Fueled by easy money policies, the economy was overheating when Herbert Hoover took office in 1929. The Fed decided to tighten the money supply by imposing two successive increases in the discount rate. These actions led to an inevitable stock market correction, forever known as "Black Tuesday," October 29, 1929.

Compounding this newly imposed restrictive monetary policy, the Hoover administration passed the Smoot-Hawley Tariff in 1930 hoping to protect the American economy. When most European countries passed retaliatory tariffs, the legislation effectively eliminated overseas trading. While not a major component of the U.S. economy, foreign trade was concentrated in a few industries and one of the most significant was farming. The collapse of farm exports led to disastrous results throughout rural America.

In *FDR's Folly*, Powell explains the continuing tight money policies of the Fed exacerbated the market contraction by placing significant pressure on banks, causing many to fail. Banks do not maintain large amounts of cash on hand. Most of their deposits are loaned out in long-term contractual obligations that are earning profits. When a run on the bank occurs, the bank is unable to call in or sell their loans to cover the massive withdrawals and thus they subsequently fail. The majority of the bank failures of the 1930s occurred in small towns where unit-banking laws prohibited branch banking. This law resulted from lobbying efforts by small town bankers who feared that competition from large city banks would drive them out of business. Unfortunately, the unintended consequence of this law restricted small country banks from diversifying their portfolios outside of their local markets. Naturally, when their client base of local farmers and businesses collapsed, the local banks collapsed right along with their customers.[2]

The most disastrous financial collapse in American history resulted, in a large part, from the mistakes made by the federal government in reacting to the crisis. Despite the many missteps, the free market was largely able to correct itself. In fact, the market contraction known as the Great Depression officially ended in the same month Franklin D. Roosevelt (FDR) became President. The peak occurred in August 1929 and the trough ending the Great Depression occurred in March 1933 (refer to Figure 12.1), according to the National Bureau of Economic Research. By the time the Great Depression ended, the market had lost over two-thirds of its value and unemployment was a staggering 25%. On March 5, 1933, Roosevelt was inaugurated for his first term as President.

Roosevelt's New Deal

The New Deal promised bold, new initiatives to stimulate economic growth. Ironically, these initiatives were not necessary because the economy was already in a recovery mode when FDR came into office. As Jim Powell points out, many countries around the world saw their industrial production begin to recover by 1932; the U.S. economy also began to show signs of recovery. The machinations of the new administration soon thwarted that recovery. With the economy improving, the Fed decided to reduce the money supply by increasing bank reserve requirements. Despite the warning signs of a falling bond market, the Fed continued raising reserve requirements for banks. This contraction in the money supply had a very depressing effect on the economy.[3]

There were new labor laws that increased payroll costs, encouraged labor strikes, and disrupted businesses. The administration imposed new tax programs such as the undistributed profits tax on corporations, a new punitive tax on farmers who produced more than the government permitted, and the creation of a Social Security payroll tax to name just a few. FDR raised the marginal tax rate for individuals to 79% while also raising corporate rates. These attacks on the private sector were integral to stalling the recovery in its tracks. These restrictive policies resulted in a less recognized but equally disturbing second depression, starting in May 1937 and ending in June 1938. Almost six years into the Roosevelt presidency, the stock market remained over one-third lower than its 1929 highs and unemployment still lingered at 19%—hardly a resounding success for FDR and his New Deal.

Whether the growing influence of the Socialist movement on the European continent, or simply homegrown resentment toward the wealthy, a genuine fear had arisen within the business community. They, perhaps more than others, understood that FDR had declared all out war on the private sector and used the economic crisis as the catalyst. He needed to find a villain to foster public support for his New Deal policies, so he targeted businesses and business executives. In other words, he pitted Americans against one another. When FDR spoke of nothing to fear but fear itself, he obviously was not referring to his own demonization of American business. He regularly attacked the private sector by imposing higher taxes, restrictive policies and intrusive regulations. The growing uncertainty within the business community was not only from continuous assaults that sapped strength from American industry, but also from the fear of not knowing what the administration was going to do next. His continual harassment froze the private sector into inaction. FDR literally guaranteed a deeper, longer, and more severe depression.

The success of his presidency had nothing to do with restoring the economy, but everything to do with perfecting interest group politics on a national scale. Jim Powell describes how FDR brought together groups of people who, previously, were just individual citizens or disgruntled employees or labor unions and other disparate factions. He pandered to them, securing their votes, and rewarded them with new government programs. Recent economic studies confirmed much of the New Deal spending did not go to the needy but to win over voters in key swing states for future elections. Special interest lobbies garnered loans and other concessions from the administration in exchange for political benefits.[4] Yes, this was the birth of modern politics.

Recalling a scene from the classic John Ford western *The Man Who Shot Liberty Valance*, a newspaper editor listens to the factual account of the events that launched the political career of their state's favorite son. Contradicting the accounts told through the years, the reality was not only less heroic but also showed the stories to be an outright lie. Upon learning the truth, the editor responded, "When legend becomes fact, print the legend."[5] Perhaps the same can be said of the FDR Presidency.

The Return to Prosperity

Although many assume the Second World War ended the Great Depression, the facts just do not bear that out. With 11 million people drafted into the armed forces, unemployment virtually disappeared. This fact had nothing to do with either the New Deal or a growing economy. While industrial production rose substantially and average weekly work hours increased, these increases had nothing to do with the New Deal or with a growing economy. Rather than growing the economy by fulfilling the needs of the consuming public, the increased production resulted from the construction of armaments and other military equipment, which actually diverted capital and resources away from the production of consumer goods.

The growth in national income during the war years had nothing to do with the New Deal or a sound economy. The accumulation of paper assets, such as money and government bonds, resulted from the consumers' inability to purchase many of the goods and products they either needed or wanted. For instance, no one was able to purchase new cars, homes or major appliances during the war because the federal government prohibited the production of such goods. Almost two-thirds of the entire labor force were either in the armed forces or directly employed by the military. The private sector workforce paid the taxes necessary to fund the war effort. With resources diverted away from the consumer, the war years actually resulted in a significant loss of wealth for the nation.

Neither the Second World War nor federal legislation ended the Great Depression. Following the war, the country returned to normalcy and the population wanted to forget the war and start building the future they fought to save. What ended the Depression? It was the veterans returning from the war, wanting to build a better life for their families. It was the pent-up demand for consumer and capital goods that were unavailable during the war. It was the elimination of the unrelenting attacks on American industry by the federal government. It was the repeal of the many onerous taxes imposed during the FDR years. It was the removal of the legislative uncertainty so prevalent throughout the FDR administration. Yes, happy days were back again.

In Retrospect

The free market, or capitalism, did not cause the Great Depression. In fact, it was the lack of faith in the free market system that led to government intervention that, almost certainly, worsened the severity of the contraction and prolonged its duration. Of more lasting impact were the politics it had wrought. FDR ushered in a new era in America that was much different from what had come before.

In his book *A Conflict of Visions*, Thomas Sowell explains that the Founding Fathers emphasized process, not results, when they wrote the Constitution. He argues the Constitution does not provide for a perfect society, which is unattainable by imperfect humans, but it provides the opportunity for people to use their natural rights to pursue their personal happiness. He acknowledges the results may yield inequalities, but the process guarantees almost everyone a chance. Sowell contends they emphasized the lessons of experience, rather than the opportunity to create a utopia. They stressed fidelity and the rules of the game more than good intentions. Until the twentieth century, most American leaders sought to protect the process, not the results.[6]

The Constitution provides equality of opportunity, not equality of outcome. In so doing, the Constitution focuses on a limited federal government whose powers are granted by the consent of the governed. The Constitution pledged the rule of law rather than the rule of the majority. The Constitution also promised individual freedoms through states' rights rather than the federal power of a centralized government.

LEARN FROM HISTORY, DON'T IGNORE IT

The New Deal policies were a failure and did not end the Depression. Nevertheless, politicians continue to build on many of FDR's concepts. They understood that the New Deal programs were, in fact, very successful politically. Sadly, many politicians have become concerned more with their political power than with their constituents. The history lesson they learned was not how to diminish the effects of a national economic catastrophe, but how to use that catastrophe to expand interest group politics. Politicians on both sides of the aisle have moved toward a populist approach, appealing to the interests and prejudices of people.

By targeting specific interest groups and campaigning on their fears, politicians successfully segregated the population into voting blocks, espousing what they believed each group wanted to hear. In so doing, politicians have increasingly attempted to "fix" the nation's ills, real or imagined, economic or social, within the political arena by either spending more and more money or enacting numerous laws and regulations. Government spending has grown to unsustainable proportions; government oversight has become government fiat; and government regulation has given way to outright government ownership.

The politicians' favorite target is the private sector and, more specifically, the free enterprise system. At the first signs of an economic slowdown, they try to convince the voting public that only the government can fix the problems in the economy. Whenever the market hits a rough patch, politicians always seem to claim it is the worst economy since the Great Depression and blame the economic woes on corrupt corporations.

Although market recessions rarely exceed 16 months, politicians seldom sit idle, allowing the economy to fix itself. "Do no harm" should be the mantra for politicians as it is for doctors. Instead, they always insist on doing something so they can take credit when the market inevitably recovers. "Why let a good crisis go to waste?" has become the rallying cry for many politicians. Targeting specific voter blocks, they reward their supporters with government programs. Populist views may deliver votes, but sound leadership drives the economy.

Despite what the politicians may say, government spending seldom creates jobs that support real economic growth. Instead, the government spends money to fund short-term employment primarily to reward their voting blocks. Taking funds from the private sector, politicians support favored groups or fund any number of local "pork-barrel" projects. Many federal programs provide only initial start-up funding. The federal government then transfers the program to state governments to manage and fund ongoing costs. Wherever the program ultimately resides, the taxpayer carries the burden.

To understand the importance of the private sector, there must be a recognition that taxes pay for every government job, every government program, and every government initiative. In order to collect taxes, companies must earn profits and individuals must earn wages. Private sector companies generate profits only when they are able to sell products to consumers. Consumers can buy products only when they have disposable income. Disposable income results from the wages earned while employed. The amount of disposable income is also a function of the taxes they pay or rather the taxes the government takes. Since the wages paid to government workers come from the taxes collected, government jobs simply redistribute funds collected from the private sector. It must be understood that private sector jobs generate the funds necessary to sustain the entire economic system.

The continuing expansion of the federal bureaucracy leads to more and more government jobs and a steady stream of new government programs. Curiously, these programs seldom shutdown and rarely do they downsize. To the contrary, the government supports many similar programs across multiple agencies and these redundant operations continue to receive funding. President Reagan observed, "No government ever voluntarily reduces itself in size. Government programs, once launched, never disappear. Actually, a government bureau is the nearest thing to eternal life we'll ever see on this earth!"

A RECIPE FOR ECONOMIC GROWTH

With your personal investment portfolio, the impact inflicted by inflation, taxes and costs can significantly reduce the real return on your portfolio. When it comes to the growth of the national economy, the same three issues hold the key.

Control Inflation

The best way to control inflation is through a strong dollar policy. A strong dollar means our currency has a stable value over time, helping to mitigate the impact of business cycles and inflationary pressures. The stability of the dollar also encourages investment not only from domestic sources but from foreign sources as well. With inflation under control, investments retain value and the strong dollar provides an excellent hedge against other currencies. Higher returns attract more capital inflows to the U.S., generating an international capital surplus or the "dreaded" trade deficit. These inflows provide American markets with greater access to capital for building new plants, expanding current capacity, investing in new ventures, and financing existing operations.

Unless offset by price changes in either foreign or domestic products, the stronger dollar does make U.S. goods less competitive due to foreign exchange rates. When this situation occurs, the U.S. imports more foreign goods and exports fewer domestic goods. This scenario may be problematic at a microeconomic level, but it is more than offset by the macroeconomic benefits to the economy as a whole. Allowing the free flow of goods across borders enables the pricing mechanism to determine the allocation of resources based on supply and demand factors and the value judgments of consumers. Recall the example of two shovels and the intrusion of government protectionism. While individual companies and their employees may be impacted, the economy as a whole improves through the efficient allocation of resources. Perhaps the company in the shovel example reallocates its internal resources and improves other garden products, thus generating greater profits. Perhaps the capital funding from external sources transfers investment capital to another project in a different industry, or it provides the necessary resources to develop a new technological advance or a medical breakthrough. All too often, the microeconomic concerns become political fodder and talking points for special interest groups that do not look at the bigger picture.

Keep Taxes Low

Maintaining low marginal tax rates for individuals and keeping corporate taxes low encourages capital investment. Even if you ignore the historical evidence, a little common sense can help provide some insight. When the government increases tax rates, the after-tax rate of return on any investment decreases whether it is a stock, a product line, a business, or a start-up venture. For instance, if you currently earn a pre-tax return of 10% on your investment and the tax rate on investment income increases from 10% to 30%, your after-tax investment return drops from 9% to 7%—a decrease of almost 25%.

Business managers most likely would try to increase the price of their products to recover that loss. Should they be unable to increase price, the next target would be to cut expenses. They may reduce carrying costs, eliminate overhead, cut jobs, or even move some or all of their jobs overseas. Due to the lower returns, investment in the business may no longer be viable and the capital outlay may be withdrawn completely. These actions are not the result of economic considerations but rather the result of government taxing policies that lead to misallocations of resources. Consider the impact of this example multiplied by thousands of investors, small businesses, and entrepreneurs trying to decide whether to risk their own capital in the economy. Lower taxes, on the other hand, encourage capital investment, risk taking and economic activity, all of which promotes economic growth.

Most individuals fail to grasp the underlying behaviors driven by the tax code. Many politicians and many in the media argue the inequities of the tax code and justify their opinions by pointing to the economic hardships occurring within certain sectors of the economy. The unfortunate reality is that pockets of underperformance are always present in such a vast and diverse economy regardless of economic conditions. When the economy is strong, politicians tend to argue compassion, asking help for those less fortunate. During a weak economy, politicians move toward a fairness argument, insisting on help for those hit hardest by the economic downturn. The one constant in all scenarios is the call to raise taxes. Is this class warfare, redistribution of wealth, or a lack of understanding economic principles?

Regardless of the specific cutoff points, everyone agrees with the concept of low-, middle-, and high-income earners. Politicians pass laws and enact programs designed to help low-income earners. To pay for many of these initiatives, the political leaders seek to raise taxes on the high-income earners. This rhetoric provides rousing campaign slogans and exciting lead stories for the evening news. In the real world however, high-income earners hire accountants, lawyers, and other financial advisors to shield much of their money from the newly raised tax rates. The only group seemingly out in the cold is the middle-income earners who must carry the burden for all. Consider the Alternative Minimum Tax (AMT) introduced in 1969. Originally, this tax targeted 155 high-income earners who avoided most if not all income taxes. The AMT tax now affects millions of middle-class Americans each year. The politicians largely ignore these unintended consequences, or do they?

While taxes obviously increase costs, regulations have the same effect but often they fly under the radar of many individuals. Whether they take the form of fees or mandatory actions to comply with new requirements, regulations increase the costs of doing business. While some regulations are necessary, many seem onerous, intended to penalize rather than to improve processes. Each business must understand the new requirements, determine how to comply with the new regulations, implement the necessary actions to be in compliance, and monitor adherence on an ongoing basis. To perform these tasks, the business needs to add staff, add equipment, or both. The newly added expenses are folded into product costs and passed on to the consumer in form of higher prices.

Manage Government Spending

Previously it was suggested the biggest difference between a business executive and a government official is one receives direction from the market while the other gives direction to the market. Another significant difference is that the business executive has a longer-term perspective, developing strategic plans to position products for future profits. Politicians, on the other hand, tend to look at the short-term, often tying programs to two-year election cycles. When the business executive encounters an unsuccessful product, he discontinues production to cut his losses. When a government program is too costly or inefficient, the politician demands new revenues to fund the program. Spending other peoples' money always seems easier than spending your own.

When the economy is strong and tax revenues are growing, this short-term focus fails to consider the impact of the bad times when tax revenues are shrinking. Unlike business executives who tighten their belts, reduce costs, and delay further investments, politicians look to expand existing programs and implement new initiatives for those newly affected segments of the population. The funding can come from additional borrowing (leading to more debt), increasing individual taxes (reducing family income), or increasing corporate taxes (reducing profits, often leading to higher prices and potentially fewer jobs).

Federal deficits and government spending affect all Americans from Wall Street to Main Street. The actual dollar amount of government spending is less important than its percentage of the Gross Domestic Product (GDP). Think of GDP as the nation's cash flow, enabling the government to meet its ongoing budget obligations and debt service. Fearing the short-term consequences of cutting or eliminating current programs from their voting blocks, politicians borrow more and more money from abroad. Government debt is not unlimited; it needs to be managed; and it must be controlled. A longer-term focus requires understanding that foreign investment will continue as long as real returns remain stable. Should the dollar lose value, real returns will fall and foreign investors may decide to flee. Domestic dollars would be needed to cover the shortfall, thus reducing the funds available to the private sector.

Figure 14.1 highlights the growth in government spending as a percentage of the Gross Domestic Product. It is approaching disastrous levels. While government spending skyrocketed during both World Wars, spending did revert to pre-war levels at the conclusion of each war. However, the spending jump that occurred during the Great Depression did not return to pre-depression levels at its conclusion. Instead, the New Deal programs permanently increased spending

FIGURE 14.1 *Government Spending as a Percentage of GDP*

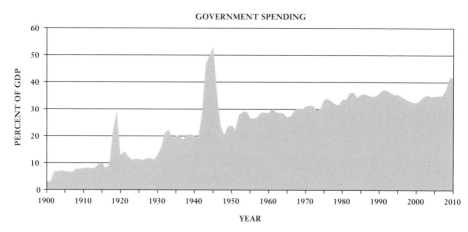

and that initiated a steady expansion of government programs. The Kennedy administration also enacted a costly piece of legislation that allowed the federal work force to become unionized. Linking public jobs at every level of the government locked-in yet another layer of permanent spending. The Obama administration further expanded the permanent spending levels with the passage of healthcare legislation. Today government spending is beyond 40% of our GDP. Significant increases are looming because the Obama healthcare legislation will not be fully implemented until 2014. This level of spending is unsustainable, and may be catastrophic.

Perhaps the most illustrative evaluation of huge government spending initiatives came from then Secretary of the Treasury Henry Morgenthau, a long time confidant of President Franklin D. Roosevelt. He wrote in his diary that if the government continued spending money at such a pace, the economy would collapse. He further lamented that despite all those spending programs, the government was not making any progress in reducing unemployment.[7]

The most disturbing element of this passage is not what he wrote but what he omitted. Revealing the folly of using massive government spending to stimulate the economy, Morgenthau, an insider of the FDR inner circle, corroborated that government stimulus does not work.

With such dramatic evidence to the contrary, the Obama administration continues to push the same failed policies of the past. Why would anyone pursue an initiative that proved to be so disastrous?

MALIGNED AND MISUNDERSTOOD

The formula for economic growth is not a revolutionary approach; it is not even a new approach. When tried, it is exceedingly successful. You may remember Reaganomics. It ushered in the Reagan Revolution and a 25-year boom. Why do we continue to ignore past successes? Why do we continue to try fixing past failures? We cannot be that uninformed; we must put aside personal agendas and work toward a stronger, growing economy benefiting all Americans.

The economic principle of supply and demand indicates higher prices result in lower demand. Logically, it follows that taxing something more reduces demand. Conversely, if you tax something less, demand increases. Marketers have long known that reductions, whether taxes or prices, increase consumer buying activities. Why do stores offer sales, why do manufacturers provide coupons, why have internet purchases soared? The government understands this principle as well. Consider so-called sin taxes on smoking, drinking, and gambling as well as the use of tariffs. The government also offers tax incentives to promote desired behavior, including deductions for mortgage interest and charitable donations—at least for now anyway.

Supply-Side Economics

Characterized in the media as tax cuts for the rich and wealthy, nothing is further from the truth. In *The End of Prosperity*, Arthur Laffer, along with fellow authors Stephen Moore and Peter Tanous, debunk this myth. The driving force behind supply-side economics is the concept of incentives.

While associated mostly with corporate executives, salary incentives drive performance in many occupations. Consider the salary of the star athlete who can carry his team to a championship, or the academic who publishes prestigious works that bring recognition to his university, or the movie star who brings large audiences to his films, or the trial lawyer who wins large settlements for his clients. Whether they receive huge salaries, collect generous residuals, negotiate a considerable percentage of gross revenues, or demand a sizeable percentage of a settlement, these individuals and their respective businesses rarely receive criticism; the media largely ignores them. Based on earnings per hour, these individuals earn far more than most business executives.

At some point however, regardless of your financial position, income tax rates can become so onerous that government tax receipts decrease. Laffer asserts that two different tax rates provide largely the same tax revenues—0% and 100% each generate zero tax receipts for the government. The first is obvious since there are no taxes collected. The second really is equally simple. If you cannot keep anything you earn, why would anyone work? With no income, there are no taxes to collect. Although logic would imply the existence of an optimum rate, Laffer prefers to focus on taxpayer reactions to changes in the tax rates. He contends taxpayer behavior is a function of the current tax rates, the timeframe for the tax rate changes, the availability of alternative options, and the existence of legal loopholes.[8]

Laffer's theory explains the narrative surrounding the example of the low-, middle-, and high-income earners. Choosing a lower rate on a large tax base expands the overall taxpayer pool, lowering the tax burden for all taxpayers whether high-, middle-, or low-income earners. Choosing a higher rate on a small tax base shrinks the overall taxpayer pool, increasing the tax burden primarily for middle-income earners who do not have the means to employ an army of financial advisors. Rather than penalizing the public with higher tax rates, the government needs to encourage positive incentives with lower tax rates. Allowing families to keep more of what they earn promotes investment, risk taking and economic activity. The same principles are evident in Steve Forbes' flat tax initiative that suggests a 17% to 18% tax rate on all income earners. It provides largely the same tax revenues as the current progressive rates. Again, larger taxpayer pools lower the overall tax rates.

Those Stubborn Facts Again
Much to the chagrin of the media, supply-side tax cuts actually do increase the percentage of taxes paid by the wealthy. The Internal

Revenue Service documents this very fact. While the media demonizes supply-side tax cuts as tax cuts for the rich, in reality the wealthy always pay more taxes under this approach, which reduces the tax burden on middle- and lower-income families. You do not find these facts reported in the general media; it simply is not a popular viewpoint, nor does it fit into their narrative.

One of the earliest proponents of lower taxes, President Calvin Coolidge, profoundly observed the relationship between tax rates and tax collections back in 1924. He said history does not confirm that higher tax rates produce larger tax revenues. In fact, he pointed out that when taxation of large incomes becomes excessive, the revenues associated with those wealthier individuals declines. He wanted to reduce the tax burden on small wage earners by collecting the largest possible tax revenues from large wage earners. President Coolidge argued that if the rates on large incomes were too high, tax collections from those with large incomes would decrease and small wage earners would end up carrying most of the tax burden. He further noted that when the tax rates are such that they produce the most revenue from large incomes, the small taxpayer benefits the most.[9]

President Coolidge makes a very important point. Lowering the marginal tax rates brings more dollars into the Treasury from the wealthy thereby lessening the burden on the small wage earner. In other words, when the politicians argue to "raise taxes on the rich" and enact higher taxes directed at the wealthy, these wealthy individuals stop investing, stop taking risk, stop innovating, and ultimately stop the economy. These wealthy individuals begin spending their money on advisors who find legal ways to reduce their tax payments. As the economy slows, the economic cycle begins to unravel—jobs are lost, unemployment rises, spending slows, goods and services decrease, prices rise, and the contraction intensifies. The politicians are adversely affecting the very people they claim to be helping!

Investment capital, labor and other resources tend to move away from higher tax areas. Simply look at the population growth in states that have no state income taxes—such as Texas and Florida—compared to the almost confiscatory rates of California and New York. Even more disturbing is the potential for foreign businesses and foreign capital to begin seeking other venues for spending their money. When domestic and foreign investment capital dries up, American jobs are soon to follow.

Rather than trying to stimulate demand by redistributing income, supply-side tax cuts target the supply of income tax payers. Allowing individuals to retain more of their income creates incentives for individuals to risk some of their capital in the hope of improving their financial situation. This incentive is not restricted to the wealthy. Supply-side tax cuts encourage investment in general, leading to economic activity and job growth. The total pool of taxpayers expands. The larger pool increases tax revenues while spreading the tax burden across larger and larger pools. When the media cites the increase in actual tax dollars collected from the lower tax brackets, they fail to explain the proportionate share of taxes paid by those in the higher and lower tax brackets. This little misdirection fails to reveal a few key facts: that the top 10% of taxpayers pay almost 71% of the all taxes collected while the bottom 50% of taxpayers pay less than 3% of the total taxes.

Stimulating the economy with more spending, tax rebates, or targeted tax cuts have little long-term benefit and limited short-term value. These short-term programs only misallocate resources. Setting the foundation for real economic growth comes from long-term policies focused on providing incentives for risk takers. Our country has been fortunate to be able to claim that each generation of Americans has been better off than their parents. This achievement did not come from attacking the wealthy, trying to push them down. It came from providing incentives to raise the wages of those in the lower- and middle-income brackets. As President John F. Kennedy so eloquently said, "A rising tide lifts all boats."

Successful tax cuts target those taxes having the most impact on restraining incentives, which are the marginal rates. The marginal tax rate is the tax you pay on the next dollar you earn. Reducing marginal rates increases your reward for working, for saving, and for risk-taking. By extension, higher rewards lead to more effort and more economic activity because an individual is able to keep the fruits of his labor, passing it on to his children and grandchildren. The wit and wisdom of President Reagan was never more powerful as when he noted, "The problem is not that people are taxed too little, the problem is that government spends too much."

A WALK DOWN MEMORY LANE

Are you still skeptical? Perhaps it is time to play a game. *Jeopardy!* is one of the longest running quiz shows in history. The game show format presents both current and historical information on a variety of topics. Except for a brief five-year period, it has been on the air continuously since its debut in 1964. The contestants are presented with answers to which they must respond with the question that would give that answer. In keeping with that practice, let's play *Jeopardy!*

THE ANSWER IS: Warren G. Harding, Calvin Coolidge, John F. Kennedy, Ronald Reagan, and George W. Bush

THE QUESTION IS: Which Presidents dramatically cut personal income tax rates?

Now let's play *Double Jeopardy!*

THE ANSWER IS: Spurred significant economic growth, increased federal tax revenues, and resulted in the rich paying significantly larger portions of the tax burden

THE QUESTION IS: What were the results of those tax cuts?

In his enlightening article "The Historical Lessons of Lower Tax Rates," Daniel J. Mitchell of the Heritage Foundation provides some rather startling information. Largely ignored by most politicians, these facts confirm lower taxes provide incentives that spur economic growth. Spin as they may in the media, higher taxes choke growth, discourage risk-taking, and inhibit job creation.

In 1920, America was still recovering from the effects of World War I. The top income tax rates rose from 7% prior to the conflict and remained at an astounding 73% going into the election. In the first election allowing women to vote nationwide, Warren G. Harding running on a campaign to "Return to Normalcy" won. Before his untimely death two years into his Presidency, Harding passed legislation reducing taxes. Succeeded by Vice-President Calvin Coolidge and elected in his own right in 1924, "Silent Cal" championed additional legislation that ultimately reduced the top marginal tax rate to 25%.

Fueled by lower tax rates, the economy responded with significant growth. The stock market expanded by almost 60% between 1921 and 1929, which is an average of more than 6% per year. The federal coffers overflowed with the dramatic growth in tax collections that increased from $719 million to $1,160 million during the period, slightly more than 60%. For those interested, the wealthy paid a considerably larger portion of the tax burden, moving from 44% in 1921 to 78% in 1928.[10]

In 1960, John F. Kennedy became President largely due to his successful appearance in the first televised U.S. presidential debate. He spoke of personal responsibility in his inaugural address, "Ask not what your country can do for you; ask what you can do for your country." His domestic program called the "New Frontier" proposed massive increases in government spending for education, medical care, and economic aid. Advocating lower taxes, the legislation did not become law until after his assassination, reducing the top marginal tax rate from a confiscatory 91% to 70% by 1965.

Stimulated by lower tax rates, the economy grew by an inflation-adjusted 42% between 1961 and 1968, which is an average of more than 5% per year. During the period, tax collections rose from $94 billion to $153 billion, posting an increase in excess of 60%. Adjusted for inflation, the increase was 33%. With tax collections from the rich rising almost 60%, the portion of the tax burden paid by the wealthy rose from 11.6% to 15.1%.[11]

In 1980, America was experiencing an economic malaise characterized by high inflation, excessive interest rates and a double-dip recession. Termed the Reagan Revolution, President Ronald Reagan would restore American morale, promote individual freedoms, and return to the fundamental principles of the Constitution. Reelected in a landslide, the voters understood it was "Morning in America." Reagan passed two major pieces of tax legislation reducing the top marginal tax rate from

70% in 1980 to 28% by 1988. The tax cuts helped produce the longest period of peacetime economic growth in American history.

Spurred by lower taxes, the economy grew by almost 4% per year during the Reagan presidency and the stock market grew an astounding 14% per year. Tax collections dramatically increased by almost 55%. Adjusted for inflation the increase was 30%. The wealthy paid a much higher percentage of the tax burden. The portion paid by the top 10% of income earners rose from 48% in 1981 to over 57% in 1988. Even more remarkable, the increase paid by the top 1% of earners rose from 17% in 1981 to over 27% in 1988.[12]

In 2000, the market continued to suffer a significant market correction driven by the implosion of the tech bubble during the Clinton administration. The economy soon experienced a severe loss of confidence due to the widespread corruption and collapse of several high profile companies. Then, the 9/11 terrorist attacks on the World Trade Center and the Pentagon shocked the nation. The economy was in freefall. Reducing the top marginal tax rate from 39.6% to 35%, President George W. Bush also lowered the tax rates for dividends from 39.6% to 15% and cut the capital gains tax from 39.6% to 20%.

The lower taxes resurrected the bull market and fueled a robust economic expansion. The economy averaged 10% annual growth from 2002 through 2007. Tax revenues increased by almost $785 billion from 2004 to 2007, the largest four-year revenue increase in American history. As before, the wealthy paid a significantly larger portion of the tax burden. The top 10% of income earners saw their portion rise from 65% in 2001 to over 70% in 2005, and the top 1% of income earners saw their portion rise from 35% in 2001 to almost 40% in 2005.[13]

It is more than just coincidental that the tax burden paid by the wealthy dropped significantly between the years 1932 and 1963. The top marginal rates during this period rose from 25% to 91%! Such high tax rates lower the tax base because the wealthy find ways to shield their income. Seeking more revenues, the government further exasperates the problem by raising taxes still higher, resulting in the middle-income earners carrying the majority of the tax burden. Five different Presidents significantly cut the marginal income tax rates, and in each instance, the results were impressive—federal tax collections dramatically increased, the wealthy paid significantly higher percentages of those income taxes, and the markets responded with remarkable growth. That is a batting average of 1.000. How can you improve on that? Why would you even try? More to the point, why are the politicians ignoring this? Double Jeopardy indeed.

THE OBAMA ECONOMY

Running on a campaign of "Hope and Change," candidate Obama promised an administration that would govern from the middle, rejecting the partisan politics of Washington. Winning super majorities in both the House and Senate, President Obama turned sharply left and followed the big government, liberal ideology of FDR. How did the actions of the Obama administration fit into our recipe for economic growth—controlling inflation, keeping taxes low, and managing spending?

Aggressive Spending

The super majorities enabled the President to enact aggressive spending programs that will impact our economy for years to come. For instance, the $900 billion Stimulus Package was supposed to rebuild the nation's infrastructure but, in reality, the majority of the money went to state governments that used it to plug budget deficits and keep bureaucrats employed. At a press conference, President Obama laughed when he told a reporter that he guessed the shovel-ready jobs were not so shovel-ready after all.

The Patient Protection and Affordable Care Act (ObamaCare) is another example. A double-count in Medicare cuts of $500 billion increased the 10-year estimated cost of ObamaCare to $1.4 trillion! Further analysis of the 2,700 pages showed still greater costs and economic burdens hidden within the legislation. The Congressional Budget Office (CBO) now projects the 10-year cost to be $1.9 trillion, far greater than the original estimates of $940 billion. It was Nancy Pelosi, then Speaker of the House, who told the representatives that they needed to pass the bill before finding out what's in the bill, and that is exactly what the House did—without a single Republican vote.

Affordable healthcare is not going to be as affordable as the President actively promoted.

Changing the rules of the Bush Troubled Asset Relief Program (TARP) legislation, the Obama administration reneged on paying down the nation's debt from the funds paid back by the original recipients. In addition, he expanded the bailouts beyond financial institutions to include General Motors and Chrysler, effectively making the federal government the owner of private sector corporations, a dangerous precedent and one that did not improve the economy overall. Further exasperating the situation, Chrysler was sold to the Italian automaker Fiat after the government bailout.

Acting quickly to pass many costly programs through his veto-proof Congress, the President secured significantly larger spending levels for future federal budgets. The baseline budgeting approach[14], enacted in 1974, automatically increases current Congressional budgets about 6% each year. Baseline budgeting allows federal spending to double every 12 years!

A real life example puts this into perspective. When the CBO scores proposed legislation, it uses baseline growth percentages as part of the analysis. Thus, if Congress had held spending flat at existing levels, the CBO scoring would have resulted in a reported budget cut of $9 trillion over 10 years, but in fact, not a single dime will be eliminated. This slight-of-hand accounting only shows a reduction in the *rate* of growth. It would be beneficial for investigative reporters to challenge those claims of Draconian cuts in spending!

Debt Financing

With a deepening recession and rising unemployment, tax revenues shrunk putting pressure on the government to fund not only their new expansive spending programs but also the many government entitlement programs already in place. The administration turned to debt financing, thus raising U.S. debt to historically high percentages of the GDP. The growing size of foreign-held debt, the expanding federal budget, and the shrinking economy raise very serious questions about our fiscal policies and future performance.

The consequences of Federal Reserve actions are also uncertain. When the quantitative easing (QE) policy to inject $1.5 trillion to get the economy moving didn't work, the Fed launched a second round of monetary easing totaling $600 billion, known as QE2. The result was a weakened dollar. While this may help U.S. exports in the short run, the longer-term effect makes both domestic and foreign investments less attractive, which hurts the recovery. With interest rates low, much of this new money went into the stock market, driving prices higher. This artificial increase in stock prices creates a bubble that can implode when the money runs out, causing a market sell-off. Flooding the system with money can also lead to inflation. As the dollar drops in value, crude materials prices increase, leading to higher producer prices, thus igniting inflationary pressures on consumer prices.

Over-Legislation and Excessive Regulation

Adding many new regulations to the massive spending initiatives has created a toxic environment of uncertainty, crippling the economic recovery, ensuring higher costs and fewer jobs in the private sector. The growing cost of energy had little to do with the Middle East turmoil and much more to do with government actions. Restrictions on drilling in the Gulf of Mexico and banning domestic drilling in Anwar and on other federal lands reduced the supply of energy, driving prices higher. Continuing to pursue such restrictive policies, the Administration also cancelled the Keystone Pipeline. Since President Obama took office, the price of a gallon of gasoline has doubled.

Establishing a carbon ceiling on businesses is both unnecessary and dangerous. The entire economy depends on oil and other fossil fuels; enacting artificial limits creates misallocations of resources, higher prices, and competitive hurdles in a global economy. In an interview, President Obama pointed out that under his plan electricity rates would skyrocket because power plants will have to retrofit their operations or shutdown. Unable to pass the Cap and Trade bill he wanted, President Obama empowered the Environmental Protection Agency (EPA) to implement his programs without Congressional approval. This is not the only example of government interference in a free market economy.

Another was the enactment of the Dodd-Frank Consumer Protection Act, granting the government unrestrained power over the financial market. The federal government can take over ailing banks, regulate activities, and even set pricing for financial services. This legislation institutionalizes the concept of "too big to fail." This new federal power froze activity in the banking industry.

A particularly alarming scenario was The National Labor Relations Board (NLRB) lawsuit against Boeing. The NLRB wanted to stop the company from moving its plant to South Carolina and force it to build a plant in Washington State. In effect, the administration did not want Boeing to create jobs in a "right-to-work" state.[15] Also alarming was the appointment of Jeffrey Immelt, CEO of General Electric, to Chair the President's Council on Jobs and Competitiveness, which, among other goals, was "to create jobs, opportunity, and prosperity for the American people."[16] Immelt's management of GE does not support the goals of this Council. General Electric plans to invest over $2.0 billion in China, move the headquarters of its X-Ray business from Wisconsin to China and has entered into a joint venture with China to develop aircraft technology in direct competition with American companies. What kind of economy will result from a federal agency bringing suit against an American company creating American jobs while another American company enters into a joint venture creating jobs overseas, competing with American firms, and providing sensitive technology to another country?

With the enactment of ObamaCare, the healthcare industry faces major adjustments with even greater economic consequences. The law mandates that businesses must provide employees with coverage that is more generous and more costly, effectively forcing businesses to either drop coverage entirely, pushing their employees into the government-sponsored insurance exchanges, or absorbing higher costs that will be passed on to the consumer. As employer-sponsored programs shrink out of existence due to rising costs, individual non-group premiums will increase so significantly that private health insurance carriers will probably cease to exist. The most likely result will be a two-tier healthcare system—one provided by the government and one provided to those able to pay for the services themselves.

Irrefutable proof of the dangers inherent with this law is that almost 1,500 companies and labor unions have received waivers from the government to delay implementation of this legislation because it is costly and onerous. Many believe the waivers were granted to avoid public outcry against the President's plan before the next election, but the point here is that government intrusion on a free market economy is inflicting significant harm to a struggling recovery and potentially causing irreparable damage to the private sector.

Taxing Schemes

Despite running on a campaign to cut taxes, President Obama continues to focus his efforts on raising taxes on successful Americans. His agenda is to raise taxes on the wealthy to address the nation's debt problem. Although citing only "billionaires and millionaires" in his speeches, the President always includes "thousandaires" in his tax plans. Often recalling the federal budget surpluses of the Clinton years, President Obama suggests the higher tax rates of that period generated those surpluses. What he fails to cite is the fact that spending levels during the Clinton years were $1.5 trillion per year compared to the current $3.5 trillion per year—almost 60% below President Obama's.

While the administration heavily promotes tax incentive plans, many do more harm than good. For instance, the famous "Cash for Clunkers" or its offspring "Cash for Appliances" did little to jump-start the economy. Deemed successful because the funds ran out, the lack of sales in succeeding months suggested the program was not as successful as noted. These short-term tax incentives did not generate new buyers; they merely induced existing buyers to purchase sooner. The net result: taxpayers funding car purchases for individuals who were going to purchase anyway.

Other programs such as tax incentives for hiring new employees, and the so-called payroll tax holiday not only wasted resources, but have not led to positive results. The primary problem with the new hire program was the assumption that businesses had a need to hire. No business arbitrarily hires additional staff without commensurate increases in sales volume. The payroll tax holiday was not only ineffective, it was misleading. It promised to lower taxes on 95% of all Americans, but that is not the entire story. Because of high unemployment and the prolonged economic downturn, the Social Security system collected less revenue than it paid out in benefits during 2010. That was the first time more was paid out than collected. Nevertheless, the President's payroll tax holiday stopped collection of the sole funding source to Social Security. It was not a tax cut, but a future increase in taxes on working families or a future reduction of benefits to the elderly or both.

The Impact of President Obama's Policies on the Economy

Let's look at the unemployment numbers. The unemployment rate dropped to 8.3% in January 2012. The administration, along with the media, presented this news with much fanfare, suggesting the economy was turning the corner and the economy was on the mend. The unfortunate truth is the unemployment rate has exceeded 8% since February 2009, which is the longest running period of high unemployment since the Great Depression. Of more concern, the CBO projects unemployment to remain above 8% through 2014.

Taking a closer look at the numbers provides valuable insight. The term "the labor force participation rate" may be unfamiliar, but it is very important. It represents the percentage of the civilian non-institutional population, age 16 or older, employed or actively seeking employment. This rate is a derived number based on a variety of sources such as cyclical, demographic, and cultural factors, some of which may be subjective. The rate adjusts the total *qualified* labor force into the total *available* labor force that is "participating" in the economy as previously defined. If the *participation rate* increases, more jobs would be required to hold the unemployment rate constant. Conversely, should the participation rate fall, fewer jobs are necessary to maintain the same unemployment rate.

This is how it works. Assume there are 150 individuals qualified to enter the labor force. For whatever reason, only 100 are *available* to work, so the *participation rate* is 66.7%. Further, assume that 90 of the 100 get jobs and 10 remain unemployed. The result is an unemployment rate of 10% (10 unemployed individuals divided by 100 people available to work). What happens if the labor *participation rate* drops to 64%? Those same 150 individuals *qualified* to enter the labor force now decrease to only 96 (not 100) *available* to work. Since the same 90 people remain employed, the new unemployed number is not 10, but only six, which results in an unemployment rate of 6.3% (six unemployed individuals divided by 96 people available to work). What is reality? The unemployment rate fell, but no increase in jobs occurred and no increase in employment took place.

Add another element: the U.S. population grows at a pace of about 1% per year. The economy needs to create approximately 100,000 jobs per month just to maintain a steady unemployment rate. For this statement to be accurate however, the labor force *participation rate* must remain unchanged. As demonstrated, even a small movement in participation has a significant impact on the reported unemployment rate.

To put this information into perspective, the average unemployment rate was 5.3% during the Bush years with an average *participation rate* of 66.2%. Democrats as well as the media attacked Bush for this weak performance and called it an economy in recession heading for a depression.

Through three years of the Obama Presidency, the average unemployment rate was 9.3% with an average *participation rate* of 64.7%. The January 2012 unemployment rate of 8.3% was accomplished with a *participation rate* of only 63.7%, a rate not seen since 1979 when President Carter was in office. The decline in the participation rate under the Obama administration was the largest drop since the end of World War II.

Let's look a little deeper at the January 2012 numbers for a more realistic assessment of the direction of the economy. Since Obama assumed office, the number of unemployed individuals has increased by 3.8 million. During this same period, the number of individuals *available* for employment has not changed. Despite population growth during that period, the numbers show that no additional individuals entered the labor force. Applying the average *participation rate* of 66% experienced since President Carter (and the participation rate in the last year of the Bush Presidency), another 5.5 million individuals need to be added to the 3.8 million unemployed. Thus, the change in unemployment during the Obama administration is more likely 9.3 million, which equates to an unemployment rate of 11.4%.

Perhaps the most devastating statement about the effectiveness of his policies came when Standard & Poor's (S&P) lowered its rating for U.S. credit. The humiliation of the U.S. credit downgrade rests squarely on the shoulders of the Obama administration. President Obama has fostered uncertainty in the marketplace and fear in the mind of the consumer.

After three years of his Presidency, the Obama legislative initiatives have led to an economic malaise evidenced by non-existent GDP growth, consistently high unemployment, a financial industry in disarray, continuing declines in manufacturing, a housing market in distress, and rising inflation. His unprecedented spending increased the national debt by $4.3 trillion in a little more than two years, which is an average increase of almost $2.0 trillion per year and more than three times the average annual amount spent by his predecessor, whom he blames for the economic woes. In any given speech, President Obama blames the economic crisis on President George Bush, the Congress, the Republicans, the banking industry, the business community, the tsunami that hit Japan, the Arab Spring, the economic problems in Europe, the Tea Party, and even bad luck.

Our recipe for economic growth focuses on controlling inflation, keeping taxes low, and managing spending. A recent *Wall Street Journal* article written by Stephen Moore reminded us of the wise counsel of noted economist Milton Friedman. Friedman explained that higher taxes never reduce deficits. Moore recalled another conversation in which he asked how America could become more prosperous. Friedman's immediate response: reduce government spending. When Moore followed up by asking how much would need to be cut, Friedman replied, "As much as possible."[17] The policies of the Obama administration suggest that the economy is a zero-sum game where the wealthy have taken a disproportionately larger piece of the pie. Our recipe for economic growth suggests building a bigger pie that will increase the share for all.

PUT YOUR FAITH IN THE FREE MARKET

One of the most important facets of a free economy is powerful cyclical trends. Those on the left view this as a core problem. During bull markets, they cite profit-hungry businesses as evil, and during bear markets, they allude to the inadequacies of the free market system. The left believes the government can do a better job. Individuals on the right look at the cyclical nature of the markets as an opportunity for new ideas, new technologies, and a rebirth of the economy. The market is free to adjust to the changing needs of the consumer who is far better equipped to spend his or her own hard-earned money than the government.

Neither government nor business is perfect. Each has a role; each must not stray into the other's territory. For instance, the unintended consequence of the rise of special interest groups has been a growing number of Americans seeking to improve themselves or their families at the expense of other Americans. Government support is helpful, but the government ought to focus on the safety net concept, encourage self-sufficiency, help the unemployed reenter the workforce, and raise the standard of living for all Americans. The measure of success is not how many people the government helps, but how many people the government puts back to work.

The private sector is not without warts. Consider the recent bailout of Wall Street when financial institutions deemed "too big to fail" received billions of taxpayer dollars, thus avoiding bankruptcy. Turning the basic risk/reward concept on its head, certain organizations incurring substantial losses did not suffer any ramifications for their missteps. The government chose the winners and losers rather than allowing the market to correct itself. This is reminiscent of the old Hollywood movie *Here Comes Mr. Jordan* where an angel removes the spirit of a pilot before the plane crashes only to find out that the pilot was not to die for another 50 years. In other words, he would have avoided the crash if given the opportunity.[18]

The real strength of capitalism lies in the entrepreneurs, the start-up ventures, and the many businesses on the streets of cities, towns, and villages across the country. These businesses are neither big nor influential but immensely powerful in generating the fuel to grow the economy. The owners unknowingly teach the rewards of hard work, customer satisfaction, and wealth creation. These businesses are the engine that employs our workers, sells our goods, expands our facilities, and ultimately drives our economy. The role of government is to provide a level playing field ensuring all businesses have an equal opportunity either to succeed or to fail. The role of government, however, is not to provide equality of outcomes and thus pick the winners and losers.

What makes America different from every other nation in the world? In less than 300 years, America has achieved a level of prosperity far exceeding any other nation in history. When speaking of American exceptionalism, it is not an ego thing. After all, Americans are no better or no worse than any other people of the world. Exceptionalism relates to America being the only member of the world community founded on a set of principles that give individuals the right to "life, liberty, and the pursuit of happiness." It is the free market system, wealth creation principles, individual freedoms, the right to own private property, the rule of law, and most importantly the limited role of government that has spurred the people of this country to overachieve and to continue building on its successes. Ordinary people achieving extraordinary results.

This concept of exceptionalism traces back to our founding. The Framers of the Constitution understood the self-destructive nature of Democracies ruled by a majority, primarily concerned with "group wants." Winston Churchill once noted, "The best argument against democracy is a five minute conversation with the average voter." Rather than the ruling majority dictating to the minority, the Constitution established a Republic ruled by laws and by a representative government recognizing the inalienable rights of individuals. The Founding Fathers created a process in which the various factions would negotiate their differences. While still allowing the majority to rule, the minority has an opportunity to voice concerns and objections. The Constitution provides the *framework for a limited government*, encouraging cooperation among different factions for the greater good of the nation.

In *The American Revolution*, author Gordon Wood points out that Thomas Jefferson was one of the first to warn us about the concept of dependence in his *Notes on the State of Virginia*, written in 1781. Jefferson wrote, "Dependence begets subservience and venality, suffocates the germ of virtue, and prepares fit tools for the designs of ambition."[19]

Almost 40 years later in the 1819 Supreme Court decision *McCulloch v. Maryland*, Chief Justice John Marshall echoed a similar thought, directing his comments directly at the government when he wrote, "The power to tax is the power to destroy."

A little over 150 years later, President Ronald Reagan updated these thoughts when he cautioned the American public, "A government big enough to give you everything you want is a government big enough to take everything you've got."

We must learn from history. Economics tells us there are no right or wrong answers, only choices. Politics tells us campaign speeches inspire, past actions inform. Life tells us nothing is free, but the cost is often hidden. In the end, we must take responsibility for the choices we make and we must own the consequences of those decisions.

PART THREE

Restoring the Promise of a Better Future

CHAPTER FIFTEEN

Financial Security for Everyone

The future ain't what it used to be.
Yogi Berra

WHAT PRESIDENTS DO really does matter. In the first year of his administration, President Obama faced a financial crisis. He chose to ignore the past economic successes of Presidents Warren G. Harding, Calvin Coolidge, John F. Kennedy, Ronald Reagan, and George W. Bush. Rather than initiating their proven policies of tax cuts and strengthening the dollar, President Obama followed the failed economic policies of FDR and the federal government spent at unsustainable levels, grew debt to unprecedented amounts, and took control of significant portions of the U.S. economy.

Intervention in the private sector led to non-existent GDP growth, high unemployment, and the first ever downgrade of U.S. debt. An inherent strength of the free market system has been its cyclical swings that reinvigorate the marketplace, encouraging technological innovations, productivity advancements, new products, and new businesses. But the path chosen by the President created an anemic recovery. Our economy is neither strong nor robust and void of significant job creation. His responses to the economic crises were similar to that of the FDR Administration, which led to a second depression following on the heels of the Great Depression. His policies of increasing taxes, creating new taxing schemes, and promoting greater regulatory intrusions have led to great uncertainty regarding the economy.

This is one history lesson all Americans would much rather read about in history books than experience in real life. The enactment of Social Security during the FDR administration is eerily similar to the current takeover of the healthcare system. The rhetoric of today's political leaders is reminiscent of those bygone days. History has a nasty way of repeating itself.

UNDERSTANDING ECONOMIC REALITIES

Most political leaders fearing for their political survival, avoid the issue of Social Security insolvency. When a new study indicates the gravity of the problem, they suggest the system can be made financially sound by simply tweaking the program, which is political-speak for increasing taxes and/or reducing benefits.

Social Security requires immediate attention. Despite what the media may say and how the political parties posture their arguments, Social Security almost certainly will look quite different in the future. The question is whether the new look will improve the system, its beneficiaries, and the economy. Change takes courage and requires leadership that seeks innovative, creative new solutions for the future.

The Origins of Social Security

Highlighting key points from *FDR's Folly*, Powell provides a glimpse into the political positioning of this program. The amount of misleading information concerning the Social Security system is astonishing. When Social Security was first proposed, President Franklin D. Roosevelt started this misdirection by misrepresenting it as a legitimate insurance program. He said,

> Get these facts straight, the act provides for two kinds of insurance for the worker. For that insurance both the employer and the worker pay premiums—just as you pay premiums on any other insurance policy. Those premiums are collected in the form of taxes. The first kind of insurance covers old age. Here the employer contributes one dollar in premium for every one dollar of premium contributed by the worker; but both dollars are held by the government solely for the benefit of the worker in his old age.[1]

Social Security is not insurance. The so-called premiums are not based on expected life spans, health considerations, or other risk factors typical of actual insurance policies. More importantly, insurance companies accumulate premiums in investment accounts to build up sufficient funds to pay off future claims when necessary.

The current concept of social insurance began in the 1880s under German Chancellor Otto von Bismarck. Initially begun as an inducement to reduce the outflow of workers to America, his program was the genesis of the European welfare state. Unable to compete with higher wages offered in America, European countries offered government-run welfare programs such as old age pensions and unemployment insurance. With the huge influx of European immigrants, it was not surprising that they called for similar welfare programs in the United States.

In the late nineteenth and early twentieth centuries, America was transforming from an agricultural to an industrial economy. Harnessing the power of electricity, building an efficient transportation system, and improving production processes led to a nation of opportunities for risk-takers and entrepreneurs. The nation experienced the power of economic expansion, the improvement in the standard of living, the creation of wealth, and the building of individual fortunes. Despite the devastation of World War I, our geographical location enabled America to prosper. America was not only the banker to the free world but also a safe haven for worldwide investment.

The ravages of the Great Depression changed the mood of the country. With companies closing their doors, jobs being lost, and families losing their savings, the appetite for government-run Social Security programs grew. By the mid 1930s, as the effects of the Depression deepened, more than half the states had enacted state-run pension plans. Inevitably, the federal government soon began to deliberate the merits of such programs. Whether a compassionate gesture for the financial security of the American people or a clever political maneuver to secure power is uncertain, but FDR recognized the potential rewards to his administration and fought tenaciously to control the outcome. Stoking the fears of privately-run pension plans, he stressed the safety of a government-run insurance program. FDR understood the political benefits of expanding the coffers of the federal government and adding another key voting block for future campaigns.

Folsom's *New Deal or Raw Deal* exposes many forgotten truths about this legislation. With the success of private pension plans and the growth of group life insurance, Senator Bennett Champ Clark of Missouri proposed an amendment allowing employers to opt out of Social Security. His proposal would require employers to match the benefits of the government plan and ensure that their costs would be no higher than the government plan. Furthermore, the plan required the placement of employee payments with an approved third party, such as an insurance company. The amendment gave the employee the right to choose either the government-run program or the private alternative. After heated debate, the Democrats, who controlled two-thirds of the Senate, passed the amendment by a vote of 51 to 35. Vehemently opposed to the Clark Amendment, FDR feared the people would select the private option thereby lessening the government's influence on the voting public. Using parliamentary tactics, FDR's supporters in the House passed their version of the bill without adding the amendment. The House-Senate conference committee ultimately submitted the bill to the President without the Clark Amendment, promising to appoint a special joint legislative committee to study the amendment. The special committee never convened and the Clark Amendment died in obscurity.[2]

Despite public pronouncements and political rhetoric touting it as an insurance program to protect Americans, when the constitutionality of Social Security was challenged in the judicial system the government reversed itself, claiming Social Security was nothing more than a tax. In *Helvering v. Davis* (1937)[3], the Supreme Court heard the government argue that Social Security was not a contributory insurance program but a tax collected for the general welfare of the public. The Supreme Court upheld the government argument and further stated in their opinion that the spending of these taxes was at the discretion of Congress.

Perhaps the most disheartening comment concerning the dubious beginnings of the Social Security system came from FDR himself. When asked about the economic problems with Social Security, he responded by saying that the questioner was correct about the economics. However, FDR went on to point out that those taxes were strictly politics and that no politician would ever be able to shutdown the Social Security program because it would lead to a political firestorm.[4]

Unintended consequences had very little to do with the results of this legislation. Perhaps our politicians were not listening, maybe they did not care, or quite possibly, it was just politics. Whatever the reason, the New Dealers knew exactly what they were doing. They knew what the impact was, and they knew what the impact would be on future generations.

Your Investment Return from Social Security

Do you ever look at "Your Social Security Statement?" The Social Security Administration mails this document to you annually, and it recaps your lifetime earnings record as well as your estimated benefits.

A recent review of a Social Security Statement indicated the contributions of an employee and those of her employer totaled $200,000. Adjusting for inflation, the real Social Security taxes were $365,000. The report also indicated that if her contributions continued at the current projected rate and if she retired at age 66, her estimated annual inflation-adjusted benefit would be $26,868—contingent, of course, on payment of another $250,000 (inflation adjusted) into the system.

A simple mathematical computation indicates that it will take almost 24 years to recoup the combined Social Security payments (divide the expected annual payment by the total inflation-adjusted contributions). In other words, she will have recovered all of the funds when she is almost 90 years of age. Of course, we all hope to live to 100, but the actuarial tables predict she will fall short of recouping her investment by seven years. Accordingly, the expected real return on her Social Security contributions is negative. Furthermore, her contributions were taxed before she paid into the system and a percentage of the benefits may be taxed when received from the system. Thus, the real after-tax expected return would be even more negative.

Unlike real insurance, no Social Security payment is distributed to a beneficiary upon her death. Instead, her spouse is allowed to receive either her Social Security benefit payment or his Social Security benefit payment, but not both. In other words, the government allows only one payment even if your spouse contributed and otherwise qualified for Social Security benefits. What was that about insurance? It sounds more like the casinos in Las Vegas where the house always wins. Look carefully at your own statement.

To make matters worse, the Social Security Statement clearly states the benefits reflect current law. Do you believe the current law is not going to change? Do you believe that if the current law does change it will be more favorable to you? Yes, that is correct; the expected return will deteriorate still further. In bold print, the statement warns "… by 2037, the payroll taxes collected will be enough to pay only about 76% of scheduled benefits." What is happening?

After learning what she may expect to receive from Social Security, she was curious about what she had given up for this so-called security blanket. Unfortunately, it only gets worse, much worse. Using the same projected contributions as in the Social Security calculations, had she placed these funds into her own retirement account following the most conservative investment program described in Part I of this book, her account would have grown to a little over $2 million as she entered retirement at age 67. She would be able to receive an annual inflation-adjusted benefit of $131,000 and retain a balance of $2.4 million at age 85. In fact, she would be able to remove that amount annually and live to 100 without running out of her savings! If she followed the life cycle investment program from Part I in its entirety, she would generate still larger returns.

Losing over $100,000 annually is a crime perpetrated by our own government. To make matters worse, the unused Social Security benefits do not pass to her heirs. Her remaining balance under the investment program would be over $2.4 million at the age of 85! This is a huge loss to her family, but an even greater one to society. One can only imagine the many opportunities lost.

The Political Positioning of Social Security

Our political leaders along with a willing media continue to perpetuate the concept of a Social Security lockbox and a Social Security trust fund. Such outrageous falsehoods are very dangerous. If you do not understand what is happening, little constructive discussion can follow. Do not be fooled into thinking the Social Security system has the protection of a trust fund. It does not. At least not in the way you think it is or in the way politicians suggest.

The lockbox is nothing more than a symbolic concept implying the government can place money in a vault today in order to pay Social Security benefits later. The trust fund is nothing more than IOUs the government has issued to itself. This is critical to understanding reality. Any Social Security surplus flows directly into the Treasury just like any other tax. In return for using these funds, the Treasury prints Social Security IOUs, or special-issue Treasury securities, for both the cash money portion and the interest that would have been earned had the funds actually been held in a trust fund.

This may sound good, but it is irresponsible to suggest any physical money has been set aside for the future payment of Social Security benefits. When these funds are required, someone will go to that lockbox, open it up, and find only IOUs!

Skeptics often ask why government bonds are good assets in a private pension fund or in an individual retirement account but not when held in the Social Security trust fund. The reason is bonds issued to intra-government accounts are not claims on additional resources. When individuals buy a government bond, they establish a financial claim against the government. When the government issues an IOU to itself, it has neither acquired anything nor created a claim against another person or entity. The truth is the trust fund holds zero financial resources to pay future benefits. The IOUs have no real economic benefit. Instead, the IOUs provide the authority to the Treasury Department to use whatever money it has on hand to pay them. Where do you think the money will come from to redeem these IOUs?

To help clarify, suppose you save a few dollars each week in a cookie jar to buy a new big-screen television. Your spouse, unknown to you, takes the dollars from that cookie jar each week to buy groceries, replacing the money with IOUs. When it comes time to purchase that television, your cookie jar contains only IOUs. Having access to the cookie jar enabled the family to spend money that was being saved for the future. "Extra cash" appeared to be available because there was money in that cookie jar—that is until the money was replaced with IOUs. This is no different from the way government has been spending your excess

Social Security payments. When you finally went to the cookie jar to retrieve the money, you found only IOUs. You saved money for a future benefit only to find that other members of your family used the money for something else. The government has been doing exactly the same thing. The family can chose to save the money again (similar to raising taxes), delay the purchase (similar to increasing the retirement age), buy a cheaper television (similar to reducing benefits), or some combination of the choices. Just like the government, your family did not acquire additional funds. Instead, they merely took the savings from one pocket to fund another, which also happens to be what the government is doing.

Politicians like to imply government pension programs, such as Social Security, are no different from private annuity companies. The facts paint a very different picture. Private annuity companies create wealth by investing the premiums they collect. These investments take many forms—homes, factories, businesses, or other tangible assets—providing the necessary revenue to pay the future pensions to the individuals paying those premiums. The government pensions, however, spend the premiums as soon as they are collected. They spend some of the premiums on the pensions for current retirees, but any remaining funds go into the general fund as current tax collections.

If this program sounds familiar, it is because it is similar to a giant Ponzi scheme. The U.S. Securities and Exchange Commission website provides the classic definition …

> A Ponzi scheme is an investment fraud that involves the payment of purported returns to existing investors from funds contributed by new investors…. With little or no legitimate earnings, the schemes require a consistent flow of money from new investors to continue. Ponzi schemes tend to collapse when it becomes difficult to recruit new investors or when a large number of investors ask to cash out.[5]

Social Security is a pay-as-you-go system. Money collected today from currently employed individuals (i.e., new investors) is distributed to those elderly individuals qualified under the program (i.e., existing investors). Bernie Madoff went to prison for running a similar program.[6]

First, the government positioned Social Security as an insurance program to gain public support and Congressional approval. Next, the government argued Social Security was a tax for the general welfare of the public to secure judicial approval from the Supreme Court. Now, the government views Social Security as an entitlement program where it determines what is appropriate, who is entitled, and when it is to be distributed. Despite our contributions and those of our employers, the American public has no legal right to the Social Security funds because the Supreme Court ruled those collections to be a tax. Seizing control of our funds, the government maintains sole authority over its use. Particularly off-putting is the government promoting itself as visionary, compassionate, and righteous.

GOVERNMENT IS NOT THE ANSWER

Okay, now you recognize the government control of the Social Security system is neither beneficial nor sustainable. Something must change, but what? Most of the suggestions to date focus on temporary fixes thus necessitating continual intervention. With the government wanting to control this large voting block, it concentrates on peripheral issues such as raising taxes or reducing benefits rather than addressing the core problem. Tinkering with the inputs or outputs cannot fix the inherent design flaws in the system. The core problem is the pay-as-you-go system itself.

Designed to Implode

With the arrival of the "baby boom" generation and the strong post-World War II economy, the expanding workforce and growing salaries provided higher and higher collections of Social Security premiums. The larger inflows of money not only fulfilled the promises made to those original retirees of the Depression-era 1930s, but encouraged politicians to increase benefits. Those politicians who supported the increases also enjoyed obvious political benefits.

Often overlooked and perhaps even ignored were those collections *not* paid out in benefits. Neither deposited into trust funds nor secured in a lockbox, the government used the excess funds to pay current expenditures or pay down existing debt. In exchange for the use of the Social Security funds, they placed IOUs in those so-called trust fund accounts and often-hyped secure lockboxes. Rather than providing good stewardship for the money given them to secure our future, the government continued to squander the excess funds on new initiatives, new programs, new entitlements, new earmarks, and new pay-offs.

Over time however, two significant changes occurred. The first was declining birthrates and the second was increasing life expectancies. The first change reduced the number of current workers paying premiums into the system while the second change increased the number of retired workers collecting benefits. Thus, the ratio of collections to payouts began to decrease substantially. The pay-as-you-go scheme began collapsing on itself, which is the way all Ponzi schemes implode. The economic downturn and high unemployment exacerbated the problems, hastening the call for action. To paraphrase Margaret Thatcher, the problem with Social Security is that you eventually run out of other people's money.

Even Today Misinformation Abounds

It seems Senator Clark was correct back in 1935. Too bad nobody listened. Private pension programs allow each individual participant to create his or her own wealth that pays the pension sometime in the future, whereas government-run programs simply transfer the responsibility of paying retired workers to the next generation. The Social Security website[7] analyzes the problems with the Clark Amendment. Those comments are misleading if not a bit disingenuous even today.

- The problem of *Adverse Selection* implies the best risks would leave the system. This is nonsense. Social Security is not, and never was, an insurance program. It is a pay-as-you-go scheme. The premiums coming in today are also going out today. The collections either pay benefits to retirees or pay for new and/ or existing federal programs. The concept of risk is a total fabrication.
- The problem of *Portability* implies when you leave your employer, your pension remains with your employer. This is

typical government misdirection. While it is true that some corporate plans do not allow departing employees to remove their funds, these traditional pension accounts provide for vesting and hold the funds until retirement age at which time distribution begins to the former employee or his beneficiaries. The government wants you to focus on portability rather than ownership of your own money.

- The problem of *Universality* suggests eligibility rules would not be the same for everyone. This is the epitome of arrogance. For example, the government taxes benefits paid to wealthier recipients. If the benefits are supposed to be universally the same, why does the government elect to ignore this concept?

- The problem of *Moral Hazard* implies companies may design phony pension schemes to avoid paying Social Security taxes. The government-run Ponzi scheme, on the other hand, avoids paying the beneficiary any money from the "so-called" Social Security insurance program, the magnitude of which dwarfs any private sector malfeasance. In the private sector, company executives go to prison for managing funds in such a fraudulent manner. In the government, politicians become heroes for spending these funds on unrelated programs.

The real question is why does the federal government not want the private sector involved? Perhaps German Chancellor Bismarck was correct when he said that a population is far more content, and far more dependent, when the government controls their pensions.

Proposals to Fix the System

When you browse the Social Security website, you find a list of the "*Provisions That Could Change the Social Security Program.*" The Social Security Office analyzes the provisions and the impact each would have on the system. This is sort of like asking an IRS agent whether you can deduct something from your tax return.

For those who may think this is an exaggeration of the truth, consider that of all the individual proposals cited on the website, 92% involve the *reduction of your benefits or an increase to your taxes*. The reductions in your benefits may be the result of reductions in the cost-of-living adjustments, the actual monthly benefits, or increases in the retirement age. Tax increases may be the result of an increase in the payroll tax rates, increases to the taxable earnings base, taxing the benefits received, eliminating deductions from the taxable base, or increasing the coverage to new groups.[8]

Of the remaining 8%, the Social Security Administration suggests investing a portion of the collected funds in equities, but ownership remains with the government. This is definitely a no-no. Despite the recent government takeover of GM, Chrysler and other targeted industries, the federal government must not take ownership positions in any private sector company. Government intervention created this very dilemma. Another proposal would allow portions of your payments to be designated for accounts linked directly to you. The proposal suggests that if this were to happen, your benefits would be somewhat reduced. Really?[9]

Politicians are concerned primarily with holding onto power by controlling our retirement funds. They propose solutions having a negative impact on the very recipients they claim to be helping. These so-called solutions are even more suspect given the Social Security system is nothing more than a Ponzi scheme. To perpetuate such a fraud is both immoral and dishonest because the system is doomed to fail. The funds eventually will run out; it is only a matter of time.

Potential solutions need to be market-based, promoting financial stability to the individual and fiscal responsibility to the government. In so doing, the solutions would encourage market growth and less government intervention—definitely a win-win.

A FREE MARKET SOLUTION BENEFITS ALL

Flawed at the outset, the Social Security system was a politically motivated initiative. Predicated on tax collections, the system guaranteed a process fraught with fiscal irresponsibility, fear mongering, and political shenanigans. FDR viewed retirees as a voting block rather than friends and neighbors. Through the years, the continuous flow of excess tax collections allowed our politicians to create new and growing entitlement programs. Spending the excess contributions as fast as collected, they rewarded key voting blocks. As with most schemes however, the perpetrators falsely assumed the ruse would last forever, or at least until they were long gone from the political scene. Shrinking collections, expanding payments, and a slumping economy exposed the ploy for what it is.

Resolving the problems with the Social Security system requires redefining the underlying relationships. The government, for instance, would no longer determine the benefits, collect the payments, and control the disposition of excess collections. Most reasonable individuals would consider such unchecked autonomy as a conflict of interest, but today we know it as the Social Security system. While the goal of individual financial security remains unchanged, the structure must evolve into a process where the participants work together. The solution is not to privatize Social Security; the solution is to optimize the system for the greater good of all Americans.

Privatization implies a focus on the individual account holder, often to the detriment of other participants. As a result, other participants influence public opinion through a campaign of fear. Common attacks include the investment capabilities of the public, the uncertainty of investment returns, the volatility of the market, the risk of losing your life savings, and the lack of any guarantees. Other negative messages certainly exist, but they are equally void of the truth.

Optimization, on the other hand, seeks to improve the process by providing incentives to all participants. For instance, how can the system maintain individual benefits while driving down costs? How can the system provide individual ownership without adversely affecting government inflows? How can the system reduce long-term government obligations without harming the economy? These are only a few of the issues needing resolution.

Under the existing system, what happens when the government can no longer raise taxes? The qualifying age for receiving benefits moves higher and higher while the benefits you earn move lower and lower. A self-sustaining program would promote financial security for the public, encourage economic stability in the private sector, and restore fiscal responsibility to the government. The following program suggests a better way. A way in which working together can lead all of us to a more secure future. Put your faith in the free market, not in the political establishment.

General Provisions

The benefits from individual ownership largely depend on the duration of the holding period and the diversification of the portfolio holdings. The most important is time. To that end, ultimate success would be dependent on changing over rapidly to individual ownership, thereby allowing the magic of compounding to grow your retirement portfolio. Accordingly, rather than giving individuals the choice of retaining the current defective scheme or moving to a self-sustaining program, the Social Security system would change in its entirety. It would require a transition period during which current retirees as well as older individuals in the workforce would be protected. These individuals do not have sufficient time to build a sizeable portfolio.

As you might expect, the government would neither hold nor manage your account. Your money goes into the private sector. The government would authorize the acceptable investment companies that may offer Private Retirement Accounts (PRAs). The individual account holders own the investments, not the investment company. The investment companies cannot commingle the funds with any other operations of the investment firm. This ownership requirement provides security and peace of mind. Excluding individual securities, Private Retirement Accounts would accept only mutual funds as approved investment vehicles thus reducing risk through diversification.

Operating expenses and fees must be reasonable and appropriate for the services provided. The fees would not exceed one-fifth or 20% of the average cost associated with similarly designed mutual funds offered in the private sector. For instance, index fund costs currently average 0.30% of assets suggesting the cost of a Private Retirement Accounts would be no more than 0.06%. The huge dollar amount of the investments held in the investment companies would generate substantial revenues despite the lower expense ratios. The government would closely regulate the investment companies to ensure adherence to all fiduciary responsibilities and regulatory requirements.

One of the major pitfalls often cited is the lack of investment knowledge on the part of the public. To alleviate this concern, each Private Retirement Account would have a portion of its portfolio holdings invested in U.S. Treasury funds. By requiring a minimum percentage, the program provides the security associated with the current system while retaining the upward potential inherent in holding equity positions.

The minimum required percentage of U.S. Treasury funds held in the portfolio of the account holder is 20% for those individuals under 35 years of age. This minimum percentage increases 10% every 10 years with the minimum percentage restriction frozen at 60% when the account owner reaches the age of 65. Insuring compliance, the investment company holding the Private Retirement Account verifies the portfolio allocations every five years beginning on the 25th birthday of the account owner.

- account owners up to 34 years old require minimum U.S. Treasury balances of 20%
- account owners 35 to 44 require minimum U.S. Treasury balances of 30%
- account owners 45 to 54 require minimum U.S. Treasury balances of 40%
- account owners 55 to 64 require minimum U.S. Treasury balances of 50%
- account owners 65 or older require minimum U.S. Treasury balances of 60%

Although individual investors may invest their funds as they choose, the treasury allocation restriction provides security and stability to the account balances. They would be able to select short-, intermediate-, or long-term treasury mutual funds. As account holders grow older, the percentage of treasury securities increases providing more protection in the event of a market downturn. For instance, should the market lose 30% of its value in a given year, a 55-year-old would likely be impacted by only one-half of that percentage or 15% on the equity portion of the portfolio, while the return on the treasury portion most likely would reduce the expected loss still further. The individual investor may increase holdings in U.S. Treasuries beyond the minimum requirements, but the recommendation is not to exceed 75% regardless of age.

Current Retirees

As stated previously, it would be best to changeover completely to a private system. However, when the funding inflows earmarked for retirees stop, there will be no funds available from which to pay benefits. The program must have certain safeguards to ensure the protection of current retirees that guarantee they would lose neither their current nor their future benefits. After all, this generation of workers did indeed contribute into the system only to see their contributions paid to the then existing retirees.

Current retirees are immediately affected by any modification, are the most concerned of any group, the most vocal in their opinions, and the most fearful of any change. For these reasons, the system effectively remains unchanged for the retirees. Their benefits continue to increase at the annual rate of inflation.

To alleviate some of their fears, several key enhancements would be part of the changeover. The most important benefit enhancement would be the retention of their deceased spouse's payments; thus, a husband or wife would no longer have to choose one or the other. There would be a minimum annual benefit increase of 1% even if inflation were non-existent. Finally, individuals who paid the maximum contribution amount into the current Social Security system for 12 years or more would receive a $1,000 monthly bonus.

New and Current Workforce Participants

Employers would continue to withhold 12.4% of their employees' salaries, with 10.2% deposited into the designated Private Retirement Account of their employees and 2.2% deposited into the Treasury. Additionally, each participant over 30 years of age would be able to add another $2,000 to his or her Private Retirement Account annually. All deposits would be taxable.

Although some may argue this favors the wealthy, the intent of this or any retirement program is to reduce the total number of individuals needing government support. Eliminating this dependency is the primary goal. The more an individual contributes to his Private Retirement Account, the less likely the individual would require government assistance during retirement, thus reducing government spending and lowering the tax burden for all Americans.

At retirement, annual distributions from the Private Retirement Account would receive preferential tax treatment. For instance, the first $50,000 of investment returns withdrawn annually would be tax-free. For distributions above this amount, 75% would be included in taxable income with the remaining 25% not taxed. The favorable tax treatment recognizes the income needs of our retired citizens while providing some protection against taxing inflation gains.

The government would establish maximum distribution percentages for the Private Retirement Accounts. Similar to current regulations for IRAs, a uniform table would determine the maximum distribution amount. To ensure the account owner does not outlive his Private Retirement Account funds, the table might target a life expectancy of 90 or 100 rather than the current life expectancy of 83. However, the program would allow Private Retirement Account owners to override the calculated distribution amounts in the early years, which are relatively low percentages, but the adjusted amount would not exceed 4% of the total account value.

Just as with current retirees, older workers also are vulnerable to system changes. Unable to establish sufficient funding in their Private Retirement Accounts, their distributions may fall short of the revised payouts established for current retirees. Should such a scenario exist, the federal government would pay the difference. In effect, the older workers would retain the current enhanced system, but they could also participate in some of the benefits of the newly designed program.

One of the major benefits of a Private Retirement Account would be the ability to leave the unused balances to your spouse, children, or other heirs. The inability to pass your account balances onto your heirs is one of the cruel realities of the current Social Security scheme. Today, individuals must choose between their government pension benefits or their spouse's. Even if each spouse paid into the system his or her entire life, the surviving spouse is only able to receive one government pension. You are not able to recover your own contributions. This is simply unfair, unethical, and immoral.

Any account transferred to an heir of the original account owner would be separate from the recipients' Private Retirement Account statement. Transferred balances must retain either the existing treasury percentage or a minimum allocation of 50%, whichever is greater. This conservative allocation provides safety while still allowing the account to grow over time. Based on the historical returns, a 50/50 portfolio generates an average annual return of approximately 7%, which is well above the historical trend of inflation.

Federal Government

The key to the Optimization Plan is the transition that transforms the system from today's pay-as-you-go Ponzi scheme to the self-funded program of tomorrow. With the elimination of pay-as-you-go, funding must occur in a more traditional manner for retiree benefit payments. The primary funding occurs from the purchase of U.S. Treasuries for the Private Retirement Account portfolios. Depending on the participants' age, those purchases can be between 20% and 60% of the participants' contributions. In addition, each worker rebalances his portfolio every five years, resulting in additional purchases of U.S. Treasuries throughout his lifetime.

In addition to these purchases, employers pay 2.2% of their employees' salaries to the government. This percentage represents the difference between the current withholding rate of 12.4% and the optimized rate of 10.2%. Thus, the business community experiences no change in the short term. The retiree payments continue much like the current system. Discontinuing the employer payments can occur when the new program becomes self-funding.

Although the purchases of U.S. Treasuries would increase the interest payments for the government, the interest costs would be more than offset by the interest savings from the eliminated Social Security trust funds. Today, the government accrues interest on the balances of the Social Security trust funds in the form of an IOU. Yes, this is another unfunded liability held for payment sometime in the future. The savings would be rather significant in the earlier years when the Private Retirement Account portfolios are just beginning. These savings coincide with the heavier payments necessary for the current retirees.

Although the shortfall in the initial year approaches $250 million, the shortfall quickly falls to a more manageable $100 million range in five years. Reductions in government spending from other discretionary programs can offset these shortfalls. Should the federal government be reluctant to curb discretionary spending, the incremental debt is a reasonable tradeoff given the substantial long-term benefits.

The optimization of the new Social Security system breaks even in approximately 15 years and it shows significant growth within 22 years. The real benefits, however, accrue both to the federal government and to the economy in the long term. For instance, the federal government would be able to eliminate the large trust fund liabilities, better known as the IOUs currently residing in the Social Security lockbox. This savings alone removes a tremendous burden from future generations while enabling the government to forgo raising taxes or reducing benefits to current and future retirees. Clearly, this is significant, but there is more.

Of equal importance is the strategic shift in funding government programs. The requirement to hold treasuries initially supports payments to the retirees. As the system becomes self-funding, the requirement to hold treasuries would be available to fund other government programs. In effect, the American people would become a growing partner in funding future government spending initiatives. With access to new borrowers, the government likely would experience downward pressure on borrowing costs, be less reliant on foreign investors, and significantly improve their financial position.

Consider the longer-term implications. In addition to fewer and fewer payment obligations, the government also would enjoy revenue opportunities. For instance, increased job creation and improved corporate profit margins would lead to greater tax revenues. The hidden treasure, however, is the huge inflow of revenue into the Treasury due to the minimum portfolio requirements. As the values of the Private Retirement Accounts grow, the purchase of more treasuries also grows in order to maintain minimum percentage requirements. The treasury percentages in the inherited Private Retirement Accounts either remains the same or increases, thus eliminating any significant redemptions. While retiree withdrawals will occur, these distributions would be small and primarily spent in the marketplace, encouraging economic activity. The majority of this new money would remain relatively stable since new ongoing purchases would offset retiree distributions.

This new inflow of capital would be a significant windfall, but the government must not squander this second chance with new entitlement programs or unnecessary spending initiatives. One thought is to provide a significant tax reduction further stimulating the economy. Another consideration is to use a portion of these funds to reduce the premium costs for the Medicare and Medicaid programs, but not to fund expansion of either. The proposal offers significant benefits to the government, the economy, and the American people.

The Private Sector
Without question, the most critical element of the Social Security system is the private sector. Yet, the private sector is the most misunderstood and often overlooked element in the equation. The skeptics point out that the success of a privately owned system depends largely on the strength of the economy and that is why the business community is so essential. Although a valid assertion, the current pay-as-you-go scheme is even more dependent on the private sector.

The funding for government spending comes from one of two sources: taxes or debt. Since the repayment of debt must occur sometime, the only real funding for government spending comes from taxes. In order for the government to collect those taxes, individuals must be earning wages in the private sector and businesses must be selling products to earn profits. This simple analysis points out the linkage between private sector jobs and the tax revenues that support the government's thirst for more and more spending. A robust private sector is essential to funding government initiatives, but it is an absolute necessity for funding the current pay-as-you-go scheme known as Social Security. Consider the impact the continuing high unemployment has on the payment of Social Security benefits. For the first time in history, Social

Security disbursements exceed Social Security tax collections in 2010. This is news no one wants to hear.

The growth of worldwide markets, increasing competition from abroad, and a resurgence of capitalism around the world have added still more challenges. American businesses are becoming less competitive due to increasing costs and higher taxes. All too often American businesses have outsourced not only manufacturing plants but back office operations as well to lower-cost locations such as China, India, and others. Although these companies may become more profitable, such actions inevitably result in fewer domestic jobs. Many businesses also invest in newer technologies and replace aging capital equipment, improving productivity that further reduces job opportunities. Larger corporations with strong balance sheets may pursue acquisitions of smaller companies, not only reducing competition but also eliminating still more jobs.

While large corporations have a decided advantage in this competitive marketplace, small businesses are the key drivers in a healthy economy, creating four out of every five jobs. These small, often obscure, companies are the mainstay of the American economy. Only a very few become the next Google or Microsoft. Many may never enjoy a second or third anniversary. Yet those companies that sustain a long-term profitable return become the backbone for economic growth, job creation, and market stability.

The value proposition between price and quality drives competitiveness. Improving quality usually requires investment and time—investment in people, equipment, or process and time for the market to recognize the quality improvement. Lowering cost, on the other hand, can happen relatively fast. The largest manageable expense on most financial statements is labor, which translates into jobs. Eliminating the 2% withholding paid to the government is helpful, but the reduction does not occur for some 30 years. A more immediate incentive would allow smaller companies an opportunity to compete while also promoting job creation. The intent of such incentives is to promote the hiring of American workers but not to negatively affect larger, multinational corporations employing workers worldwide.

The Optimization Plan links tax incentives to employing U.S. citizens. With tax reform remaining a campaign issue in both political parties, this proposal can work regardless of future tax changes. For instance, under the current tax code, companies employing only American workers would see their corporate income tax rate drop to 10%. As the percentage of American workers decreases, the corporate income tax rate for that firm would increase until it returns to the current 35% level. The current corporate tax rates may look like this:

- 10% corporate tax for a 100% U.S. citizen workforce
- 15% corporate tax for a 95% U.S. citizen workforce
- 20% corporate tax for a 90% U.S. citizen workforce
- 25% corporate tax for a 85% U.S. citizen workforce
- 30% corporate tax for a 80% U.S. citizen workforce
- 35% corporate tax for less than a 80% U.S. citizen workforce

Should future corporate tax rates change, the incentive model can adjust accordingly. Rather than penalizing companies for their indiscretions, this proposal rewards them for their actions. While some corporations with overseas footprints may qualify for these favorable rates, the primary beneficiaries would be small businesses that are the drivers of job creation. Designed as a win-win for all participants, the proposal provides benefits for businesses, labor unions, government, and the American public. Businesses benefit from the tax reductions making them more competitive and more attractive for investment dollars. Labor benefits from improved job opportunities. The government collects more tax revenues due to the larger taxpayer base and higher corporate profits, and they disburse fewer entitlement payments due to lower unemployment and fewer individuals taking early retirement. Another potential benefit may be lower consumer prices resulting from increased competition.

To offset this lost opportunity for large U.S. multi-national corporations, the proposal advocates changing the repatriation tax. The U.S. currently boasts the highest corporate tax rate in the world. Unlike most countries, the U.S. taxes profits earned overseas. The tax laws, however, do allow businesses to defer paying taxes on foreign-sourced income until those monies come back into the U.S., referred to as repatriation. Rather than acting as a deterrent to overseas investing, this tax law encourages corporations to keep their profits overseas, building new plants, expanding current operations, and creating more jobs—overseas! The elimination of this repatriation tax promotes a better allocation of resources because corporations would make decisions based on actual business activity rather than the artificial constraints of the U.S. tax code. Re-evaluating their business models, some corporations may prefer to stop the costly practice of moving their facilities overseas and perhaps focus their capital on building better distribution networks to transfer their products globally. The tax code needs to be neutral towards business decision-making thereby making economic factors the driving force in the process.

For those insisting on penalties, such an approach is neither recommended nor encouraged. The use of negative incentives leads to unexpected and often unfavorable consequences. Repatriation is just one example. Long-term behavior modification is more successful with positive incentives. After all, you do attract more flies with honey.

To avoid the unintended consequences inherent with many well-meaning government programs and to calm the fears of those who may question the veracity of corporate executives, certain limitations would be necessary to thwart potential manipulation. For instance, the percentage calculation of U.S. workers would be the average hours for the year, not a point-in-time figure such as year-end. The calculation would include all temporary workers, part-timers, consultants, and other contract workers to reduce abuse. Corporate acquisitions and divestitures would have a five-year look back and a seven-year carryforward to avoid potential restructuring opportunities. Firms with greater than 40% of their sales to a single company would include their staff in the headcount calculations to avoid possible legal gerrymandering. The responsibility for the accuracy of the data resides with the reporting company and their external auditors, with significant fines and penalties assessed to both parties for incorrect reporting regardless of the intent.

The government also must have incentives to employ U.S. workers when they spend their tax dollars. Since any fees or penalties would become additional taxes to their constituents, another form of incentive is necessary. Any federal, state, or local government agency employing outside companies must disclose the percentage of non-U.S. workers within those companies according to the same parameters used in the private sector. Failure to meet the same percentage standards as the private sector would escalate their disclosure requirements and increase the level of their scrutiny. Should the percentages exceed 10% for instance, an outside audit must disclose how and to whom the government spends its tax collections. Total transparency is the currency of the realm for government agencies, and it would be a very powerful inducement indeed.

As Social Security benefit payments approach or exceed the tax revenues collected, the length of time necessary for this Optimization Plan to become self-funding naturally increases. Individual ownership remains the best solution, but it may require more time to achieve the goal of being self-sufficient. The underlying problem of the current Social Security scheme magnifies itself when unemployment rises significantly. With fewer people employed, fewer tax dollars are coming into the government at the very time benefit payments are on the rise. The shortfall highlights the inadequacies of the pay-as-you-go scheme for all to see. While vilifying Bernie Madoff for his role in stealing some $60 million, the government avoids its own culpability for the millions and millions of dollars it misdirected from the taxpayers over the years. In fact, the government seeks to continue and expand this travesty on the public.

WAKING AN ECONOMIC POWERHOUSE

Any sustainable, long-term program must have at its core the health of the economy. The key driver for a healthy economy is a private sector creating jobs, providing paychecks, and earning profits to sustain not only Social Security but also the entire federal government.

Figure 15.1 presents the annual projections for optimizing the Social Security system. The largest deficit of almost $250 million occurs in the first year. The deficit drops by 20% in the next two years and another 25% in the following two years. In the sixth year, the deficits decrease another 33% and level-off near $100 million for the next 10 years. While not small, these deficits are manageable. Should the government choose

FIGURE 15.1 *Optimizing the Social Security System*

ALL DOLLAR FIGURES IN MILLIONS

Number Of Years	Currently Retired (a)	Newly Retired (b)	Corporate Purchases (c)	U.S. Treas Purchases (d)	New UST Int Costs (e)	Saved UST Int Costs (f)	Net Position (g)
1	($626)	($114)	$124	$254	($0)	$116	($245)
2	($493)	($213)	$125	$258	($0)	$118	($206)
3	($389)	($311)	$127	$262	($1)	$120	($191)
4	($313)	($350)	$129	$266	($1)	$121	($147)
5	($252)	($413)	$131	$271	($1)	$123	($142)
6	($203)	($446)	$133	$276	($2)	$125	($118)
7	($163)	($492)	$135	$281	($3)	$127	($116)
8	($129)	($539)	$137	$286	($4)	$129	($121)
9	($102)	($570)	$139	$292	($5)	$131	($116)
10	($80)	($592)	$141	$297	($6)	$133	($106)
11	($62)	($615)	$143	$304	($8)	$135	($103)
12	($49)	($636)	$146	$311	($9)	$137	($101)
13	($38)	($648)	$148	$318	($12)	$139	($95)
14	($31)	($634)	$150	$387	($14)	$141	($0)
15	($25)	($644)	$152	$406	($16)	$143	$16
16	($20)	($652)	$155	$428	($19)	$145	$36
17	($16)	($624)	$157	$452	($21)	$147	$95
18	($13)	($615)	$159	$473	($40)	$149	$114
19	($11)	($603)	$162	$386	($44)	$152	$42
20	($8)	($581)	$164	$400	($49)	$154	$79
21	($7)	($548)	$166	$416	($54)	$156	$130
22	($5)	($553)	$169	$433	($60)	$159	$142
23	($4)	($511)	$172	$449	($77)	$161	$190
24	($3)	($495)	$174	$685	($84)	$163	$441
25	($2)	($499)	$177	$731	($91)	$166	$481
26	($1)	($461)	$179	$791	($99)	$168	$577
27	($1)	($457)	$182	$850	($107)	$171	$638
28	($1)	($437)	$185	$949	($191)	$173	$679
29	($0)	($425)	$188	$621	($206)	$176	$353
30	($0)	($410)	$190	$654	($221)	$179	$392
31	($0)	($411)	$193	$697	($238)	$181	$423
32	($0)	($377)	$196	$740	($255)	$184	$488

NOTES ON CALCULATIONS

(a) currently retired payments includes current retirees, retiree spouses who continue receiving benefits after the death of their spouse, and the bonus payment to retirees contributing the maximum amount for 12 or more years

(b) newly retired is based on a $36,000 average annual salary with 15% of the population contributing the maximum amount plus an additional annual $2,000 contribution for individuals over 30 years of age (approximately one-third of the population)

(c) corporate payments represents the 2.2% reduction in the existing withholding amounts; these payments can be eliminated when the program becomes self-funding

(d) U.S. Treasury purchases are the minimum required purchases within the PRA accounts, which includes the initial purchases and the periodic portfolio adjustments required every five years but excludes the bonus payments due to the likelihood those monies would be spent (if not, the net position would improve)

(e) new U.S. Treasury interest costs represent the interest paid on the U.S. Treasury holdings within the PRA accounts

(f) saved U.S. Treasury interest costs represent the annual interest that should have been earned on the historical balances of the U.S. Social Security Trust Funds

(g) equals the sum of columns (a) through (f)

to reduce other discretionary spending, the deficits shrink even further. After 16 years, the projections turn into surpluses and average nearly $90 million over the next 10 years. At this point, the surpluses escalate almost tenfold with expected projections averaging well into the $400 million range and some years exceeding $600 million. In less than a quarter century, the Optimization Plan becomes self-sufficient, restores solvency, and rebuilds confidence in the system.

Based on these projections, the government would get a redo, a mulligan, a new start. The cancellation of the unfunded Social Security liabilities and the elimination of ongoing Social Security payments would strengthen the dollar creating a favorable investment climate. The large windfall of tax revenues would allow the government to reduce taxes further, stimulating economic growth. The flow of capital into the private sector would encourage investment in new technologies, new capital spending, and new products invigorating long-term growth and prosperity. Reduced tax rates would encourage business investment, business development, and foreign investors. Job growth would increase almost immediately.

- Mutual fund companies would need to invest in infrastructure and customer service
- Public accounting firms most likely would increase staff to manage the new work assignments and the growth in mutual fund assets
- Even the public sector would see job growth to support regulation and oversight responsibilities

To perpetual cynics who traffic in negativity and fear, the Optimization Plan mitigates the most often cited concerns to individual ownership in a positive, pro-active approach. Requiring minimum percentage of U.S. Treasuries lessens the fear that the public lacks investment knowledge. Temporary corporate contributions and the purchases of U.S. Treasuries moderate the fear that the funding of the transition is not achievable. Rewarding companies employing American workers with tax incentives eases the fear that too many American jobs are being lost. Historical returns and time-tested principles diminish the fear that the market is too risky. Guaranteed government payments and two government pensions alleviate the fear that current retirees and those nearing retirement would sacrifice benefits. Optimization promotes benefits for all participants with the most important being the health of the overall economy.

LEARNING THE FACTS EXPOSES THE FICTION

Suggesting private ownership of Social Security accounts undoubtedly would escalate the political rhetoric and raise a media firestorm. Critics surely will begin to demonize big business, condemn the potential investment risks, and criticize the cyclical nature of the stock market. Preying on emotions and inflaming the fears of uncertainty directs public opinion away from the real issue—the fear that politicians may lose their golden goose.

The story that needs to be told is that the government continues to take our money only to penalize us when we want it returned. Since its inception, the tax collections have far exceeded the benefit payments of the Social Security system. Why is no one asking about where those excess tax collections have gone? Where is the outrage? With individual ownership of Social Security accounts, the government would lose access to those excess funds, thereby losing much of their influence over the public, losing some of their power over the economy, and focusing much more attention on their spending initiatives. By eliminating this back door access to excess Social Security payments, the government would need to justify spending in the light of day. Dare we say transparency?

One can only wonder what the result would have been had the Clark Amendment passed in 1935 and the Social Security collections went into private pension plans rather than government run schemes. Surely, the Social Security long-term liabilities would not exist. Perhaps much of the federal discretionary spending would not be present. Maybe the government bureaucracy would not be as large. Most likely, the economy would be larger, stronger, and more competitive. The private sector may have discovered new medical advances, developed more technological innovations, or produced greater productivity breakthroughs.

While no one can say for sure what would have been, it certainly provides much speculation and an interesting topic for discussion. The one undeniable fact, however, is the government would not have had access to those stealth Social Security funds. Would the government have pursued much of its discretionary spending programs without those funds? Would the public have accepted increases in income taxes to fund those discretionary programs? Would there have even been a need for those programs?

While individual ownership is not without concerns, no incremental risk exists between the Optimization Plan and the current pay-as-you go scheme. To the contrary, individual ownership is far superior. This must be clear and understood. Since the future is unknown, even the most meticulously researched plans may encounter unexpected events. Accordingly, preparation for possible contingencies is helpful.

The Optimization Plan is no different. The largest risk to successful implementation occurs during the initial transition when a sustained loss in tax revenues would cause a shortfall in meeting Social Security disbursements. Should the government be unwilling or unable to sustain such shortfalls in the near term, an effective contingency plan would be to target the Treasury percentages held in the Private Retirement Accounts. Raising the required minimums would increase the flow of money into the treasury. Increasing future minimums and shortening the periods between these adjustments are other options. To offset the expected slower growth in the Private Retirement Accounts, individuals would be able to increase their personal contributions beyond the proposed limits of $2,000 and they may start contributing before 30 years of age, which also adds to the Treasury inflows. Such moves would only be temporary.

For those opponents still fearing the worst, consider the consequences should the individual ownership plan fail. The government would takeover benefit payments for retirees by resuming the control of taxing the income of current workers and the profits of existing businesses. True, the government may raise the qualifying age, reduce some benefits and increase taxes. Hey, wait a minute! This is exactly what the government is doing today with the current pay-as-you-go scheme.

The plain and simple truth is the Optimization Plan adds no additional risk, but it does offer substantial and meaningful rewards. While focusing on private ownership, the Optimization Plan provides incentives to the private sector—greater profits; to the public—more job growth; to the government—higher tax revenues; and to the economy—additional investment opportunities. We can build a foundation of financial security, fiscal responsibility, and economic prosperity.

A successful program may raise other concerns. The wealth created within the Private Retirement Accounts may become quite large. After several generations, the transfer of unused account balances to heirs may create significant long-term liabilities for the government. The majority of these inherited accounts will represent permanent long-term liabilities that, most likely, will be passed from one generation to another without significant redemptions. A mechanism to reduce this long-term government liability may be necessary. Considerations include taxing inherited accounts beginning with the fourth or fifth transfer. Another would be taxing inherited accounts in excess of a certain value but only after several transfers. These provisions would ensure a fiscally sound Social Security system. An added benefit of a successful program would be the real possibility that many more people would have the financial security to retire earlier. This would lead to more employment opportunities for younger individuals, thereby creating a positive stimulus to the economy.

The choice is clear: a government pay-as-you-go scheme dependent upon tomorrow's paycheck or an Optimization Plan based on a free market system. The former, devised by politicians thirsting for power, is a powder keg about to implode. The latter forges a coalition among the participants helping improve the financial security for all Americans. You decide where to place your hard-earned money.

ON THE HOME FRONT

The history lessons of the Great Depression, FDR, and World War II provide a glimpse into the character of the American people. Through some of the darkest days in our history, the American spirit never wavered, the American Dream never faltered, and the American worker never surrendered.

World War II ushered America into a global conflict with fighting taking place in distant lands around the world. Sometimes forgotten is that the home front also joined in the fight. Rationing, recycling, and victory gardens became their battlegrounds, but perhaps the most deafening call came from the songs performed at the War Bond Rallies seen throughout the country.

One such song entitled "Everybody Every Payday" written by Tom Adair and Richard Uhl captured the spirit and patriotism of those who stayed behind. Like so many other songs from that time, it called on all Americans to help ensure the future of the U.S.A. They believed that everyone could pitch in to help save the nation regardless of profession, job, or position in life. The song urged all working Americans to take 10% from every paycheck and buy U.S. Savings Bonds.[10]

As with those tumultuous days of the Second World War, the American people again may be asked for 10% from every paycheck. This war, however, is taking place entirely on the home front—in the homes of millions and millions of American families, fighting for financial security.

Our politicians need to understand the link between a growing, prosperous private sector and a strong, supportive government. Allowing the business community to flourish not only ensures the government a steady stream of tax revenues but it also fosters a spirit, an inner strength within its people to achieve success. The government must grasp the concept "less is more"—a limited government providing the legal framework to assure fair competition and opportunities for all, a tax system rewarding success and wealth creation, and a fiscal policy promoting a strong dollar to encourage investment and job creation. We can reprise another popular song from those historic years written by Cliff Friend and Charles Tobias. The song captures our current resolve, just as it did when originally written, "We did it before and we *will* do it again."[11]

CHAPTER SIXTEEN

One Portfolio at a Time

The doors of wisdom are never shut.
Benjamin Franklin

BUILDING A SOUND financial future is not limited to developing an investment portfolio. We also must lay the groundwork for a sound economy. After all, the economy ultimately provides financial security as well as national security for all families.

BUILDING YOUR INVESTMENT PORTFOLIO

We started on a journey to make you a better, more informed investor and hopefully that objective was accomplished. Making the complex understandable is not an easy task; but even if only a single individual has been helped, the effort will have been worthwhile.

The primary focus was to provide you with an actionable investment model based on historical financial trends, proven investment strategies, and basic user-friendly guidelines. The model places a significant premium on patience rather than action. Historical evidence clearly indicates *the most costly investment mistakes come not from being in the market when the market falls dramatically, but from being out of the market when the market surges upward.*

The challenge to succeed in the investment arena does not rely solely on what you do. It also depends on what you do *not* do as an investor. The investment model provides a balanced framework, enabling solid returns with minimal risk throughout your lifetime. Experience is perhaps the greatest teacher, but it can be a very expensive education for an investor. For instance, the experienced investor always thinks risk first before considering reward. You would do well to remember time and patience have a strange way of making ordinary investors look like investment geniuses.

BUILDING THE FOUNDATION
FOR ECONOMIC GROWTH

A second, but equally important, objective was to provide you with some insight into the dynamic nature of our free market system. Whether it is the many factors affecting the cyclical changes in the market, or the multiplicity of interrelated transactions occurring every minute of every day, or the political pressures influencing the dangerous growth in deficit spending, even the most casual observer can appreciate the sophisticated nature of the economy. The free market system is extremely large, exceptionally complex, and exceedingly nuanced.

Choose Successful Strategies

Despite substantial historical evidence to the contrary and without a single instance of success, our politicians continue to pursue a deficit-driven economy laden with government regulations and targeted attacks on business. This approach leads to a sluggish, financially strapped economy that severely limits our ability to compete in the global marketplace. While individual consumers determine the winners and losers in a free market system, politicians decide who wins in a government-run economy. Somehow, that just does not seem right.

History can teach us much if we only look. Continued attempts to repeat failed policies of the past when successful policies exist upon which to build is neither wise nor rational. Why do many of our political leaders reject an approach that has worked every time it has been tried—a policy of low marginal tax rates? Five different Presidents have enacted such policies, and each time they have delivered an economic juggernaut generating significant job growth and substantially greater tax revenues. If it is not broken, why fix it?

Avoid the Trappings of Political Speak

Perhaps the answer lies in the concept of Gross Domestic Product. GDP is often used as a proxy for the standard of living in an economy. GDP refers to the value of all final goods and services produced within a country. One method of measuring GDP is the expenditure approach where GDP is the sum of four components represented by the calculation: GDP = C + I + G + Xn. *Consumption* (C), normally the largest component, represents total consumer spending by individual households. *Investment* (I) represents total business spending including new factories, office buildings, machinery, equipment, inventories, and home purchases. *Government* (G) represents the total spending by federal, state, and local governments on final goods and services. *Net Exports* (Xn) is the difference between total exports and total imports, and it can be either positive or negative.

Many politicians contend that government spending *increases* GDP. Further, they insist that more spending leads to a still higher GDP, and that increased GDP values enable increased deficit spending. This circular logic leads to spending on steroids!

Rather than being a model from which policies are to be developed, the expenditure formula is simply a static, point-in-time calculation. It does not prove that a given action will have a predictable result. Such thinking either ignores completely, or discounts considerably, the impact human behavior has on various components of the calculation. The expenditure method totals the various inputs, but it does not provide any insight into cause-and-effect outcomes.

Such logic is consistent with the short-term thinking of politicians. Many tend to do what looks good today regardless of what the long-term consequences may be because they want to be re-elected. They believe that long-term impacts will come too late to be politically damaging, or they assume their constituents will either forget or not make a connection between them and the consequences, or both. Simply stated, our politicians are disconnected from economic realties.

Understand Sound Principles

Human behavior is at the very core of supply-side economics. While it may be true that people tend to react in unpredictable ways, the proper incentives do drive actions that are more predictable. Lowering high marginal tax rates generates more disposable income, encourages more consumer spending, promotes greater business investment, and generally improves overall consumer confidence. As history confirms, these actions produce significantly higher tax revenues, considerably greater amounts of taxes collected from the wealthy, and a strong, robust economy. A thriving economy allows the government to increase spending through the organic growth of an expanding tax base. Sound fiscal policies promote a stronger, sustainable economic climate capable of absorbing those inevitable disasters, natural or man-made, that are just over the horizon.

In his analysis of supply-side economics, Art Laffer points out that lower rates on a large tax base expands the overall taxpayer pool, lowering the tax burden for all taxpayers whether high-, middle-, or low-income earners. Proponents of the flat tax provide further evidence that lowering tax rates promotes economic investment while maintaining federal tax revenues.

Enacting two simple changes can focus attention on the tax burden carried by the American public. The first change would be to move federal and state elections from the first Tuesday after the first Monday in November to the first Tuesday following April 15th. Such a change would place the tax issue front and center for each election. The second change would be to stop the practice of withholding taxes from individual paychecks and begin sending monthly invoices to every employee for the payment of those taxes. This second change would highlight the difference between your real paycheck and the staggering amount taken from you to pay taxes. Of course, neither will happen.

Perhaps the government could save both time and money by following the advice of Bob Hope who quipped, "I have the perfect simplified tax form for the government. Why don't they just print our money with a return address on it?"

BUILDING LONG TERM PROSPERITY

In a country founded on the principles of self-reliance and self-governance, why is private ownership of our own individual Social Security accounts deemed controversial? In a country founded on the rule of law, why can the government administer the largest Ponzi scheme ever devised with absolute immunity? Why indeed?

Enacted during the FDR Administration, the Social Security system achieved instant credibility. Convincing the public it was an insurance-based product, FDR knew it was a tax-driven, politically motivated scheme designed to give the government enormous power over the public. The Social Security system was a charade from the very beginning. Compounding this initial problem, elected politicians through the years continued to siphon off the excess Social Security tax collections to fund a never-ending list of government programs and an expanding bureaucracy. In exchange for borrowing this money, the government established a Social Security trust fund filled with IOUs.

Failing to foresee the demographic changes and then hoping for a reversal of the trend, politicians finally realized that declining birthrates coupled with increasing life expectancies posed a significant problem. Rather than exposing Social Security for the hoax it is, politicians began to increase the tax rates, extend the eligibility age, and pursue other modifications to delay the opening of that trust fund lockbox. The only item the politicians neglected to adjust was their usage of the excess tax collections. Rather than fearing the private ownership of Social Security, the American public should fear the consequences of not owning their individual accounts.

The Optimization Plan changes the focus of the system from a government-centric scheme to a retiree-driven model. Focusing on incentives, the Social Security Optimization Plan provides all workers, affluent or not, an investment framework based on historical facts and time-tested principles. Incentives for the business community include increased profits and improved competitiveness. Incentives for the government include the elimination of future Social Security liabilities, increased tax revenues, and restoration of sound fiscal policies. The incentives for the American public include rising employment opportunities and a path to a more secure future.

Most promising is the fact that it can rekindle a partnership among the American people, the private sector, and the government. Working together for the common good of all was one of the key principles envisioned by the Founding Fathers. The Constitution provides for *a limited federal government while strengthening individual freedoms.* Thomas Jefferson noted, "It is error alone which needs the support of government. Truth can stand by itself."

LOOKING TO THE FUTURE

As you prepare to embark on your own, remember the three wise men. No, not those three wise men. These three: *Benjamin Graham,* who explained that achieving satisfactory investment results is easier than most people realize. *Warren Buffett,* who expressed a basic concept for all investors large and small—rule number one is not to lose money and rule number two is not to forget rule number one. *John Bogle,* who urged both new and experienced investors alike to stay the course.

There is a fourth wise man or woman and that would be you. You will work a lifetime for your money, and now you want your money to work a lifetime for you. You must have strength, courage, and conviction to make a difference and to build a stronger, more secure future.

A future that begins now.

Chapter One: Get in the Game!

1. One of the longest running and most successful comedies in the history of radio, *The Jack Benny Program* was heard on NBC from 1932 through 1948 and CBS from 1948 through 1955. Due to the high income tax rates at the time, Benny moved his entire program to CBS. Although making a terrific salary, most of the money was lost to taxes. CBS proposed buying his entire company for a reported $2 million and paying him a smaller salary. The more notable supporting cast members included Mary Livingstone, his girlfriend (and real life wife), Phil Harris, his heavy-drinking bandleader, Eddie Anderson, his gravel-voiced butler Rochester, Dennis Day, his scatterbrained singer, and Don Wilson, his rotund announcer. The program successfully transitioned into television as *The Jack Benny Show* running from 1950 through 1965.

2. *The Money Pit* was released in 1986 and starred Tom Hanks and Shelley Long. *Mr. Blandings Builds His Dream House* was released in 1948 and starred Cary Grant and Myrna Loy. A newer update was entitled *Are We Done Yet?* and was released in 2007 starring Ice Cube and Nia Long.

Chapter Two: Recognize the Theories

1. Hillary Waugh, *Mysteries and Mystery Writing*, (Cincinnati, Ohio: Writers Digest Books, 1991), pp. 18–19.

Chapter Three: Building Blocks

1. John C. Bogle, *Common Sense on Mutual Funds* (New York: John Wiley & Sons, Inc., 1999), pp. 37–56.

2. William J. Bernstein, The Four Pillars of Investing (New York: McGraw Hill, 2002), p. 200.

3. John C. Bogle, *Common Sense on Mutual Funds* (New York: John Wiley & Sons, Inc., 1999), pp. 304–314.

4. Ty Cobb elected to Baseball's Hall of Fame in 1936, an original member. His plaque reads, "Tyrus Raymond Cobb. Detroit, Philadelphia American League 1905–1926. Led American League in batting 12 times and created or equaled more major league records than any other player. Retired with 4,191 major league hits." www.baseballhalloffame.org

5. John C. Bogle, *John Bogle on Investing: The First 50 Years* (New York: McGraw Hill, 2001), pp. 62–63.

6. Ibid., p. 63.

7. Jeremy J. Siegel, *Stocks For The Long Run, Fourth Edition* (New York: McGraw Hill, 2008), pp. 12–16.

8. Yogi Berra was elected to Baseball's Hall of Fame in 1972. His plaque reads, "Lawrence Peter 'Yogi' Berra. New York, American League 1946–1963. New York, National League 1965. Played on more pennant winners (14) and World Champions (10) than any player in history. Had 358 home runs and lifetime .285 batting average. Set many records for catchers including 148 consecutive games without an error, voted American League Most Valuable Player 1951–54–55. Managed Yankees to pennant in 1964." www.baseballhalloffame.org

9. Rex Stout, *The Doorbell Rang*, (1965).

10. Chairman's Letter, *Berkshire Hathaway, Inc. 1987 Annual Report*

11. George Santayana, *"The Reason in Common Sense"* from *The Life of Reason* published in five volumes from 1905 to 1906.

12. Rex Stout, *In the Best of Families*, (1950).

Chapter Four: Gaining Perspective

1. From the movie *Charlie Chan in Egypt*, 1935

2. From the movie *Charlie Chan at the Circus*, 1936

Chapter Five: Think Risk First

1. *Morningstar Mutual Funds Resource Guide, Morningstar Mutual Funds* (Chicago, Illinois: Morningstar Inc., 2009), pp. 9–19.

2. "Vanguard Long-Term U.S. Treasury" page, *Morningstar Mutual Funds* (Chicago, Illinois: Morningstar Inc., 2010), p. 1579.

3. Arthur Conan Doyle, *The Valley of Fear*, 1915.

Chapter Six: The All Important Next Step

1. Hillary Waugh, *Mysteries and Mystery Writing*, (Cincinnati, Ohio: Writers Digest Books, 1991), pp. 97–98.

2. *Morningstar Mutual Funds Resource Guide.* (Chicago, Illinois: Morningstar Inc., 2009), pp. 9–19.

3. "Vanguard 500 Index" page, *Morningstar Mutual Funds* (Chicago, Illinois: Morningstar Inc., 2010), p. 281.

Chapter Seven: Putting the Pieces Together

1. Linus Van Pelt, Lucy's brother, is one of the many memorable characters created for the Peanuts comic strip written and illustrated by the late Charles M. Schultz (1922–2000). First appearing in September 1952, his famous security blanket arrived years later. The first strip appeared on October 2, 1950 with the introduction of Charlie Brown, and two days later Snoopy made his first appearance. The rest of the gang followed: Schroeder (May 1951), Lucy (March 1952), Pig Pen (July 1954), Sally (August 1959), Peppermint Patty (August 1966), Woodstock (April 1967 but not named until June 1970), Franklin (July 1968), and Marcie (July 1971).

Chapter Eight: Looking for More

1. Thomas Easton, "The Ultimate Buy-and-Hold," *Forbes Magazine*, June 14, 1999.

2. Robert D. Arnott and Clifford S. Asnass, "Surprise! Higher Dividends = Higher Earnings Growth." *Financial Analysts Journal*, Vol. 59, No. 1, January/February 2003.

3. Ping Zhou and William Ruland, "Dividend Payout and Future Earnings Growth." *Financial Analysts Journal*, Vol. 62, No. 3, pp. 58–69, June 2006.

4. Stanley Block, "The Dividend Puzzle: The Relationship between Payout Rates and Growth." *AAII Journal*, (Chicago, Illinois: American Association of Individual Investors, May 2009), pp. 6–7.

5. Benjamin Graham, *The Intelligent Investor, Fourth Revised Edition*, (New York: Harper & Row Publishers, 1973), p. 54.

6. Ibid., p. 280.

7. Ibid., p. 287.

Chapter Nine: What If You Win the Lottery?

1. Joe Jackson was a defendant in the infamous Black Sox scandal that accused eight players from the Chicago White Sox of throwing the 1919 World Series to the Cincinnati Reds. After leaving a Grand Jury hearing, Jackson was reported to have been asked by a youngster, "It ain't true, is it, Joe?" Whether a true story or not, over the years this saying has become part of baseball legend. All eight were acquitted by the Grand Jury, but Kenesaw Mountain Landis, the Commissioner of Baseball, banned all eight players from the game.

2. The information on opening an account with the U.S. Treasury is available in greater detail at the following website: www.treasurydirect.gov/indiv/

3. Ibid.

Chapter Ten: Dos and Don'ts

1. Laura Hillenbrand, *Seabiscuit*, (New York: Random House, Inc., 2001), p. xii.

2. Ibid., p. 257.

3. Ibid., p. 268.

4. Ibid., p. 274.

5. Arthur Conan Doyle, "*The Adventure of the Beryl Coronet,*" *The Strand Magazine*, May 1892.

6. Benjamin Graham, *The Intelligent Investor, Fourth Revised Edition*, (New York: Harper & Row Publishers, 1973), p. vii.

Chapter Eleven: Pundits Can Be Detrimental to Your Wealth

1. John Naisbett is the author of *Megatrends* published in 1982.

Chapter Twelve: When Doing Nothing May Be the Best Move

1. National Bureau of Economic Research maintains a website at www.nber.org that offers the use of their "U.S. Business Cycles Expansions and Contractions" chart when appropriately referenced. The website also provides a history of the organization and a "Frequently Asked Questions" section explaining their approach.

2. Jeremy J. Siegel, *Stocks For The Long Run, Fourth Edition* (New York: McGraw Hill Inc., 2008), pp. 215–216.

Chapter Thirteen: The Significance of Scarcity

1. Willis L. Peterson, *Principles of Economics: Micro* (Homewood, Illinois: Richard D. Irwin, Inc., 1971), p. 2.

2. For a more thorough discussion on economics, Thomas Sowell has written an excellent book called *Basic Economics: A Citizen's Guide to the Economy*. Written in an easy to understand style, Sowell provides an informative, thought-provoking analysis on this complicated subject.

3. Thomas Sowell, *Basic Economics: A Citizen's Guide to the Economy* (New York, New York: Basic Books, a member of the Perseus Books Group, 2004), pp. 132–137.

4. John Steele Gordon, *An Empire of Wealth: The Epic History of American Economic Power* (New York: HarperCollins Publishers, Inc., 2004) pp. xiii–xiv.

Chapter Fourteen: Building on Success

1. Three books have been written that critically detail the Presidency of Franklin D. Roosevelt and the policies of the New Deal. Each is well-written and well-documented providing serious scholars with an objective evaluation of those tumultuous times.

   a) *FDR's Folly: How Roosevelt and His New Deal Prolonged the Great Depression* written by Jim Powell (New York: Crown Forum, a division of Random House, Inc., 2003).

   b) *The Forgotten Man: A New History of the Great Depression* written by Amity Shlaes (New York: Harper Collins Publishers, 2007).

   c) *New Deal or Raw Deal? How FDR's Economic Legacy Has Damaged America* written by Burton Folsom Jr. (New York: Threshold Editions, a division of Simon & Schuster, Inc., 2008).

2. Jim Powell, *FDR's Folly: How Roosevelt and His New Deal Prolonged the Great Depression* (New York: Three Rivers Press, a member of the Crown Publishing Group and a division of Random House, Inc., 2003), pp. 30–32.

   From *FDR's Folly* by Jim Powell, copyright © 2003 by Jim Powell. Used by permission of Crown Forum, an imprint of Crown Publishers, a division of Random House, Inc.

3. Ibid., pp. 222–224.

   From *FDR's Folly* by Jim Powell, copyright © 2003 by Jim Powell. Used by permission of Crown Forum, an imprint of Crown Publishers, a division of Random House, Inc.

4. Ibid., pp. 99–101.

   From *FDR's Folly* by Jim Powell, copyright © 2003 by Jim Powell. Used by permission of Crown Forum, an imprint of Crown Publishers, a division of Random House, Inc.

5. From the movie, "The Man Who Shot Liberty Valance" starring John Wayne, James Stewart, and Lee Marvin; directed by John Ford, produced by Willis Goldbeck and John Ford, and distributed by Paramount Pictures, 1962.

6. Thomas Sowell, *A Conflict of Visions* (New York: William Morrow, 1987), pp. 58–62.

   [As referenced by Burton Folsom Jr., *New Deal or Raw Deal? How FDR's Economic Legacy Has Damaged America* (New York: Threshold Editions, a division of Simon & Schuster, Inc., 2008), p. 255.]

7. John M. Blum, *From the Morgenthau Diaries: Years of Crisis, 1928–1938* (Boston: Houghton Mifflin, 1959), I, 242; *New York Times*, March 3, 1936.

   [As referenced by Burton Folsom Jr., *New Deal or Raw Deal? How FDR's Economic Legacy Has Damaged America* (New York: Threshold Editions, a division of Simon & Schuster, Inc., 2008), p. 180.]

8. Arthur B. Laffer, Stephen Moore, and Peter J. Tanous, *The End of Prosperity* (New York: Threshold Editions, A Division of Simon & Schuster, Inc., 2008), pp. 30–31.

9. Jude Wanniski, Supply-Side U, *Lesson #6*, Spring 1998

   [As referenced by Arthur B. Laffer, Stephen Moore, and Peter J. Tanous, *The End of Prosperity* (New York: Threshold Editions, A Division of Simon & Schuster, Inc., 2008), pp. 51–52.]

10. Daniel J. Mitchell, Ph.D., *"The Historical Lessons of Lower Tax Rates"* (The Heritage Foundation, Washington, D.C., Backgrounder # 1086, July 19, 1996), p. 3.

11. Ibid., p. 3.

12. Ibid., p. 4.

13. Arthur B. Laffer, Stephen Moore, and Peter J. Tanous, *The End of Prosperity* (New York: Threshold Editions, A Division of Simon & Schuster, Inc., 2008), pp. 144–151.

14. Baseline Budgeting fixes the current spending levels as the base upon which future funding is determined. This process assumes the current spending levels are appropriate and no additional evaluation is necessary. This approach rewards spending rather than placing incentives on saving.

15. Right-to-work states enacted laws that allow a person to work at any place of employment without being forced to join a union as a condition of that employment.

16. Information taken from the President's Council on Jobs and Competitiveness website located at www.whitehouse.gov/administration/advisory-boards/jobs-council/

17. Stephen Moore, "*The Man Who Saved Capitalism*" The Wall Street Journal, New York, July 31, 2012, p. A13.

18. *Here Comes Mr. Jordan*, released in 1941, starred Robert Montgomery as Joe Pendleton (the boxer/pilot), Claude Rains as Mr. Jordan, Edward Everett Horton as the errant angel, and James Gleason as Joe's trainer. The movie was remade in 1978 as *Heaven Can Wait* starring Warren Beatty, and again in 2001, as *Down to Earth* starring Chris Rock.

19. Gordon S. Wood, *The American Revolution: A History* (New York: The Modern Library, a division of Random House, Inc. 2002), p. 94.

Chapter Fifteen: Financial Security for Everyone

1. P. J. O'Brien, *Forward with Roosevelt* (Chicago: John Winston, 1936), pp. 92, 93.

   [As referenced by Jim Powell, *FDR's Folly: How Roosevelt and His New Deal Prolonged The Great Depression* (New York: Three Rivers Press, a member of the Crown Publishing Group and a division of Random House, Inc., 2003), pp. 179-180.]

2. Burton W. Folsom, Jr., *New Deal or Raw Deal? How FDR's Economic Legacy Has Damaged America* (New York: Threshold Editions, a division of Simon & Schuster, Inc., 2008), pp. 117–118. Reprinted with the permission of Threshold Editions, a division of Simon & Schuster, Inc., from *New Deal or Raw Deal?* by Burton W. Folsom. Copyright © 2008 by Burton Folsom. All rights reserved.

3. *Helvering v. Davis* , 301 U.S. 619, 635 (1937).

4. Frank Freidel, *Franklin D. Roosevelt: A Rendezvous with Destiny* (Boston: Little, Brown, 1990), p. 150.

> [As referenced by Burton Folsom, Jr., *New Deal or Raw Deal? How FDR's Economic Legacy Has Damaged America* (New York: Threshold Editions, a division of Simon & Schuster, Inc., 2008), p. 117.] Reprinted with the permission of Threshold Editions, a division of Simon & Schuster, Inc., from *New Deal or Raw Deal?* by Burton W. Folsom. Copyright © 2008 by Burton Folsom. All rights reserved.

5. Additional information is available at the Official website of the U.S. Securities and Exchange Commission: www.sec.gov/answers/ponzi.htm

> The U.S. Securities and Exchange Commission website defines a Ponzi scheme as follows:

> A Ponzi scheme is an investment fraud that involves the payment of purported returns to existing investors from funds contributed by new investors. Ponzi scheme organizers often solicit new investors by promising to invest funds in opportunities claimed to generate high returns with little or no risk. In many Ponzi schemes, the fraudsters focus on attracting new money to make promised payments to earlier-stage investors and to use for personal expenses, instead of engaging in any legitimate investment activity.

> The website also explains why Ponzi schemes collapse.

> With little or no legitimate earnings, the schemes require a consistent flow of money from new investors to continue. Ponzi schemes tend to collapse when it becomes difficult to recruit new investors or when a large number of investors ask to cash out.

> Ponzi schemes, sometimes referred to as pyramid schemes, exchange money for enrolling other people into the scheme without any product or service delivered. The basic concept is an individual invests his money with a "guaranteed" earnings potential. As other people join the program through word-of-mouth recommendations, their "investments" pay the original or previous investors while they, in turn, convince others to join. Thus, the scheme continues to grow, but it is unsustainable. Eventually, new participants will decrease thereby reducing payments and uncovering the fraud. The website points out the collapse may be relatively slow should the existing participants reinvest money.

6. Sentenced on June 29, 2009 to a maximum prison term of 150 years, Bernie Madoff pleaded guilty to 11 federal crimes. He also admitted to perpetrating a massive Ponzi scheme defrauding thousands of investors including high-net-worth individuals, hedge funds, financial institutions, and other businesses as well. The estimated losses were in excess of $65 billion.

7. Additional information is available at the Official website of the Social Security Administration: www.ssa.gov

8. Ibid.

9. Ibid.

10. "Everybody Every Payday" written by Tom Adair and Richard Uhl, 1942; recorded commercially in November 1942 by Barry Wood, Tommy Tucker, and Guy Lombardo through a temporary lifting of the Petrillo recording ban. This version performed by Barry Woods accompanied by Mark Warrow's Orchestra and the Lyn Murray Chorus with Martin Block as narrator in an electrical transcription from late 1942. From the album *"Something for the Boys"* (VJC-1036) distributed by Vintage Jazz Classics, 1992.

11. "We Did It Before (And We Can Do It Again)" written by Cliff Friend and Charles Tobias, 1941; introduced by Eddie Cantor on his December 10th radio program, then interpolated into his concurrent Broadway musical *Banjo Eyes*. This version performed by Clyde Lucas and his Orchestra in New York, December, 1941. From the album *"Something for the Boys"* (VJC-1036) distributed by Vintage Jazz Classics, 1992.

INDEX

AAII Journal, 138

A&E Network, 23

A&P, 205

Account fees, 32

Adams, Dr. Galen (Doc), 126

Adair, Tom, 283

Adventures of Sherlock Holmes, The (Doyle), 61

Alternative Minimum Tax (AMT), 232

American Exceptionalism, 251

American Revolution, The (Wood), 251

Anderson, Rochester, 12

Apple, 95, 129, 142, 209

Arness, James, 126

Arnott, Robert, 137

Arthur Andersen, 27

"As Time Goes By", 155, 156

Asness, Clifford, 137

Astor, Mary, 110

Average duration of unemployment, 201

Average prime rate, 199

Average weekly hours manufacturing, 194

Average weekly initial claims unemployment, 195–196

Balance of trade, 212

Baseline budgeting, 243

Basic Economics (Sowell), 202

Benchmark strategy, 21, 170

Benny, Jack, 12, 13

Bergman, Ingrid, 155

Bernstein, William, 33

Berra, Yogi, 47, 254

Beta, 20, 21, 71, 95, 136, 137

Bid-ask spread, 32, 33, 92, 135

Biggers, Earl Derr, 52

Biofuels, 215

Bismarck, Chancellor Otto von, 256, 264

Black, Fischer, 20

Black Tuesday, 223

Blaine, Rick, 155

Block, Stanley, 138

Boeing, 142, 245

Bogart, Humphrey, 110, 155

Bogle, John, 21, 25, 26, 44, 134, 289

Bogle on Investing (Bogle), 44

Bonds, individual issues

  investment ladder, 157–158, 159–164, 165–167

  pricing of, 66–68, 188

  risk, 69–70

  vs. mutual funds, 158–159

  yield calculation of, 68–69

Bonds, mutual funds

  analysis of, 70–75

  overview, 62–63

  vs. individual issues, 158–159

Book value, 95, 144, 147

Britt, Jeremy, 61

Brokerage commissions, 32

Bruce, Nigel, 61

Buffett, Warren, 17, 33, 45, 49, 111, 118, 119, 147, 173, 175, 177, 289

Building permits, new housing, 196–197

Bush, George W., 239, 241, 243, 248, 249, 254

Bush TARP legislation, 243

Business cycle, 145, 148, 182, 185–187, 188, 190, 191, 196, 199, 201, 230

Business risk, 28, 44

California, 237

Call risk, 28

Cap and Trade Bill, 244

Capital asset pricing model (CAPM), 20, 136

Capitalization standards, 215

Carter, Jimmy, 192, 248

Casablanca, 155, 156

Cash for Appliances, 246

Cash for Clunkers, 246

Castle-in-the-air theory, 18–19

Cather, Orrie, 24

Chan, Charlie, 52, 60

Change in consumer price index for services, 199

Change in labor cost per unit of output, 200

Charles, Nick, 84

Charles, Nora, 84

Charlie Chan in Shanghai, 52

Chaykin, Maury, 23

China, 211, 215, 245, 274

Chrysler, 210, 213, 243, 265

Churchill, Winston, 221, 251

Cisco, 142, 209

Clark Amendment, 257, 263, 280

Clark, Senator Bennett Champ, 257, 263, 280

Clinton, Bill, 241, 246

Clinton, Hillary, 27

Closed-end fund, 56, 99

Cobb, Ty, 40

Coca Cola, 95, 142, 136, 209

Coleman, Benita, 12

Coleman, Ronald, 12

Commercial and industrial loans outstanding, 200

Common Sense on Mutual Funds (Bogle), 25

Conflict of Visions (Sowell), 227

Congressional Budget Office (CBO), 242, 243, 247

Conrad, William, 126

Constitution, 213, 227, 228, 240, 251, 257, 288

Consumer installment credit to income, 199–200

Consumer price index (CPI), 66, 79, 189, 190, 199

Coolidge, Calvin, 237, 239, 240, 254

Core (taxable) portfolio, 53, 63, 77, 130

Cost: What Everyone Forgets, 31–33

Credit risk, 28, 63, 70

Cronkite, Walter, 220

Crude materials prices, 188, 189, 244

Currency risk, 28, 44, 91

Curtiz, Michael, 155

Daly, John, 220

Death of a Doxy (Stout), 23

Debt to total capital, 149–150

Debtor nation, 212

Deferred sales charges, 32, 74, 97

Dillon, Marshall Matt, 126, 153

Discount rate, 223

Divergence, 190

Diversification: What Everyone Tries To Do, 42–45

Dividends, 17, 18, 24, 25, 26, 34, 35, 47, 55, 57, 88, 124, 134, 141, 145, 151, 173, 188, 207, 241

    double taxation, 48, 146

    DRIP, 139–140, 143

    key to successful investing, 137–139

    targeted goals, 144, 151

    valuation factor, 146–147

Dodd, David, 17

Dodd-Frank Consumer Protection Act, 245

Dollar-cost averaging, 124, 139, 173, 174

Dow Jones Industrial Average (DJIA), 138, 205

Doyle, Arthur Conan, 61

DRIPs, 139–140, 143

Dupin, C. Auguste, 22

Durkin, Fred, 24

Easton, Thomas, 134

Einstein, Albert, 34, 173

Economic growth, leading factors
    inflation, 230–231
    taxes, 231–232
    government spending, 232–235

Economic risk, 28, 44

Efficient frontier, 20

Efficient market theory, 19–20

Elements of a detective story, 16

Empire of Wealth, An (Gordon), 221

Employees on non-agricultural payrolls, 197

End of Prosperity, The (Laffer, Moore, Tanous), 235

Enron, 27

Environmental Protection Agency (EPA), 244

Equities, individual issues
    considerations, 127–130
    incorporating into the model, 130–133
    investment criteria, 134–140
    selling, 150–153
    targeting candidates, 140–146
    valuation factors, 146–150

Equities, mutual funds
    analysis of, 94–99
    elimination factors, 99–101
    types
        active and passive funds, 91–93

domestic and international funds, 90–91

fund cap sizes, 85–87

growth and value funds, 88

hybrid funds, 89–90

mix and match, 93–94

specialty funds, 89

Eversharp, 210

"Everybody Every Payday" (Adair & Uhl), 283

Exchange fees, 32

Exchange-traded funds, 71, 99

Expenditure Method GDP, 285–286

Exxon Mobil, 86, 95, 142

Fannie Mae, 62

FDR's Folly (Powell), 223, 255

Federal funds, 194

Federal Government
    financing, 217–219
    role of, 213–217

Federal Reserve, 27, 28, 45, 64, 65, 159, 164, 194, 244

FedEx, 136, 142, 209

Fer-de-Lance (Stout), 23

Fiat, 243

Fidelity funds, 58

Financial Analysts Journal, 137

Financial risk, 28, 44

Firm foundation theory, 17

Firm risk, 28, 57, 127, 153

Flat yield curve, 192

Florida, 237

Folsom Jr., Burton, 223, 257

Football pools, 13

Forbes Magazine, 134

Forbes, Steve, 236

Ford, John, 226

Forgotten Man, The (Shlaes), 223

Founding Fathers, 227, 251, 288

Four Pillars of Investing, The
  (Bernstein), 33
Franklin, Benjamin, 8, 284
Freddie Mac, 62
Friedman, Milton, 45, 216–217, 249
Friend, Cliff, 283
Fundamental analysis, 17, 19, 25, 26

General Electric (GE), 95, 142,
  143, 209, 245
*General Theory of Employment, Interest
  and Money, The* (Keynes), 18
Ginnie Mae, 62, 63
GM, 210, 213, 265
Goizueta, Robert, 209
Goodrich, Frances, 84
Goodwin, Archie, 23, 24, 34
Google, 95, 209, 274
Gordon, John Steele, 221
Government guaranteed
  mortgages, 215
Graham, Benjamin, 17, 49, 140, 154,
  177, 184, 288
Great Depression, 46, 103, 168, 186,
  233, 247, 254, 256, 282
  causes, 222–224
  how it ended, 226–227
  in retrospect, 227–228
  New Deal, 224–226
Great Recession, 182
Greenstreet, Sidney, 23, 110
Gross Domestic Product (GDP),
  184, 185, 187, 196, 198, 204, 218,
  219, 221, 233, 234, 243, 249, 254,
  285, 286
Gross National Product (GNP), 196
Guinness, 210
Gunsmoke, 126
Gutman, Kaspur, 110

Hackett, Albert, 84
Hammett, Dashiell, 84, 110
Harding, Warren G., 239, 240, 254
Heineken, 210
Helvering v. Davis (1937), 257
Here Comes Mr. Jordan, 250
Heritage Foundation, 239
Hillenbrand, Laura, 168, 169
*Historical Lessons of Lower
  Tax Rates, The* (Mitchell), 239
Holmes, Sherlock, 61, 62, 83, 170
Honda, 210
Hoover, Herbert, 223
Hope and Change, 242
Hope, Bob, 48, 287
House Without a Key, The
  (Biggers), 52
Howard, Charles, 168
Hutton, Timothy, 23
Hydrox cookies, 210

IBM, 95, 142, 209, 210
Immelt, Jeffrey, 245
Index mutual funds
  benchmark target, 54–55
  benefits, 55–56
  bonds, 75–77
  selection process, 58–59
Index of consumer expectations, 196
Index of coincident indicators,
  197–199
Index of industrial production, 198
Index of lagging indicators, 199–201
Index of leading indicators, 192–197
Index of supplier deliveries, 195
India, 215, 274
Individual securities,
  characteristics, 57
Inflation cycle, 188–189, 201
Inflation risk, 45, 69, 70

Inflation: What Everyone Must Surrender, 45–47
Inspector Cramer, 24
Intel, 95, 142, 209
Intelligent Investor, The (Graham), 140, 154, 177
Interest rate analysis, 189–192
Interest rate risk, 28, 69
Interest rate spread, 194
International investments, 44, 90–91, 99
International trade, 210–213
Investment life cycle, 53–54, 58, 79, 111, 112, 125, 130, 138, 172
Investment model
    life cycle program, 112–115
    with equity funds only, 103–108
    with individual stocks, 130–133
    with treasury funds only, 77–81
    with lottery winnings, 157–159
Irrational Exuberance (Shiller), 18

Japan, 211, 249
Jefferson, Thomas, 251, 288
Jeopardy!, 239, 242
Johnson & Johnson, 56, 95, 142, 209
Junk bonds, 62

Kennedy, John F., 234, 238, 239, 240, 254
Keynes, John Maynard, 18
Keystone Pipeline, 244
Kroc, Ray, 209

Labor force participation rate, 247, 248
Labor resources, 205–207
Laffer, Arthur, 235, 236, 287
Leverage risk, 28, 44
Lintner, John, 20
Linus, 117

Loaded funds, 99
Lotus 123, 210
Loy, Myrna, 84
Lund, Ilsa, 155

Madoff, Bernie, 261, 277
Malkiel, Burton G., 19
Maltese Falcon, The, 110
Man Who Shot Liberty Valance, The, 226
Management fees, 32, 74, 97
Manufacturing and trade sales, 198–199
Manufacturers' consumer new orders, 194–195
Manufacturers' non-defense new orders, 197
Mark-to-market, 216
Market contraction, 43, 45, 51, 55, 56, 61, 62, 78, 86, 87, 88, 89, 92, 94, 112, 114, 118, 135, 137, 139, 172, 174, 182, 185, 186, 187, 188, 191, 192, 199, 201, 223, 224, 226, 227, 237, 250, 268
Market expansion, 35, 51, 61, 62, 88, 92, 93, 94, 112, 139, 174, 185, 186, 187, 188, 196, 199, 201, 229, 234, 241, 249, 256, 265, 273, 284
Market peak, 38, 55, 185, 186, 187, 196, 224
Market risk, 14, 20, 28, 38, 44, 57, 127, 153, 158, 208
Market timer, 51, 100, 121, 136, 176, 201
Market trough, 38, 55, 185, 186, 224
Markowitz, Harry, 20
Marshall, Chief Justice John, 252
Marx, Karl, 205
McCulloch v. Maryland (1819), 252
McDonalds, 142, 206, 209
Medicare, 242, 273
Merck, 142, 143, 209
Mexico, 205, 244

MGM, 84, 85

Microsoft, 86, 95, 129, 142, 209, 274

Miele, 210

Minimum wage, 206

Mitchell, Daniel J., 239

Modern portfolio theory, 20–21

Momentum, 188, 190, 196, 197, 198

Money Pit, The, 14

Money supply, 45, 182, 192, 193–194, 223, 224

Montgomery Ward, 205

Moore, Stephen, 235, 249

Morgenthau, Henry, 234

Morning in America, 240

Morningstar, 59, 70, 71, 75, 86, 90, 94, 95, 98, 102, 105

Mr. Blandings Builds His Dream House, 14

Mr. Market, 49–50, 129, 154, 174

Mrs. Fields, 209

Municipal bonds, 63, 175

Murders in the Rue Morgue, 16

Mutual funds, characteristics, 58–59

Mysteries and Mystery Writing (Waugh), 16, 84

NAFTA, 210

Naisbett, John, 180

National Bureau of Economic Research, 185, 186, 187, 224

National Labor Relations Board (NLRB), 245

Negative yield curve, 193

Nero Wolfe Mystery, A, 23

New Adventures of Sherlock Holmes, The, 61

New Deal, 223, 224–226, 228, 233, 257, 258

New Deal or Raw Deal? (Folsom), 223, 257

New England Patriots, 77

New Frontier, 240

New York, 237

New York Giants, 77

9/11, 27, 241

No load funds, 32, 58 173

Normal distribution curve, 29, 38

Notes on the State of Virginia, 251

Obama, Barack, 213, 234, 235, 242–249, 254

Obama Economy

  aggressive spending, 242–243

  debt financing, 243–244

  impact on the economy, 247–249

  over legislation and excessive regulation, 244–246

  taxing schemes, 246–247

Oland, Warner, 52

P&G, 86, 95, 136, 142

Panzer, Saul, 24

Patient Protection and Affordable Care Act (ObamaCare), 100, 242, 245

Patton, General George S., 100

Payroll Tax Holiday, 246, 247

Peanuts, 117

Pelosi, Nancy, 242

Perot, Ross, 210

Perrier, 214

Personal income less transfer payments, 198

Peterson, Willis, 202

Pfizer, 95, 142, 143, 209

Pimlico Racetrack, 168

Poe, Edgar Allan, 16, 22

Polaroid, 210

Political risk, 28, 44

Pollard, Red, 168

Ponzi scheme, 261, 263, 264, 265, 287

Portfolio Selection (Markowitz), 20

Positive yield curve, 190, 191

Povich, Shirley, 169

Powell, Jim, 223, 224, 225, 255

Powell, William, 84, 85

Power (magic) of compounding, 34, 36, 40, 55, 57, 58, 77, 85, 96, 103, 124, 134–136, 139, 144, 151, 173, 174, 175, 267

President's Council on Jobs and Competitiveness, 245

Price to cash flow ratio (P/CF), 95, 150

Price to earnings ratio (P/E), 25, 150

Pricing mechanism, 203, 207, 230

Prime rate, 199

Profit margin, 148–149, 189, 272

Profit motive, 209–210

Protectionism (trade), 211, 230

Provisions That Could Change the Social Security Program, 263–265

Purchase fees, 32

Quantitative Easing (QE), 244

Rains, Claude, 155

Random Walk Down Wall Street, A, (Malkiel), 19

Random Walk Theory, 19

Rathbone, Basil, 61

Ratio manufacturing inventories to sales, 200

Reaganomics, 235

Reagan Revolution, 235, 240

Reagan, Ronald, 33, 48, 202, 229, 235, 238, 239, 240, 241, 252, 254

Recessionary yield curve, 191–192

Redemption fees, 32, 74, 97

Reinvestment risk, 28, 69, 157, 162, 165

Renault, Captain Louis, 155

Repatriation Taxes, 275–276

Return on equity (ROE), 95, 147–148, 149

Return to Normalcy, 240

Return: What Everyone Wants, 24–27

Reversion to the mean, 40, 46

Right-to-Work state, 245

Risk: What Everyone Fears, 27–31

Roland, William, 137

Roosevelt, Franklin D. (FDR), 223–228, 234, 242, 254, 255, 256, 257, 265, 282, 287

Rule of 72, 37

Russell, Kitty, 126

Sales charges, 32, 58, 73, 74, 96, 97, 101, 171

Sales revenue, 148

Samsung, 210

Santa Anita Racetrack, 169

Santayana, George, 51

Saturday Evening Post, 12

Savings vs. investment capital, 52–53

Schering-Plough, 142, 143

Seabiscuit, 168, 169, 177

Seabiscuit (the book and the movie), 168

Sears, 205

Security Analysis (Graham, Dodd), 17

Shakespeare, William, 110, 141

Sharpe, William, 20

Shiller, Robert, 18

Shlaes, Amity, 223

Siegel, Jeremy, 46, 134, 186

Smith, Adam, 222

Smith, Tom, 168, 169

Smithwick's, 210

Smoot-Hawley Tariff, 223

Social Security, current system
   investment return, 258–259
   misinformation, 263–264
   origins, 255–258
   positioning, 259–262
   problems, 262–263
   proposals, 264–265
Social Security lockbox, 259, 260,
   262, 263, 272, 288
Social Security, Optimization Plan
   current retirees, 269
   federal government, 271–273
   general provisions, 267–269
   learn the facts, 280–282
   new and current workforce
      participants, 269–271
   private sector, 273–277
   projected results, 277–280
Social Security statement, 258–259
Social Security trust funds, 259,
   260, 262, 263, 271, 272, 278, 288
Social Security trust IOU's, 260,
   261, 263, 271, 272, 288
Soviet Union, 216, 221
Sowell, Thomas, 202, 209, 227
Spade, Sam, 110
Speculators (intermediaries),
   207–208
S&P 500 Stock Index, 21, 95, 137,
   138, 195
Stebbins, Sergeant Purley, 24
Stimulus package, 242
Stock market cycle, 9, 14, 85, 112, 118,
   145, 176, 182, 187, 188, 201
Stocks for the Long Run (Siegel),
   46, 186
Stout, Rex, 23
STRIPS (Separate Trading of
   Registered Interest and Principal
   of Securities), 66
Super Bowl, 16, 77

Supply-side economics, 235–236, 237,
   238, 286, 287
Systematic risk, 20

T. Rowe Price funds, 58
Tanous, Peter, 235
Taxes
   investment impact, 53, 54, 58, 66,
      71, 77, 91, 96, 101, 115, 121, 125, 130,
      131, 162, 171
   general, 24, 28, 34, 43, 45, 46,
      47–48, 52, 57, 146, 158,159, 162,
      198, 201,222, 230, 231–232, 249,
      252, 285, 286, 287
   government collections, 63, 215,
      217, 218, 219, 225, 226, 227, 229,
      233, 235, 236, 237, 238, 239, 240,
      241, 242, 243, 246–247
   social security, 254, 255, 257, 258,
      259, 260, 261, 262, 264, 265, 266,
      269, 270, 272, 273, 274, 275, 276,
      277, 279, 280, 281, 282, 283, 288
Taxes: What Everyone Learns
   to Despise, 47–48
Technical analysis, 18, 19, 25, 26
Tempest, The (Shakespeare), 110
Texas, 237
Thatcher, Margaret, 263
Theory of Investment Value, The
   (Williams), 17
Thin Man, The (Hammett), 84, 85
Timing risk, 28
Timing: What Everyone
   Misunderstands, 34–42
TIPS (Treasury Inflation Protected
   Securities), 65, 70, 71, 79, 165
Tobias, Charles, 283
Toler, Sidney, 52
Too big to fail, 245, 250
Toyota, 210, 214

Treasury yield curves, 78, 161,
    189–192, 194
Troubled Asset Relief Plan
    (TARP), 243
Twain, Mark, 181
12b-1 fees, 32, 74, 97
Tyco, 27
Tylenol, 214

Uhl, Richard, 283
United Auto Workers, 206
UPS, 209
U.S. credit downgrade, 64, 249, 254
U.S. Treasuries
    in your portfolio, 82–83
    market overview, 64
    market structure, 64–65
    individual accounts, 65–66
Unsystematic risk, 20

Vanguard Funds
    corporation started, 21
    corporation structure, 58–59
    investment portfolio, balanced,
        112–115
    investment portfolio, equities,
        103–108
    investment portfolio, treasuries,
        77–84
    Morningstar, 500 Index Fund, 95
    Morningstar, Long Term
        Treasury Fund, 71

Wall Street Journal, 249
War Admiral, 169
Washington, George, 222
Washington Post, The, 169
Watson, Dr. John H., 61
Waugh, Hillary, 16, 84, 85
Wealth of Nations, The (Smith), 222
Welch, Jack, 209

Wholesale or producer prices, 189
Williams, John Burr, 17
Winters, Roland, 52
Wolfe, Nero, 23, 24, 34, 49, 51
Wood, Gordon, 251
WorldCom, 27
World War I, 222, 233, 239, 256
World War II, 45, 155, 222, 226, 227,
    233, 248, 262, 282, 283
Wyeth, 142, 143

You Are There, 220

Zenith, 210
Zero-coupon treasury bonds, 66
Zero-sum game, 92, 101, 170, 171, 249
Zhou, Ping, 137

ABOUT THE AUTHOR

You have worked a lifetime for your money.
Now it's time for your money to work a lifetime for you.

After earning an MBA from Northwestern University, Bob spent most of his career in the financial ranks of some of the largest and most respected companies in America, including American Hospital Supply Corporation, Baxter International, Citibank and Citigroup. He now ventures into the nuanced world of investing to remove much of the mystique, debunk some of the hype and provide helpful, actionable information. For over 20 years, he has helped friends and associates improve their investment portfolios. The results are the inspiration for this book. Bob resides with his wife, Sue, in a north shore suburb of Chicago, Illinois.

THE TYPEFACE

JANSON is the typeface used in this book. For many years it was believed that Anton Janson, a Dutchman, created it while working in Leipzig as a typefounder. He practiced this art from 1668–1687. More recently, it has been proven that it was not Janson but the Hungarian, Nicholas Kis (1650–1702), who produced this text face while he was an apprentice to the master typefounder, Dirk Voskens, also a Dutchman practicing in Amsterdam. Janson is recognized as a premier example of Dutch Baroque serif faces. It was revived in 1937 by Chauncey H. Griffith, who modified the design from Kis's original matrices.